Casanova's Journey Home
and
Other Late Stories

Studies in Austrian Literature, Culture, and Thought

Translation Series

Arthur Schnitzler

Casanova's Journey Home
and
Other Late Stories

Translated and with an Afterword by
Norman M. Watt

ARIADNE PRESS
Riverside, California

Translated from the German

Library of Congress Cataloging-in-Publication Data

Schnitzler, Arthur, 1862-1931.
    [Short stories. English. Selections]
    Casanova's journey home and other late stories / Arthur
Schnitzler ; translated and with an afterword by Norman M. Watt.
    p. cm. -- (Studies in Austrian literature, culture and
thought. Translation series)
    ISBN 1-57241-074-4
    1. Schnitzler, Arthur, 1862-1931--Translations into English.
I. Watt, Norman M. II. Title. III. Series.
PT2637.N5A28 2002
833'.8--dc21

                  00-058659

Cover Design:
Art Director: George McGinnis
Designer: Corrine Bachman

Contents

Acknowledgments

I would like to thank several individuals, each of whom contributed significantly to the genesis of this volume: first of all, my present colleagues Eric Nelson and Maggie Odell, and my former colleague Margaret Reese Goold, for their careful reading of early drafts and helpful editing suggestions; Friederike Kölbl Nelson, for her advice on Austrian sources and Austrianisms; Donald Bratland and Adam Moore, for their invaluable work in formatting the texts; and finally, Donald Daviau and Jorun Johns of Ariadne Press—Don for helping to get the project underway in the first place and for offering frequent encouragement, and Jorun for stepping in at the last moment and seeing everything through to the end.

Northfield, Minnesota
May 2000

Casanova's Journey Home

In the fifty-third year of Casanova's life, when the restlessness of approaching old age had long since replaced the adventurous spirit of his youth as the force that propelled him around the world, he began to feel such an intense longing in his heart for his native city of Venice that he began to draw nearer to it in ever tightening circles, like a bird gradually descending from its airy heights to die. During the past ten years of his exile he had frequently sent petitions to the Great Council requesting permission to return; but while defiance, obstinacy, and sometimes even a wrathful pleasure in the task itself had previously guided his pen as he composed these masterful missives, the almost humble, pleading tone of his words in recent times seemed by contrast to express more and more unmistakably a painful longing and a genuine remorse on his part. And since the sins of his earlier years—his freethinking in particular, which the city fathers of Venice found much harder to forgive than his licentiousness, brawling, or generally comic-spirited swindles—were gradually fading from memory, and the story of his amazing escape from the city's Lead Chambers, told by him on innumerable occasions at monarchs' courts and aristocrats' palaces, at high society festivities and houses of unsavory reputation, was beginning to neutralize any other remaining vilifications associated with his name, he felt all the more assured that his petition would be granted. Only recently, in fact, had men of high station sent letters to him in Mantua, where he had been staying for the past two months, and these gave the aging adventurer reason to hope, at a time when his inner and outer brilliance were both beginning to fade, that his fate would soon be decided favorably.

Since his finances had dwindled considerably, Casanova had decided to spend the days until his reprieve arrived in the modest but respectable inn where he once had lived in happier years; here he whiled away his time—leaving unmentioned the less intellectual diversions he was not capable of giving up completely—by composing a disputation against the blasphemous Voltaire, the publication of which was intended to make his position and reputation in Venice unassailably secure among all right-thinking people immediately upon his return.

As he was walking outside the city gates one morning trying to put the finishing touches on a devastating sentence directed against the godless Frenchman, a strange, almost physically painful unrest suddenly came over him. The life of tedious habituation he had been leading for all of three months—his morning walks out into the countryside, the evenings spent gambling with the putative Baron Perotti and his pockmarked mistress, the attentions of the no longer exactly young, though still fiery proprietress of the inn where he was staying, and even his study of the writings of Voltaire and his work on a bold rejoinder that he was reasonably satisfied with so far—all this seemed to him now, in the gentle, all too sweet breezes of this late summer morning, to be equally meaningless and repulsive. He muttered a profanity without really knowing who or what it was he was cursing; then, as if invisible eyes were mocking him from the surrounding solitude, he grasped the handle of his dagger and, casting hostile looks in all directions, suddenly turned back toward the city with the intention of preparing his departure without further delay. Certain that his mood would improve the moment he was even a few miles closer to his longed-for place of origin, he quickened his step to be sure of getting a seat on the express mail coach that would be heading east before sunset. Aside from that there wasn't much else he had to do; he certainly wouldn't bother stopping by Baron Perotti's to say goodbye, and half an hour would be more than enough time to pack his few belongings for the trip. He considered his two threadbare outfits, the shabbier of which he was wearing at the moment, and his once elegant shirts that were now a patchwork of mends; these things, along with a few fancy little boxes, a gold watch on a chain, and a number of books, were the sum total of his possessions. He thought of bygone days, when he had traveled from place to place in a splendid coach with a servant—though admittedly not of the most trustworthy variety—as an elegant gentleman lavishly supplied with all sorts of necessary and unnecessary items, and tears of helpless rage filled his eyes.

A young woman with a whip in her hand rode by in a small cart in which her drunken husband lay snoring among sacks and various household goods. She looked at Casanova's contorted face as he came striding along the highway under the chestnut trees, their blossoms now withered, muttering incomprehensibly under his breath. Her expression was curious and mocking at first, but his return stare, angry and full of fire, startled her, and as she turned to look back at him as he passed by, her eyes took on a pleased, lascivious expression. Casanova, well aware that anger and hatred do more to maintain the appearance of youth than gentleness and affection, knew instantly that he would only have to shout something suggestive to bring her cart to a halt, at which point he would be able to do whatever he liked with the young woman. But although this realization improved his humor momentarily, it didn't seem worth the effort to him to postpone his plans even for a few minutes for the sake of such a minor adventure, and so he allowed the farm cart and its occupants to continue creaking along unhampered through the dust and haze of the highway.

The shadow cast by the trees did little to relieve the sun's scorching intensity as it climbed higher in the sky, and Casanova had no choice but to gradually slow his pace. His clothes and shoes were coated with a layer of dust so thick that it was no longer possible to see how worn they were, so that anyone observing his dress and bearing would have taken him for a gentleman of standing who just happened to have been in the mood to leave his fancy carriage at home for a change. He had already reached the city gate close to the inn where he was staying when a ponderous, country-style carriage came rumbling toward him. The man sitting in it, portly, well-dressed, and still relatively young, held his hands folded over his stomach, and his eyes were blinking as if he were about to nod off. He happened to glance in Casanova's direction, and suddenly his expression took on an unexpectedly lively sparkle—his whole being, in fact, seemed over-come by a kind of joyous excitement. Getting up out of his seat too quickly, he fell back into it, then got up again and gave the coachman a poke in the back to make him stop the carriage. As it continued to roll on for a short distance, he turned around to keep from losing sight of Casanova, waved to him with both hands, and finally called out his name three times in a thin, high-pitched voice. Only now did Casanova recognize the man; stepping over to the carriage, which had come to a stop in the meantime, he grasped the hands that were stretched out toward him and smiled.

"Is this possible, Olivo? Can it really be you?"

"Yes, it's me, Signor Casanova—so you still recognize me?"

"Why wouldn't I? You do seem to have put on a little girth since your wedding day—that was the last time I saw you—but I suppose I've changed a fair amount over the past fifteen years, too, if not in quite the same way."

"Why no," Olivo exclaimed, "you've hardly changed at all, Si-gnor Casanova! By the way, it's been sixteen years—as of just a few days ago. And as you can probably imagine, we talked about you for quite a while on that occasion, Amalia and I . . ."

"Did you really?" Casanova said warmly. "So the two of you still think about me once in a while?"

Olivo's eyes grew moist. He was still holding Casanova's hands in his and gave them an emotional squeeze.

"We owe you so much, Signor Casanova! Do you think we could ever forget our benefactor? And if we ever—"

"Let's not talk about that," Casanova interrupted. "How is Si-gnora Amalia? And how is it possible that in the two months I've been in Mantua now—I've been leading a fairly solitary existence, of course, but still, I do as much walking as I ever did—how is it that I've never run into you, either one of you, not even once?"

"That's easy to explain, Signor Casanova. We don't live in the city any more and haven't for a long time; I never really liked it here, no more than Amalia did. But do me the honor of getting into my car-riage now, Signor Casanova. We'll be at my place in an hour."

Casanova declined with a slight motion of his hand.

"Please don't say no. Amalia will be so happy to see you again, and so proud to introduce our three children to you. That's right, Signor Casanova, three. All girls. Thirteen, ten, and eight . . . so none of them is old enough yet, if you don't mind my saying this, to—to have her head turned by Casanova."

Olivo laughed good-naturedly and was on the point of simply pulling him into the carriage. But Casanova shook his head. For a moment he had been tempted to give in to his understandable curiosity and take Olivo up on his offer, but then, beginning to feel keenly impatient again, he explained that unfortunately he had no choice but to leave Mantua before nightfall due to important business. What possible reason could he have for going to Olivo's house, after all? Sixteen years was a long time! Amalia certainly wouldn't have grown younger and more beautiful in all those years, and their thirteen-year-old daughter would hardly show much interest in him at his age. And as for Olivo himself, the opportunity of admiring the once lean and studious young man in his rural surroundings as a lethargic, peasantish father of a family didn't hold sufficient interest for him to consider delaying a journey that would bring him another ten or twenty miles closer to Venice.

But Olivo, who didn't seem of a mind to let Casanova's refusal go unchallenged, insisted on at least dropping him off at his inn for the time being, an offer that he couldn't very well turn down. A few minutes later they had arrived. The proprietress, a well-endowed woman in her mid-thirties, greeted Casanova in front of the inn with a look that couldn't help but make even Olivo aware of the amorous relationship that existed between them. She gave Olivo a friendly shake of the hand, explaining to Casanova that he regularly supplied her with a reasonably priced semi-sweet wine from his estate. Olivo immediately began to lament that the Chevalier de Seingalt (this was how the proprietress had greeted him, and Olivo didn't hesitate to make use of this title as well) had been so cruel as to reject the invitation of an old friend he hadn't seen in years for the ridiculous reason of having to leave Mantua that very day and not a day later. The proprietress' disconcerted look immediately told Olivo that she was hearing this for the first time, whereupon Casanova decided it was time to explain that he had in fact only pretended having to leave so as not to burden his friend's family with a completely unexpected visitor. Still, it was true that he was under some constraint—obligation, even—to finish an important piece of writing in the next few days, and he knew of no more suitable place at which to do this than this excellent inn, where he had a cool, quiet room all to himself.

At this, Olivo declared that no greater honor could be granted his modest home than to have the Chevalier de Seingalt complete his work there; the seclusion of the countryside could only be conducive to an undertaking of that sort. There would be no lack of scholarly books and reference works, either, if Casanova needed them, since Olivo's niece, his late stepbrother's daughter—still just a girl, but extremely erudite in spite of her young age—had arrived at their place with a whole crate full of books a few weeks before. And if occasional guests appeared in the evening, the chevalier wouldn't have to pay any attention to them at all, unless he happened to be in the mood for some pleasant conversation or a little card-playing after the efforts of the day.

No sooner had Casanova heard about the young niece than he decided to have a look at her at close range. Feigning uncertainty, he finally gave in to Olivo's insisting, but emphasized that he couldn't be gone from Mantua for more than one or two days and implored his kind proprietress to have a messenger bring him any letters that might arrive without delay, since these could be of the utmost importance.

With all the arrangements made and Olivo extremely gratified, Casanova went up to his room and got ready to leave. A quarter of an hour later he came down to the dining room, where he found his old friend engaged in a lively conversation of a business nature with the proprietress. Standing up and finishing his glass of wine, Olivo gave her an understanding wink and promised to return the chevalier safe and sound, though probably not as soon as tomorrow or the next day. Casanova himself suddenly seemed distracted and anxious to leave; his farewell to his friendly proprietress was so cool that she, standing next to the carriage door, whispered a parting word in his ear that was anything but sweet.

As the two men drove along the dusty road under the blazing noonday sun out into the countryside, Olivo told the story of the last several years of his life in tedious detail and in no particular order. He had bought a tiny piece of land near the city shortly after his marriage and opened a small grocery, then gradually added to his property holdings and begun to farm; finally, three years ago, with God's blessing and through his own and his wife's hard work, he had reached the point where he was able to purchase the debt-ridden Count Marazzani's old and somewhat dilapidated palazzo along with the vineyards that were part of the estate. He and his wife and children now led a comfortable life on this noble soil, though certainly not in a manner befitting a count. And all this he ultimately owed to the hundred and fifty pieces of gold that Casanova had given his bride, or actually her mother. Without the magical power of this gift, his life would likely be the same today as it had been at that time—he would still be teaching reading and writing to ill-mannered brats; moreover, he probably would have become an old bachelor and Amalia an old maid . . .

Casanova let him talk on, though he was barely paying attention. The affair he had been involved in in those days, simultaneously with several other more memorable ones, ran through his mind; since it had been the least interesting of all of them, it had affected his heart as little at the time as it had subsequently his memory. On a trip from Rome to Turin or Paris—he couldn't remember which anymore—he had made a stopover in Mantua and caught sight of Amalia one morning in church; her pretty, pallid, somewhat tear-stained face had appealed to him, and he had addressed a question to her in a friendly, gallant tone. Affectionately trusting as they all were toward him in those days, she had been glad to pour out her heart to him. She had fallen in love with a poor schoolteacher and, her own circumstances being rather meager as well, both his father and her mother had adamantly refused to consent to a union as hopeless as theirs promised to be. Casanova had immediately declared his willingness to take the matter in hand. First of all he had arranged to have himself introduced to Amalia's mother, who, as an attractive widow of thirty-six, could still lay claim to the attentions of men. Casanova and she were

soon on such intimate terms that his advocacy was able to attain anything with her. And once she had given up her negative stance, Olivo's
father, a shopkeeper who had fallen on hard times, was also ready to
grant his approval—especially since Casanova, introduced to him as
a distant relative of the mother of the bride, generously agreed to pay
for the wedding expenses and contribute to the dowry. As for Amalia,
her noble benefactor had appeared to her like a messenger from some
higher world, and she couldn't help demonstrating her gratitude to
him in a way that her own heart commanded; and when, her cheeks
aglow, she tore herself away from Casanova's final embrace on the
night before her wedding, the thought never occurred to her that she
might have wronged her husband-to-be, who after all owed his good
fortune entirely to this wonderful stranger's kindness and high-minded
spirit. Whether Amalia had ever made a confession to Olivo concerning the extraordinary token of gratitude that she had granted her benefactor, whether Olivo had perhaps viewed her sacrifice as a matter of
course and accepted it without any subsequent jealousy, or whether
the event had been kept secret from him until that very day—Casanova
had never troubled himself about this, nor did he now.

It was getting hotter and hotter. The carriage's suspension was
poor and its cushions hard; it rumbled and jerked along pitifully, and
Olivo's good-natured chatter began to bore Casanova. He went on
and on in his thin voice, informing the chevalier about the fertility of
his soil, his wife's excellent qualities, the wonderful way his children
had turned out, and the cordial, untroubled dealings he maintained
with the farmers and noblemen of the neighborhood. Annoyed,
Casanova asked himself why he had accepted an invitation that could
bring him nothing but inconvenience and possibly even disappointment. Longing for his cool room at the inn in Mantua where he could
have been working quietly on his piece against Voltaire at that very
moment, he decided on the spot to get out of the carriage at the
tavern just ahead, hire whatever conveyance was available, and ride
back to town. But suddenly Olivo let out a loud shout and began to
wave both hands as he always did when he was excited. Grabbing
Casanova by the arm, he pointed to a carriage next to theirs that had
come to a stop at the same moment, as if the whole thing had been

prearranged. Three little girls jumped down from the other carriage one after the other, so that the narrow board they had been using as a seat went flying into the air and flipped over.

"These are my daughters," Olivo said not without pride, then added, as Casanova was about to get out of his seat, "just stay where you are, my dear chevalier, it's only a quarter of an hour to my place now. For that length of time we'll all be able to squeeze into my carriage. Maria, Nanetta, Teresina, this is the Chevalier de Seingalt, an old friend of your father's—come over here and kiss his hand. If it hadn't been for him, you wouldn't have"—he caught himself in mid-sentence and whispered to Casanova, "I almost said something stupid." Then, speaking out loud again, he modified what he had been going to say: "Without him a lot of things would be different now!"

The daughters, black-haired and dark-eyed like Olivo, still had a childish look about them, even Teresina, the eldest. They observed the stranger with an open, somewhat peasantish curiosity, and Maria, the youngest, was all set to follow her father's instructions and actually kiss his hand. But Casanova wouldn't hear of it; instead, he took each of them, one after the other, by the head and kissed them on both cheeks. While this was going on Olivo exchanged a few words with the young driver who had brought his daughters this far in his cart, whereupon the man touched his horse with his whip and drove off along the highway toward Mantua.

The girls sat down on the seat across from Olivo and Casanova, laughing and squabbling in a teasing way; they sat there tightly squeezed together, all speaking at the same time, and since their father never stopped talking himself, it wasn't easy at first for Casanova to make sense of their conversation. He heard one name clearly, that of a Lieutenant Lorenzi. Teresina announced that the lieutenant had ridden past them a short while before, had promised to pay the family a visit that evening and asked the girls to greet their father from him. The children went on to report that their mother had considered coming along with them to meet their father, but had decided to stay home with Marcolina after all because of the terrible heat. Marcolina herself had still been in bed when they left the house; they had thrown berries and hazelnuts at her from the garden through her open window, otherwise she would probably still be asleep.

"That's unusual for Marcolina," Olivo said, turning to his guest; "as a rule she's sitting in the garden by six o'clock if not earlier, and she stays there studying till noon. We did have guests yesterday, of course, so we were up somewhat later than usual; we had a little card game going, too, though not the kind the Signor Chevalier is used to, I don't suppose—we're simple people and we don't really want to take anyone's money away. And since our esteemed abbot usually plays too, you can imagine that things don't get too terribly sinful, Signor Chevalier."

As soon as the abbot was mentioned, the girls laughed and started telling each other all kinds of stories that made them laugh even more. Casanova merely nodded absently; in his mind's eye he saw Signorina Marcolina, whom he hadn't even met yet, lying on her white sheets across from the window, her blanket pulled down and her body half-naked, defending herself with drowsy hands against the flying berries and hazelnuts—and his senses were overcome by a foolish passion. He had no more doubt that Marcolina was Lieutenant Lorenzi's mistress than if he himself had observed the two of them in the most intimate embrace, and his readiness to hate this unknown Lorenzi was as great as his desire for the as yet unseen Marcolina.

Rising above the gray-green foliage, a square tower appeared in the trembling noonday haze. A moment later the carriage turned off the highway onto a side road; vineyards sloped gently uphill on the left, while the crowns of ancient trees hung over the top of a garden wall on the right. The carriage pulled up to the wide-open gate, the passengers got out, and at a wave from Olivo the coachman drove on past the weather-beaten double doors toward the stable. A broad path lined with chestnut trees led up to the house, which at first glance appeared somewhat bleak, even neglected. The first thing that caught Casanova's eye was a broken window on the second floor, and he couldn't help noticing that the walls of the broad, squat tower that perched rather gracelessly on the building were crumbling in places as well. By contrast, the front door was finely carved, and the interior, as Casanova noticed as soon as he stepped into the entrance hall, was well-maintained and definitely in far better condition than the exterior would have led anyone to believe.

"Amalia!" Olivo called out loudly, his voice echoing from the vaulted ceiling. "Come down as fast as you can! I've brought you a guest—and what a guest!"

But Amalia, though not yet visible to the new arrivals below who had just stepped out of the bright sunlight into semi-darkness, had already appeared at the head of the stairway. Casanova, his sharp eyes still able to penetrate even the dark of night, caught sight of her before her husband did. He smiled, sensing at once that his smile made his face look younger. Amalia hadn't become the least bit plump as he had feared and still looked slender and youthful. She recognized him instantly.

"What a surprise—I can't tell you how happy I am!" she cried out without a trace of embarrassment. Rushing down the stairs, she offered Casanova her cheek to kiss, whereupon he, without a moment's hesitation, hugged her like a dear old girl friend.

"Amalia," he said, "do you really expect me to believe that Maria, Nanetta, and Teresina are your own flesh and blood daughters? It would be possible, of course, given the length of time—"

"And in every other way too, Chevalier," Olivo added, "you can take my word for it!"

"So you're late because you ran into the chevalier, Olivo?" Amalia gazed at their guest, her eyes intoxicated with memories.

"That's right, Amalia. But I hope there's still something left to eat in spite of that."

"Well, we certainly didn't sit down at the table all by ourselves, Marcolina and I, as hungry as we were."

"Would you mind being patient just a little while longer?" Casanova requested. "I'd like to get some of the dust of the road off my clothes and myself."

"I'll take you to your room right away," Olivo said. "I hope you'll find it satisfactory, Chevalier, almost as satisfactory as your inn in Mantua . . ." he winked and added in a muted voice, "even though there might be a thing or two missing here."

He led Casanova up the stairs to the gallery that ran around all four sides of the entrance hall, and from there to the far corner, where a narrow wooden staircase wound its way upward. When they had reached the top, Olivo opened the door to the tower; standing on the threshold and uttering polite phrases, he offered the space to Casanova as a modest guest room. A maid came up with his valise, then went back down the stairs with Olivo, leaving Casanova standing alone in a medium-sized room that contained all the necessities but was otherwise relatively empty. Four tall, narrow arched windows offered a distant view in all directions of the sun-drenched plain, with its green vineyards, brightly-colored meadows, yellow fields, gleaming roads, houses in pastel hues, and shady gardens. Paying no further attention to the view, Casanova got ready quickly, less out of hunger than from a tormenting desire to see Marcolina face to face as soon as possible; he didn't even change his clothes, since he intended to wait until evening before appearing in greater splendor.

As he entered the wood-paneled dining room on the ground floor and looked around the beautifully-set table, he caught sight of a slender young woman in a simple gray flowing dress with a dull sheen sitting with the host and hostess and their three daughters. The expression on her face as she looked back at him was perfectly natural, as if he were a member of the household or someone who had been a guest here a hundred times already. Her eyes showed nothing of the glow that had so often greeted him in former days, when he, still an unknown, had made his entrance in the captivating splendor of his youth, or later, in the dangerous good looks of his mature years. This lack of reaction was nothing new to Casanova, of course, nor had it been for years; still, even in more recent times the mention of his name had usually been enough to elicit an expression of belated admiration from the lips of a woman, or at the very least a slight twinge of regret at not having encountered him a few years earlier. On this occasion, however, as Olivo introduced him to his niece as Signor Casanova, Chevalier de Seingalt, she smiled no differently than she would have at the mention of some ordinary name devoid of any sense of adventure and mystery. And even when he sat down next to her and kissed her hand, and his eyes sent a shower of sparks of delight and desire raining down on her, her expression betrayed nothing of the quiet satisfaction that might, after all, have been expected as a fitting response to the glowing homage he had just paid her.

After a few polite opening phrases, Casanova gave his table partner to understand that he had heard about her scholarly endeavors and asked her which field in particular she was interested in. She replied that for the most part she was pursuing the study of higher mathematics, to which Professor Morgagni, the famous scholar at the University of Bologna, had introduced her. Casanova expressed his amazement at this interest, certainly unusual among attractive young ladies of grace and good breeding, in a subject that was so difficult and at the same time so prosaic. But Marcolina replied that in her opinion higher mathematics represented the most imaginative branch of knowledge—it could even be said, in fact, that it was the one that was truly divine in nature. When Casanova asked her to explain this novel view in greater detail, Marcolina modestly declined, commenting that those present, and especially her dear uncle, might well be more interested in hearing about the experiences of a well-traveled friend who hadn't been heard from for such a long time than in listening to a philosophical discussion. Amalia agreed wholeheartedly with this, and Casanova, always glad to give in to requests of this kind, mentioned offhandedly that he had mostly been involved with secret diplomatic missions in recent years, and that these had taken him, to mention only the larger cities, to Madrid, Paris, London, Amsterdam, and St. Petersburg. He spoke of his encounters and conversations, some serious and some amusing, with men and women of every imaginable station in life; he was careful to include the friendly reception he had received at the court of Catherine of Russia, and gave a very comical account of how Frederick the Great had come close to making him a teacher at a cadet school for the sons of Pomeranian landed gentry—a danger he had escaped by beating a hasty retreat. He told these and many other stories as if they had taken place in the recent past and not, as was really the case, years or decades before; he invented occasional details, not really conscious himself of these greater and smaller lies, and enjoyed his own good humor along with the rapt attention of his audience. And as he went on talking and improvising in this fashion, he almost got the feeling that even today he really was the radiant, brazen Casanova, the favorite child of fortune who had traveled the world with beautiful women and been honored by the special favor of wordly and ecclesiastical rulers, a man who had squandered, gambled, and given away thousands—rather than some poor devil who had seen better days and was supported by trivial amounts of money sent by former friends in England and Spain—money that in recent times sometimes failed to appear, so that he had to rely on the few miserable coins he won from Baron Perotti or the baron's guests; he even forgot, in fact, that what seemed to him to be his greatest goal was to return to the city of his fathers—the city that had first imprisoned him and, following his escape, declared him an outlaw and banished him—and to end his once so resplendent existence there as the least of its citizens, as a clerk, as a beggar, as a nothing.

Marcolina listened to him attentively along with the others, but reacted no differently than if someone had been reading a moderately entertaining story out of a book to her. No one would have suspected from the expression on her face that the man sitting across from her was Casanova himself, who had experienced all these things and many others he wasn't telling about—that the lover of a thousand women was sitting across from her and that she *knew* this. Amalia's eyes, though, glowed with a different light. For her, Casanova had remained the same man he had always been; his voice sounded as seductive to her as it had sixteen years before, and he himself sensed that it would cost him only a word, if that, to resume their former affair whenever he wanted. But of what interest was Amalia to him now? It was Marcolina he desired, more than any woman ever before! He could almost see her naked body through the dull sheen of her dress as it flowed around her; he sensed the bloom of her budding breasts, and when she bent over at one point to pick up the handkerchief that had fallen to the floor, Casanova's burning fantasy ascribed such a lascivious significance to her movement that he almost thought he would lose consciousness. Marcolina was quick to notice that he had inadvertantly faltered for a moment in the midst of his narration and that his eyes had begun to flutter strangely, and he saw in hers a sudden consternation, a protest, even a trace of disgust. He quickly regained his composure and was about to continue telling his story with renewed animation when a corpulent clergyman entered the room; Olivo greeted him as Abbot Rossi, and Casanova immediately recognized him as the same person he had met twenty-seven years earlier on a market boat sailing from Venice to Chioggia.

"You had a bandage over one eye at the time," said Casanova, who seldom missed an opportunity to show off his excellent memory, "and there was a farmer's wife wearing a yellow scarf on the boat who recommended a medicinal ointment to you, and a young pharmacist with a very hoarse voice who just happened to have some with him."

The abbot nodded and smiled, feeling flattered. Then, with a sly expression on his face, he walked right up to Casanova as if he had a secret to tell him. Instead, he announced in a very loud voice, "And you, Signor Casanova, were there with a wedding party . . . I don't know if you were one of the guests or even the best man, but in any case the bride was giving you much fonder looks than she was the groom . . . A wind came up and it got rather turbulent, and you began to recite an extremely racy poem."

"The chevalier certainly did that only to calm the storm," Marcolina said.

"I've never credited myself with magical powers of that sort," Casanova replied, "although I can't deny that people stopped worrying about the storm once I started to recite the poem."

The three girls had surrounded the abbot with expectant looks on their faces. Soon he was taking large quantities of exquisite candies out of his enormous pockets and stuffing them into the children's mouths with his fat fingers. While this was going on, Olivo gave the abbot a detailed report of how he had happened to meet Casanova again. Lost in memories, Amalia kept her glowing eyes riveted on her beloved guest's dark, lordly face. The children ran out into the garden and Marcolina got up and watched them through the open window. The abbot extended greetings from Marchese Celsi, who, if his health permitted, planned to come by that evening with his wife to pay his esteemed friend Olivo a visit.

"That's perfect," Olivo said, "we'll be able to have a nice little card game in honor of the chevalier. I'm expecting the Ricardi brothers as well, and Lorenzi's coming—the children happened to see him today when he was out riding."

"He's still here?" the abbot asked. "A week ago there was talk of his having to leave to join his regiment."

Olivo laughed. "I suspect that the marchesa got Lorenzi's colonel to give him a leave," he said.

"I'm surprised that any Mantuan officers are being granted leaves now," Casanova interjected, then continued with his fabrication. "Two acquaintances of mine, one from Mantua and the other from Cremona, left with their regiments last night headed for Milan."

"Is there going to be war?" Marcolina asked from the window. She had turned around; her face was in shadow and her expression impossible to read, but there was a slight tremor in her voice that no one but Casanova was likely to have noticed.

"It might not come to anything," he said lightly, "but since the Spaniards are acting belligerent, we have to be prepared."

Olivo frowned. "Do we really even know whose side we'll be fighting on, the Spanish or the French?" he asked, putting on an air of importance.

"I don't suppose Lieutenant Lorenzi cares one way or the other," the abbot said, "as long as he finally has a chance to test his heroism."

"He's already done that," Amalia said. "He fought in the Battle of Pavia three years ago."

Marcolina remained silent. Casanova knew all he needed to. He walked over to her and looked out the window, taking in the garden in one sweeping glance. All he could see was the broad overgrown meadow where the children were playing, bordered by a dense row of tall trees toward the wall.

"What a beautiful estate," he said, turning to Olivo. "I'd be interested in seeing the rest of it."

"I'd like nothing better, Chevalier, than to take you through my vineyards and fields," Olivo replied. "To tell you the truth, in fact—just ask Amalia—ever since I bought this little place, I've wanted nothing more than to welcome you here, on my own land, as my guest some day. I was on the point of writing you ten different times to invite you to come. But who could ever be sure that a message would reach you? If someone said they'd seen you in Lisbon recently, it was a sure thing that you'd left for Warsaw or Vienna in the meantime. And now I find you again, by some miracle, just as you're on the point of leaving Mantua, and I'm able to lure you into coming here— let me tell you, Amalia, it wasn't easy—and you act so stingy with your time that you—can you believe this, Monsignore, he doesn't want to grant us more than two days!"

The abbot was in the process of letting a slice of peach dissolve in his mouth with great relish. "Perhaps the chevalier can be persuaded to stay longer," he said, casting a quick glance at Amalia. Casanova took this as an indication that she had confided more fully in him than in her husband.

"I'm afraid that won't be possible," Casanova replied stiffly. "My fellow citizens of Venice, you see—it wouldn't be right for me to keep this a secret from my friends here who have shown such concern for my life and well-being—are on the verge of making amends for the injustice they did me years ago—somewhat belatedly, but with all the more honor attached—and I won't be able to say no to their urgings any longer without looking ungrateful or even vindictive." With a slight movement of his hand he fended off the curious though re-spectful question he saw forming on Olivo's lips, then added quickly: "Well, Olivo, I'm ready. Show me your little empire."

"Wouldn't it be advisable to wait until a cooler part of the day?" Amalia interjected. "I'm sure the chevalier would prefer to rest a bit now, or take a walk in the shade?" Her eyes flashed at Casanova in timid supplication, as if her fate would be decided for a second time during this pleasure stroll.

There were no objections to Amalia's suggestion, and everyone went outside. Marcolina ran on ahead of the others, across the sun-shiny meadow to where the children were hitting shuttlecocks back and forth, and immediately joined in their game. She was barely taller than the oldest of the three girls, and now, with her loose curls flow-ing around her shoulders, she looked like a child herself. Olivo and the abbot sat down on a stone bench at the edge of the gravel path close to the house. Amalia continued along the path with Casanova. When they were out of earshot of the others, she began to speak in tones of long ago, as if she had never spoken to him in any other way: "So you're here again, Casanova! How I've longed for this day—I knew it would finally come." "It's pure coincidence that I'm here," Casanova said coldly. Amalie simply smiled. "Call it what you want. You're here! In all these sixteen years I've been dreaming about nothing but this day!"

"One has to assume," Casanova replied, "that you dreamt about a few other things during that time as well—and that you didn't only dream about them."

Amalia shook her head. "You know that's not true, Casanova. And you didn't forget me, either—otherwise, seeing what a rush you're in to get to Venice, you wouldn't have accepted Olivo's invitation!"

"What can you possibly be thinking, Amalia? That I came here to deceive that good, decent husband of yours?"

"Why are you talking like this, Casanova? When we make love again, it won't be deceiving, and it won't be a sin!"

Casanova laughed out loud. "It won't be a sin? Why won't it be? Because I'm an old man?"

"You're not old. For me you can never be old. It was in your arms that I felt ecstasy for the first time, and I know that it's my fate to experience it for the last time with you!"

"The last time?" Casanova repeated in a mocking tone, despite feeling somewhat touched. "My friend Olivo may well have some objections to that."

"With him it's—" Amalia began, blushing, "it's an obligation . . . all right, even pleasure; but ecstasy it is not, and never has been."

They stopped before the end of the gravel path, neither seeming to want to go near the meadow where Marcolina and the children were playing, then turned as if by prior agreement and walked back to the house in silence. A window on the narrow side of the ground floor was standing open. In the dim light at the far end of the room Casanova saw a bed curtain that had been partially pushed to one side, and beyond that the foot end of the bed. A pale, gauzy garment was draped over the chair next to it.

"Marcolina's room?" Casanova asked.

Amalia nodded. "Do you find her attractive?" she asked, her tone sounding innocently cheerful.

"Of course. She's beautiful."

"Beautiful and virtuous."

Casanova shrugged his shoulders as if indicating that he hadn't asked about that. "If you were seeing me today for the first time, Amalia," he said, "would you still be attracted to me?"

"I don't know if you look any different today than you did back then. I see you—the way you were then. The way I've seen you ever since, even in my dreams."

"Look at me, Amalia! These wrinkles on my forehead . . . the folds of skin on my neck! And these deep furrows that run from my eyes to my temples! And here, look, I'm missing a tooth on this side." He opened his mouth wide in a distorted grin. "And my hands, Amalia! Just look at them! Fingers like claws . . . little yellow spots on the nails . . . and these veins—blue and swollen—they're the hands of an old man, Amalia!"

She took both his hands as he held them up to her, and in the shadows next to the path she kissed them with reverence, first one and then the other.

"And tonight I mean to kiss your lips," she said in a devotedly tender tone that enraged him.

Not far from them, at one end of the meadow, Marcolina lay in the grass, her hands behind her head, looking up as the shuttlecocks the children were hitting flew over her. Suddenly she stretched out an arm and grabbed at one of them. She caught it and laughed out loud, and immediately the children pounced upon her; her hair flew wildly as she tried unsuccessfully to defend herself. Casanova began to tremble.

"You will kiss neither my lips nor my hands," he said to Amalia, "and your waiting for me and dreaming about me will come to nothing unless—I have Marcolina first."

"Are you crazy, Casanova?" Amalia cried out in an agonized voice.

"No more than you are," Casanova said. "You're crazy because you think you've found the lover of your youth in me, an old man, and I'm crazy because I've taken it into my head to have Marcolina.

But maybe both of us are fated to get our sanity back. Marcolina will make me young again—for you. Plead my cause with her, Amalia!"

"You're out of your mind, Casanova, it's impossible. She won't have anything to do with *any* man."

Casanova laughed. "How about Lieutenant Lorenzi?"

"Lorenzi? What do you mean?"

"He's her lover, I know he is."

"You're wrong about that, Casanova. He asked her to marry him, and she refused. And he's young—he's handsome—I almost think he's even more handsome than you ever were, Casanova!"

"He asked her to marry him?"

"Ask Olivo if you don't believe me."

"Either way, it doesn't matter. What do I care if she's a virgin or a slut, a bride-to-be or a widow—I want her, I want her!"

"I can't give her to you, my friend."

Casanova sensed a tone of pity in her voice. "Now you know what a disgraceful reprobate I've become, Amalia! Ten years ago, even five, I wouldn't have needed anyone to help me, to plead for me, even if Marcolina had been the goddess of virtue herself. And here I am now, trying to turn you into a madam. If I were rich . . . with ten thousand ducats I could . . . But I don't even have *ten*. I'm a beggar, Amalia."

"You wouldn't get Marcolina even for a hundred thousand. What does she care about money? She loves her books, the sky, the meadows, the butterflies, playing games with children . . . And her inheritance, as small as it is, is more than enough for her."

"Oh, if only I were a king!" Casanova cried, declaiming a bit as he sometimes did, especially when tormented by genuine passion. "If I had the power to throw people in prison, to have them executed . . . But I'm nothing. I'm a beggar—and a liar. I've been begging the Venetian authorities for a job, a scrap of bread, a place to call home! Look at what's become of me. Don't you think I'm disgusting, Amalia?"

"I love you, Casanova!"

"Then get her for me, Amalia! You can do it, I know you can. Tell her whatever you want to. Tell her I've threatened you and your family, tell her you think I'm capable of setting your house on fire!

Tell her I'm a madman, a dangerous madman who's escaped from an insane asylum, and that the embrace of a virgin could make me sane again. Yes, tell her that!"

"She doesn't believe in miracles."

"What? She doesn't believe in miracles? Then she doesn't believe in God either. That's even better! I'm in the good graces of the Archbishop of Milan—tell her that! I can destroy her! I can destroy all of you. That's true, Amalia! What are these books that she reads? Some of them must have been forbidden by the church. Let me have a look at them—I'll write down their titles. One word from me . . ."

"Be quiet, Casanova, she's coming! Don't give yourself away! Be careful how you look at her! Never, never—listen to what I'm telling you, Casanova—never have I known anyone more pure in spirit. If she had the least presentiment of what I've just had to listen to, she would feel dirty; and you would never get to see her again for as long as you're here. Talk to her, Casanova. Go ahead, talk to her. You'll end up asking her for forgiveness—and me too."

Marcolina and the children had caught up with them; the children went running on into the house, while she herself stopped in a gesture of apparent politeness to Casanova. Amalia made a pointed exit. And Casanova did indeed feel as if a breath of austerity and chastity were wafting toward him from Marcolina's pale, half-opened lips and smooth forehead, framed now by her light brown pinned-up hair. He was conscious of a sensation he rarely felt in the presence of a woman, one he hadn't even felt in Marcolina's presence inside the house before—a kind of awe, of submission without desire, that came flowing through his soul. Speaking with a reserve of the kind that people manifest when addressing those of higher station, a deference that couldn't help but seem flattering to her, he asked whether she was planning to devote the approaching evening hours to her studies again. She replied that she wasn't in the habit of studying with any regularity when she was in the country; still, she couldn't prevent certain mathematical problems she happened to be working on from pursuing her in her leisure hours as well, and this, in fact, had happened to her just now as she was lying on the grass looking up at the sky. Feeling encouraged by her friendliness, Casanova asked her jokingly what sort of lofty yet importunate problem it had been, but she replied in a somewhat scornful tone that it didn't have the least to do with the renowned cabala with which the Chevalier de Seingalt was known to achieve great things, and that for this reason it wouldn't mean much to him. He was annoyed that she spoke of the cabala in such a clearly disapproving tone, even though he himself, in his admittedly rare moments of deep reflection, was aware that this strange number mysticism had no meaning and no claim to legitimacy—that in a sense it had no basis in reality, but was used only by cheats and jokesters (a role he himself had played from time to time, and always masterfully) to dupe gullible people and fools. This notwithstanding, he tried now against his own inner conviction to defend the cabala to Marcolina as a completely valid and serious science. He talked about the divine nature of the number seven as referred to in Holy Scripture, the profoundly prophetic meaning of the number pyramids and the new system of constructing them that he himself had propounded, and the frequent fulfillment of his predictions based on this system. Hadn't his construction of one such number pyramid in Amsterdam just a few years earlier induced the banker Hope to assume the insurance liability for a merchant ship believed lost at sea, and hadn't this brought him a profit of two hundred thousand gulden in gold?

Casanova was still so adept at presenting his fraudulently ingenious theories that, as had happened so often before, he began to believe all the nonsense he was spouting and even dared to end his remarks by claiming that the cabala represented less a branch of mathematics than its metaphysical perfection. Marcolina, who had listened attentively and with apparent seriousness up to this point, looked at him now with a half pitying, half mischievous expression on her face.

"My esteemed Signor Casanova," she said (this time, apparently intentionally, she did not address him as 'Chevalier'), "you seem to find it important to present me with a choice example of your world-renowned talent as an entertainer, and I'm genuinely grateful to you for that. But of course you know as well as I do that the cabala has nothing to do with mathematics, that it in fact represents an outright violation of the true essence of that branch of knowledge and bears the same resemblance to it as does the muddled, deceitful prattle of the sophists to the clear and exalted teachings of Plato and Aristotle."

"Be that as it may," Casanova replied quickly, "you will have to concede, my beautiful and learned Marcolina, that even the sophists should in no way be considered as utterly despicable and foolish as one would assume them to be from your all too severe criticism. It is certainly justifiable, to cite an example from our own day, to characterize Monsieur Voltaire, in his entire manner of thinking and writing, as a prime example of a sophist; yet in spite of that it would never occur to anyone, not even me, who confesses to being his decided opponent—in fact, I won't deny that at this very moment I'm in the process of writing a piece in opposition to him—it would never occur even to me to deny his extraordinary talent the recognition it deserves. And let me hasten to add that I have not let myself be influenced, as some might think, by the extravagant courtesy that Monsieur Voltaire had the kindness to show me on the occasion of my visit to Ferney ten years ago."

"How charming of you, Chevalier, to be so well-disposed as to judge the greatest intellect of the century with such charity."

"A great intellect," Casanova exclaimed, "even the greatest, you say? To call him that seems to me inadmissible, if for no other reason than that despite all his genius he is an irreligious man, a downright atheist. And an atheist can never be a great intellect."

"I don't see how the one rules out the other, Signor Chevalier. But first of all you'll have to prove that Voltaire can indeed be considered an atheist."

Casanova was in his element now. In the first chapter of his disputation he had compiled a great number of passages from Voltaire's works, most notably the notorious *Pucelle*,[1] that seemed to him particularly well-suited for proving the author's atheism. Thanks to his excellent memory he was able to quote them literally now and cite his own counterarguments. But in the person of Marcolina he had encountered an adversary almost his equal in breadth of knowledge and mental acuity, and one far superior to him in ingenuity and clarity of expression, if not in eloquence. Quick-witted and adroit, she interpreted the passages that Casanova sought to present as proofs of

Voltaire's skepticism, love of mockery, and irreligiosity, as just as indicative of the Frenchman's scholarly and literary genius and of his ardent, untiring striving for truth. She was even fearless enough to offer the opinion that doubt, mockery, and even a lack of religious faith, when associated with so much knowledge, absolute sincerity, and courage, had to be more pleasing in the eyes of God than the humility of the pious, which usually was nothing more than a cover for their inability to think logically, and at times even—and here there were plenty of examples—for their cowardice and hypocrisy.

Casanova listened to Marcolina with growing amazement. In the face of her objections he realized more and more that his own fluctuating spiritual disposition of recent years, which he had become accustomed to thinking of as religious belief, was on the verge of disintegrating completely. Feeling incapable of winning her over to his view, he resorted to the general observation that opinions such as those Marcolina had just expressed were liable to undermine seriously the existing order of the church, to say nothing of the foundations of the state. He then made a clever transition to politics, an area in which he could be relatively sure of having a certain edge over Marcolina because of his experience and cosmopolitan background. Since she had little knowledge of the important personalities or the ins and outs of diplomacy and the court, she could not very well contradict Casanova on individual points, even when she felt inclined to mistrust the reliability of what he was saying; all the same, her comments made it absolutely clear to him that she had no great regard for either the rulers of this earth or for forms of government as such, and that she was convinced that the world, from its lowest to its highest social strata, was not so much controlled by self-interest and love of power as it was thrown into confusion by them.

Casanova had rarely encountered such independence of thought in a woman, let alone in one who certainly hadn't yet reached the age of twenty. Feeling a touch of melancholy, he thought back to happier bygone days when he himself, consciously and with a certain self-satisfied boldness, had ventured along the same intellectual paths he now saw Marcolina taking—the difference was that she seemed to be completely unaware of her boldness. Utterly captivated by her way of thinking and expressing herself, he came close to forgetting that his companion was a young, beautiful, and extremely desirable creature— and this was all the more amazing, considering that he was completely alone with her on the path, now cast in deep shadow, and a good distance from the house.

Suddenly, interrupting herself in mid-sentence, Marcolina called out brightly, almost joyfully, "Here comes my uncle!" . . . And Casanova whispered to her as if he had let an opportunity slip, "Too bad. I wish we could have gone on talking like this for hours, Marcolina!" — As he spoke these words, he could sense a rekindled desire glowing in his eyes, and Marcolina, who had adopted an almost intimate tone during their conversation despite her mocking attitude, immediately assumed a more distant bearing again, her look expressing the same protest, even revulsion, that had already wounded Casanova once so deeply that day. Am I really so loathsome, he asked himself anxiously? No, he said, answering his own question, that's not the problem. It's that Marcolina—isn't a woman. She's a scholar, a philosopher, one of the wonders of the world, if you like—but she's not a woman. — He understood immediately, however, that he was only saying this to try and deceive himself, to offer himself some consolation, to spare himself pain—and he also knew that this attempt was futile.

Olivo had come up to them. "Well," he said to Marcolina, "wasn't it a good idea of mine to invite Signor Casanova to the house? Now there's finally someone here for you to have intelligent conversations with, the way you do with your professors in Bologna, I would imagine."

"And even among them, dearest uncle," Marcolina replied, "there isn't a single one who would dare to challenge Voltaire himself to a duel!"

"What? Voltaire? The chevalier is challenging him to a duel?" Olivo exclaimed, uncomprehending.

"Your witty niece is referring to the disputation I've been working on recently, Olivo. Something to while away my idle hours. I used to have more sensible things to do."

"The air will be nice and cool for your walk," Marcolina said, paying no attention to his remark. Nodding curtly, she said goodbye and hurried across the meadow toward the house. Casanova forced himself not to look after her.

"Is Signora Amalia coming with us?" he asked.

"No, my esteemed Chevalier," Olivo replied, "she has a lot of things to see to in the house—this is the time of day she gives the girls their lessons, too."

"What a fine, hard-working wife and mother! You're to be envied, Olivo!"

"Yes, I tell myself the same thing every day," Olivo answered, his eyes growing moist.

They walked along the narrow side of the house. Marcolina's window was still standing open, and the gauzy, light-colored garment shimmered from deep within the dimly-lit interior. They continued along the broad chestnut-lined path until they reached the road, which was now completely in shadow. Walking slowly uphill next to the garden wall, they turned off at a right angle at the point where the vineyards began. Olivo led his guest between tall grapevines heavy with bunches of dark-blue grapes to the summit of a hill. There he gestured contentedly back toward his house, now a considerable distance below them. Casanova thought he saw a feminine figure moving back and forth past the window in the tower.

The sun had almost reached the horizon, but it was still relatively hot. Drops of perspiration ran down Olivo's cheeks, while Casanova's forehead remained perfectly dry. Moving on slowly and heading downhill now, they came to luxuriant meadowland where grapevines wreathed their way from one olive tree to the next and tall yellow ears of grain waved gently between the rows of trees.

"The sun's blessing," Casanova said appreciatively, "a thousand times over."

Once again, and at even greater length than before, Olivo told the story of how he had acquired this beautiful piece of land bit by bit and how a few good harvests and vintages had made him a well-to-do, even rich man. But Casanova was lost in thought and reacted only now and again with some polite question or other to show Olivo that he was paying attention. His host chattered on and on about everything under the sun, though it wasn't until he got onto the subject of his family and, finally, Marcolina, that Casanova began to listen attentively. He didn't find out much more than he already knew, however. Marcolina's father, Olivo's stepbrother, had been a doctor in Bologna, and her mother had died young; even as a child she had begun to amaze everyone she encountered in her father's house with the early awakenings of her mental acuity, so that people had had time and occasion enough to become accustomed to her brilliance. Her father had died a few years before, and ever since then—except for the summer months, which she always spent at her uncle's—she had been living with the family of a famous professor at the University of Bologna, the Professor Morgagni whom Casanova had already heard about and who had the audacity to want to turn his pupil into a great scholar. There had been a number of marriage offers, one from a businessman in Bologna, another from the owner of a nearby estate, and finally Lorenzi's; all of these she had rejected, and it appeared that she truly was of a mind to devote her life entirely to the service of learning. As Olivo talked on, Casanova felt his desire growing boundlessly, and the realization that it was as foolish as it was hopeless brought him to the edge of despair.

They left the fields and meadows behind and, walking out onto the road, heard the sounds of shouted greetings coming toward them from an approaching cloud of dust. A carriage came into view, and they caught sight of an elegantly-dressed older gentleman sitting inside next to a woman who was somewhat younger, voluptuous, and highly made-up.

"The marchese," Olivo whispered to his companion. "He's on his way to my house."

The carriage stopped. "Good evening, my excellent friend Olivo!" the marchese called. "May I ask you to introduce me to the Chevalier de Seingalt? I have no doubt, you see, that I have the pleasure of being in his presence at this very moment."

Casanova bowed slightly. "Yes, I am Casanova," he said.

"And I am the Marchese Celsi—and this is the marchesa, my wife." The marchesa extended her fingertips to Casanova, who put them to his lips.

The marchese had piercing greenish eyes and thick red eyebrows that grew together in the middle, none of which lent his narrow, waxen face a particularly friendly look.

"Well, my good friend Olivo," he said, "we're going to the same place, namely to your house. And since it's not even a quarter of an hour's stroll from here, I'll get out and walk with you." He turned to the marchesa, who had been taking Casanova's measure with lascivious eyes the whole time.

"I assume you have nothing against riding the short distance alone," he said.

Then, without waiting for his wife's answer, he waved to the coachman, who immediately whipped up his horses as if he had some reason for getting the marchesa away from there as quickly as possible. In a moment the carriage had disappeared in a cloud of dust.

"As you can see," said the marchese, who was a few inches taller than Casanova and unnaturally lean, "the news has already gotten around that the Chevalier de Seingalt is here and is staying at his friend Olivo's house. It must be an elevating feeling to be the bearer of such a famous name."

"You're very kind, Signor Marchese," Casanova replied. "I certainly haven't given up the hope of acquiring a name such as you describe, though at this moment I still feel far from that goal. A piece that I'm currently working on will hopefully bring me somewhat closer to it."

"We can take a shortcut here," Olivo said, setting out along a path through the fields that led directly to the wall of his garden.

"A piece," the marchese repeated in an indeterminate tone, "may I ask what sort of piece you're referring to, Chevalier?"

"Since you ask me that, Signor Marchese, I feel compelled to ask you what kind of fame it was you were referring to before."

Casanova looked arrogantly into the marchese's piercing eyes. Even though he knew very well that neither his fantastic novel *Icosameron* nor his three-volume *Refutation of Amelot's History of the Government of Venice* had brought him any literary fame to speak of, it was important to him to demonstrate that he recognized no other kind as worthwhile, and so he intentionally misunderstood all the rest of the cautiously probing remarks and allusions made by the marchese, who had no trouble picturing Casanova as a well-known seducer of women, a gambler, a businessman, a political emissary, or all sorts of other things, but certainly not as a writer, and all the less so because he had never heard a single word about either the chevalier's refutation of Amelot's work or his *Icosameron*. The marchese finally remarked, with a certain polite embarrassment, "At any rate, there's only one Casanova."

"That's not true either, Signor Marchese," Casanova replied coldly, "I have brothers and sisters, and the name of one of my brothers, the painter Francesco Casanova, might well sound familiar to the ear of an art connoisseur."

It was apparent that the marchese could not be counted among the connoisseurs of this type either, and so he turned the conversation to the subject of various acquaintances who had stayed with him in Naples, Rome, Milan, and Mantua, on the assumption that Casanova might occasionally have spent time with some of them. In this connection he mentioned, among others, Baron Perotti, though in a somewhat disdainful tone, and Casanova had to admit that he sometimes did a little gambling at the baron's house. "Just for fun," he added, "for half an hour or so before going to bed. Otherwise I've more or less given up that particular pastime."

"I'd be sorry if that were the case, Signor Chevalier," the marchese said, "because I have to confess that it's always been my dream to compete with you—both in gambling and—in my younger years—in other areas as well. Did you know, by the way, that I arrived in Spa—how long ago was that, I wonder—on precisely the same day, even the same hour, as you left? Our carriages drove past each other. And my luck was just as bad in Regensburg—I stayed in the very same room there that you had vacated an hour earlier."

Casanova felt somewhat flattered in spite of himself. "It really is unfortunate that people sometimes encounter each other too late in life," he said.

"It's still not too late," the marchese exclaimed enthusiastically. "As far as certain other things are concerned, I'll gladly concede victory to you in advance, and it doesn't bother me much; but when it comes to gambling, my dear Chevalier, perhaps both of us have reached that certain age—"

Casanova interrupted him. "That certain age—you may be right. But I'm afraid that precisely in the area of gambling I'm no longer entitled to the pleasure of competing with a partner of your standing, since"—this he said in the tone of a dethroned ruler—"since despite all my fame, my esteemed Signor Marchese, I've never amounted to much more than a beggar."

The marchese involuntarily lowered his eyes before Casanova's proud look, then shook his head in disbelief as if in response to an odd kind of joke. Olivo, however, who had been following the whole conversation avidly, accompanying his extraordinary friend's masterfully adroit responses with approving nods, wasn't able to hide his expression of alarm. The three men had come to a narrow wooden door in the wall at the back of the garden; Olivo turned the key in the squeaky lock and, letting the marchese step through into the garden ahead of him, grabbed Casanova by the arm.

"You'll take back what you just said, Chevalier, before you set foot in my house again," he whispered to him. "The money I've owed you for sixteen years is waiting for you. I just didn't dare to . . . You can ask Amalia . . . It's all counted out already. I was planning on waiting until you were leaving—"

Casanova interrupted him gently. "You don't owe me anything, Olivo. Those few pieces of gold were, as you know, a wedding present that I, as a friend of Amalia's mother . . . But why are we even talking about this? What do I care about a few ducats? I'm at a turning point in my life," he added in an intentionally loud voice, so that the marchese, who had stopped to wait for them, could hear.

Olivo exchanged looks with Casanova to make sure that he approved, then said to the marchese, "You see, the chevalier has been called back to Venice, his home city, and he'll be leaving in a few days."

"Or to be more precise," Casanova said as they drew closer to the house, "they've been appealing to me for some time now to come back, and their pleas are getting more and more urgent. But in my view, those lordly senators took their time getting to that point. Now it's their turn to be patient."

"A proud stance," the marchese said, "and one that you are absolutely justified in taking, Chevalier!"

Leaving the path and crossing the meadow, which was completely in shadow now, they saw the small company of people standing near the house waiting for them. Everyone got up and began walking towards them, the abbot taking the lead between Marcolina and Amalia; the marchesa followed after, next to a tall, clean-shaven young officer in a silver-laced red uniform and shiny riding boots who could be none other than Lorenzi. The way in which he spoke to the marchesa, glancing at her white, powdered shoulders as if they were a familiar sample of other attractive items no less well-known to him, and even more than this, the marchesa's smiling gaze up at him and her half-closed eyelids, could leave even those with less experience with no doubt as to the nature of the relationship between them, nor about their lack of concern to keep it a secret from anyone. They continued their quiet but animated conversation until they were standing face-to-face with the new arrivals.

Olivo introduced Casanova and Lorenzi. Each took the other's measure with a brief, cold look that seemed to assert their mutual antipathy; then both smiled fleetingly and bowed without offering a hand to shake, since each would have had to take a step toward the other to do this. Lorenzi was a handsome man with a thin face and, considering his youthfulness, strikingly severe features; there was an indefinable flicker in the depths of his eyes, warning anyone of Casanova's experience to proceed with caution. For a split-second he wondered who it was that Lorenzi reminded him of, then realized that he was seeing a vision of himself from thirty years before. Can it be that I've returned in his body, he wondered? But then I would have to have died already . . . A shudder went through him: Haven't I been dead for a long time in any case? What's left of the Casanova who was young, handsome, and happy?

He heard Amalia's voice. It seemed to come from far away, although she was standing right next to him asking how he had enjoyed his walk. Speaking loudly enough for everyone to hear, he lavishly praised the productive, well-tended estate he had just explored with Olivo. Meanwhile, the maid was beginning to set the extra-long table that had been carried out onto the grass; with a great deal of bustle and giggling, Olivo's two elder daughters helped by bringing dishes and glasses and whatever else was needed from the house. It was coming on for dusk, and a gentle cooling breeze was blowing through the garden. Marcolina hurried over to the table to finish what the children had started in consort with the maid and to remedy the things they hadn't gotten right. The others strolled around the meadow and along the paths in casual groupings. The marchesa treated Casanova with great courtesy, asking among other things if he would tell the famous story of his escape from the Lead Chambers of Venice; she was well aware, of course—as she added with an ambiguous smile—that he had survived much more dangerous adventures, though to tell these might well be something of a dubious proposition. Casanova replied that while he had indeed been involved in various sorts of difficult situations, both serious and amusing, he had never really gotten to know first-hand the one walk of life whose purpose and very essence was synonymous with danger; for even though he had been a soldier on the Island of Corfu for a few months during a time of unrest many years before—really, was there any profession on earth that fate had not thrust him into?!—he had never had the good fortune to participate in an actual campaign as Lieutenant Lorenzi was about to, something that made him feel almost envious.

"You seem to be better informed than I am, Signor Casanova," Lorenzi said, his voice sharp and defiant—"better even than my colonel, who just granted me an indefinite extension of my leave."

"Did he now!" the marchese exclaimed with uncontrolled fury. "And just imagine, Lorenzi," he added in a mocking tone, "we—I should say my wife—was so sure that you were going to be leaving that she already invited one of our friends, the singer Baldi, to come and stay with us the beginning of next week."

"That's a nice coincidence," Lorenzi replied unperturbed, "Baldi and I are good friends, we'll get along fine." He turned to the marchesa, his teeth flashing. "Don't you agree?"

"I would advise both of you to do so," she said, smiling brightly, then walked over to the still empty table and took a seat. Olivo and Lorenzi joined her on either side, and Amalia sat down across from them between the marchese and Casanova, who had Marcolina on his left at one of the narrow ends; the abbot sat at the opposite end of the table next to Olivo.

The food was simple but extremely palatable, just as it had been at lunch. The two elder daughters, Teresina and Nanetta, served the guests and filled their glasses with excellent wine from Olivo's slopes; both the marchese and the abbot thanked the girls with playfully crude caresses that a father who was stricter than Olivo might not have found acceptable. Amalia seemed not to notice; she was pale and wore a gloomy expression on her face, like a woman who was determined to grow old since being young no longer had any meaning for her. Is this all that's left of my power over women? Casanova thought bitterly as he looked at her from the side. But maybe it was only the light that had transformed Amalia's expression and made it look so sad. A single broad beam from a lamp inside the house fell on the guests, who otherwise made do with the dusky glow of the sky. The sharp black outlines of the treetops cut off the view, reminding Casanova of a mysterious garden where, many long years ago, he had once waited for a lady love in the middle of the night.

"Murano," he whispered to himself, trembling. "There's a garden that belongs to a religious order on an island close to Venice," he added out loud. "The last time I was there was a few decades ago; the nighttime fragrances were exactly the same as they are here now."

"I suppose you were a monk at one time, too?" the marchesa asked jokingly.

"Almost," Casanova replied with a smile. He told the true story of how he had received minor orders from the Patriarch of Venice at the age of fifteen, but soon decided to put his clerical garb aside. The abbot made mention of a nearby convent and strongly urged Casanova to pay it a visit if he hadn't already. Olivo agreed emphatically, praising the somber old building, its pleasant location, and the changing scenery along the way. Incidentally, the abbot continued, Sister Seraphina, the abbess—an extremely learned woman and a duchess by birth—had written him a letter (the nuns in this particular convent were under a vow of perpetual silence) in which she had mentioned the erudite young Marcolina and expressed a desire to meet her face to face.

"Well, Marcolina," Lorenzi said, addressing her directly for the first time, "I hope you won't be seduced into trying to emulate this duchess-abbess in every respect."

"Why should I be?" Marcolina replied brightly. "Freedom can be maintained without taking vows—more easily, in fact, because vows mean compulsion."

Casanova sat next to her, not even daring to touch her foot slightly or press his knee against hers; if he were forced to witness that horrified, disgusted expression on her face yet a third time—this he knew with certainty—he would unfailingly be driven to some act of madness. As the meal progressed and the empty glasses grew in number, the conversation became more animated and began to extend around the whole table; all at once Casanova heard Amalia's voice, coming again, as it seemed, from far away: "I spoke with Marcolina—"

"You spoke with—" An insane hope flared up in him.

"Keep your voice down, Casanova. We didn't talk about you, only her and her plans for the future. And I'll tell you one more time: She will never give herself to any man."

Olivo, who had put away considerable quantities of wine, suddenly got up from his chair with his glass in his hand and said a few awkward words about the great honor that had been granted his house by virtue of the visit of his esteemed friend the Chevalier de Seingalt.

"Where is this Chevalier de Seingalt you're referring to, my good friend Olivo?" Lorenzi asked in his sharp, defiant voice.

Casanova's first impulse was to throw his full glass of wine in the impertinent lieutenant's face; but Amalia touched his arm lightly and said, "There are still many people, Signor Chevalier, who know you only as Casanova, your older and more famous name."

"I wasn't aware that the King of France had conferred nobility on Signor Casanova," Lorenzi said in an earnest, insulting tone.

"I was able to spare the king the effort," Casanova replied calmly, "and I hope that you will be willing to accept an explanation that the Mayor of Nuremberg found unobjectionable when I offered it to him in connection with another matter that needn't concern us here." The others remained tensely silent. "Everyone knows that the alphabet is common property," he went on. "I picked out several letters that I liked and made myself a nobleman without being under obligation to a ruler who would hardly have been able to acknowledge my claims. I am Casanova Chevalier de Seingalt. I would be sorry for your sake, Lieutenant Lorenzi, if this name did not meet with your approval."

"Seingalt—an excellent name," the abbot said, then repeated it a few times as if he were trying out the aftertaste on his lips.

"And there's no one in the world," Olivo exclaimed, "who has more right to the title of chevalier than my noble friend Casanova!"

"Furthermore, Lorenzi," the marchese added, "as soon as your fame resounds as far and wide as that of Signor Casanova, Chevalier de Seingalt, we will not hesitate, if you should so desire, to call you 'chevalier' as well."

Casanova, annoyed at the unwanted support from all sides, was about to ask that the others refrain so that he could get on with the point at issue on his own, when two old men in barely respectable clothing stepped out of the darkness of the garden and came up to the table. Happy to have the edge taken off a dispute that was threatening to become serious and spoil the merriment of the evening, Olivo gave them a noisily cordial welcome. The new arrivals were the Ricardi brothers, two bachelors who had once lived in high style, as Casanova soon learned from Olivo, but who had had little success in a variety of enterprises and had finally moved back to the neighboring village, their place of birth, where they lived in a miserable little rented house. An odd pair, but inoffensive enough. The two Ricardis expressed their delight at renewing their acquaintance with the chevalier, whom they had met in Paris years before. Casanova didn't remember the occasion. Or had it been Madrid? . . . "That's possible," he said, but he knew that he had never seen them before. Only the younger-looking of the two said anything; the other one looked like he was ninety years old and accompanied his brother's remarks with incessant nodding and an addled grin.

Everyone rose from the table; the children had already left some time before. Lorenzi and the marchesa strolled across the meadow in the dusky light, and Marcolina and Amalia soon could be seen through the open parlor windows, apparently getting things ready for the card game. What's going on here, Casanova wondered, as he stood alone in the garden. Do they think I'm rich? Are they out to fleece me? All these preparations, the marchese's courteous manner, the abbot's obsequiousness even, and the arrival of the Ricardi brothers, somehow seemed suspicious to him; and couldn't Lorenzi be part of the conspiracy, too? Or Marcolina? Or even Amalia? Is this whole business, he thought fleetingly, a trick my enemies are playing on me to complicate my return to Venice—to make it impossible the very moment I'm ready to leave? But he immediately realized that this idea was completely nonsensical, if for no other reason than that he no longer had any enemies. He was a poor old fool who had seen better days and had ceased to be a danger to anyone; who would even care if he returned to Venice or not? Through the open windows he saw the men busily arranging themselves around the table, on which a deck of cards and full wine glasses had been set out, and he realized beyond any doubt that nothing more was planned here than the usual innocent card game at which a new player would, of course, certainly be welcome.

Marcolina brushed against Casanova as she walked past him and wished him good luck.

"You're not going to stay?" he asked. "Not even just to watch the game?"

"What point would there be in that? Good night, Chevalier de Seingalt—I'll see you tomorrow."

Voices called out into the garden. "Lorenzi" — "Signor Chevalier" — "We're waiting." Standing in the shadow of the house, Casanova could see the marchesa trying to pull Lorenzi away from the meadow to the darkness of the trees. Once there, she pressed her-

self against him passionately, but Lorenzi tore himself away roughly
and hurried toward the house. He met Casanova at the entrance and,
with a kind of mock politeness, allowed him to enter first. Casanova
accepted without responding.

The marchese set up the first bank. Olivo, the Ricardi brothers,
and the abbot wagered such small amounts that the whole game
seemed like a joke to Casanova, even now, when his entire wealth
consisted of only a few ducats. And the marchese's grandiose expression as he gathered in the money or paid it out, as if large amounts
were involved, struck him as all the more ridiculous. Lorenzi, who
hadn't been part of the game at first, suddenly threw a ducat onto the
table and won; he then bet his two ducats and won a second and a
third time, and after that he kept winning with only occasional interruptions. The others continued to wager their small coins as before,
and the two Ricardis in particular grew highly indignant when the
marchese appeared not to be treating them with the same respect as
Lieutenant Lorenzi. The brothers bet together on each hand; beads of
perspiration rolled down the older one's forehead as he was dealt his
cards, while the other stood behind him, talking at him incessantly as
if he had unerring advice to offer. Every time his taciturn brother
gathered in their winnings his eyes brightened, and when they lost he
looked heavenward in despair. The abbot remained relatively indifferent, uttering only occasional comments of an aphoristic nature,
such as "Neither luck nor women can be coerced," or "The earth is
round, heaven is vast." Every now and then he shot sly, encouraging
looks at Casanova, and then Amalia, who was sitting across the table
next to her husband, as if he wanted to get the former lovers to pair
off again. But Casanova's only thought was that Marcolina was slowly
undressing in her room at that very moment, and that if her window
was open her white skin would be shimmering out into the night.
Seized by a mind-numbing desire, he was on the verge of getting up
from his seat next to the marchese and leaving the room; the marchese,
however, took his stirring as an indication that he wanted to join in
the game.

"Ah, finally!" he said. "We knew that you wouldn't remain a mere
spectator, Chevalier."

He dealt him a card, and Casanova bet all the money he had with him, which was just about all he had to his name. It amounted to about ten ducats, though he didn't count it; he simply let it slip out of his moneybag onto the table and hoped that he would lose it in one round. This would then be a sign, a good omen, though he wasn't really sure of what—possibly of his imminent return to Venice, or a chance to look at Marcolina with no clothes on; but before he had time to make up his mind which it was, the marchese had already lost the hand to him. Casanova let his winnings ride as Lorenzi had, and luck stayed with him too, just as it had with the lieutenant. By now the marchese was no longer paying any attention to the other players; insulted, the silent Ricardi brother got up, while the other one wrung his hands—then the two of them went and stood in one corner of the room looking devastated. The abbot and Olivo were more easily appeased; the first ate candies and repeated his little sayings, while the other watched the course of the game excitedly. Soon the marchese had lost five hundred ducats, with Casanova and Lorenzi sharing in the winnings.

The marchesa got up and gave the lieutenant a sign with her eyes before leaving the room; her hips swayed as she walked, which Casanova found repulsive. Amalia followed after her, creeping along at her side like a submissive old woman. Now that the marchese had lost all his cash, Casanova took over the bank, insisting to the marchese's displeasure that the others join the game again. The Ricardi brothers were back at the table in a flash, eager and excited; the abbot had had enough and shook his head, and Olivo joined in purely in acquiescence to his noble guest's wishes. Lorenzi's luck continued; when he had won a total of four hundred ducats, he got up from the table.

"I'll be glad to offer anyone another chance tomorrow. For now, though, I'd like to ask your permission to leave—I have to be getting home."

"Home," the marchese exclaimed with a derisive laugh, "that's not bad!" He turned to the others. "The lieutenant's staying at my place, you know. And my wife already left some time ago. Enjoy yourself, Lorenzi!"

"You know very well that I'm riding straight to Mantua," Lorenzi replied without batting an eye, "and not to your palazzo, where you were kind enough to put me up yesterday."

"Ride wherever you want to—straight to hell, for all I care!"

Lorenzi paid his respects to the others with extreme politeness and left without giving the marchese a suitable response, which amazed Casanova. The chevalier went back to turning cards up again and had such a streak of luck that the marchese soon owed him a few hundred ducats. What's the point, Casanova wondered at first. Gradually, though, the allure of the game took hold of him again. I'm not doing badly, he thought . . . I'll have a thousand soon . . . and that could turn into two thousand. And the marchese will pay what he owes. I wouldn't mind at all making my entrance into Venice with a small fortune in hand. But why Venice? Being rich again means being young again. Money is everything. Now I'll be able to buy them again, at least. Who, though? There's only one I want . . . She's standing at the window naked—I know she is . . . she's waiting after all . . . suspecting that I'll come . . . she's standing at the window to drive me crazy. And I'm here.

Meanwhile, his face expressionless, he kept on dealing cards to the marchese, Olivo and the Ricardis, every so often slipping the brothers a gold piece they were in no way entitled to. They made no objections. From the darkness outside came a sound like the hoofbeats of a horse galloping along the road. Lorenzi, Casanova thought . . . The noise reverberated from the garden wall like an echo, then gradually faded away. Soon Casanova's luck began to turn against him. The marchese's bets grew steadily larger, and by midnight Casanova was as poor as he had been before—even poorer, in fact, since he had lost the few gold pieces he had started with as well. Pushing the cards aside, he rose with a smile.

"Thank you, gentlemen."

Olivo stretched his arms out to him. "My friend, let's keep playing . . . A hundred and fifty ducats, have you forgotten? — No, not just a hundred and fifty! Everything I have, everything I am—everything, everything!"

Olivo hadn't stopped drinking the whole evening and was slurring his words. Casanova turned down his offer with an exaggeratedly elegant gesture.

"There's no coercing women or luck," he said, bowing towards the abbot, who nodded contentedly and clapped his hands.

"I'll see you tomorrow, then, my esteemed Chevalier," the marchese said. "The two of us will take Lieutenant Lorenzi's money away from him again."

The Ricardis insisted that the game go on. The marchese, in a jovial mood now, set up a bank for them, and they got out the gold pieces that Casanova had helped them acquire. In two minutes the marchese had won everything back and firmly refused to go on playing with them if they couldn't produce any cash. They wrung their hands, and the older brother began to cry like a child; the younger one kissed him on both cheeks to calm him down. The marchese asked if his carriage had returned yet, and the abbot said that he had heard it drive up half an hour before. The marchese offered to give the abbot and the Ricardi brothers a ride home, and everyone left.

Once the others had gone, Olivo took Casanova's arm and assured him over and over again in a teary voice that everything in the house belonged to him, Casanova, and that he was free to do whatever he liked with it. They walked past Marcolina's window. It was closed now and covered with a grating as well, and curtains hung down on the inside. There had been times, Casanova thought, when such things were of no use or didn't mean anything. They stepped inside the house. Olivo insisted on accompanying his guest up the rather creaky stairway to the tower room, where he gave him a farewell embrace.

"We'll pay a visit to the convent tomorrow," he said. "But sleep as long as you like; we won't be leaving too terribly early—in fact, we'll arrange everything to suit you. Good night."

He left, closing the door quietly behind him, but his footsteps resounded from the stairway through the entire house.

Casanova stood by himself in the subdued light of two candles, letting his eyes wander around the room from one window to the next. The countryside stretched out in a bluish haze, looking almost the same in each of the four directions: broad plains with slight rises, and only in the north the indistinct outlines of mountains; here and there occasional houses, farms, some relatively large buildings as well. From one of these, on slightly higher ground, a light was shining; Casanova assumed that this was the marchese's palazzo.

Apart from the wide, free-standing bed, the room contained nothing but the long table on which the two candles stood burning, a few chairs, and a dresser with a gold-framed mirror above it; careful hands had straightened up the room, and Casanova's traveling bag had been unpacked. The well-worn locked leather portfolio containing his papers lay on the table, along with a few books that he needed for his work and had brought along for that reason; writing utensils had been laid out for him too. Since he didn't feel the least bit sleepy, he took his manuscript out of the portfolio and sat in the candlelight reading through what he had last written; he had stopped in the middle of a paragraph, so it was easy for him to pick up the thread.

Taking pen in hand, he quickly wrote a few sentences, then stopped again suddenly. What's the point, he said to himself, as if he had just realized some terrible truth. Even if I were sure that what I've written so far and will continue to write would turn out to be magnificent beyond compare—yes, even if I could actually succeed in demolishing Voltaire and outshining his fame with mine—wouldn't I gladly burn all these papers in spite of all that if I were granted the privilege of holding Marcolina in my embrace now instead? Wouldn't I be prepared to vow never again to set foot in Venice—even if its citizens were about to welcome me back in triumph? Venice! . . . He repeated the word, and it rang out around him in all its splendor— and in an instant it had regained its old power over him. The city of his youth rose up before him, bathed in all the magic of memory, and his heart swelled with a tormented, boundless longing—greater, he believed, than any he had ever felt before. Never to return home seemed to him the most impossible of all sacrifices that fate could require of him. How could he go on in this miserable, vapid world without the hope, the certainty of seeing his beloved city again? After years and decades of wandering and adventure, after all the happiness and misery he had experienced, after the honor and disgrace, the triumphs

and humiliations he had gone through, he finally needed a place to
rest, a home. And could there be any home for him but Venice? Or
any happiness except in knowing that he had a home again? An out-
cast in foreign lands, he had long since been unable to achieve any
lasting happiness. At times he was still able to summon the strength
to grasp hold of it, but he could no longer maintain this hold. His
power over people, women and men alike, was gone. Only in situations where he represented some past memory was his word, his voice,
his gaze still able to captivate; in the real present, however, none of
this had any effect. His time was past!

And now he admitted something else to himself, something he
had previously tried his best to keep hidden: that even his literary
achievements, including the disputation against Voltaire on which he
had pinned all his hopes, would never achieve widespread success. It
was too late for this, too. If he had had the time and patience in
younger years to devote himself more assiduously to his writing, he
was certain that he would have been a match for the best of the poets
and philosophers; and it was equally true that, given greater persever-
ance and caution than were his by nature, he could have become the
most competent of financiers or diplomats. But what had happened
to all his patience and caution, all his plans for the future, whenever a
new amorous adventure had beckoned? Women—women everywhere!
At any given moment he had been willing to throw everything away
for them; whether aristocratic or lower-class women, passionate or
frigid women, virgins or sluts—for him, all the honors of this world
and all the bliss of the next had always been for sale for a night of love
in a different bed. — But did he have any regrets about whatever else
in life he might have missed as a result of his eternal quest, this never
(or always) finding, this earthly-divine flight from desire to pleasure
and from pleasure to desire? No, he regretted nothing. He had lived a
life such as no other man had—and wasn't he still living it after a
fashion? He still encountered women everywhere, although they might
not exactly lose their minds over him any longer as they once had. —
And Amalia? — He could have her anytime he wanted—at this very
moment, in her drunken husband's bed. And the proprietress of his
inn in Mantua—wasn't she in love with him, tenderly, jealously, as if

he were a handsome boy? — And Perotti's pock-marked, but shapely mistress, intoxicated by the name Casanova, a name that seemed to shower sparks of lust from a thousand nights on her—hadn't she begged him to grant her one single night of love, and hadn't he spurned her like a man who was still able to choose according to his own pleasure? — Then, of course, there was . . . Marcolina—women like Marcolina were beyond his reach now. Or—might she always have been? Women of that type certainly existed. He may have encountered one at some point in his life, but since there had always been others who were more willing, he had never wasted so much as a day sighing in vain. And since not even Lorenzi had been able to win over Marcolina—since she had refused the offer of a man who was as handsome and as brazen as he, Casanova, had been in his younger years— it might just be possible that she was indeed the embodiment of that wondrous being whose existence on earth he had previously doubted: the virtuous woman. And he let out a ringing laugh that echoed through the room. "That inept fool!" he shouted, as he often did during soliloquies of this sort. "He didn't know how to make the most of the situation. Or the marchesa won't let him go. Or did he take up with her only because he couldn't get that scholar, that philosopher Marcolina?!"

And suddenly an idea came to him: I'll read my disputation against Voltaire to her tomorrow! She's the only person I can count on to truly appreciate it. I'll convince her . . . she'll be full of admiration. Of course she will . . . "Excellent, Signor Casanova! Your writing style is brilliant, old man! So help me, you've destroyed Voltaire . . . you ingenious Methuselah!" He went on in this way, hissing out the words and running back and forth in the room as if he were in a cage. A tremendous rage had taken hold of him, against Marcolina, against Voltaire, against himself, against the whole world. He summoned his last ounce of self-control to keep himself from shouting at the top of voice. Finally he flung himself down on the bed, still dressed, and lay there, staring with wide-open eyes at the beams in the ceiling; here and there he saw the silvery gleam of spider webs in the glow of the candles. Then, as sometimes happened to him before falling asleep after a gambling spree, images of playing cards began racing past him at a fantastic speed. Finally he sank into a brief and dreamless sleep, then woke again and lay there listening to the mysterious silence all around him. The windows of his room stood open to the east and south; delicate, sweet fragrances came wafting in from the garden and the fields, and he could hear indeterminate noises from far and wide, harbingers of the approaching dawn. Casanova was unable to lie still any longer; an insistent yearning for change took hold of him, enticing him out into the open. Birds called to him with their songs and the cool morning breeze brushed his forehead. He opened the door quietly and tiptoed down the stairway; the nimbleness he had demonstrated on so many occasions allowed him to negotiate the wooden steps without the slightest creak. Then he made his way down the stone staircase to the ground floor and through the dining room, where half-filled glasses still stood on the table, and from there out into the garden. Since his footsteps made a sound on the gravel, he immediately stepped onto the grass, which stretched out endlessly in the early dawn light. Next he crept along the path toward the side of the house where Marcolina's window would come into his line of vision. It was closed and covered with its grating and curtain just as he had last seen it. Casanova sat down on a stone bench barely fifty paces away from the house. He heard a carriage drive by on the other side of the garden wall, then all was quiet again. A fine gray vapor rose from the meadow, giving it the look of a diaphanous, nebulous pond with blurred edges. He thought again of that night long ago in the cloister garden on the island of Murano—or had it been a different garden, a different night? He wasn't sure any longer which one— perhaps a hundred nights were all running together in his memory into a single one, just as on some occasions a hundred women he had loved became a single one, an enigmatic figure floating through his wondering mind. And wasn't one night ultimately like any other, after all? And one woman like any other? Especially when it was over? And the word "over" kept hammering in his temples, as if it was destined from this point on to become the pulse beat of his lost existence.

He thought he heard something rustling along the wall behind him. Or was it just an echo? Yes, that was it—the noise itself was coming from the house. All at once Marcolina's window was standing open, the grating pushed back and the curtain gathered up to one side; a shadowy figure appeared from out of the darkness of the room— it was Marcolina herself. She stepped up to the window sill in her white, high-buttoned nightgown as if to breathe in the pleasant morning air. In an instant Casanova had slid down off the bench; mesmerized, he looked past it through the branches by the path at Marcolina, whose eyes appeared to be submerged in the dawn, heedless, looking in no particular direction. A few seconds later she finally seemed able to compose her still drowsy self and let her glance wander slowly to the right and left. Next she bent over the window sill, her long, flowing hair trailing down, as if searching for something on the gravel, and immediately after that she turned her head upward toward a window on the floor above. Once again she stood for a while without moving, her hands propped against the window frame on both sides as if she were nailed to an invisible cross. Only then, as if suddenly illuminated from inside her, did her indistinct facial features become clearer to Casanova. A smile played around her lips, then froze instantly. She put her arms down, and her mouth moved strangely as if she were whispering a prayer. Once again her eyes surveyed the garden, slowly searching; then she gave a quick nod, and at that same moment someone who must have been crouching at her feet till then swung himself over the window sill and landed outside: Lorenzi. He virtually flew over the gravel to the broad path, crossing over it not ten paces away from Casanova, who lay under the bench holding his breath, then hurried toward the back of the garden beyond the path, where a narrow strip of grass ran alongside the wall, and was soon out of sight. Casanova heard a door sigh on its hinges—it had to be the same one he had come through the previous evening with Olivo and the marchese to get into the garden—and then all was quiet. Marcolina had remained at the window completely motionless the whole time. As soon as she was sure that Lorenzi had gotten away safely, she breathed a deep sigh of relief, then closed the grating and the window; the curtain fell shut as if by its own power, and everything was as it had been before—except that in the meantime, as if it no longer had any reason to hesitate, dawn had begun to break over the house and garden.

Casanova, too, was still lying there under the bench as before, his arms stretched out in front of him. After a while he crawled over to the middle of the path and continued from there on all fours until he had reached a spot where he couldn't be seen either from Marcolina's window or any of the others. He stood up, his back aching, stretched his body and then his arms and legs, and finally regained his senses. Only now, in fact, did he become his true self again; he felt as if he had been transformed from a beaten dog back into a human being, condemned now to feel the blows not as bodily pain, but as a terrible disgrace. Why, he said to himself, didn't I go up to the window while it was still open and climb over the sill into her room? Could she have resisted? Could she have allowed herself to, that hypocrite, that liar, that slut? He went on calling her names as if it were his right, as if she had sworn a lover's oath to be faithful to him and then deceived him. He vowed to confront her in person, to accuse her to her face in the presence of Olivo, Amalia, the marchese, the abbot, the maid and the servants of being nothing but a lascivious little whore. As if rehearsing, he ran through every little detail of what he had just witnessed, taking pleasure in inventing all kinds of extra things to humiliate her even more: she had stood naked at the window, she had let her lover fondle her indecently as the morning breezes played about them.

But now that he had taken the edge off his anger for the moment, he considered whether there might not be some better use for his new knowledge. Wasn't she in his power now? Couldn't he use threats to force her to give him what she wouldn't give willingly? But this disgraceful plan immediately collapsed of itself, less because Casanova saw it as disgraceful than because he knew it would be pointless and futile in her case. Why would Marcolina care if he threatened her? She was answerable to no one and cunning enough, if it came down to it, to drive him from her doorstep as a slanderer and blackmailer. And even if she were willing for some reason to pay with her body to keep her affair with Lorenzi a secret (he knew, of course, that this was beyond the realm of possibility), wouldn't he, Casanova, a lover who was a thousand times more desirous of bestowing bliss than receiving it, find this forced pleasure an unspeakable torture that would drive him to madness and self-destruction?

Suddenly he found himself standing by the garden door. It was locked, so Lorenzi had to have a duplicate key. Who, then, he wondered for a moment, had gone thundering off through the night on a galloping horse after Lorenzi had left the card game? Someone he had hired beforehand, apparently. Casanova couldn't help smiling in approval . . . they were worthy of each other, Marcolina and Lorenzi, the philosopher and the officer. And both of them still had brilliant careers ahead of them. Who will Marcolina's next lover be, he wondered? The professor in Bologna whose house she lives in? Oh, what a fool I am—he already is, has been for a long time . . . Who else has there been? Olivo? The abbot? Why not?! Or the young servant who was standing by the gate gawking when we drove up yesterday? Every one of them! I'll swear to it. But Lorenzi doesn't know. I have that advantage over him.

Yet deep down inside, Casanova was not only convinced that Lorenzi had been Marcolina's first lover, he even suspected that this had been their first night together. But this didn't keep him from continuing his spitefully lewd imaginings as he walked along the wall by the edge of the garden. Soon he was standing once again at the door to the parlor, which he had left open; it was clear to him that for the moment he had no alternative but to sneak back undetected to his room in the tower. He crept up the stairs as quietly as he could and, once there, let himself sink into the easy chair where he had been sitting before; the pages of his manuscript lay on the table and seemed to be awaiting his return. His glance fell automatically on the sentence he had left half-finished before: "Voltaire will be immortal, that is certain; but he will have paid for his immortality with that part of himself which is immortal; his wit has consumed his heart, just as doubt has his soul, and so—"

At that moment the reddish rays of the morning sun came flooding in and the page he was holding in his hand began to glow; feeling defeated, he put it back down on top of the others. Noticing suddenly how dry his lips were, he poured himself a glass of water from the bottle standing on the table; it was lukewarm and had a sweetish taste. Disgusted, he turned his head to one side; a pale old face with disheveled hair hanging down over the forehead stared out at him from the mirror above the chest. With self-tormenting pleasure he let the corners of his mouth droop even more limply, as if he were performing some hackneyed role in a play. Running his hand through his hair to make the strands look even more disorderly, he stuck his tongue out at his reflection in the mirror, croaked out a string of nonsensical, abusive names in an intentionally hoarse voice, and finished by blowing the pages of his manuscript off the table like a badly-behaved child. Then he began to swear at Marcolina again, and after heaping the most obscene insults possible on her he whispered through his teeth: Do you think your pleasure will last for long? You'll get fat and wrinkled and old just like the other women you once shared your youth with—you'll become an old woman with flaccid breasts and dry gray hair, toothless and bad-smelling . . . and finally you'll die! You might even die young! Then you'll decompose—and be food for worms.

As his final revenge against her, he tried to imagine her dead. He saw her lying in an open coffin dressed in white, yet he was unable to visualize any signs of physical deterioration in her body; on the contrary, her truly ethereal beauty worked him into a frenzy again. Before his closed eyes the coffin became a nuptial bed; Marcolina lay there blinking her eyes and smiling, and then, with a mocking expression, tore the white garment away from her delicate breasts with her slender hands. But as he stretched his arms out and was about to throw himself on her and embrace her, the vision dissolved into nothingness.

There was a knock on the door; he awoke with a start out of his stupor and saw Olivo standing next to him.

"Don't tell me you're at your desk already?!"

Casanova composed himself instantly. "I'm in the habit of devoting the early morning hours to my writing," he said. "What time has it gotten to be?"

"Eight o'clock," Olivo replied. "Breakfast is waiting in the garden. Whenever it suits you, Chevalier, we can start out on our trip to the convent. But look at the way the wind has scattered your papers around!"

Casanova made no objections as he bent down to pick them up off the floor. Walking over to the window, he saw that the breakfast table had been set up on the grass in the shade of the house. Seated around it, dressed in white, were Amalia, Marcolina, and the three little girls. They all shouted their morning greetings up to him, but he saw only Marcolina; holding a plate of early-ripe grapes in her lap and popping one after the other into her mouth, she smiled up at him, her eyes bright and friendly. All his contempt for her, all his anger and hatred melted away in his heart; he knew only that he loved her. Intoxicated by the sight of her, he stepped back into the room, where Olivo was still kneeling on the floor gathering the scattered pages from under the table and chest. Casanova insisted that he stop and asked to be left alone so that he could get ready for their outing.

"There's no hurry," Olivo said, brushing the dust off his breeches, "we'll easily be back in time for lunch. By the way, the marchese asked if we could start our game today early in the afternoon; apparently he wants to be home before dark."

"It really doesn't matter to me when the game starts," Casanova said, arranging his papers in their portfolio, "I certainly won't be part of it."

"Yes, you will," Olivo declared in a decisive tone not typical of him. He placed a roll of gold pieces on the table. "This is in repayment of my debt, Chevalier—late, but with a grateful heart."

Casanova made a dismissive gesture.

"You must accept this," Olivo insisted, "or I'll be deeply insulted; besides, Amalia had a dream last night that will induce you . . . but I'll let her tell it to you herself."

Having said this, he hastily left the room. Casanova went ahead and counted the gold pieces nonetheless; there were a hundred and fifty, the exact number he had given the bridegroom, or the bride, or her mother—he wasn't sure himself anymore—fifteen years earlier. The most sensible thing to do, he said to himself, would be to put the money in my bag, say goodbye and leave the house, if possible without seeing Marcolina again. But have I ever done what's sensible? He wondered if a message from Venice might not have arrived in the meantime . . . P52His excellent proprietress, of course, had promised to forward anything to him immediately . . .

Meanwhile, the maid had brought up a large pottery jug full of cold spring water; Casanova washed his entire body and felt very refreshed. Then he put on the better of his two outfits, a formal one he would have worn the previous evening if he had had time to change. On the other hand, he was quite content to be able to appear before Marcolina today in more elegant garb and, in a sense, as a different person.

He made his entrance into the garden in a glossy silk gray coat adorned with embroidery and broad Spanish silver lace, a yellow vest, and cherry-red silk breeches. His bearing was noble, though not quite proud; a condescending yet at the same time affable smile played around his lips, and his eyes seemed to sparkle with the fire of inextinguishable youth. He was disappointed to find the garden empty now except for Olivo, who invited him to sit down next to him at the table and make do with a modest breakfast. Casanova feasted on milk, butter, eggs, and white bread, followed by peaches and grapes that seemed more exquisite to him than any he had ever tasted before. The three girls came running across the grass toward the table. Casanova kissed each of them, then gave the thirteen-year-old a few little caresses of the kind she had put up with from the abbot the day before; but the sparks that suddenly glimmered in her eyes, as Casanova was quick to recognize, had been ignited by a pleasure different from that of an innocent child's game.

Olivo was pleased to see how well the chevalier was getting on with the children.

"And you mean to say you're still going to leave us tomorrow?" he asked with shy affection.

"This evening," Casanova said, but with a playful wink. "You know after all, my dear Olivo, the senators in Venice—"

"Haven't done a thing to deserve you," Olivo interrupted him forcefully. "Let them wait. Stay with us till the day after tomorrow— no, stay for a week."

Casanova slowly shook his head. He was holding little Teresina by the hands and pretending to keep her trapped between his knees; with a smile that no longer had anything childlike about it, she slithered easily out of his grasp. Just then Amalia and Marcolina came out of the house wearing shawls over their light dresses, Amalia's black and Marcolina's white. Olivo urged both of them to help convince their guest to stay.

"It's not possible," Casanova said, a note of exaggerated severity in his voice, when neither Amalia nor Marcolina could find anything to say in support of Olivo.

As they strolled along the path under the chestnut trees toward the gate, Marcolina asked Casanova if he had made any significant progress on his writing the previous night; Olivo had told her that he had found the chevalier early that morning still hard at work. For a moment Casanova contemplated giving her a sarcastically ambiguous answer that would have made her suspicious without betraying his own hand; but considering the negative consequences that any premature remark might have, he restrained himself and replied politely that he had only made a few revisions, and that these had been the result of their stimulating conversation of the day before.

They climbed into the carriage, which was inelegant and poorly upholstered but otherwise comfortable. Casanova sat across from Marcolina and Olivo across from his wife, but the vehicle was so spacious that even with all the shaking back and forth there was no chance of any unintentional contact between the occupants. Casanova asked Amalia to tell him her dream. She gave him a friendly, almost gracious smile; any trace of hurt feelings or anger had vanished from her face.

"I saw you in a carriage, Casanova, a majestic one drawn by six dark horses, riding up to a white building. Or I should say, the carriage came to a stop and I didn't know who was in it yet—and then you got out, dressed in a magnificent white formal jacket embroidered in gold that was almost more magnificent than the one you have on today (the expression on her face contained a touch of friendly mockery)—and you were wearing—this is the absolute truth—the same narrow gold chain you have on now, and I swear I've never seen you wearing it before! (This chain and the gold watch attached to it, along with the gold box set with semiprecious gems that Casanova was fingering like a toy at the moment, were the last such items of any value that he had been able to keep in his possession.) — An old man who looked like a beggar opened the carriage door—it was Lorenzi; but you, Casanova, you were young, very young, even younger than you were in bygone days. (She said "in bygone days," unconcerned that the expression brought all her memories fluttering back to her with a rush of wings.) You nodded greetings all around, even though there was no one in sight far and wide, and stepped through the door; it closed behind you with a bang, but I couldn't tell if it was the storm that had blown it shut or if Lorenzi had slammed it; the noise was so loud that the horses shied and raced off with the carriage. Next I heard shouting from the side streets as if people were trying to save themselves, then it was quiet again, and you appeared at one of the windows—I knew now that it was a gambling casino—and you looked down and nodded greetings all around again, even though there was no one there. Then you turned your head and looked over your shoulder as if someone were standing behind you in the room, but I knew that there was no one there either. At that point I suddenly caught sight of you at another window on a higher floor, where exactly the same thing happened, then higher again, and still higher—the building looked like it was growing infinitely tall; and everywhere you appeared you looked down and nodded to the people below the way you had before and talked to people standing behind you who weren't really there at all. And Lorenzi kept running up the stairs after you because you hadn't thought to give him any money. He never caught up to you, though . . ."

Amalie grew silent.

"What happened next?" Casanova asked.

"Lots of things, I'm sure, but I've forgotten them," Amalia said.

Casanova was disappointed. Whenever he related a dream himself, or some real occurrence for that matter, he always tried to give the story he was telling some shape and meaning.

"Dreams turn things around so strangely," he said, sounding somewhat dissatisfied. "Me, a rich man, and Lorenzi an old man and a beggar!"

"Lorenzi's wealth doesn't amount to much," Olivo said. "His father certainly has enough money, but the two of them don't get along all that well."

Without having to make the effort of asking any questions, Casanova soon learned that Olivo and his family had met the lieutenant through the marchese, who simply had brought him along to Olivo's house one day a few weeks earlier. An experienced man like the chevalier, Olivo went on, didn't have to be told in so many words how things stood between the young officer and the marchesa; and in any case, since her husband didn't have any objections to their relationship, there was no reason why disinterested parties should be concerned about it either.

"I have to wonder if the marchese is as accepting as you seem to think, Olivo," Casanova said. "Haven't you noticed the anger and contempt he shows the lieutenant? I wouldn't bet on things turning out smoothly between them."

Even now Marcolina's expression and bearing betrayed nothing. She seemed to be quietly enjoying the scenery and not showing the least bit of interest in any of the talk about Lorenzi. The road they were on took them around frequent curves and gradually climbed through a forest of olive trees and evergreen oaks; as the pace of the horses got slower and slower, Casanova decided to get out and walk alongside the carriage. Marcolina spoke about the beautiful scenery around Bologna and the evening walks she often took with Professor Morgagni's daughter, then mentioned that she was planning to go to France the coming year; she had been corresponding with the famous mathematician Saugrenue at the University of Paris and wanted to meet him in person.

"Maybe I'll allow myself the pleasure of stopping by Ferney on the way," she said smiling, "to find out from Voltaire himself how he reacted to the disputation of his most dangerous opponent, the Chevalier de Seingalt."

Casanova's hand was resting on the side rail next to Marcolina's arm, and her puffy sleeve brushed against his fingers.

"How Voltaire reacts to my disputation will be less important than how posterity does," he replied coolly. "Only subsequent generations will have the right to make the final judgment."

"Do you really believe that final judgments can be made concerning the matters at issue here?" she asked, looking serious.

"I'm surprised to hear that question coming from you, Marcolina, given that your philosophical and, if the term is at all appropriate here, religious opinions, though hardly indisputable in my view, seem to be absolutely firmly rooted in your soul—assuming that you acknowledge the existence of the soul."

Paying no attention to the barbs in Casanova's remark, Marcolina looked calmly up at the expanse of dark-blue sky above the treetops.

"Sometimes, especially on days like this," she replied—and for Casanova, the only one who knew her secret, a tremor of exaltation from the depths of her newly awakened woman's heart resonated in her voice—"it seems to me that everything that people call philosophy and religion is nothing but a play on words—a nobler kind of play, of course, but more pointless, too, than any other kind. To grasp infinity and eternity will always be denied us; our path goes from life to death. What else can we do but live in accordance with the law that has been planted in each of our hearts—or possibly in opposition to that law? Rebellion, after all, comes from God just as much as submission does."

Olivo looked at his niece in awestruck admiration, then anxiously turned to Casanova, who was searching for a response that would make it clear to Marcolina that she was affirming and denying God in the same breath, as it were—or that God and the devil were the same for her. He sensed, however, that he had nothing to counter her sentiments with but empty words—and even these weren't coming to him today. His strange facial contortions seemed to reawaken in Amalia the crazed threats he had made the day before, and she hastened to speak: "Still, Marcolina truly is religious, Chevalier, believe me."

Marcolina smiled, her mind elsewhere. "We all are in our own way," Casanova said courteously, looking off into space.

A sudden bend in the road, and the convent stood before them, with slender crowns of cypresses towering above the high outer wall. The gate had opened at the sound of the approaching carriage, and a gatekeeper with a long white beard greeted the guests serenely and let them pass through.

As they walked between the columns of an open arcade that bordered on either side on a completely overgrown, dark green garden, they were met with a cool unwelcoming breeze blowing from the gray and unadorned prison-like walls of the convent building itself. Olivo pulled the bell-cord, and there was a shrill ring that died away immediately; a heavily-veiled nun opened the door silently and conducted the guests to a large, austere reception room containing nothing more than a few plain wooden chairs; the back of the room was closed off by a heavy iron grating, beyond which everything was submerged in obscure semi-darkness. His heart full of bitterness, Casanova thought back to an incident that had begun in quite similar surroundings and still seemed to him to have been one of the most wonderful experiences he had ever had: he saw before him the figures of the two nuns from Murano who had become close friends through their love for him and who together had brought him incomparable hours of pleasure. And as Olivo began in a whisper to speak about the strict discipline demanded of the nuns here, who were not allowed to show their faces unveiled in the presence of a man and were condemned to eternal silence once they had been accepted as novices, a smile began to play about Casanova's lips, then instantly froze into a grimace.

The abbess suddenly emerged from the half-light and greeted her guests silently. With an exceedingly gracious nod of her veiled head, she accepted Casanova's thanks for being permitted to visit the convent along with the others; then, as Marcolina was about to kiss her hand, she enclosed her in her arms instead. Motioning everyone to follow her, she led them through a small side room to a corridor that formed a square around a garden in full bloom. In contrast to the overgrown one they had passed by on their way in, it appeared to be tended with special care, and the many opulent, sun-drenched beds offered a wondrous play of bright and fading colors. Blending in with the heavy, almost stupefying fragrances that streamed from the flowers' calyxes was another especially mysterious one, unlike anything Casanova could remember ever having smelled before. Just as he was on the verge of commenting on this to Marcolina, he noticed that the puzzling fragrance that so aroused his heart and senses was emanating from her; the scarf she had been wearing around her shoulders was now draped over one arm, allowing the fragrance of her body to rise more freely from the neck of her dress and join with those of a hundred thousand flowers, similar to them in essence and yet unique.

The abbess, silent as before, led her visitors back and forth along narrow winding paths between the beds as if they were walking through an ornamental labyrinth. The joy she felt in showing the others the colorful splendor of her garden was apparent in the lightness and rapidity of her gait; like the leader of a lively round dance, she seemed determined to make them dizzy as she strode on faster and faster ahead of them. Suddenly, then—it seemed to Casanova as if he were waking up from a confused dream—they all found themselves back in the reception room again. Dark figures hovered about on the other side of the grating; no one could have said whether there were three or five or twenty veiled women moving aimlessly back and forth behind the closely-spaced bars like ghosts startled out of their rest, and only Casanova's acute night vision was able to pick out human forms at all in the dense gloom. The abbess conducted her guests to the door, silently gave them a sign indicating their dismissal, and vanished into thin air before they even had time to express their thanks. Then, as they were about to leave the room, a woman's voice resounded from the area beyond the grating—"Casanova"—just the name, yet uttered with an expression different from any that Casanova could remember ever having heard before. Was it someone he had once loved, or someone he had never seen, who had just broken her sacred vow to breathe his name into the air for the last time—or the first? Had that trembling voice expressed the bliss of unexpected reunion, the pain of irretrievably lost love, or the lament at the fulfillment, too late and to no purpose, of an ardent desire of long ago? Casanova had no way of knowing this; all he knew was that today, for the first time ever, his name—as often as he had heard it whispered tenderly, stammered passionately, shouted joyfully—had penetrated his heart with the full resonance of love. Yet precisely for this reason he felt that any further curiosity would be both ignoble and pointless—and the door closed behind him on a mystery that he would never solve. No one said a word as they walked through the arcade toward the gate, and if the others hadn't intimated through their cautious, fleeting glances that they too had heard the brief cry, they might all have imagined that their ears had been playing tricks on them. Casanova followed along behind everyone else, his head bowed as if he had just said a sad farewell.

The gatekeeper was given a few coins, and the guests got into the carriage and set out immediately for home. Olivo looked embarrassed and Amalia's mind was off somewhere else; Marcolina appeared unaffected, but her attempt at starting up a conversation with Amalia about household concerns struck Casanova as much too forced. Olivo had to answer in his wife's place, with Casanova soon joining in as well. The chevalier was extremely well-versed in matters of food and wine and saw no reason to keep his knowledge and experience in this area to himself rather than displaying it as yet another proof of his manifold capabilities. Amalia awoke from her dreamy state now too; following the almost fairy-tale-like yet disturbing adventure they had just had, everyone, and most of all Casanova, seemed to feel immensely at ease to have returned to a normal, down-to-earth environment, and as the carriage drove up to Olivo's house and the smells of roasting meat and all sorts of spices came wafting towards them, Casanova was just in the process of describing a Polish meat pie in the most wonderfully appetizing way and feeling flattered that even Marcolina was listening to him with a kind of charming, housewifely interest.

As he sat with the others over lunch, he was surprised himself at his strangely calm, almost contented mood. He flirted with Marcolina in the joking, light-hearted manner that was considered acceptable between an elegant older gentleman and a well-bred young lady of good family. She made no objections to this and responded to his compliments with perfect grace. It was difficult for him to imagine that his refined luncheon companion could be the same Marcolina whose presumed lover he had seen taking flight from her window the night before; and it was just as hard for him to believe that this delicate young miss who loved to roll around in the grass with other half-grown girls maintained a scholarly correspondence with the famous Saugrenue in Paris. But he immediately chided himself for having such a dull imagination. Hadn't he realized on countless occasions that different and even seemingly opposing qualities coexisted in perfect harmony in the soul of every person who was truly alive? He himself, in enormous turmoil and despair only a short while before and prepared to do terrible things—how gentle and indulgent he was now, in the mood for silly little jokes that made Olivo's daughters shake with laughter at times. It was only his ravenous hunger, something that invariably came over him in the wake of intense emotional agitation, that made him realize that his spiritual balance was still far from being restored.

When the maid came in with the last course of the meal, she had a letter for the chevalier with her that a messenger from Mantua had just delivered. Olivo, noticing that Casanova had grown pale with excitement, ordered food and drink for the messenger and then turned to his guest.

"Don't mind us, Chevalier," he said, "go ahead and read your letter."

"If you'll excuse me," Casanova replied. He got up from the table with a slight bow, then walked over to the window and opened the letter with feigned indifference. It was from Signor Bragadino, an old bachelor who had been like a father to him in the days of his youth. Now over eighty years old and a member of the Great Council for the past ten years, he appeared to be pleading Casanova's cause in Venice with greater enthusiasm than the chevalier's other supporters. The letter, in extremely graceful, if somewhat shaky handwriting, ran as follows:

"My dear Casanova. Today I am finally in the agreeable position of being able to send you some news that I hope will satisfy your wishes for the most part. At its last meeting, which took place yesterday evening, the Great Council not only declared itself prepared to grant you permission to return to Venice, but also expressed the wish that you expedite this return as much as possible, since it intends to take advantage immediately of the active gratitude you have pledged in numerous letters. Alhough you may not be aware of this, my dear Casanova (since we have been deprived of your presence for such a long time), the internal conditions of our beloved city have taken a rather disturbing turn in both a political and moral sense in recent times. I am referring to the existence of secret organizations directed against our sovereign constitution; these, in fact, seem to be planning a violent overthrow, and as is the nature of things, the participants in these organizations—which one could also describe, using a harsher term, as conspiracies—are for the most part certain freethinking, ir-religious elements, dissolute in every sense. We are informed that the most shocking and downright treasonable conversations take place on public squares and in coffeehouses, to say nothing of private loca-tions; but only in the rarest of cases have we been able to catch the guilty parties in the act or to establish evidence against them subse-quently, since confessions obtained by torture have proven to be so unreliable that some of the members of our Great Council have ex-pressed the opinion that it would be better to refrain from such cruel and often counterproductive methods of investigation in future. There is certainly no dearth of individuals willing to offer their services to the government for the good of the state and in the interest of main-taining the public order; but since these people are precisely the ones who are generally well-known as staunch supporters of the existing constitution, it is unlikely that anyone would allow himself to be carried away in their presence to the point of making an incautious remark, let alone a treasonable speech. In light of this, one of the senators whom I will leave nameless for the moment expressed the view in yesterday's meeting that a person widely known as a free-thinker and as lacking in moral principles—not to mince words, that a man like you, Casanova, as soon as he turned up in Venice again, would without a doubt meet with immediate sympathy in the ques-tionable circles I referred to above, and eventually, assuming a certain amount of skill on his part, would gain their unqualified trust. Those elements that the Great Council in its untiring efforts on behalf of the public welfare is most concerned to render harmless and punish in an exemplary fashion would, in my opinion, of necessity seek you out, as if guided by a law of nature. And so, my dear Casanova, if immediately upon returning home you were to find yourself prepared, in the context of what has been indicated above, to try and establish contact with the elements I have described, to associate with them in a friendly manner as someone who tends in the same direction, and to supply the senate with immediate and detailed reports of anything that might seem suspicious to you or otherwise worthy of our interest, we would consider this not only proof of your patriotic zeal, but also an unmistakable indication of your complete renunciation of all those propensities for which you were once made to suffer in the Lead Chambers—with severity, to be sure, but, as you yourself realize today (if we may believe the assurances you have given us in your letters), not without some justification. In recompense for your services we would be disposed to offer you initially a monthly salary of two hundred and fifty lire, exclusive of extra remuneration in individual cases of special importance, in addition to which, of course, all costs stemming from the performance of your services (for example, expenses incurred for food and drink for one individual or another, small gifts for female companions, etc.) would be reimbursed without hesitation or parsimoniousness. I am not unaware that you will have certain scruples to overcome before being able to reach the decision that accords with our wishes; but permit me as your old and sincere friend (who was once young himself) to ask you to consider that it can never be counted as dishonorable for a person to render his beloved homeland any service necessary for its security and continued existence, even if this be a type of service which citizens of a superficial, unpatriotic turn of mind typically consider less respectable. I would also like to add that you, Casanova, are certainly a good enough judge of character to be able to tell a talker from a criminal, or a scoffer from a heretic; and so it will be within your discretion to show mercy in cases that warrant it, and to hand over to the authorities only those you believe to be deserving of punishment. But above all else, keep in mind that if you were to reject the gracious offer of the Great Council, the fulfillment of your fondest wish—to return to your home city—would be deferred for a long time, in fact for an unforeseeable period of time, I'm afraid, and that I myself as an old man of eighty-one years, if I may be permitted to mention this as well, would in all probability have to forgo the pleasure of ever seeing you again. Since for understandable reasons your appointment is to be of a confidential rather than a public nature, I request that your response, which I pledge to communicate to the Great Council at its next meeting one week from today, be addressed to me personally and with the greatest possible dispatch, since, as I indicated above, applications arrive here daily from persons who are in some cases highly trustworthy and who, out of love of country, offer the Great Council their services of their own free will. Needless to say, there is hardly one among them who could compare with you, my dear Casanova, in experience and intelligence; and if in addition to this you take my fondness for you into account as well, I can scarcely doubt but that you will joyfully accept the call that has gone out to you from an office so venerable and well-intentioned. Until then, I remain in constant friendship your devoted Bragadino.

P.S. I will be pleased, immediately upon receiving word of your decision, to issue a bill of exchange in the amount of two hundred lire to the banking institution Valori in Mantua for the defrayal of your travel expenses. The above."

Though Casanova had long since finished reading the letter, he kept it held high in front of him to hide the deathly pallor of his contorted face. The clattering of plates and tinkling of glasses continued as before, but no one said a word. Finally Amalia spoke out in a timid voice:

"The food is getting cold, Chevalier, won't you come and have something?"

"No thank you," Casanova said, letting his face show again; he looked calm now, thanks to his extraordinary skill at dissimulating. "I've just received excellent news from Venice and I have to send my reply back immediately. I hope you'll excuse me for leaving the table so abruptly."

"Do just as you like, Chevalier," Olivo said. "But don't forget that our game begins in an hour."

Casanova went up to his room and sank into a chair; his whole body broke out in a cold sweat, he was shaken with chills, and a feeling of disgust rose within him so that he thought he would choke on the spot. At first he wasn't able to formulate his thoughts clearly, and his entire energy went to keeping himself under control, although he couldn't have said from doing what. After all, there was no one here in the house he could vent his enormous rage on, and he quickly realized the lunacy of his vague notion that Marcolina was somehow involved in the unspeakable humiliation he had suffered. When he had pulled himself together somewhat, his first thought was to take revenge on the reprobates who had assumed that he would be for hire as a police spy. He thought about sneaking into Venice in some disguise or other and stealthily doing in all those good-for-nothings—or at least the one who had come up with this miserable plan. Could it even have been Bragadino himself? Why not? Here was an old man who had become so shameless that he dared to write this letter to Casanova, so feeble-minded that he thought that he, Casanova, a man he had known so well at one time, would stoop to becoming a spy! Ah, he clearly no longer knew who Casanova was! No one knew this, in Venice or any other place. But they would find out. Granted, he was no longer young and handsome enough to seduce virtuous maidens—and hardly skillful and agile enough to slip out of prisons and perform acrobatics on rooftops—but he was still smarter than all the rest of them! And once he was in Venice he would be to able to do whatever he pleased; it was simply a matter of getting there. It might not even be necessary to kill anyone at all; there were many other types of revenge more clever, more devilish, than ordinary murder. If he merely acted as if he were accepting the councilmen's offer, it would be the easiest thing in the world to destroy the people he wanted to destroy, and not those the Great Council had it in for and who were certainly the worthiest of all the Venetians! The idea! Simply because they were enemies of this vile government, because they were considered heretics, they were to be imprisoned in those same Lead Chambers where he himself had languished twenty-five years ago, or even be executed?! He hated the government a hundred times more than they did, and with greater reason; he had been a heretic his whole life and still was today, with a more sacred conviction than any they might have! He had, in fact, merely been acting out a complicated comedic role to *himself* in recent years—out of boredom and disgust. He,

Casanova, believe in God?! What kind of god was it who was gracious to the young but deserted the old? What kind of god could transform himself into the devil whenever he felt like it, change wealth to poverty, happiness to misery, pleasure to despair? You toy with us—and we're supposed to pray to you? To doubt in your existence is the only means we have—of not blaspheming you! — I command you not to exist! Because if you *do* exist, I must curse you!

He sat up and raised his clenched fists to the heavens. Unconsciously, a hated name formed on his lips: Voltaire! Yes, now Casanova was in the right state of mind to finish his disputation against the wise old man of Ferney. Finish it? No, he was really only beginning it now! A new disputation, a different one! One in which he would take the ridiculous old codger to task as he deserved—for his caution, his half-measures, his groveling. Voltaire, an unbeliever? And yet all that anyone heard in recent times was how wonderfully he got along with the clergy and the church, that he even went to confession on holy days! Voltaire, a heretic? He was nothing but a windbag, a cowardly braggart! But the terrible day of reckoning was drawing near, after which there would be nothing left of the great philosopher but a clever little scribbler. He'd been so full of himself, this admirable Monsieur Voltaire . . . "Ah, my dear Monsieur Casanova, I am very upset with you. What do I care about the works of this Monsieur Merlin?[2] You are to blame for my spending four hours with these inanities." — It's a matter of taste, my excellent Monsieur Voltaire! Merlin's works will still be read after your *Pucelle* has long since been forgotten . . . and people might still have some regard for my sonnets then, too, which you gave back to me with an utterly insulting smile and not a word of comment. But these are minor things. We won't let literary touchiness complicate a matter of such great import. Philosophy is what is at issue here—and God! Let's cross our swords, Monsieur Voltaire; just please do me the favor of not dying too soon.

Casanova was already thinking of beginning his new work on the spot when it occurred to him that the messenger was waiting for his answer. His hand flew across the page as he composed a letter to the old fool Bragadino, a letter full of false humility and feigned delight: he accepted the gracious decision of the Great Council with grateful joy and would expect the bill of exchange by return mail so as to have the privilege of prostrating himself before his benefactors, especially his highly esteemed and fatherly friend Bragadino, as soon as possible.

As he was sealing the letter, there was a soft knock on the door; the oldest of Olivo's young daughters, the thirteen-year-old, stepped into the room and announced that the other players had already assembled and were waiting impatiently for the chevalier to come and join in the game. Her eyes glowed strangely, her cheeks had reddened, and her bluish-black hair, as thick as a woman's, flowed around her temples; her childlike mouth was half-open.

"Have you been drinking wine, Teresina?" Casanova asked, taking one long step toward her.

"Yes, I have—the Signor Chevalier noticed so quickly?"

She turned redder still and ran her tongue along her lower lip in apparent embarrassment. Casanova grabbed her by the shoulders, breathing his hot breath in her face, pulled her over to his bed and threw her down on it; she looked at him, her eyes large and helpless, their glow extinguished. She opened her mouth as if to scream, but Casanova's expression was so threatening that she froze and let him do whatever he wanted with her. He kissed her with tender passion and whispered: "Don't tell the abbot about this, Teresina, not even in confession. And when you have a lover later on, or a fiancé, or even a husband, he doesn't need to know about it either. In fact you should always lie, to your father and mother and sisters, too—so that you may prosper on earth. Remember that."

He uttered these blasphemies, and Teresina took his hand and kissed it like a priest's, apparently believing that he had just given her his blessing.

Casanova laughed out loud. "Let's go, my little woman," he said, "we'll make our appearance in the parlor arm in arm!" She acted coy at first, but smiled contentedly nonetheless.

It was high time for them to be leaving, since Olivo was just coming up the stairway, hot and frowning; it immediately occurred to Casanova that the marchese or the abbot had probably been making indelicate jokes about Olivo's daughter being gone so long and caused him some misgivings. His expression brightened as soon as he saw Casanova standing in the doorway, his arm hooked playfully, so it seemed, in Teresina's.

"I'm sorry I've kept everyone waiting, my dear Olivo," Casanova said, "I had to finish writing my letter first." He held it up to Olivo as if displaying the evidence.

"Take this to the messenger," Olivo said to Teresina, stroking back her slightly tousled hair.

"Here, Teresina," Casanova added, "give him these two gold pieces, too, and tell him to hurry back to Mantua so that the letter will get there soon enough to be sent on to Venice today—and have him tell the proprietress of my inn . . . that I'll be back this evening."

"This evening?" Olivo exclaimed. "That's out of the question!"

"Well, we'll see," Casanova said condescendingly. He turned to Teresina again. "Here's a gold piece for you, too," he said. When Olivo objected, he added, "Put it in your savings box, Teresina; the letter you have in your hand is worth a few *thousand* gold pieces."

Teresina ran off and Casanova nodded with satisfaction; he had already slept with her mother and grandmother and found it especially amusing to pay the little temptress for her favors in the presence of her own father.

By the time Casanova walked into the parlor with Olivo the game was already underway. He responded to the enthusiastic greetings of the others with serene dignity and sat down across from the marchese, who was holding the bank. The windows facing the garden were open, and Casanova heard voices approaching; Marcolina and Amalia walked by, glanced briefly into the parlor, and then were gone again. As the marchese turned over the cards, Lorenzi turned to Casanova.

"I have to compliment you, Chevalier," he said with extreme politeness, "you were better informed than I was; our regiment has indeed been given marching orders. We leave late tomorrow."

The marchese seemed astonished. "And you're only letting us know now, Lorenzi?"

"It's not all that important."

"Maybe not to me," the marchese said. "It is to my wife, though—don't you suppose?" His laugh was repulsively hoarse. "Though actually it does matter to me a bit, too—considering that I lost four hundred ducats to you yesterday—and now there might not be enough time for me to win it back!"

"The lieutenant won money from us, too," the younger of the Ricardis said. The older, silent one looked over his shoulder at his brother, who was standing behind him as he had the day before.

"Luck and women—" the abbot began, and the marchese finished for him: "Coerce them if you can."

Lorenzi tossed his gold pieces onto the table with a devil-may-care attitude.

"There's my money, Marchese. If you like, I'll bet it all on one card, so that you won't have to go chasing after it for so long."

Casanova suddenly felt a certain sympathy for Lorenzi that he couldn't quite account for, but given the considerable faith he placed in his powers of presentiment, he was convinced that the lieutenant would be killed in the first armed encounter that he faced.

The marchese refused to accept Lorenzi's high wager, and the lieutenant didn't insist; and so the game began at a modest level, with the other players, too, continuing to place their small bets as they had the day before. Over the next fifteen minutes the stakes grew higher, and before another quarter of an hour had gone by, Lorenzi had lost his four hundred ducats to the marchese. As far as Casanova was concerned, luck didn't seem to be bothering about him one way or the other; he won, then lost, then won again in an almost comically regular pattern. Lorenzi took a deep breath when his last gold piece had made its way over to the marchese and rose from the table.

"Thank you, gentlemen. I suspect that this was my last game"— he hesitated a moment or two—"for a long time in this hospitable house. If you'll allow me, my esteemed Signor Olivo, to say goodbye to the ladies before I leave for the city—I'd like to arrive there before dark and get things ready for my departure tomorrow."

You barefaced liar, Casanova thought. In the middle of the night you'll be back here—with Marcolina! His rage flared up inside once again.

"What's this?" the marchese exclaimed irritably. "It's still several hours till evening, and we're supposed to stop playing already? If you like, Lorenzi, my coachman can drive home and tell the marchesa that you'll be late."

"I'm riding to Mantua," Lorenzi replied impatiently.

The marchese paid no attention and kept talking. "There's still plenty of time. Get out your own money, whatever little you have." He flung a card in his direction.

"I don't have a single gold piece left," Lorenzi said wearily.

"What?!"

"Not one," Lorenzi repeated, looking disgusted.

"No matter," the marchese exclaimed in a suddenly friendly tone with an unpleasant edge to it. "You can owe me ten ducats—even more, if necessary."

"All right, one ducat," Lorenzi said, drawing his cards. The marchese's beat his. Lorenzi kept on playing as if it were perfectly natural and soon owed the marchese a hundred ducats. Casanova took over the bank and had even better luck than the marchese. By now it had turned into a game with only three players again, but this time the Ricardi brothers didn't protest; they became admiring observers along with Olivo and the abbot. No one said a word; only the cards spoke, and they spoke clearly enough. As the luck of the game would have it, every last coin ended up on Casanova's side of the table; in an hour's time he had won two thousand ducats from Lorenzi—except that all the money had come out of the marchese's pocket, leaving him with nothing himself now. Casanova offered him however much he wanted, but the marchese shook his head.

"Thank you," he said, "enough is enough. The game is over for me."

Out in the garden the children were laughing and shouting to each other. Casanova was able to pick out Teresina's voice; he was sitting with his back to the window but didn't turn around. Once again, for Lorenzi's sake, he tried to get the marchese to continue playing, though he didn't know himself why he was doing it. The marchese replied with an even more decisive shake of the head. Lorenzi got up from the table.

"I'll take the liberty, Signor Marchese, of paying you the amount I owe you in person by twelve o'clock noon tomorrow."

The marchese gave a short laugh. "I'd like to know how you're going to do that, Signor Lieutenant Lorenzi. There's not a person in Mantua or anywhere else who would lend you *ten* ducats, let alone two thousand, and especially not now that you're going off to war tomorrow with no guarantee that you'll be coming back."

"You'll have your money at *eight o'clock* tomorrow morning, Signor Marchese—word of honor."

"Your word of honor," the marchese said coldly, "isn't worth even one ducat to me, to say nothing of two thousand."

The others held their breath. But Lorenzi, showing no signs of particular agitation, simply replied, "You will give me satisfaction, Signor Marchese."

"With pleasure, Signor Lieutenant," the marchese answered, "as soon as you've paid what you owe me."

"I'll vouch for the amount, Signor Marchese," Olivo said, stammering a bit and looking terribly distressed. "Unfortunately I don't have enough cash on hand at the moment—but there's my house, my property—" He made an awkward circular gesture with his hand.

"I don't accept your offer," the marchese said. "For your sake— you would lose your money."

Casanova saw that all eyes were on the gold coins piled in front of him on the table. What if I were to vouch for Lorenzi, he thought— or pay what he owes? The marchese couldn't refuse that . . . Isn't it even almost my obligation? It's the marchese's gold, after all . . .

But he kept his silence. He sensed the vague beginnings of a plan developing in his mind, and he would have to allow ample time for it to ripen.

"You'll have your money before nightfall today," Lorenzi said. "I'll be in Mantua in an hour."

"Your horse might break its neck," the marchese replied, "and you too—maybe even on purpose."

"In any event," the abbot said in an annoyed tone, "the lieutenant can't conjure up the money by magic!" The two Ricardi brothers laughed, but broke off again instantly.

"It's clear that the first thing you have to do is allow Lieutenant Lorenzi to leave," Olivo said, turning to the marchese.

"If he puts something up for security," the marchese declared, his eyes flashing as if the idea gave him some special pleasure.

"That's not a bad idea," Casanova said, somewhat lost in thought as his plan began to take form. Lorenzi pulled a ring off his finger and put it on the table. The marchese picked it up.

"This should be good for a thousand."

"And this one?" Lorenzi flung another ring at the marchese.

"The same again," he said nodding.

"Are you satisfied now, Signor Marchese?" Lorenzi asked, getting ready to go.

"I'm satisfied," the marchese replied with a smirk, "all the more so, since these rings are stolen."

Lorenzi turned around quickly, raised his fist above the table, and was about to bring it smashing down on the marchese. Olivo and the abbot grabbed his arm and held it tightly.

"I know these two stones," the marchese said, without changing his position in the least, "even though they've been reset. Look at this emerald, gentlemen, it has a slight flaw, otherwise it would be worth ten times as much. The ruby is perfect, but not very large. Both stones are from a piece of jewelry I gave my wife myself at one time. And since I can hardly imagine that the marchesa had the stones made into rings for Lieutenant Lorenzi, they can only be—along with the rest of the piece, presumably—stolen. Well then, Signor Lieutenant, this is sufficient as security for the moment."

"Lorenzi!" Olivo exclaimed, "you have the word of all of us that no one will ever find out what has just happened here."

"And no matter what Signor Lorenzi may have done," Casanova said, "you, Signor Marchese, are the greater villain."

"I certainly hope so," the marchese replied. "Anyone who has lived as long as you and I, Signor Chevalier de Seingalt, can't let himself be outdone—in villainy, at least—by anyone else. Good evening, gentlemen."

The marchese got up out of his chair and made his exit. No one responded to his words of farewell. For a short time it was so quiet that the children's laughter, coming in from the garden again, seemed excessively loud. And who could possibly have found anything to say at that moment that would have spoken to Lorenzi's innermost being? The lieutenant was still standing there, his arm raised above the table as before. Casanova, the only one who had kept his seat, instinctively felt a certain aesthetic pleasure in this now pointless, yet nobly threatening gesture that had turned to stone, as it were, and transformed the young man's entire body into a statue. Finally Olivo made a gesture of apparent pacification; the Ricardis began to move toward Lorenzi as well, and the abbot seemed to be trying to bring himself to say something to him. Suddenly a brief tremor ran through his body; he made an imperious gesture of protest to ward off any attempted intrusion into his affairs, then nodded politely and left the room unhurriedly. Casanova, who had just wrapped the gold that lay on the table in front of him in a silk scarf, got up and followed on his heels. Even without seeing the expressions on the others' faces, he sensed that they all assumed he was hastening off to do what they had been expecting of him all along: to place the money he had won at Lorenzi's disposal.

He caught up with the lieutenant on the chestnut-lined path that led from the house to the gate.

"Would you allow me to walk with you, Lieutenant Lorenzi?" he asked casually.

Lorenzi looked straight ahead. "Whatever you like, Signor Chevalier," he replied in a haughty tone hardly appropriate to his situation, "but I'm afraid you won't find me very talkative."

"Well, then, Lieutenant," Casanova said, "maybe you'll find me all the more so. If it's all right with you, we'll take the path through the vineyards where we won't be disturbed."

They turned off the road onto the same narrow footpath along the garden wall that he and Olivo had taken the day before.

"You assume quite correctly," Casanova began, "that I'm of a mind to offer you the money you owe the marchese; not as a loan, because—if you'll forgive me—I'd consider that an all too risky business. It would be more like a form of compensation, though certainly of much lesser value, for a favor you might be able to do me."

"I'm listening," Lorenzi said coldly.

"Before I say anything else," Casanova replied in the same tone, "I'm going to state a condition that you will have to agree to if this conversation is to continue."

"Name your condition."

"I want you to give your word of honor that you'll listen to me without interrupting, even if what I have to say to you strikes you as strange, arouses your displeasure, or even shocks you. I'm perfectly aware how unusual my proposal is, Lieutenant Lorenzi, and once you've heard what it is, it will be completely up to you to accept it or not. You are to answer simply yes or no—and whichever it turns out to be, no one will ever find out what was discussed here—by two men of honor who may well both be lost souls."

"I'm ready to hear your proposal."

"You accept my conditions?"

"I won't interrupt you."

"And you'll answer only yes or no without saying another word?"

"Yes or no, and not another word."

"All right, then," Casanova said. As they slowly climbed the hill through the grapevines beneath the sultry late afternoon sky, he began:

"Let's consider the situation according to the rules of logic, we'll understand each other best that way. It's clear that you can't possibly come up with the money you owe the marchese by the set deadline; and there can be no doubt, either, that he's firmly resolved to destroy you if you don't pay him back. Since he knows more about you than he revealed today (here Casanova dared to say more than he needed to, but he was fond of making this sort of brief and not necessarily safe foray along an otherwise predetermined path), the fact is that you are completely in this villain's power and your fate as an officer and a gentleman would be sealed. That's the situation seen from one perspective. On the other hand, as soon as you've paid back what you owe him and he has returned the rings that . . . came into your possession however they did, you'll be saved; and being saved means in this case that you will once again be in control of a future that you had as much as put to an end, a future that—given your youth, your good looks, your fearlessness—will be full of distinction, fame, and fortune. A prospect such as this, especially when all that beckons on the other side is inglorious, humiliating ruin, strikes me as magnificent enough to warrant the sacrifice of certain compunctions that you've never actually had yourself. I know, Lorenzi," he added quickly, as if he were expecting a reply and wanted to cut it off, "you don't have any compunctions at all, any more than I have or ever had; and what I am about to ask of you is something that I myself wouldn't hesitate to agree to for a moment if I were in your position—just as, in fact, I've never shied away from doing base deeds, or rather, things that the fools of this earth like to describe that way, whenever fate or even my own whim demanded it. At the same time I've always been willing, just as you have, Lorenzi, to put my life on the line for less than nothing, and that makes up for everything else. I'm willing to do that now, too—if it should turn out that you don't like my proposal. We're cut from the same cloth, Lorenzi, we're brothers in the spirit, which is why we can bare our innermost selves to each other, proud and naked, with no false modesty. Here's my two thousand in gold—or rather yours—if you can arrange for me to spend the night with Marcolina in place of you. Let's not stop here, Lorenzi, let's continue our stroll."

They walked through the fields under the low olive trees, where the grapevines, heavy with fruit, hung from one tree to the next. Casanova went on talking without a break.

"Don't give me your answer yet, Lorenzi, I have more to say. If it were your intention to make Marcolina your wife, or if Marcolina's own hopes and desires ran in that direction, then what I've proposed, though certainly not evil, would of course be hopeless and therefore pointless. But as sure as yesterday's night of love was the first between you (this supposition, too, he expressed as an unquestionable certainty), the one tonight—to the extent that it's humanly possible to know such things, and even as far as you and Marcolina were able to foresee—was destined to be your last for a very long time to come, and probably forever. And I am completely convinced that if the man she loves wished it and if it would save him from certain destruction, Marcolina herself would be prepared without a moment's hesitation to grant this one night to his rescuer. After all, she too is a philosopher and just as free of compunctions as either of us. But even though I'm absolutely sure that she would stand the test, I have no intention of subjecting her to it, because to make love to a submissive woman who is full of inner resistance is something that, especially in this instance, would not fulfill my needs. I want to enjoy this rapture—a rapture that ultimately seems so great to me that I would pay for it with my life—not only as her lover, but as her beloved. You have to understand this, Lorenzi. This is why Marcolina may not be allowed to have the slightest suspicion that I am the one she is holding in her heavenly embrace; she must have absolutely no doubt that it's *you* she's taking in her arms. It's your task to lay the groundwork for this deception, and mine to carry it out. It shouldn't be particularly diffi-cult for you to convince her that there are reasons why you have to leave her room before dawn, and I'm sure that you'll be able to come up with a pretext for your remaining absolutely silent during your love-making this time. And to rule out any chance of her discovering the truth later on, at a suitable moment I'll act as if I hear a suspicious noise outside, take my cloak—yours, that is, which you will have to lend me for this purpose—and disappear through the window. And she'll never see me again. What I will do beforehand, of course, is make it look like I'm already leaving tonight; then, halfway to Mantua, I'll tell the coachman that I've forgotten some important papers and have him drive back; I'll slip into the garden through the door in the wall at the back—you'll supply me with the key, Lorenzi—and go from there to Marcolina's window, which will open suddenly at mid-night. I will have taken off my clothing, including my shoes and stock-ings, in the coach, so that all I'll be wearing is your cloak—that way nothing will be left behind at my sudden departure to give either you or me away. You'll get your cloak back along with the two thousand ducats at my inn in Mantua tomorrow morning at five o'clock, and then you'll be able to throw the money at the marchese's feet even before the time you indicated. I give you my solemn oath on this. And now I've said all that I had to say."

He stopped suddenly and stood there on the path. Sunset was approaching; a gentle breeze grazed the tops of the yellow ears of grain, and a reddish evening glow spread over the tower of Olivo's house. Lorenzi had stopped walking too; not a muscle stirred in his pallid face as he looked steadily off into the distance past Casanova's shoulder. His arms dangled limply, while Casanova, ready for anything, held onto the handle of his rapier as if his hand had just happened to light there. Several seconds passed, and Lorenzi remained rigid and silent; he seemed lost in quiet contemplation, but Casanova continued to keep his guard up. Holding the scarf containing the money in his left hand and still gripping the handle of his rapier in his right, he spoke again:

"You've kept my condition like a gentleman, Lorenzi. I know that it wasn't easy for you; you and I may not have any compunctions about things, but the world we live in is so poisoned by them that we can't completely remove ourselves from their influence. In fact, I have to admit that while you were on the verge of grabbing me by the throat a time or two over the last fifteen minutes, I was toying with the idea of simply giving you the two thousand ducats the way I would a friend. A *good* friend, I really should say, because I've rarely felt such a strange feeling of empathy for a person from the first moment on as I have for you. But if I had yielded to that magnanimous impulse, I would have regretted it enormously a second later—the same way that you, Lorenzi, would come to the maddening realization, a second before firing a bullet into your brain, that you were a fool beyond all measure to have thrown away a thousand nights of love with countless different women for one single night, after which no more nights— or days—would follow."

Still Lorenzi said nothing; his silence lasted for seconds, for minutes, and Casanova began to wonder how much time he should give him. Just as he was on the point of turning away with a curt nod by way of indicating that he considered his proposal rejected, Lorenzi, still without saying a word, reached with his right hand slowly into the pocket of his tailcoat; Casanova, still ready for anything, took a step backward as if he were about to duck, and Lorenzi—handed him the key to the garden door. Casanova's movement had unquestionably betrayed a stirring of fear, and this brought a disdainful smile to Lorenzi's lips that vanished in an instant. Casanova was able to control his rising anger and keep it to himself, realizing that a violent outburst could undo everything. Bowing slightly, he took the key.

"I assume I can consider this a yes," he said simply. "An hour from now—by then I expect you will have made your arrangements with Marcolina—I'll be waiting for you in my room in the tower, where you'll leave me your cloak and I'll give you the two thousand ducats in return. I've decided to do it this way partly as an indication of my trust, but also because I really don't know where I would keep the money tonight."

They each went their separate ways without any further formalities. Lorenzi took the same path back and Casanova walked to the village tavern, where he put down a substantial deposit for a carriage that would be waiting at Olivo's house at ten o'clock that evening to take him to Mantua.

A short time later, after hiding his gold in a safe place in his room for the time being, Casanova walked out into the garden. Given his mood at the moment, he found the scene he encountered there strangely touching, even though it wasn't at all unusual in itself. Olivo was sitting next to Amalia on a bench at the edge of the grass, his arm draped around her shoulder. The three girls, looking tired from the games they had played that afternoon, were camped out at their feet; Maria, the youngest, had her little head on her mother's lap and seemed to be asleep; at her feet lay Nanetta, stretched out on the grass with her arms under her neck; Teresina leaned against her father's knees while his fingers tenderly caressed her curls. As Casanova drew nearer, her eyes greeted him not with the look of lustful consent that he had unconsciously expected, but with an open smile of childlike closeness, as if what had taken place between them a few hours before had been nothing but an inconsequential game. Olivo's face brightened and Amalia gave him a nod of warm gratitude. It was perfectly clear to Casanova that they were greeting him as someone who had just done a noble deed and who expects others to be tactful enough to refrain from saying even a single word about it.

"Are you really still planning on leaving us tomorrow, my dear Chevalier?" Olivo asked.

"Not tomorrow," Casanova replied, "it's this evening I'm leaving, as I said before." As Olivo was about to raise another objection, he added with a regretful shrug, "The letter that arrived from Venice today unfortunately leaves me with no other choice. The invitation I've been issued is so honorable in every way that my noble benefactors would view any delay in my return as a terrible, inexcusable discourtesy."

Having said this, he asked for permission to go back to his room and get ready for his trip, after which he would be able to spend the last hours of his stay in the circle of his kind friends without any further disruptions.

Paying no heed to their protestations, he went back into the house and up the stairs to his room. There he exchanged his splendid clothing for the simpler outfit that would have to do for the trip and packed his traveling bag, listening more and more tensely with each passing minute for Lorenzi's footsteps. Then, even before it was time, there was a sharp knock on the door and Lorenzi stepped in, wearing his capacious dark-blue riding cloak. Without a word he let it slip off his shoulders and drop to the floor, where it lay like a shapeless piece of cloth between the two men. Casanova got the gold pieces from their hiding place under his bed pillow and spread them out on the table. He counted out the coins as Lorenzi watched, a process that didn't take very long since many of them were of denominations higher than one ducat. Next he put the amount agreed upon in two bags and handed them to Lorenzi; this left Casanova himself with about a hundred ducats. Lorenzi put the bags in his coat pockets and was about to leave without a word.

"Wait, Lorenzi," Casanova said. "Who knows whether we might not meet again at some point in our lives. If so, let's not have it be an angry meeting. This was a business transaction like any other, and we're even."

He extended his hand to him. Lorenzi refused it and finally spoke his first words:

"I don't remember there being anything about this in our agreement."

Lorenzi turned and left. So, my friend, Casanova thought, we're that precise, are we? Then I can be all the more certain that I won't end up being cheated. — He hadn't for a moment considered this possibility seriously, however, knowing from his own experience that people like Lorenzi have their own special kind of honor; its laws couldn't be recorded in neat, numbered paragraphs, but there was virtually never a doubt from one situation to the next as to what they were.

He placed Lorenzi's cloak on top of the other things in his traveling bag, locked it, and put the remaining coins in his moneybag. He looked all around the room he had been staying in and would probably never see again; then, hat and rapier in hand and ready to leave, he went down to the parlor where he found Olivo, his wife, and the children sitting at the table waiting for supper. Marcolina came in from the garden side at the same moment as Casanova entered the room, which he took as a providential sign; she returned his greeting with a casual nod. The meal was served; conversation was slow and laborious at first, as if the mood of departure had put a damper on everyone. Amalia seemed noticeably more occupied with the children than usual and constantly concerned that they not have too much or too little on their plates. At no one's particular urging, Olivo spoke about an insignificant lawsuit with a neighboring property owner that had been decided in his favor, then mentioned an upcoming business trip that would take him to Mantua and Cremona. Casanova expressed the hope of seeing his friend in Venice in the not too distant future. By some strange coincidence Olivo had never been there, though Amalia had seen the magnificent city many years before when she had been just a child. She didn't remember anything about how she had gotten there; her only memory, in fact, was of an old man dressed in a scarlet cloak who had gotten out of a rather long black boat, stumbled, and fallen flat on his face.

"You haven't been to Venice either?" Casanova asked Marcolina, who was sitting directly across from him looking over his shoulder into the darkness of the garden. She shook her head without saying anything. And Casanova began to think: If only I could show it to

you, the city where I once was young! Oh, if only you had been young
with me . . . And another thought came to him, almost more futile
than the previous one: What if I were to take you there now with me?
But at the same time as all these unspoken thoughts were running through his heart and mind, he had begun to talk about the city
of his youth with that ease of manner that he was able to conjure up
even in moments of extreme inner agitation. He spoke artfully and
dispassionately, as if he were trying to describe a painting—until, his
tone now unintentionally warmer, he was suddenly telling the story
of his own life; he himself was at the center of the scene, which only
now began to glow with vibrancy. He spoke of his mother, the famous actress for whom the great Goldoni, her admirer, had written
his exquisite comedy *La Pupilla*;[3] he told of his depressing stay in the
pensione of a skinflint named Dr. Gozzi, of his boyhood love for the
gardener's daughter who later ran off with a lackey, of his first sermon
as a young ecclesiastic, after which he had found a few amorous notes
along with the usual coins in the sexton's collection basket, and of the
nasty practical jokes that he, a violinist in the orchestra of the Teatro
San Samuele, had played with a few of his like-minded fellow musicians, sometimes masked, sometimes not, in the streets, taverns,
dancehalls, and casinos of Venice. But even during the telling of these
wild and sometimes morally questionable stunts, he never used of-
fensive language, speaking instead in a poetical, lofty manner as if he
were trying to be considerate of the children—who, like all the others, Marcolina not excepted, listened raptly to his every word.

But it was getting late, and Amalia sent her daughters off to bed.
Before they went Casanova kissed each one with great tenderness,
Teresina no differently than the two younger ones, and they all had to
promise to pay him a visit in Venice with their parents soon. Though
he became somewhat less restrained once the children were gone, there
still was not a suggestive reference or a trace of vanity in anything he
described, and everyone had the feeling that they were listening to a
love-sick sentimental fool rather than a dangerous, impetuous seducer
and adventurer. He went on to tell about the strange mystery woman
who had traveled with him for weeks disguised as an officer before
suddenly disappearing one morning; about the noble-minded shoe

repairman's daughter in Madrid who, between lovemaking sessions, tried again and again to turn him into a pious Catholic; about the beautiful Jewish woman from Turin named Lia, who looked more splendid on horseback than any princess, and the sweetly innocent Manon Balletti, the only woman he had come close to marrying; about the inept singer he had booed in Warsaw, the ensuing duel with her lover, General Branitzky, and his flight from the city; about La Charpillon, the scheming courtesan who had made such an utter fool of him in London; about a boat ride during a storm at night that had almost cost him his life, across the lagoons to the island of Murano to see the nun he adored; about a gambler named Croce who, having lost a fortune in Spa, bade him a teary farewell on the highway and set out on foot for St. Petersburg—dressed just as he was, in silk stockings and an apple-green velvet jacket and carrying a cane. He told about actresses, singers, milliners, countesses, dancers, ladies-in-waiting; about gamblers, officers, princes, ambassadors, financiers, musicians, and adventurers. And so wondrously captivated by the relived magic of his own past were his senses, so complete was the triumph of all his glorious, though irretrievably lost experiences over the pathetic shadow-existence of his present life, that he was on the point of relating the story of a pretty, fair-skinned girl who had confided her sad tale of love to him in the semi-darkness of a church in Mantua, oblivious to the fact that this same person, now sixteen years older, was sitting across the table from him as the wife of his friend Olivo—when suddenly the maid entered, treading heavily, and announced that his carriage was waiting at the gate. And with his incomparable talent for adapting to a situation immediately whenever he had to, whether asleep or awake, he got up to say his goodbyes. Once again he cordially invited Olivo, who was too moved to speak, to come and visit him in Venice with his wife and children. He embraced him, then walked up to Amalia with the same thing in mind, but she kept him at a distance and simply held out her hand, which he kissed deferentially. Finally he turned to Marcolina.

"You should write down everything you told us tonight, Signor Chevalier," she said, "and lots of other things, too. Just the way you did with your escape from the Lead Chambers."

"Do you really mean that, Marcolina?" he asked, as shy as a young author. She smiled in gentle mockery.

"I have a suspicion," she said, holding her hand out to him, "that a book of that sort could be much more entertaining than your disputation against Voltaire."

That may well be true, he thought, but kept it to himself. Who knows, maybe I'll follow your advice some day. And you yourself will be the last chapter, Marcolina. — This idea, and beyond that, the thought that this last chapter would be taking place that very night, made his eyes flash so strangely that Marcolina slipped her hand out of his just as he was bending over to kiss it. Without a trace of emotion, whether disappointment or anger, Casanova turned to go, indicating at the same time with one of his characteristically clear, simple gestures that no one, not even Olivo, should accompany him.

He strode quickly along the path under the chestnut trees to the carriage; after giving the maid a gold piece for stowing his traveling bag inside, he got in himself and the carriage drove off.

The sky hung heavy with clouds. Once the carriage had passed through the village, where faint candles were still glimmering here and there behind dilapidated windows, all that remained to cast light in the surrounding darkness was the yellow lantern at the front of the wagon shaft. Casanova opened the traveling bag that lay at his feet and took out Lorenzi's cloak; spreading it over himself, he undressed with all due caution under its protective cover. He locked the clothing he had taken off in the bag along with his shoes and stockings, then pulled the cloak more tightly around him and called out to the coachman:

"Hey, we have to go back!" The coachman turned around, annoyed.

"I left my papers in the house. Did you hear what I said? We have to go back."

The coachman, a lean, gray-bearded, bad-tempered man, seemed to hesitate.

"I'm not asking you to do this for nothing, of course," Casanova added. "Here!"

He put a gold piece in his hand, at which the man nodded, mumbled something, and then, whipping his horse unnecessarily, turned the carriage around.

When they passed through the village again all the houses lay dark and silent. After a short stretch along the highway, the coachman began turning onto the narrower, gradually rising road that led to Olivo's property.

"Stop right here!" Casanova shouted, "I don't want you to drive too close and wake everyone up. Wait here at the corner. I'll be back soon . . . And if it should happen to take longer, you'll get an extra ducat for every hour!"

The man now had some idea of what the situation was, as the chevalier could tell by the way he nodded to him.

Casanova got out of the carriage and, hurrying on, soon disappeared from the coachman's view. Walking past the locked entrance gate, he continued along the wall to the corner where it made a right-angle turn up the hill, and easily found the path through the vineyards that he had already taken twice by daylight. He stayed close to the wall and kept following it when it made another right angle turn about halfway up the hill. He was treading on soft meadow grass now, and his only concern was not to overshoot the garden door in the darkness of the overcast night. He ran his hand along the smooth stone wall until his fingers felt rough wood, and soon he was able to distinguish the door's narrow outlines. Finding the lock quickly, he inserted the key and turned it, then stepped into the garden and locked the door behind him again. On the far side of the meadow, the house with its tower seemed an incredible distance away and soared to an equally incredible height. He stood quietly for a moment and looked in all directions; what would have been impenetrable darkness for other eyes amounted only to deep twilight for his. The gravel on the path hurt his bare feet, so he decided to risk cutting across the grass, and this also deadened the sound of his footfalls. His steps were so light that he felt like he was floating. — Were things any different when I followed similar paths as a young man of thirty? Don't I feel the same burning desire I felt then, and all the youthful juices flowing through my veins? Am I not still Casanova, as I was then? . . . And since I'm Casanova, why should that deplorable law known as aging, a law that others are subject to, amount to anything in my case! — And growing steadily bolder, he said to himself: Why am I sneaking to Marcolina in disguise? Isn't Casanova more than Lorenzi, even though he's thirty years older? And wouldn't she be the very woman to comprehend this incomprehensible fact? . . . Was it really necessary to commit a small act of duplicity and to mislead someone else into committing an even greater one? Wouldn't I have reached the same goal by being a little more patient? Lorenzi will be gone tomorrow, and I would have stayed on . . . Five days . . . three—and she would have been mine—she would *knowingly* have been mine.

He stood pressed against the side of the house next to Marcolina's still tightly shut window, his thoughts racing on. Well, is it too late to do it that way? . . . I could come back—tomorrow, the day after . . . and begin the job of seduction—as an honorable man, so to speak. This night would be a foretaste of future ones. Marcolina wouldn't even need to find out that it was me tonight—or not until later— much later. —

The window was still shut tight, and nothing was stirring behind it. It probably wasn't quite midnight yet. Should he let his presence be known somehow? Maybe knock gently on the window? But that could make Marcolina suspicious, since nothing like that had been agreed upon. He would simply have to wait. It couldn't be much longer now. The idea crossed his mind, not for the first time, but just as fleetingly as before, that she might recognize him instantly and see through the deception before it had run its course; this, however, was not so much a serious concern as a natural, rational consideration of a possibility so distant that it faded into a haze of improbability. A rather ridiculous incident passed through his mind, one from twenty years earlier that had involved an ugly old woman in Solothurn; he had spent an exquisite night with her, imagining her to be a beautiful young woman he was in love with—and to make matters worse, the woman had sent him an impertinent letter the next day taunting him about the slip-up that had been so welcome to her and that she her-self had advanced with shameful cunning. Thinking back to the incident made Casanova shudder with disgust. This of all things he shouldn't have thought about at this moment, and he drove the repulsive image from his mind.

But wasn't it midnight by now? How long was he supposed to stand here pressed against the wall, shivering in the chilly night air? Or was he waiting to no end? Had he been duped after all? Two thousand ducats for nothing? And Lorenzi behind the curtain with her, mocking him? — Unconsciously he took firmer hold of the rapier he was holding pressed against his naked body under the cloak. With someone like Lorenzi, after all, one had to be prepared for the most unpleasant surprise imaginable. But then —

At that moment he heard a low, creaking noise, and realized that the grating covering Marcolina's window was being pushed back. A moment later the two wings of the window opened wide, though the curtain inside was still pulled shut. Casanova remained motionless for a few seconds, until an invisible hand gathered the curtain together and raised it on one side; for Casanova this was a signal to swing himself over the sill into the room and immediately shut the window and grating behind him. The folds of the curtain had fallen down over his shoulders, and he had to crawl out from under them first; he would have been standing there in complete darkness then, had not a faint glimmer from the depths of the room, an indeterminate distance away and seemingly sparked by his own gaze, shown him the way. Only three strides—and longing arms stretched out toward him; he put his rapier down, let the cloak slip off his shoulders, and sank into ecstasy.

From Marcolina's rapturous sighs, the tears of bliss that he kissed from her cheeks, the repeated surges of passion that his tender touches called forth, he soon realized that she was sharing in his delights— delights that seemed to him of a higher nature, of a new and different kind than he had ever before enjoyed. Passion turned to adulation, the deepest rapture to a profound sense of being alive; here, finally, in Marcolina's embrace, was the fulfillment he had so often been foolish enough to believe he had experienced before but never really had. In his arms he held the woman he could squander himself upon, yet still feel himself inexhaustible, in whose embrace the last moment of abandon and the next of desire flowed together into a single moment of unimaginable spiritual euphoria. Weren't life and death, time and eternity all one when he kissed her lips? Wasn't he a god? Weren't youth and old age merely a fable, a human invention? The familiar and the exotic, glamor and misery, fame and oblivion—were these not insubstantial distinctions for the use of the restless, the lonely, the vain—and meaningless, if one was Casanova and had found Marcolina? It seemed undignified to him and more and more ridiculous with each passing moment that he should abide by the fainthearted resolve he had made earlier and flee like a thief, silent and unrecognized, from this wondrous night. In the certain feeling of being both the giver of joy and the receiver, he felt ready to hazard revealing himself to her, even though he was aware that he would be taking a great gamble by doing so, and that if he lost he had to be prepared to pay with his life. Still cloaked in impenetrable darkness, he could put off his confession until the first light of morning broke through the heavy curtain. Then Marcolina's reaction would determine his fate, his very life.

But wasn't it precisely this silently blissful, sweetly oblivious lovemaking that bound Marcolina to him more and more inextricably with each kiss? Hadn't the wondrous delights of this night transformed what had begun as deception into truth? Didn't she herself, this deceived, beloved, matchless woman, already feel a shiver of presentiment that it wasn't Lorenzi, a mere boy, a nonentity—that it was a man, that it was Casanova, whose divine fires were consuming her? He began to think it possible that he would not have to go through the moment of confession that he both longed for and feared. He dreamt of Marcolina herself, trembling, enraptured, transfigured, whispering his name to him. And then, when she had forgiven him—no—when she had received his forgiveness—he would take her with him, immediately, that very hour; together they would leave the house in the gray of morning, together they would get into the carriage that was waiting by the curve in the road . . . and together they would drive off, and he would keep her with him forever, he would crown his life's work by winning the youngest, most beautiful, most intelligent woman through the tremendous power of his inextinguishable being—at a time of life when other men were preparing for a dismal old age, he would make her his own for all time. Because she *was* his, like no other woman before her. He glided along with her through mysterious, narrow canals fronted with palaces, feeling once again at home in their shadow, and under arched bridges over which dimly-seen figures darted to and fro; some of them waved over the balustrade in their direction and were gone again before they had gotten more than a glimpse of them. Now the gondola put in to shore alongside marble steps leading up to Senator Bragadino's splendid house, the only one that was festively lit; masked people ran up and down the stairs—some of them stopped out of curiosity, but who could recognize Casanova and Marcolina behind their masks? They entered a large room where several people were playing cards. All the senators including Bragadino stood around the table in their crimson robes. When Casanova entered, they all whispered his name as if they were terrified; they had recognized him from the flash of his eyes behind his mask. He didn't sit down, nor did he take any cards, and yet he was playing. He won; he won all the gold that was lying on the table, but there wasn't enough, and the senators had to make out bills of exchange; they lost their wealth, their palaces, their crimson robes— they were beggars, crawling around after him in rags and kissing his hands, and in the dark-red adjoining room there was music and dancing. Casanova wanted to dance with Marcolina, but she was gone. The senators in their crimson robes were sitting around the table as before; but now Casanova knew that it wasn't cards that were at stake, but defendants in court, some of them guilty, some of them innocent. Where was Marcolina? Hadn't he been holding onto her wrist tightly the whole time? He rushed down the stairs to where the gondola was waiting; row on, row on, through the confusion of canals; of course the oarsman knew where Marcolina was, but why was he wearing a mask, too? That hadn't been customary in Venice in former times. Casanova wanted to take him to task about this, but he didn't dare. Is this how cowardly old men become? And on and on—what a gigantic city Venice had grown to be in the last twenty-five years! Finally the houses receded and the canal became wider—they glided on between islands, till the walls of the convent of Murano, where Marcolina had fled to, rose before them. The gondola was gone—

now he had to swim—oh, it felt so good! In the meantime, of course, the children back in Venice were playing with his gold pieces; but what did he care about gold? . . . The water changed back and forth from warm to cool; it dripped from his clothes as he climbed up the bank to the wall. — Where is Marcolina? he asked in a loud, resounding voice in the reception room, as only a ruler is allowed to do. I'll call her, the duchess-abbess said, then melted away. Casanova walked, flew, flitted back and forth like a bat, keeping to the iron grating. If I'd only known before that I could fly. I'll teach Marcolina, too. Women were hovering around behind the bars. Nuns—yet they were all wearing worldly clothing. He knew this, although he couldn't see them, and he also knew who they were. There was Henriette, the mystery woman, and the dancer Corticelli, and the bride Cristina, and the beautiful Dubois and that damned old woman from Solothurn and Manon Balletti . . . and a hundred others—Marcolina was the only one who wasn't among them! You lied to me, he shouted to the gondolier, who was waiting down by the water in his gondola; he had never hated anyone on earth as much as this man, and he vowed to himself that he would take an extreme form of revenge on him. But wasn't it stupid of him to have looked for Marcolina in the convent on Murano when she'd left on a trip to visit Voltaire? It was a good thing he could fly, since he didn't have enough money left to pay for a carriage. And he swam off. But now it wasn't pleasant any more, the way he had thought it would be; it was getting colder and colder, and he was adrift on the open sea, far from Murano, far from Venice— not a ship anywhere in sight, and his heavy, gold-embroidered clothes were pulling him under. He tried to take them off, but that was impossible, since he was holding the manuscript he was going to present to Monsieur Voltaire in his hand; water was filling his mouth and his nose, a deathly fear came over him, he flailed about, he struggled to breathe, he cried out and opened his eyes with effort.

A ray of morning light was coming in through a narrow crack between the curtain and the window frame. Marcolina stood at the foot end of the bed, holding her white nightgown against her chest with both hands and looking at Casanova with an expression of unspeakable horror on her face. In an instant he was fully awake. Instinctively he stretched out his arms to her as if he were pleading. Marcolina made a gesture of fending him off with her left hand, at the same time clutching her nightgown to her breast even more frantically than before. Casanova raised himself halfway, supporting himself on the mattress with both hands, and stared at her. He was no more able to avert his gaze from her than she was from him. His expression was filled with rage and shame, hers with shame and horror. And Casanova knew what she was seeing, because he could see himself as if an invisible mirror were hanging there in the air, and he saw what he had seen the day before in the mirror in his tower room: a mean-spirited yellow face with deeply engraved wrinkles, narrow lips, and piercing eyes that looked all the more devastated at this moment from the excesses of the past night, the agitation of his early-morning dream, and the shock of waking to reality. And what he read in Marcolina's expression was not 'thief—lecher—reprobate,' which he would infinitely have preferred; he read only one thing, and this dashed him to the ground in greater humiliation than any other insult could have—he read the words that were the most terrible of all to him, words that pronounced the final verdict over him: old man.

If it had been in his power at this moment to destroy himself with some magic word, he would have done it, simply to avoid having to crawl out from under the blanket and display himself to Marcolina completely naked, a sight she could not help but find more abhorrent than that of a disgusting animal. She, however, apparently regaining her senses again and wanting to give him an opportunity to do what was unavoidable as quickly as possible, turned her face to the wall; he took advantage of this moment to get out of the bed, pick his cloak up off the floor, and wrap it around himself. Then, his rapier in hand and feeling that he had escaped the greatest disgrace—being made to look ridiculous—he began to consider whether he might not come up with a few choice words, as he had done on so many other occasions, that would cast this lamentable situation in a new light and even turn it to his favor somehow. Given what had happened, there could be no doubt in Marcolina's mind that Lorenzi had sold her to him; but no matter how much she might hate her scoundrel of a lover at this point, Casanova sensed that he himself, the cowardly thief, could not but seem a thousand times more hateful to her. There was another approach, though, that might be more likely to give him a degree of satisfaction: to humiliate Marcolina by saying suggestive, mockingly indecent things to her. But this spiteful idea faded away, too, as the horrified look on her face gradually changed to one of infinite sadness; it seemed to say that not only had Casanova defiled Marcolina's femininity—no, it was as if this night had witnessed the egregious, unforgivable violation of trust by cunning, of love by lust, of youth by old age. To Casanova's great torment, her look rekindled all that was good in him for a brief moment, and he turned away. Without looking back at Marcolina again, he went to the window, pulled the curtain to one side, and opened both window and grating; then, with a glance around the garden that seemed still to be slumbering in the dim morning light, he swung himself over the sill and onto the grass. Since someone in the house might already be awake and see him from one of the windows, he kept away from the grassy area and disappeared into the protecting shadows of the walkway. He stepped out through the garden door and barely had locked it behind him when someone came up to him and blocked his way. The oarsman . . . was his first thought—because now he suddenly realized that the gondolier in his dream had been none other than Lorenzi. There he stood, his red coat with silver lacing burning through the dim morning light. What a beautiful uniform, Casanova thought in his confused and exhausted brain, it looks almost new. And it's definitely not paid for . . . These practical considerations brought him back to reality, and as soon as he became conscious of the true situation, he felt glad. Assuming his proudest stance and veiled by his cloak, he grasped the handle of his rapier more firmly.

"Don't you think, Signor Lieutenant Lorenzi," he said in his most affable tone, "that you're a little late with this idea?"

"Not at all," Lorenzi replied—and in this moment he was more imposing than anyone Casanova had ever seen—"since only one of us will be leaving this place alive."

"You're rushing this, Lorenzi," Casanova said in an almost gentle tone. "Shouldn't we postpone it until Mantua, at least? I would be honored to have you ride along with me in my carriage. It's waiting at the bend in the road. There would be something to say for observing the formalities, too . . . especially in this case."

"No formalities are necessary. It's you or me, Casanova—and now, not later."

He drew his rapier, and Casanova shrugged his shoulders.

"Whatever you like, Lorenzi. But I have to point out to you that I will be forced to compete in rather inappropriate attire."

He threw open his cloak and stood there naked, holding his rapier playfully in one hand. A wave of hatred rose up in Lorenzi's eyes.

"I will not allow you to be at a disadvantage to me," he said, and quickly began removing every article of his own clothing.

Casanova turned away and covered himself with his cloak again for the time being; it had become perceptibly cool, even though the sun's rays were beginning to penetrate the morning haze. The few sparse trees that stood on top of the hill cast long shadows over the grass. What if someone were to happen by this way, Casanova wondered for a moment. But the path that ran along the wall to the rear garden door was probably used only by Olivo and his family. It occurred to Casanova that he might be experiencing the last minutes of his life now, and he was surprised at how completely calm he was. Monsieur Voltaire is going to be lucky, he thought fleetingly; but deep inside he cared absolutely nothing about Voltaire, and he wished that his mind could have conjured up a more pleasant image than the old hack's repulsive, birdlike face. Incidentally, wasn't it odd that there weren't any birds singing in the treetops on the other side of the wall? That probably meant a change in the weather. But what did he care about the weather? He would have preferred to think about Marcolina and the raptures he had enjoyed in her arms—raptures that he was about to pay for dearly. Dearly? — The price wasn't bad at all! A few years of his old man's life—in misery and debasement . . . What did he have left to do in the world? . . . Poison Signor Bragadino? Would that be worth the effort? Nothing was worth the effort . . . Funny, how few trees there were up on that hill. He started to count them. Five . . . seven . . . ten . . . Don't I have anything more important to do than this? —

"I'm ready, Signor Chevalier!"

Casanova turned around quickly. Lorenzi stood facing him, as magnificent in his nakedness as a young god. Any trace of ignoble thoughts or feelings had been wiped from his face; he seemed equally ready to kill or to die. — What if I were to throw down my weapon, Casanova thought. Or if I were to embrace him? He let his cloak slip down off his shoulders and stood there like Lorenzi, trim and naked. In accordance with the rules of fencing, Lorenzi lowered his rapier in salutation, and Casanova responded in the same manner; a moment later they crossed swords, and silvery morning light glistened from blade to blade. How long has it been, Casanova wondered, since I was last involved in a duel? But none of his more serious contests came to mind now; all he could remember were the frequent practice sessions he had engaged in ten years earlier with Costa, his valet— that good-for-nothing who had later absconded with a hundred and fifty thousand lire of his. Even so, Casanova thought, the man was a competent fencer—and I haven't forgotten anything of the art my- self! His arm was sure and his hand quick and his vision as sharp as ever. Youth and old age, nothing but a myth, he thought . . . Am I not a god? Aren't we both gods? If only someone could see us now! — I can think of a few women who would pay for the privilege.

Their blades bent, the tips of their swords whirred; a faint rever- beration sang out in the morning air after each touch of steel on steel. Was this a fight? No, it was a tournament! . . . Why this look of horror, Marcolina? Aren't we both worthy of your love? He is merely young, but I am Casanova! . . . And Lorenzi fell to the ground, pierced through the heart. The rapier slipped out of his hand, and he opened his eyes wide as if in utter astonishment; he raised his head, his mouth twisting in pain, then let it drop again; his nostrils flared, he gave a soft gasp . . . and he was dead.

Casanova bent over and knelt beside him. He saw a few drops of blood oozing from the wound; he put his hand up close to Lorenzi's mouth, but he wasn't breathing. A shiver ran through Casanova's body, and he got up and covered himself with the cloak. Walking over to the corpse again, he looked down at the young man's body lying stretched out in incomparable beauty on the grass. A soft rustle dis- turbed the silence; it was the morning breeze blowing through the treetops on the other side of the garden wall. What to do now, Casanova wondered. Call someone? Olivo? Amalia? Marcolina? But why? No one is going to bring him back to life! — He deliberated for a while with the cold composure that was always at his command at the most dangerous moments of his life. — It might be several hours before anyone finds the body, possibly even evening, or longer still. By then I'll have gained some time, and that's all that need concern me. —

He was still holding his rapier in his hand; noticing blood glistening on it, he wiped it off on the grass. He considered dressing the body again, but that would have cost him valuable minutes that he wouldn't be able to recover. Bending down once more, he closed the dead man's eyes as if making a final sacrificial offering.

"You're the lucky one," he said aloud, and then, in a dreamlike daze, he kissed him on the forehead.

He got up quickly and hurried along the wall, turned the corner and went down the hill toward the road. The carriage was standing at the crossing where he had left it and the coachman had fallen fast asleep in his seat. Taking extreme care not to wake him, Casanova climbed in gingerly, then called out and poked him in the back at the same time.

"Hey! Are you finally going to wake up?"

The coachman gave a start and looked all around, surprised to see that it was already light, then whipped up the horses and drove off. Casanova leaned far back in his seat, covered by the cloak that had once belonged to Lorenzi. As they passed through the village there were only a few children on the street; the men and women were apparently already at work in the fields. After all the houses were behind them, Casanova began to breathe more easily; opening his traveling bag, he took out his clothes and began to get dressed under the cloak, feeling somewhat concerned that the coachman might turn around and notice his passenger's strange maneuverings. But nothing happened and Casanova was able to finish dressing undisturbed. Once this was done, he stowed Lorenzi's cloak in his bag and draped his own around his shoulders. He looked up at the sky, which had grown overcast in the meantime. He wasn't at all tired; on the contrary, he felt extremely alert and self-possessed. He thought over his situation, and however he looked at it, he came to the conclusion that while there certainly was cause for some concern, things were not as dangerous as a more fearful individual might have believed. Though there was a good likelihood that he would immediately be suspected of having killed Lorenzi, no one would doubt that it had taken place during an honorable duel. Furthermore, he had been set upon by Lorenzi and forced to fight, and no one could consider it a crime that he had defended himself. But why had he left him lying on the grass like a dead dog? No one could find fault with him for that, either; it had been his perfect right, almost his duty, to take flight immediately. Lorenzi wouldn't have done any differently. But couldn't Venice turn him over to the authorities? As soon as he arrived he would place himself under the protection of his patron Bragadino. By doing that, though, wouldn't he be admitting to having done something that might otherwise never come to light, or that he, at least, wouldn't be charged with? Was there any proof at all against him? Hadn't he been issued a formal call to come to Venice? Who could say that he had fled? The coachman, possibly, who had waited by the road half the night? A few extra gold pieces would silence him.

Casanova's thoughts kept running through his mind in circles. Suddenly he was sure he heard the gallop of horses' hooves behind the coach. So soon? was his first thought. He put his head out the window and looked back; the road was empty. They had driven by some farm buildings, and it had been the echo of the hoofbeats of his own coachman's horses that he had heard. For a while he was so relieved to have been mistaken that he was convinced that all possible dangers were behind him for good now.

The towers of Mantua loomed in the distance . . . "Faster, faster," he whispered, not wanting his words to be heard. But the coachman, close to his destination now, allowed the horses to race on as fast as they wanted to in any case. Soon they were at the same gate that Casanova had passed through with Olivo not two days before on their way out of the city; he gave the coachman the name of his inn, and a few minutes later the signboard with its golden lion came into view and Casanova jumped out of the carriage. The proprietress stood in the doorway, vivacious and smiling broadly, and seemed not indis-

posed to greet him like a sorely missed lover returning after an unwanted absence. Casanova, however, pointed in annoyance at the
coachman as if he were an inconvenient witness, then immediately
sent him off to eat and drink to his heart's content.

"A letter from Venice came for you last evening, Signor Chevalier," the proprietress said.

"Another one?" Casanova asked. He ran up the stairs to his room
with the proprietress right behind him. In extreme agitation, he opened
the sealed letter that lay on his table. Are they withdrawing their offer, he wondered fearfully? But once he had read the brief note his
face brightened again. It was from Bragadino, who had enclosed a
voucher for two hundred and fifty lire so that Casanova wouldn't
have to delay his trip for even a day longer, assuming that he had
decided to come. He turned to the proprietress in pretended annoyance, explaining to her that he had no choice, unfortunately, but to
continue his trip immediately, since he would otherwise run the risk
of losing the position that his friend Bragadino had arranged for him
in Venice—one for which there were a hundred other applicants. But,
he added quickly, noticing threatening clouds developing on her forehead, after arriving there he would simply secure his position and
accept his mandate—as secretary to the Great Council of Venice—
and then, once officially in office, he would immediately ask for a
leave of absence for the purpose of putting his affairs in Mantua in
order, and this, of course, they could not deny him; he would even
leave most of his belongings here at the inn—and then, then it would
be entirely up to his dear, charming sweetheart whether she was willing to give up her hostelry and follow him to Venice as his wife . . .

She flung her arms around his neck and asked him, her eyes bathed
in tears, if she couldn't at least bring a good breakfast up to his room
before he left. He realized that she had a farewell celebration in mind,
and although he wasn't the least bit interested in this, he agreed nonetheless just to be finally rid of her. Once she had left, he put his most
essential clothes and books in his bag and went down to the restaurant, where he found the coachman enjoying a sumptuous meal. He
asked him whether he would be willing—for an amount double the
usual charge—to leave right away with the same horses and take him

to the nearest postal station on the road to Venice. The coachman agreed on the spot, and for the moment Casanova was freed of his greatest worry. The proprietress came in, her face red with anger, and asked him if he had forgotten that his breakfast was waiting for him in his room. Casanova replied very calmly that he certainly hadn't forgotten and asked her, since he was short on time, to take his voucher to the bank and pick up the two hundred and fifty lire for him. As she ran off to get the money, Casanova went up to his room where the food had been set out for him and began devouring it with a veritably animal-like voracity. He kept right on eating when she came back, pausing simply to put the money she had brought him in his pocket. She sat down at his side affectionately, and when he had finished eating he turned to her. Thinking that her time had finally come, she stretched out her arms to him with unmistakable intent; he embraced her impetuously, kissed her on both cheeks, and held her close to him—and just as she seemed ready to yield to him completely, he tore himself away so forcibly that she fell backwards into the corner of the sofa.

"I have to go," he said, "goodbye!" The expression on her face, a mixture of disappointment, anger, and helplessness, struck Casanova as so exquisitely funny that he couldn't keep himself from laughing out loud as he shut the door behind him.

The coachman could hardly have failed to notice that his passenger was in a hurry, but felt under no obligation to wonder why. In any case, he was sitting on the box ready to go when Casanova came out of the inn, and as soon as the chevalier had gotten into the carriage he whipped the horses vigorously and drove off. Sensing that it would be best not to drive straight through the city, he circled around it and then returned to the highway on the opposite side. It was three hours till noon, and the sun still wasn't very high in the sky. It's quite possible, Casanova thought to himself, that they haven't even found Lorenzi's body yet. He was barely conscious that he was the one who had killed the lieutenant, and was only glad to be getting farther and farther away from Mantua and finally have a respite of peace. . . He fell into the deepest sleep of his entire life—one that, in a sense, lasted two days and two nights, since his memory proved unable to retain as separate events the short pauses needed for changing horses, during which he sat in taverns, walked back and forth in front of postal buildings, exchanged casual bits of conversation with postmasters, innkeepers, customs guards, and travelers. Later in his life, his remembrance of these two days and nights would fuse with the dream he had dreamt in Marcolina's bed, and even the duel fought by two naked men on the green grass in the early morning sunshine somehow became part of it. Puzzlingly enough, at times he was not Casanova in the dream, but Lorenzi; not the victor, but the vanquished; not the one in flight, but the dead man, his pale youthful body touched only by the morning breeze; and neither of them, he himself or Lorenzi, were any more real than the senators in their crimson-red cloaks who had crawled around him on their knees like beggars, nor were they any less real than the old man he had seen somewhere leaning on the railing of a bridge at dusk and to whom he had tossed a few coins from the carriage. If Casanova's power of reasoning hadn't allowed him to distinguish between what he had experienced and what he had dreamt, he could easily have imagined that he had fallen into a confused dream in Marcolina's arms and only awakened from it on catching sight of Venice's campanile.

Looking over from Mestre on the third day of his trip, he saw the bell tower for the first time again after more than twenty years of longing—a gray stone shape, rising solitary in the early morning light as if still a great distance away. But he knew that only two hours separated him now from the beloved city where he once had been young. He paid the coachman, without knowing whether he was the fourth, fifth, or sixth since Mantua, and then, followed by a boy who carried his baggage, hurried off through the squalid streets to the harbor; the market boat would be leaving for Venice at six o'clock that morning just as it had twenty-five years before. The boat seemed to have been waiting just for him; he had barely taken his seat on a narrow bench among shopkeepers, workers, and women bringing their wares to the city, when it began to move away from the embankment. The sky was overcast; mist hung over the lagoons, and there were smells of stagnant water, damp wood, fish, and fresh fruit in the air. The campanile loomed taller and taller, other towers emerged through the haze, the domes of churches became visible; morning sunbeams shone in his direction, reflecting off a roof somewhere, two roofs, several; the buildings were distinct from one other now and taller; ships large and small came bobbing out of the fog, and greetings were exchanged from one to the other. The chatter around him grew louder. A small girl asked him if he wanted to buy some grapes; he ate the bluish fruit, spitting the skins overboard behind him the way his fellow Venetians were doing, and got into a conversation with a man who expressed his pleasure that the weather finally seemed to be taking a turn for the better. What, it had been raining here for three days? He hadn't heard anything about it; he had come from the south, Naples, Rome . . . The boat was already passing through the canals on the edge of the city; dirty houses stared at him from grimy windows that looked like strange dull eyes; the boat made two or three stops and a few young people got off, one with a large portfolio under his arm, along with some women carrying baskets. Now they were coming to more pleasant sections of the city. Wasn't that the church where Martina had gone for confession? — And that house—wasn't that the one where he had brought Agatha, pale and deathly ill, back to rosy-cheeked health using certain methods of his own? — And in that other one he had beaten the good-for-nothing brother of a captivating girl named Silvia black and blue . . . and that little yellowish house over there in the side canal, where a bare-footed fat woman was standing on the steps as the water washed over them . . . Before he could remember which phantom from his distant past belonged there, the boat had turned into the Grand Canal and was now slowly continuing along the broad waterway between palaces. As he thought back to his dream, it seemed to him that he had come this same way just the day before.

He got off the boat at the Rialto Bridge, having decided to find himself a room and leave his baggage there before going to see Signor Bragadino; he knew of a small, inexpensive inn in the neighborhood, though he couldn't recall its name. He found the building more decrepit, or at least more neglected than he had remembered it; a grouchy, unshaven waiter gave him a rather unpleasant room that looked over to the windowless wall of a house across the way. But Casanova didn't want to lose any time, and since he had spent almost all his available cash during the trip, the low price of the room was very welcome. He decided to stay there for the time being and set about brushing off the dust and dirt from his long trip. Next he debated for a while whether he should change into his lavish outfit; then, concluding that his more modest one would suit the occasion better after all, he finally left the inn.

It was only a hundred paces, along a narrow little street and over a bridge, to Bragadino's small, elegant palazzo. A young servant with a rather impertinent look on his face came to the door. When Casanova announced himself, he acted as if he had never heard the famous name before; a moment later, however, he returned from his master's apartment looking somewhat more pleasant and invited the guest to step inside. Bragadino was having breakfast at a table near an open window; he started to get up, but Casanova wouldn't let him.

"My dear Casanova," Bragadino exclaimed, "how happy I am to see you again! Who would have thought that we would ever see each other again?"

He held out both hands to him, and Casanova grasped them as if he were going to kiss them, though he didn't; he responded to his host's cordial greeting by expressing his impassioned gratitude in the rather pompous style that was never absent from his manner of expression in such situations. Bragadino invited him to have a seat and asked him first of all if he had had breakfast. Hearing that he hadn't, Bragadino rang for the servant and gave him the appropriate instructions. Once the servant had left, Bragadino expressed his gratification that Casanova had accepted the offer of the Great Council unconditionally; his decision to offer his services to his fatherland would certainly not be disadvantageous to him. Casanova declared that he would consider himself a fortunate man if he were able to win the satisfaction of the Great Council.

So he went on, keeping what he was thinking to himself. Not that there was any hatred towards Bragadino left in him; what he felt was more a kind of sympathy for the old, old man who was sitting across from him, his mind no longer clear, his gray beard growing sparse, his eyes red around the edges, his cup trembling in his thin hand. When Casanova had last seen him, Bragadino would have been about as old as Casanova himself was today, and even then he had already seemed ancient to him.

The servant came in and served breakfast to Casanova, who needed little encouragement to go ahead and indulge his appetite, since he had only had an occasional quick bite to eat on his trip. — Yes, indeed, he had traveled day and night from Mantua, so eager had he been to demonstrate his allegiance to the Great Council and his eternal gratitude to his noble patron (he offered this by way of excusing himself for the almost indecent gusto with which he was gulping down his steaming hot chocolate). The myriad sounds of life came in through the window from the nearby canals, with the calls of the gondoliers hovering in their monotone above all the others; somewhere, not very far away, possibly in the palace directly opposite—wasn't it Signor Fogazzari's?—a beautiful, rather high-pitched woman's voice was singing coloratura runs; the voice presumably belonged to someone very young, someone who hadn't even been born yet when Casanova had made his escape from the Lead Chambers.

He ate zwieback with butter, eggs, and cold meat, excusing himself continually for his insatiable appetite as Bragadino looked on contentedly.

"I love to see young people enjoying their food," he said. "And as far as I can remember, my dear Casanova, you've always done that!"

He was reminded of a meal they had had in the early days of their acquaintanceship—or to be more precise, a meal at which, just as today, he had looked on admiringly as Casanova ate. In those days, not long after his young friend had thrown out the doctor whose incessant bloodletting had almost sent poor Bragadino to his grave, he himself had been in no condition to eat . . .

They talked about times long past . . . yes, life in Venice had been better back then. — "Not everywhere," Casanova said, smiling faintly and thinking of the Lead Chambers. Bragadino made a motion with his hand as if to say that this was not the time to be thinking about such minor annoyances. In those days, too, incidentally, he had done all he possibly could to help Casanova, but unfortunately he hadn't been able to keep him out of prison. If only he had been a member of the Council of Ten back then! —

The conversation turned to political matters, and the old man, enlivened by the subject, seemed to regain all the alertness and vigor of his younger years; Casanova learned many noteworthy things about the disturbing intellectual movement that a segment of Venetian youth had been involved in recently and about the unmistakable signs of dangerous revolutionary activities that were beginning to manifest themselves. This proved to be good preparation for his visit to a café that evening, following a day spent sequestered in his dismal room at the inn putting his papers in order and burning some of them for the sole purpose of calming his emotional distress. The Café Quadri on St. Mark's Square was reputed to be the main gathering place of the freethinkers and revolutionaries; Casanova was recognized there immediately by an old musician, the former conductor at the Teatro San Samuele where he had played violin thirty years earlier. This provided him with a natural, unforced introduction to a group of mostly younger people whose names he remembered from his morning conversation with Bragadino as being those of especially suspicious characters. His own name, however, didn't appear to impress the group at all in the way he might have expected; apparently most of them knew nothing of Casanova other than that he had been imprisoned in the Lead Chambers a long time ago for some reason or other, possibly even guiltlessly, and that he had escaped from there under great peril. The book in which he had described his escape so vividly many years before was not, however, completely unknown these days, though no one seemed to have read it with the attention it deserved. Casanova found it rather amusing to think that it was completely in his power at any moment to help each and every one of these young men to gain some first-hand knowledge about living conditions in the Lead Chambers and about the difficulty of escaping from them. But he had no intention of letting anyone know that he was thinking such nasty thoughts or even of hinting that he was; instead, he played his usual charming, innocuous role, and soon was regaling the others in his inimitable fashion with all sorts of funny adventures that had taken place during his last trip from Rome to Venice—stories that, though relatively true for the most part, actually went back fifteen or twenty years.

While his audience was listening in rapt attention, someone arrived with various items of news, including the murder of an officer from Mantua near the estate of a friend he had been visiting; the robbers had stolen everything including the victim's clothes. Since attacks and murders of that sort were no rarity in those days, the incident didn't arouse any particular interest in the group, and Casanova went on with his story at the point where he had been interrupted, as if the murder was of as little concern to him as it was to the others; he came up with even funnier, bolder ways of expressing himself than before, in fact, now that he had been freed from a feeling of unrest that he hadn't quite been willing to acknowledge previously.

It was past midnight when he said a brief farewell to his new acquaintances and walked out onto the broad, empty square alone; above him the starless but restlessly flickering sky hung heavy with mist. He found his way through the cramped little streets with the sureness of a sleepwalker, not really aware that he hadn't done this for a quarter of a century; he walked along between dark walls and over narrow footbridges, under which the blackish canals flowed toward the eternal sea, until he reached his shoddy little inn. After repeated knocking the door finally opened, languorously, inhospitably; a few minutes later, as painful exhaustion weighed on his body without granting it release and a bitter aftertaste seemed to rise to his lips from his innermost being, he threw himself still half-dressed onto the uncomfortable mattress where, after twenty-five years of exile, he would have his first, longed-for sleep in his homeland—a sleep that finally came at the break of dawn, heavy and dreamless, to take pity on the old adventurer.

NOTE

Casanova did actually visit Voltaire in Ferney, but nothing in the novella that is connected with this—in particular his writing of a disputation directed against Voltaire—is based on fact. It is historically accurate, however, that Casanova found himself compelled to offer his services as a spy to his native city of Venice between the age of fifty and sixty; more detailed and accurate accounts of this and several other of the famous adventurer's earlier experiences mentioned in passing in the novella can be found in his *Memoirs*. Other than these incidents, the entire story of *Casanova's Journey Home* is purely fictitious.

A. S.

Fräulein Else

"Are you sure you don't want to play any more, Else?"—"No, Paul, I'm really too tired. I'll be seeing you. Goodbye, Frau Mohr."—*"Oh, Else, I wish you'd call me 'Frau Cissy'. Or better yet, just 'Cissy,' plain and simple."*—"Goodbye, Frau Cissy."—*"But why are you leaving already, Else? It's still a good two hours till the evening repast."*—"Could you just play singles with Paul, Frau Cissy? I'm really not much fun today."—*"Don't mind her, Frau Mohr, she's not in one of her most agreeable moods today.—Looks wonderful on you, Else, by the way—being disagreeable, I mean. To say nothing of your red sweater."*—"I hope blue will agree with you better, Paul. 'Bye."

That wasn't a bad exit. I hope they don't think I'm jealous.—I'm positive there's something going on between them, cousin Paul and Cissy Mohr. There's nothing in the world I could care less about.—Now I'll turn around and wave to them. Wave and smile. Do I look more agreeable now? Oh, they're already playing again. I'm a better player than Cissy Mohr, actually, and Paul isn't exactly a matador, either. He looks good, though, with his collar open and that bad-boy expression of his. If only he weren't so affected. You don't need to worry, Aunt Emma . . .

What a gorgeous evening! Today would have been perfect weather for a climb up to the Rosetta chalet. Mt. Cimone is so majestic against the sky!—We would have left at five in the morning. I would have felt woozy at first, of course, as usual. But that never lasts long.—There's nothing more delightful than hiking at dawn.—That one-eyed American at the chalet looked like a boxer. Maybe someone knocked his eye out in a boxing match. I really wouldn't mind marrying someone and moving to America, but not an American. Or I

could marry an American and we'd live in Europe. A villa on the
Riviera. Marble steps down to the sea. I'm lying naked on the
marble.—How long has it been since we were in Mentone?[1] Seven or
eight years. I was thirteen or fourteen. Ah, yes, back then we were in
better circumstances.—It was really silly to postpone the hike. We
would have been back by now if we'd gone.—When I left to play
tennis at four the special delivery letter from Mama that they'd telegraphed me about still hadn't arrived. I wonder if it's here yet? I could
easily have played another set.—Why are these two young men nodding at me? I don't even know them. They've been staying at the hotel
since yesterday, their table is over by the window on the left side of
the restaurant, where those Dutch people used to sit. Did I look disagreeable when I nodded back to them? Or self-centered? I'm not like
that at all. What was it that Fred said on the way home from
"Coriolanus"?[2] Self-sufficient. No, self-assured. You're self-assured,
Else, not self-centered.—That's a clever way of putting it. He's always
coming up with things like that.—Why am I walking so slowly? Am
I worried about Mama's letter after all? Well, I hardly expect it to
contain anything pleasant, of course. Special delivery! I wonder if I'll
have to go back home. Oh, Lord, what a life! Even with my red silk
sweater and silk stockings. Three pairs! The poor relation, invited to
spend her vacation with her rich aunt. I'm sure she regrets it already.
Do you want me to give it to you in writing, dear aunt, that I wouldn't
dream of getting involved with Paul? Or anyone else, for that matter.
I'm not in love. Not with anyone. And I never was. Not even with
Albert, although for a week I thought I was. I don't think I'm capable
of falling in love. That's strange, actually. Because I'm definitely sen-
sual. Self-assured and disagreeable, too, though, thank goodness. I
think the only time I was ever really in love was when I was thirteen.
With van Dyck—or the Abbé des Grieux, actually, and Marie Renard,[3]
too. And when I was sixteen, at Lake Wörther.—Well, no, that wasn't
anything. Why bother trying to figure it out, I'm not writing my
memoirs. I don't even keep a diary the way Bertha does. I like Fred,
but that's the extent of it. Maybe if he were more elegant. I really am
a snob. Papa thinks so, too, and he teases me about it. Oh, dear Papa,
I worry so much about you. I wonder if he's ever had an affair? Defi-

nitely. Lots of them. Mama's pretty dense, really. She doesn't have any idea what I'm like. No one else does, either. Fred?—well, not much more than an idea. It's a heavenly evening. The hotel looks so festive. So many people having a good time, nobody with any problems. Like me, for example. Ha, ha! Too bad. I would have been well-suited to the carefree life. Things could be so beautiful. Too bad. There's a red glow on Mt. Cimone. An alpenglow, Paul would say. That's far from an alpenglow. It's so beautiful it makes me want to cry. Oh, why do I have to go back to the city!

"Good evening, Fräulein Else."—"Good evening, madam."—*"Been playing tennis?"*— She can see that, why does she ask? "Yes, madam. And is madam having a nice stroll?"—*"Yes, my usual evening stroll along the Rolleweg. It's so pleasant the way the path runs through the meadows. During the day it's almost too sunny."*—"Yes, the meadows here are wonderful. Especially from my window in the moonlight."

"Good evening, Fräulein Else. Good evening, madam."—"Good evening, Herr von Dorsday."—*"Been playing tennis, Fräulein Else?"*— "You're so perceptive, Herr von Dorsday."—*"Don't mock, Else."*—Why didn't he call me 'Fräulein Else'?—*"Anyone who looks as good as you do with a tennis racket can wear it, so to speak, as if it were a piece of jewelry."*—Jackass, I'm not even going to respond to that. "We played all afternoon. Just three of us, unfortunately. Paul, Frau Mohr, and myself.—*"At one time I was a rabid tennis player."*—"Not any more?"— *"I'm too old for that now."*—"Old? In Marienlyst there was a sixty-five-year-old Swede who played every evening from six to eight. And the year before that he had even played in a tournament."— *"Well, I'm not sixty-five yet, thank God, but unfortunately I'm not a Swede, either."*— Why 'unfortunately'? I suppose he thinks that was a joke. It would be best for me simply to smile politely and leave. "Good evening, madam. Goodbye, Herr von Dorsday." Why is he bowing so low and making eyes like that? Calf's eyes. I wonder if I insulted him with the story about the sixty-five-year-old Swede. Well, what does it matter. Frau Winawer must be an unhappy woman. Close to fifty, I'm sure. Those bags under her eyes—looks like she's cried a lot. Terrible to be that old. Herr von Dorsday is being nice to her. He's walking along with her now. He's still not bad-looking, with his little gray-flecked

goatee. But I don't find him very appealing. Always putting on such airs. What good does it do you to have an expensive tailor, Herr von Dorsday? Dorsday! I'll bet that wasn't always your name!—Here comes Cissy's sweet little daughter with her governess. "Hello there, Fritzi. Bonsoir, Mademoiselle. Vous allez bien?"—"*Merci, Mademoiselle. Et vous?*"—"What's this, Fritzi, you're carrying a hiking stick? Don't tell me you're going to climb Mt. Cimone!"—"*Of course not, I'm not allowed to go up that high yet.*"—"Next year you will, though. Bye, Fritzi. A bientôt, Mademoiselle."—"*Bonsoir, Mademoiselle.*"

She's pretty. I wonder why she's a governess? And for Cissy, of all people. What a bitter fate. Oh, Lord, it could happen to me, too. No, I'd definitely find something better than that. Better?—Delightful evening. "The air is like champagne," Dr. Waldberg said yesterday. And the day before that someone else said it, too.—Why is everyone sitting inside when the weather's so beautiful? It's beyond me. Or are they all waiting for special delivery letters? The desk clerk saw me before; if a special delivery letter had arrived for me he would have brought it to me right away. So it's not here yet. Thank goodness. I'm going to have a little catnap before dinner. Why does Cissy always say 'evening repast'? Stupid affectation. They suit each other, Cissy and Paul. Oh, I wish the letter were here already. I suppose it'll come during the 'evening repast.' And if it doesn't, I'll toss and turn all night. I slept so miserably last night, too. Of course it's just about that time. That's why I've got this pain in my legs. Today's the third of September. So probably on the sixth. I'll take some Veronal[4] tonight. No, I won't get addicted to it, dear Fred, you don't need to worry. I always get so personal with him in my thoughts.—People should try everything, even hashish. Brandel, that navy ensign, brought some back from China, I think. Do you drink hashish or do you smoke it? They say people have marvelous visions. Brandel invited me to drink hashish with him—or smoke it. Kind of fresh. But nice-looking.—

"*Excuse me, Fräulein, a letter for you.*"—The desk clerk! So it did come! I'll turn around very casually now. After all, it could be a letter from Karoline, too, or from Bertha, or Fred, or Miss Jackson. "Thank you very much." No, it's from Mama, all right. Special delivery. Why didn't he just say so right away? "Oh, special delivery!" I'll wait and

open it in my room so I can read it without being disturbed.—There's
the marchesa. She looks so young in this dim light. She must be forty-
five. Where will I be when I'm forty-five? Maybe dead already. I hope.
She's smiling at me so sweetly, the way she always does. I'll nod a little
as she walks past—not that I feel especially honored to have a marchesa
smile at me.— *"Buona sera. "*—She said 'buona sera' to me—now I at
least have to nod to her. Did I overdo it? She's so much older than I
am, after all. What a majestic walk she has. Is she divorced? I have a
nice walk, too. But I'm aware of it. Yes, that's the difference. An Italian could be dangerous for me. Too bad that handsome dark-haired
man with the Roman look has left already. "He looks like a filou,"[5]
Paul said. Good Lord, I have nothing against filous, quite the contrary.—Here we are, number seventy-seven. A lucky number, actually. It's an attractive room. Delicately-grained pine. There's my vir-
ginal bed.—Now it really has become an alpenglow. But I won't agree
with Paul if he says it again. Paul is shy, actually. A doctor, a gynecologist, even! Maybe that's why. In the woods the other day, when we
were so far ahead of everyone else, he could have been a little more
daring. But he wouldn't have gotten anywhere. Actually, no one has
ever really been daring with me. Possibly that one time three years
ago at Lake Wörther, in the mineral baths. Daring? No, he was downright indecent. But handsome. Apollo Belvedere. I didn't really quite
understand what was happening back then. Well, of course not—I
was sixteen years old. My heavenly meadow! My very own! If only I
could take it back to Vienna with me. A trace of mist. Autumn? Of
course, it's the third of September in the mountains.

Well, Fräulein Else, aren't you finally going to decide to read the
letter? It might not even have anything to do with Papa. It could be
about something my brother has been up to. Maybe he's gotten engaged to one of his flames. A chorus girl or someone who works in a
shop selling gloves. No, no, he's too sensible to do that. I don't know
much about him, really. When I was sixteen and he was twenty-one
we were almost close friends for a while. He talked a lot about a girl
named Lotte. Then he stopped all of a sudden. This Lotte must have
jilted him or something. And ever since then he's kept things to himself.—Now the letter's open, and I didn't even know I was doing it.

I'll sit on the window sill and read it. I'll have to be careful not to fall out. As has been reported to us from San Martino, a terrible accident took place in the Hotel Fratazza there. Fräulein Else T., a beautiful nineteen-year-old girl, daughter of the well-known lawyer . . . People would say, of course, that I'd done myself in because of unrequited love or because I was pregnant. Unrequited love—no, I don't think so.

"My dear child"—I especially want to see what she says at the end.—"And so once again, don't be upset with us, my dear, good child. I send you my"—Good God, don't tell me they've all killed themselves! No, of course not, Rudi would have sent a telegram then.— "My dear child, you can imagine how sorry I am to come crashing into your nice vacation"—as if I weren't always on vacation—"to unfortunately tell you such an unpleasant piece of news."—Mama's writing style is terrible—"But after careful consideration there remains no other choice for me. So, to make a long story short, this business of Papa's has reached a critical point. I'm at my wit's end."—Get on with it!—"It's a matter of a relatively trivial amount—thirty thousand gulden,"—trivial?—"which we have to come up with in three days, otherwise all is lost." Good God, what is she saying?—"Just imagine, my beloved child, Baron Höning"—what, the district attorney?—"had Papa come to his office early this morning. I don't need to tell you how highly the Baron thinks of Papa, how fond he is of him, even. A year and a half ago—it was touch and go then, too—he spoke with Papa's major creditors personally and got things settled at the last minute. But this time absolutely nothing can be done if the money isn't forthcoming. And apart from the fact that we'll all be ruined, there'll be a scandal the likes of which has never been seen before. A lawyer, after all, a famous lawyer who—no, I can't even write it down. I'm fighting back tears the whole time. You know, of course, my child—you're no simpleton—that we've been in similar situations, God help us, a few times before, and the family has always helped us out. The last time it was even more, a hundred and twenty thousand. But on that occasion Papa had to sign a statement that he would never turn to our relatives for help again, and especially not Uncle Bernhard."—Would you get to the point? What are you driving at? What do you expect *me* to be able to do?—"The only relative we might still consider would be Uncle Viktor, but unfortunately he's on a trip to the North Cape of Norway or to Scotland"—isn't *he* lucky, the disgusting man—"and absolutely can't be reached, at least for the moment. To turn to business associates, especially Dr. Sch., who has helped Papa out several times"—good Lord, it's that bad!—"is out of the question, since he's gotten married again"—all right, would you finally tell me what you want me to do!—"And then your letter came, my dear child, in which you mention Dorsday, among other people, who happens to be staying at the Fratazza, too—and it seemed to us as if fate were beckoning. You remember, no doubt, how often Dorsday came to visit us in earlier years"—not that often, really—"it's pure chance that we haven't seen much of him for two or three years; they say he's involved in a rather serious relationship— nothing very refined, just between you and me."—Why 'just between you and me'?—"Papa still plays whist with him every Thursday at his men's club, and last winter he saved Dorsday a nice piece of money in a lawsuit against another art dealer. Furthermore—why shouldn't you know this—he's helped Papa out once already."—I thought so.—"That time it was a mere bagatelle, eight thousand gulden,—but thirty thousand doesn't actually amount to much for Dorsday, either. And so I was thinking, perhaps you could do your loved ones a favor and talk to Dorsday."—What?—"He's always been especially fond of you."— Can't say I've noticed. He stroked my cheek once, when I was twelve or thirteen. 'Already a grown-up young lady.'—"And since Papa fortunately hasn't approached him again since the eight thousand, he won't refuse us this act of kindness. Not long ago he's supposed to have made eighty thousand just by selling a single Rubens to someone in America. It goes without saying, of course, that you shouldn't mention that."—Do you think I'm an idiot, Mama?—"But otherwise you can be very open with him. If it comes up, you can even mention that Baron Höning called Papa in to see him. And that the thirty thousand will definitely keep the worst from happening, not just for the moment, but, God willing, for always."—Do you really believe that, Mama?—"Because the Erbesheimer case, which is looking extremely favorable, will certainly earn your Papa a hundred thousand—though obviously he can't ask the Erbesheimers for anything at this point. So I beg you, my child, speak with Dorsday. I assure you that it won't be difficult. Papa could simply have sent him a message by telegraph—we seriously considered that—but it's really so much better, my child, to speak with someone in person. The money has to be there by twelve o'clock on the sixth; Dr. F."—Who's Dr. F.? Oh, of course, Fiala.—"is adamant. Of course personal animosity is involved here, too. But since, unfortunately, money from a trust fund is involved,"—good God! Papa, what have you done?—"we have no choice. And if the money isn't in Fiala's hands by twelve noon on the fifth, a warrant of arrest will be issued—or rather, that's how long Baron Höning is willing to delay issuing it. So Dorsday would have to have the money transferred by telegraph from his bank to Dr. F. Then we'll be saved. If not, God only knows what will happen. Believe me, you won't be compromising yourself in the least, my dear child. Papa, of course, had his misgivings at first. He even made two other attempts with different parties. But he came back home in utter despair."—Is Papa really capable of despair?—"Maybe not even so much because of the money, but because people are treating him so shamefully. One of them was Papa's best friend at one time. I'm sure you know who I mean."—I don't have the vaguest idea. Papa has had so many best friends, but in reality not a single one. Warnsdorf, maybe?—"Papa came home at one o'clock, and now it's four in the morning. He's finally asleep, thank God."—If only he wouldn't wake up, that would be the best thing for him.—"I'll take this letter to the post office as early in the morning as possible and mail it special delivery, so you should get it on the morning of the third."—How did Mama imagine this was going to work? She never has any idea about things like this.—"So speak with Dorsday right away, I implore you, and let us know by telegraph how it turns out. Whatever you do, don't let Aunt Emma know that anything's wrong; it's sad enough that a person can't turn to her own sister in a case like this, but it would be just like talking to a stone. My dear, dear child, I'm so sorry that you have to deal with such things at your tender age, but believe me, Papa is the least to blame in this whole business."—Who's to blame, then, Mama?—"Well, let's hope to God that the Erbesheimer case will signify a change in our lives in every respect. We just have to get beyond these next few weeks. It would be utter mockery if something terrible happened because of thirty thousand gulden, wouldn't it?"—She doesn't seriously believe that Papa would . . . But wouldn't—the other possibility be even worse?—"I'll close now, my child. I hope that no matter what happens"—no matter what happens?—"you'll be able to stay in San Martino through the holidays, at least till the ninth or tenth. You certainly don't need to come back for our sake. Say hello to your aunt and just keep being nice to her. And so once again, don't be upset with us, my dear, good child. I send you my"—Yes, yes, I've read all that.

So I'm supposed to put the touch on Herr Dorsday. This is insane. How does Mama picture me doing this? Why didn't Papa just get on the train and come here? That wouldn't have taken any longer than the special delivery letter. But maybe they would have stopped him at the station—attempted escape— —this is so horrible! And the thirty thousand won't help. It's the same story, over and over again. For seven years now! No, longer. And who could tell from looking at me? No one, and Papa doesn't let anything show, either. And yet everyone knows about it. I have no idea how we've been able to hold on. You can get used to anything. And at the same time we actually live quite well. Mama is truly amazing. That dinner on New Year's day last year, for fourteen people—unbelievable. But my two pairs of evening gloves, on the other hand, what a scene that was. And then she almost cried when Rudi needed three hundred gulden a while back. Papa always keeps his good humor, though. Always? Oh no, oh no. That expression on his face when we were at Figaro not long ago—all of a sudden he looked completely empty. It scared me. It was as if he were a different person. But afterwards we ate at the Grand Hotel and he was in his usual sparkling mood again.

And here I am holding this letter in my hand. It's crazy! I'm supposed to talk to Dorsday? I'd be utterly ashamed.— —Me, ashamed? Why? I'm not to blame.—Should I talk to Aunt Emma? Absolutely not. She probably doesn't have that much money at her disposal anyway. My uncle is such a skinflint. Oh, Lord, why don't I have any money? Why haven't I ever earned any? Why haven't I learned how to do anything? Oh, I've learned some things, all right. Who could say that I haven't learned anything? I play the piano, I can speak French and English and a little bit of Italian, I've gone to art history lectures—haha! And even if I had learned something more sensible, what good would it do me? I would never have saved thirty thousand gulden.— —

The alpenglow is gone. The evening isn't splendid any more. This whole place is sad. No, it's not the place—*life* is sad. And here I am sitting calmly on the window sill. And Papa's going to be put in prison. No, never, I can't let that happen. I'll save him. Yes, Papa, I'm going to save you. It's very simple, actually. A few nonchalant words—this is just right for me, I'm so 'self-assured'—haha, I'll make Herr Dorsday think that it's an honor for him to lend us money. And it is, too.— Herr von Dorsday, might you have a moment's time for me? I just got a letter from Mama, it seems that she's in an awkward situation at the moment—or rather, Papa is—'Well, of course, my dear Fräulein, with the greatest of pleasure. How much do they need?' If only I didn't find him so unpleasant. The way he looks at me, too. No, Herr Dorsday, your elegance doesn't fool me, and neither do your monocle and your noblesse. You could just as well deal in old clothes as in old paintings.—Else, Else, what's gotten into you!—Oh, I can say that if I want to. No one can tell by looking at me. I'm even blond, reddish blond, and Rudi looks just like an aristocrat. Of course with Mama you notice right away, at least when she talks. Not with Papa, though. Anyway, *let* them notice. I don't try to hide it, and Rudi does even less. Quite the opposite. What would Rudi do if Papa got put in prison? Would he shoot himself? Oh, that's ridiculous! Shootings and prison, none of that really happens, you only read about it in the newspaper.

The air is like champagne. In an hour it'll be time for dinner, for the 'evening repast.' I can't stand Cissy. She doesn't take the least interest in her little girl. What should I wear? My blue dress or my black one? The black one might be more appropriate for tonight. Is it too low-cut? They call it 'toilette de circonstance' in French novels. I have to look absolutely stunning when I talk to Dorsday. After dinner, nonchalantly. His eyes will be locked onto my neckline. Disgusting man, I hate him. I hate everyone. Why does it have to be Dorsday, of all people? Is there really no one in this world who has thirty thousand gulden but Dorsday? How about if I were to talk to Paul? He could tell Aunt Emma he has gambling debts—she would definitely be able to come up with the money then. Almost dark already. Night. Dark as the grave. I'd like best of all to be dead.—That's not the least bit true. How about if I were to go down right now and talk to Dorsday before dinner, even? Oh, this is so awful!—Paul, if you get me the thirty thousand you can have anything you want from me. That sounds like it came right out of a novel again. The noble-minded daughter sells herself for her beloved father and ends up having fun doing it. Disgusting! No, Paul, even for thirty thousand you're not getting anything from me. Maybe for a million? For a palace? A pearl necklace? If I ever get married I'll probably do it for less. Is that so bad, after all? Fanny essentially sold herself, too. She told me her husband makes her flesh crawl. Well, Papa, how about if I were to auction myself off tonight? To save you from going to prison. Scandal!—I definitely have a fever. Or has it started already? No, I'm feverish. Could be from the air. Like champagne.—Would Fred be able to suggest anything if he were here? I don't need any advice. There's nothing to give advice about, anyway. I'll talk to Herr Dorsday from Prešov,[6] I'll put the touch on him, I, self-assured Else, the aristocrat, the marchesa, the beggar, the swindler's daughter. How did I end up this way? Other girls aren't as good mountain climbers as I am, they aren't as daring—sporting girl, as the English say. I should have been born in England, or as a countess.

There are all my clothes hanging in the wardrobe! Is the green loden outfit even paid for, Mama? Only a down payment, I think. I'll put on my black dress. They couldn't take their eyes off me yesterday. Even the pale little man with the gold pince-nez. I'm actually more interesting than beautiful. I should have gone on the stage. Bertha's had three lovers already, no one holds that against her . . . In Düsseldorf it was the theater director. In Hamburg it was a married man; she lived in the Hotel Atlantic, in a suite with a bathroom. I think she's even proud of it. They're all so stupid. I'll have a hundred lovers, a thousand, why not? This neckline isn't low enough; if I were married

it could be lower.—Glad I ran into you, Herr von Dorsday, I just
happened to get a letter from Vienna . . . I'll take the letter along just
in case. Should I ring for the girl? No, I'll get ready by myself. If I
were rich, I'd never travel without a lady's maid.
Time to turn on the light. It's getting cool. Shut the window. Pull
the curtains?—No need to. No one's standing on the mountain over
there with a telescope. Too bad.—I just happened to get a letter, Herr
von Dorsday. —Would it be better to wait till after dinner? People are
in a more relaxed mood then. Dorsday, too. And I could drink a glass
of wine beforehand. But if this business were over and done with
before dinner I'd enjoy the food more. Pudding à la merveille, fromage
et fruits divers. And what if Herr von Dorsday says no?—Or if he gets
fresh, even? Oh no, no one has ever gotten fresh with me. There was
that navy ensign Brandel, of course, but he didn't mean anything by
it.—I've lost some weight again. I look good like this.—Dusk gazes
into the room. Gazes in like a ghost. Like a hundred ghosts. The
ghosts rise up from my meadow. How far are we from Vienna? How
long have I been away now? I'm so alone here! I don't have a girl
friend, I don't have a boy friend, either. Where are they all? Who will
I marry? Who's going to marry a swindler's daughter?—Just received
a letter, Herr von Dorsday.—'Oh, it's really nothing, Fräulein Else, I
sold a Rembrandt yesterday, you don't need to thank me, Fräulein
Else.' And then he tears a check out of his checkbook and signs it
with his gold fountain pen; and tomorrow morning I go back to Vienna
with the check. I'll go one way or the other, even without the check.
I'm not staying here any longer. I couldn't, how could I possibly?
Here I am, living the life of an elegant young lady, and Papa's got one
foot in the grave—no, in the penitentiary. My next-to-last pair of silk
stockings. No one will notice this little tear just below the knee. No
one? Who knows. Don't be indecent, Else.—Bertha is nothing but a
slut. But is Christine the least bit better? Her future husband has that
to look forward to. I'm sure Mama has always been a faithful wife. I
won't be faithful. I'm self-assured, but I won't be faithful. Filous are
dangerous for me. I'll bet the marchesa's lover is a filou. If Fred really
knew what I was like, that would be the end of his feelings for me.—
'You could have become anything you wanted to, Fräulein—a pia-

nist, an accountant, an actress—you have so much potential. But your life has always been too easy.' Too easy. Haha. Fred overestimates me. Actually I don't have talent for anything.—Who knows? I could have done as well as Bertha, certainly. But I lack energy. Young lady from a good family. Ha, good family. Her father embezzles trust fund money. Why are you doing this to me, Papa? If you at least had some of it left! But to gamble it all away on the stock market! Is that even worth the effort? And thirty thousand more certainly won't do you any good. For a few months at best. Eventually he's going to have to run away. A year and a half ago things had almost reached that point. Then help came, just in time. But sooner or later help won't come—and what will become of us then? Rudi will go to Rotterdam and get a job in Vanderhulst's bank. But how about me? Find a wealthy husband. Fine, if that was what I was interested in! I really look beautiful today. Probably because I'm so agitated. Who am I beautiful for? Would I be happier if Fred were here? No, Fred simply isn't right for me. He's not a filou! But I'd take him if he had money. And then some filou would come along—and the misery would be complete.—I think you'd like to be a filou, Herr von Dorsday; from a distance you even look like one sometimes. Like a jaded vicomte, like a Don Juan—with your silly monocle and your white flannel suit. But a filou you're not, not in the least.—Do I have everything? Am I ready for the 'evening repast'?—But what will I do for an hour if I don't run into Dorsday? He might be taking a walk with that unhappy Frau Winawer. Oh, she can't be that unhappy, she doesn't need thirty thousand gulden. I'll just sit in an easy chair in the lobby and look impressive; I'll cross my legs—no one will see the tear below the knee—and glance through the *London Illustrated News* and the *Vie parisienne*. Maybe a billionaire has just arrived.—It's you or no one, Fräulein.—I'll take my white shawl along, I look good in it. I'll drape it casually around my magnificent shoulders. Who do I have them for, these magnificent shoulders? I could make some man very happy. If only the right man would turn up. But I don't want to have any babies. I'm not motherly. Marie Weil is motherly. Mama is motherly, Aunt Irene is motherly. I have a noble forehead and a beautiful figure.—'If you'd let me paint you the way I'd like to, Fräulein Else.'—Yes, you'd like that, all right, wouldn't you. I don't even know what his name was any more. It wasn't Titian, I can tell you that—the audacity of him!—I've just received a letter, Herr von Dorsday.—A little more powder on my neck and throat, a drop of Verveine on my handkerchief, close the wardrobe, open the window again. Ah, it's so beautiful I could cry! I'm nervous. Well, wouldn't anyone be nervous under these circumstances? The Veronal container is next to my underwear. I could use new underwear, too. That'll be another scene. Oh, Lord.

Mt. Cimone looks so sinister, so gigantic—as if it were about to fall on me! Still not a star in the sky. The air is like champagne. And the fragrance from the meadows! I'm going to live in the country. I'll marry a landowner and have children. Dr. Froriep might have been the only man I would have been happy with. How wonderful those two evenings were, first at Kniep's and then at the artists' ball. Why did he suddenly disappear? As far as I was concerned, at any rate. Because of Papa, maybe? Probably. I'd like to shout 'hello' out into the air before I have to go downstairs and mingle with those awful people again. But who would I be shouting to? I'm completely alone. No one else can imagine how terribly alone I am. Hello, my beloved! Who? Hello, my husband-to-be! Who? Hello, my boy friend! Who?— Fred?—Not a chance. I'll leave the window open. Even though it's going to get cool. Turn off the light. There—oh, yes, the letter. I'd better take it along just in case. I'll put my book on the night table— I'll definitely read some more of *Notre Coeur* tonight, no matter what happens. Good evening, most beautiful young lady in the mirror, remember me kindly, goodbye . . .

Why am I locking the door? Nothing gets stolen here. I wonder if Cissy leaves her door open at night? Or does she wait and unlock it when he knocks? Am I sure about this? Well, of course. Then they lie in bed together. Repulsive. I won't share the same bedroom with my husband and my thousand lovers.—Not a soul on the stairway, never is around this time. My steps are echoing. I've been here for three weeks now. I left Gmunden on the twelfth of August. Gmunden was boring. Where did Papa get the money to send Mama and me to the country? Und Rudi traveled around for a good four weeks. God knows where. He barely wrote twice the whole time. I'll never understand how we get by. Mama doesn't have any jewelry left, of course.—Why did Fred spend only two days in Gmunden? I'll bet he has a mistress, too! Although I can't quite imagine it. I can't imagine *anything*. He hasn't written me for a week now. He writes nice letters.—Who's that sitting at the little table there? No, it's not Dorsday. Thank God. I couldn't possibly say anything to him now, before dinner.—Why is the desk clerk looking at me so strangely? I wonder if he could have read Mama's letter? I think I'm going crazy. I'll have to tip him again soon.—That blond woman there is already dressed for dinner, too. How can anyone be so fat!—I'm going to go outside and stroll up and down in front of the hotel for a little while. Or should I go to the music room? Isn't that someone playing? A Beethoven sonata! How can anyone be playing a Beethoven sonata here! I've been neglecting my piano playing. When I'm back in Vienna I'm going to practice regularly again. I'll change my life in lots of ways. We'll all have to do that. Things can't go on like this. I'll have a serious talk with Papa— if there's still time. There will be, there will be. Why haven't I ever done that? In our house people deal with everything by joking about it, even though no one is in a joking mood. We're all actually afraid of each other, each of us is alone. Mama is alone, because she's not very bright and doesn't know anything about anyone—not about me, not about Rudi, not about Papa. But she doesn't sense that, and Rudi doesn't either. He's certainly a nice, elegant young man, but when he was twenty-one he showed more promise. It'll be good for him to go to Holland. But where will I go? I'd like to leave and be able to do what I want to. If Papa runs off to America I'll go with him. I'm so completely confused . . . The desk clerk must think I'm out of my mind, sitting here on the arm of a chair staring off into space. I'll light a cigarette. Where's my cigarette case? Up in my room. But where? The Veronal is by my underwear. But what did I do with the cigarette case? Here come Cissy and Paul. She finally has to change for the 'evening repast,' otherwise they would have gone right on playing in the dark.—They don't see me. I wonder what he's saying to her? Why is she laughing in that idiotic way? It would be fun to write an anonymous letter to her husband in Vienna. Would I be capable of doing a thing like that? Never. Who knows? Now they've noticed me. I'll nod to them. She's annoyed that I look so pretty. She looks so embarrassed.

"Well, hello, Else. You're dressed for dinner already?"—Why did she say 'dinner' this time and not 'evening repast'? She's not even consistent.—"That's right, Frau Cissy." *"You look absolutely ravishing, Else, I'm really tempted to make a pass at you."* —"Save yourself the effort, Paul, and give me a cigarette instead."—*"With the greatest pleasure."*—"Thank you. How did your match turn out?"—*"Frau Cissy beat me three times in a row."*—"Oh, but he was distracted. By the way, Else, did you know that the Crown Prince of Greece is arriving here tomorrow?"*—What do I care about the Crown Prince of Greece? "Is he really?" Oh, Lord—Dorsday with Frau Winawer! They're waving. Now they're walking on. I nodded back much too formally. Not at all the way I usually do. Oh, I'm such an awful person!—*"Looks like your cigarette has gone out, Else."*—"So it has. Can you give me a light? Thanks."—*"Your shawl is so pretty, Else, it looks fabulous with your black dress. But I'd better go and change, too."*—I wish she wouldn't leave, I'm afraid of Dorsday.—*"And I'm having the hairdresser come at seven, she's marvelous. She works in Milan in the winter. Goodbye for now, Else, goodbye, Paul."*—*"My respects, Frau Mohr."* —"Goodbye, Frau Cissy."—She's gone. It's a good thing that Paul's staying, at least. *"May I sit down with you for a moment, Else, or am I disturbing your dreams?"*—"Why my dreams? Maybe my realities." In other words, nothing at all. It would be better if he'd leave. I've simply got to talk to Dorsday. He's still standing there with that unhappy Frau Winawer; he's bored, I can see it in his face, he wishes he could come over to me.—*"So you have realities you don't want to be disturbed in, do you?"*—What's he saying? He can go to the devil. Why am I giving him such a flirtatious smile? He's not the one I have in mind at all. Dorsday's looking over this way out of the corner of his eye. Where am I? Where am I?—*"What's bothering you today, Else?"*—"Why do you think something's bothering me?"—*"You're so mysterious, alluring, seductive."*—"Don't talk nonsense, Paul."—*"A person could almost lose his senses just looking at you."*—What's gotten into him? How can he talk to me like that? He's handsome. The smoke from my cigarette keeps getting trapped in his hair. But he's of no use to me now.—*"You're looking right past*

me, Else. Why is that?"— I'm not going to answer. He's of no use to me now. I'll put on my most hateful expression. I simply can't talk to him now.— *"You're off somewhere far away in your thoughts."*—"I suppose I might be." He doesn't exist for me. Has Dorsday noticed that I'm waiting for him? I'm not looking in his direction, but I know he's looking at me. *"Well, goodbye, Else."*— Thank God. He's kissing my hand. He's never done that before. "'Bye, Paul." Where did I get this dripping voice? He's going, the hypocrite. He probably has to arrange something with Cissy for tonight. I wish them lots of pleasure. I'm going to put my shawl around my shoulders and get up and go out in front of the hotel. It's bound to be a little chilly. Too bad that my coat—oh, wait, I had the desk clerk hang it up in the closet behind the counter this morning. I can feel Dorsday's gaze on my neck through my shawl. Frau Winawer is going up to her room now. But how do I know that? Mental telepathy. "Excuse me, please —"— *"The young lady would like her coat?"*—"Yes, please."— *"The evenings are indeed a bit cool already, Fräulein. That happens here so suddenly."*—"Thank you." Should I really go outside? Of course, what other choice is there? I'll go over to the door, at least. Here they come now, one after the other. The man with the gold pince-nez. The tall blonde in the green vest. They're all looking at me. Pretty, that petite woman from Geneva. No, it's Lausanne she's from. It's really not so cool after all.

"Good evening, Fräulein Else."— Oh, God, it's him. I won't say anything about Papa. Not a word. Not until after we've eaten. Or maybe I'll go to Vienna tomorrow. I'll go and see Dr. Fiala myself. Why didn't I think of that right away? I'm going to turn around and act as if I didn't know who it was behind me. "Oh, Herr von Dorsday."— *"You were going for a walk, Fräulein Else?"*—"Oh, not a walk, really, just a little stroll before dinner."— *"That's still almost an hour away."*—"Really?" It's not at all cool. The mountains are blue. It would be funny if he suddenly asked me to marry him.— *"There is absolutely no more beautiful spot on earth than right here."*— "Do you think so, Herr von Dorsday? Just please don't say that the air here is like champagne."— *"No, Fräulein Else, I only say that above two thousand meters. And we're barely sixteen hundred and fifty above sea level here."*—"Does that make such a big difference?"— *"It certainly does.*

Have you ever been in Engadin?"—"No, I never have. So the air is really like champagne there?"—*"One could almost put it that way. But champagne isn't my favorite drink. I prefer this region. If for no other reason than the splendid forests."*— How boring he is. Doesn't he notice? He apparently doesn't know quite what to talk to me about. It would be easier with a married woman. One little indecent remark, and the conversation continues.—*"Are you staying for any length of time here in San Martino, Fräulein Else?"*— I'm acting like an idiot. Why am I giving him such a flirtatious look? And he's already begun to smile in that certain way. Lord, how stupid men are. "That depends partly on what my aunt decides." That's not the least bit true. I can go back to Vienna alone if I want to. "Probably till the tenth."—*"I suppose your mother is still in Gmunden?"*—"No, Herr von Dorsday. She's back in Vienna already. She's been back for three weeks. Papa's in Vienna, too. He took barely a week's vacation this year. The Erbesheimer case has been a lot of work for him, I think."—*"I can well imagine. But your father is probably the only one who can get Erbesheimer off the hook . . . It's a partial success already that the case has been turned into a civil suit."*— This is good, this is good. —"I'm pleased to hear that you have favorable presentiments, too."—*"Presentiments? How so?"*—"Well, that Papa will win the case for Erbesheimer."—*"Now, I wouldn't go so far as to maintain that with any certainty."*— What, is he backing off already? I'm not going to let him get away with that. "Oh, I think highly of presentiments and premonitions. Just imagine, Herr von Dorsday, I got a letter from home this very day." That was rather inept. He looks a bit taken aback. Keep going, don't swallow. He's a good old friend of Papa's. Don't stop, don't stop. It's now or never. "Herr von Dorsday, you just spoke so kindly of Papa that it would really be despicable of me to be less than candid with you."— His eyes are getting so big. Oh, Lord, he's starting to understand. Keep going, keep going. "You see, you were mentioned in the letter, too, Herr von Dorsday. It's a letter from Mama, actually."—*"Ah."*—"It's really quite a sad letter. You know how things are with my family, Herr von Dorsday." — I have tears in my voice, for heaven's sake. Keep going, keep going, there's no turning back now. Thank God. "To make a long story short, Herr von Dorsday,

things have come to that point again."— He's wishing he could van-
ish into thin air now. "It's only a matter of—a bagatelle. Really, just a
bagatelle, Herr von Dorsday. And yet, from what Mama writes,
everything's at stake." I'm blabbing on like some stupid cow. — *"Please
calm yourself, Fräulein Else."*— He said that so nicely. But all the same,
he doesn't need to be touching my arm.— *"So what actually is the
matter, Fräulein Else? What does your mother say in her sad letter?"*—
"Herr von Dorsday, Papa"— My knees are shaking. "Mama wrote
that Papa"—*"Good Lord, Else, what's wrong? Wouldn't you like to—
here's a bench. May I help you into your coat? It's gotten chilly."*—"Thank
you, Herr von Dorsday. Oh, it's nothing, really nothing at all." Now
I'm sitting here on the bench all of a sudden. Who is the lady walking
by there? I have no idea. If only I didn't have to keep talking. The way
he's looking at me! How could you ask me to do this, Papa? It wasn't
right of you, Papa. But now I've started. I should have waited till after
dinner. — *"Fräulein Else?"*— His monocle is dangling. It looks so silly.
Should I answer him? I have to. All right, quickly, so that I can put
this behind me. What can happen to me, anyway? He's a friend of
Papa's.—"Oh, Lord, Herr von Dorsday, you're such an old friend of
the family." I did that very well. "And it probably won't surprise you
to hear that Papa is in a very awkward situation again." How peculiar
my voice sounds. Is that really me talking? Am I dreaming? I'm sure
my face looks completely different than it usually does, too. — *"That
doesn't surprise me a great deal, to be sure. You're right about that, dear
Fräulein Else—although I'm very sorry to hear it."*— Why am I looking
up at him with this pleading expression? Smile, smile. That's better.
— *"I feel a genuine bond of friendship with your father, with all of you."*—
He shouldn't look at me like that, it's indecent. I'm going to talk to
him differently and stop smiling. I have to act more dignified. "Well,
Herr von Dorsday, now you have the opportunity to demonstrate
your friendship to my father." I have my old voice back, thank God.
"You see, Herr von Dorsday, it seems that all our relatives and acquaintances—most of them haven't come back to the city yet—otherwise Mama wouldn't have hit on the idea.—You see, when I wrote
to Mama not long ago I happened to make reference—among other
things, of course—to your being here in San Martino."—*"I suspected*

*immediately, Fräulein Else, that I would not constitute the sole topic of
your correspondence with your mama."*—Why is he standing there press-
ing his knees against mine? Oh, I'll just put up with it. What's the
difference! Once a person has sunk so low. "Here's the situation: it's
Dr. Fiala who seems to be making things difficult for Papa this time."—
"Ah, Dr. Fiala."— He apparently knows what this Dr. Fiala is like.
"Yes, Dr. Fiala. And the amount in question is supposed to be, rather
has to be in his hands on the fifth, that's the day after tomorrow, at
twelve noon, if Baron Höning isn't to—just imagine, the baron had
Papa come see him in private, he's so fond of him, you know." Why
did I mention Höning, that wasn't at all necessary.— *"You're telling
me, Else, that arrest would otherwise be unavoidable?"*—Why the stern
tone? I won't answer, I'll just nod. "Yes." There I went and said 'yes'
after all. *"Hm, this is indeed—serious, this is really very—such a highly
talented, brilliant fellow.—And how much is the sum in question, Fräulein
Else?"*—Why is he smiling? He says it's serious and then he smiles.
What does this smile mean? That it doesn't matter how much it is?
And what if he says no? I'll kill myself if he says no. Come on now,
I'm supposed to say the amount. "What, Herr von Dorsday, haven't I
said how much it is yet? A million." Why did I say that? Now is
hardly the time for making jokes, is it? But then he'll be pleased when
I tell him how much less it *really* is. Look how big his eyes have gotten! Does he really think it's possible that Papa could ask him—"Herr
von Dorsday, forgive me for making a joke, at this moment of all
times. I'm truly not in a joking mood." That's right, go ahead and
press your knees against mine, you can take that liberty with me. "Of
course it's not a million, it's only thirty thousand gulden in total,
Herr von Dorsday, and it has to be in the hands of Dr. Fiala by noon
on the day after tomorrow. Mama wrote me that Papa tried every
possibility, but as I mentioned before, none of our relatives who might
be able to help out have come back to Vienna yet." Oh, God, how
humiliating this is! "Otherwise it would never have occurred to Papa
to turn to you, that is, to ask me—" Why isn't he saying anything?
Why is his face so expressionless? Why doesn't he say yes? Where are
his check book and fountain pen? Oh Lord, he won't say no, will he?
Should I get down on my knees and beg him? Oh, God! Oh, God!—

"On the fifth, you said, Fräulein Else?"— Thank God, he's talking again. "Yes, that's right, Herr von Dorsday, the day after tomorrow, at twelve noon. So that would mean—I don't think there would be time to take care of it by mail at this point."— *"No, of course not, Fräulein Else, we'd have to do it by telegraph."*—'We'—that's good, that's very good.— *"In any case, that's the least of the problems. How much did you say it was, Else?"*— He heard perfectly well what I said, why is he tormenting me? "Thirty thousand, Herr von Dorsday. A trivial amount, actually." Why did I say that? How stupid. But he's smiling. Silly girl, he's thinking. Such a charming smile. Papa is saved. He would even have lent him fifty thousand, and we could have bought all sorts of things. I would have bought new underwear. How contemptible I am. That's what this leads to. — *"Not quite as trivial, my dear girl,"*— Why is he calling me 'dear girl'? Is that good or bad? — *"as you might imagine. Even thirty thousand gulden has to be earned."*— "I'm sorry, Herr von Dorsday, I didn't mean it that way. I was only thinking how sad it is that Papa—because of an amount like that, because of a bagatelle"— Oh, Lord, I'm getting all in a muddle again. "You simply can't imagine, Herr von Dorsday—even though you do know something about our circumstances—how terrible this is for me and especially for Mama." He's put one foot on the bench. Is that supposed to be elegant—or something else? — *"Oh, I can indeed imagine, dear Else."*— His voice sounds so different, so peculiar. — *"I've said to myself more than a few times: the man's brilliant—it's too bad, it's really too bad about him."*— Why did he say 'too bad'? Isn't he going to give us the money? No, he just meant it in a general kind of way. Why won't he finally say yes? Or maybe he doesn't think he has to say it in so many words. The way he's looking at me! Why has he stopped talking? Oh, it's because those two Hungarian women are walking by. At least he's taken his foot off the bench now and isn't leaning over in that indecent way. His tie is too loud for a man his age. Does his mistress pick them out for him? Nothing very refined, 'just between you and me,' Mama wrote. Thirty thousand gulden! I'm smiling at him, for heaven's sake. Why am I smiling? Oh, I'm such a coward. — *"And if one could at least assume, my dear Fräulein Else, that the money would really help. But—you're such a clever young lady, Else—what would*

thirty thousand gulden amount to? A mere drop in the ocean." — Oh God, isn't he going to give us the money? I have to get this terrified look off my face. Everything is at stake. I've got to say something reasonable now, something really convincing. "Oh, no, Herr von Dorsday, this time it wouldn't be just a drop in the ocean. The Erbesheimer case is coming up soon, don't forget that, Herr von Dorsday, and it's already as good as won. You had that same feeling yourself, Herr von Dorsday, isn't that true? And Papa has other cases, too. And besides, I'm intending—please don't laugh, Herr von Dorsday—to have a talk with Papa, a very serious one. He thinks a lot of me. I can say with confidence that if there is any person capable of exerting an influence on him, then that person is me, that's right, me."—*"You're a touching, charming creature, Fräulein Else."*—His voice has that sound again. It's so repulsive when men start to sound like that. Even Fred. — *"In truth, a charming creature."*—Why did he say 'in truth'? That's so tasteless. They only say that in the Burgtheater. —*"But as much as I'd like to share your optimism—once the cart has gotten into a rut—"* — "But that's not the case, Herr von Dorsday. If I didn't believe in Papa, if I weren't completely convinced that the thirty thousand gulden—" I don't know what else I can say. I can't literally beg from him. He's considering it. Apparently. Maybe he doesn't know Fiala's address? Ridiculous. This situation is intolerable. I'm sitting here like some poor sinner. He's standing in front of me, boring into my forehead with his monocle and not saying a word. I'm going to get up now, that'll be best. I won't let myself be treated like this. Papa can go ahead and kill himself. I'll kill myself, too. It's a disgrace to live this way. It would be best if I jumped off that mountain over there, then it would be over and done with. It would serve you right, every one of you. I'm getting up. —*"Fräulein Else"*—"Forgive me for troubling you about this matter, Herr von Dorsday. I can of course completely understand your refusal."—There, it's done with, I'm going. —*"Please stay, Fräulein Else."*— Stay? Why am I supposed to stay? He's going to give us the money. Yes. Definitely. He has to. But I'm not going to sit down again. I'll just stand here as if it were only for half a second. I'm slightly taller than he is. —*"You didn't wait for my answer, Else. On one earlier occasion I was in a position, forgive me, Else, for bringing it up in this context*—he wouldn't have to say Else so often—*to help your Papa out of a predicament. To be sure with an even more—trivial amount than this time, and I didn't delude myself in the least with the hope of ever seeing it again. And so there really wouldn't be any reason for me to withhold my assistance this time. And especially when a young girl like you, Else, when you yourself approach me as intercessor—* — What is he getting at? His voice doesn't have that sound any more. It sounds different now. The way he's looking at me—he'd better be careful!! —*"And so, Else, I'm prepared to—Dr. Fiala will have the thirty thousand gulden in his hands at twelve noon on the day after tomorrow—under one condition."*— I can't let him say it, I can't! "Herr von Dorsday, I, I personally guarantee that my father will pay back the amount as soon as he has received his fee from Erbesheimer. Up till now the Erbesheimers haven't paid him anything. Not even a retainer—Mama herself wrote me—" — *"Don't say that, Else, one should never guarantee anything on behalf of another person—one shouldn't even do it for oneself."* — What does he want? His voice has that sound again. No one has ever looked at me like this before. I sense what he wants. He'll be sorry if he— *"An hour ago I wouldn't have thought it possible that it might ever occur to me to set a condition in a situation such as this. And now I'm doing it nevertheless. Yes, Else, a man is quite simply only a man, and it isn't my fault that you're so beautiful, Else."*— What does he want? What does he— *"Perhaps tomorrow or the next day I would have requested the same thing of you that I now wish to request, even if you hadn't asked me for a million, excuse me, thirty thousand gulden. But under any other circumstances, of course, you would hardly have granted me the opportunity of speaking with you privately for so long."*—"Oh, but I've really taken up too much of your time, Herr von Dorsday." I did that well. Fred would be pleased. What's this? He's grabbing my hand? What does he think he's doing? — *"I'm sure you've known for a long time, Else."* — He can't go on holding my hand like this! Oh, thank God, he's let it go. Not so close, not so close. *"You wouldn't be a woman, Else, if you hadn't noticed. Je vous désire."*— He could have said it in German, this Herr Vicomte. —*"Do I have to say anything more?"*— "You've already said too much, Herr von Dorsday." And I'm still standing here. Why? I'm

going to walk away, just walk away without saying goodbye. — *"Else!*
Else!"— Now he's next to me again. — *"Forgive me, Else. I was making*
a joke, too, just as you did before about the million gulden. And, like you,
I'm not asking as much either—as you feared, I unfortunately have to
say—so that the lesser request might come as a pleasant surprise to you.
Please, Else, stay a moment longer."— And I'm really staying. Why?
Here we are, face to face. Shouldn't I simply have slapped him? Couldn't
I still do it? The two Englishmen are walking by. Now would be the
time. Precisely because they're here. Why can't I do it? I'm a coward,
I'm destroyed, I'm humiliated. What will he want instead of a million? A kiss, maybe? That we could talk about. A million is to thirty
thousand as—what ludicrous equations there are. — *"If you should*
ever really need a million, Else—I am certainly not a rich man—then we
would have to see. But for now I am easily satisfied, as you are. For now
the only thing I want is to—see you."— Is he crazy? He's looking right
at me!—Oh, no, so *that's* the way he means it! I should just slap him,
the beast! Am I blushing, or have I turned pale? You want to see me
naked? A lot of men would like to. I'm beautiful when I'm naked.
Why can't I just slap him? His face is gigantic. Why are you so close to
me, you beast? I don't want your breath on my cheeks. Why don't I
just leave him standing here? Has he put me under a spell? We're
looking each other in the eye like mortal enemies. I'd like to tell him
what a beast he is, but I can't. Or don't I really want to? — *"You're*
looking at me as if I were crazy, Else. Perhaps I am somewhat. There's a
kind of magic that emanates from you, that you're not even aware of
yourself, Else. I hope that you sense, Else, that my request is not meant to
insult you. I say 'request,' even though I realize that it looks desperately
similar to extortion. But I am not an extortionist, I am simply a man
who has had certain experiences—among others, that everything in the
world has its price—and that a person who gives his money away if he is
in a position to get something in return is an absolute fool. And—the
thing I want to buy this time, Else, as much value as it unquestionably
has—you will be none the poorer for selling it. And that it would remain
a secret between you and me, that I swear to you, Else, by—by all the
charms whose unveiling would so delight me."— Where did he learn to
talk like that? It sounds like it's out of a book. — *"And I also swear to*

you that I will not try to draw any advantage from the—situation that is not specified in our agreement. I ask nothing more of you than to be permitted to stand in reverence before your beauty for a quarter of an hour. My room is on the same floor as yours, Else, number sixty-five, easy to remember. The Swedish tennis player you mentioned earlier today was sixty-five years old, was he not?"— He's crazy! Why am I letting him go on like this? I feel paralyzed. — *"But if for any reason it doesn't suit you to visit me in room sixty-five, Else, then I would suggest a little walk after dinner. There's a clearing in the woods, I discovered it completely by chance the other day, scarcely five minutes from the hotel. It's looking to be a wonderful, summery evening, almost warm, and the light of the stars will array you in splendor."*— He's talking the way he would to a slave. I'll spit in his face. — *"I don't want you to give me your answer right away, Else. Think it over. After dinner you will be kind enough to inform me of your decision."* — Why did he say 'inform'? What an idiotic word— inform! — *"Think it over, take your time. Perhaps you will understand that it is not simply a business transaction that I am proposing to you."*— What else is it, you repulsive-sounding beast! — *"Possibly you will sense that you are speaking with a man who is rather lonely and not especially happy, one who perhaps deserves some consideration."* — Affected beast. Talks like a bad actor. His manicured fingers look like claws. No, no, I won't do it. Why can't I tell him that? Kill yourself, Papa! What is he doing with my hand? My arm has gone completely limp. He's putting my hand to his lips. They're hot. Disgusting! My hand is cold. I feel like knocking his hat off. Wouldn't that be funny! Haven't you kissed your fill yet, you beast?—The lamps in front of the hotel are already on. There are two windows open on the third floor. The one where the curtain is moving is mine. Something on top of the wardrobe is catching the light. There's nothing there, it's only the brass hinges. — *"Goodbye for now, Else."*— I'm not going to answer. I'm standing here perfectly motionless. He's looking me in the eye. My expression is impenetrable. He can't tell anything from it. He doesn't know if I'll come or not. I don't know either. All I know is that everything's over. I feel half dead. He's leaving. A little bent over. Beast! He feels me staring at his back. Who is he nodding to? Two ladies. He nods to people as if he were a count. Paul should challenge him to a

duel and kill him. Or Rudi. What does he take me for? The man has
no shame! Not on your life, never. You won't have any other choice,
Papa, you'll have to kill yourself.—This couple must just have come
back from a hike. Attractive, both of them. Do they still have time to
change before dinner? I'll bet they're on their honeymoon, or maybe
they're not even married. I'll never have a honeymoon. Thirty thousand gulden. No, no, no! There must be thirty thousand gulden somewhere in the world! I'll go to Fiala. I can still get there in time. Mercy,
mercy, Herr Doktor Fiala. With pleasure, my girl. Step right into my
bedroom.—Do me a favor, Paul, ask your father for thirty thousand
gulden. Tell him you have gambling debts and that you'll have to
shoot yourself otherwise. Glad to, dear cousin. I'm in room so-and-
so, I'll be expecting you at midnight. Oh, Herr von Dorsday, how
modest your demands are. For the time being. He's changing clothes
now. Tuxedo. So let's decide. Moonlit meadow or room number sixty-
five? Will he accompany me to the woods in his tuxedo?

Dinner's not for a while yet. I'll take a little walk and give myself
time to think things over. I'm a lonely old man, haha. Heavenly air,
like champagne. Not cool at all any more—thirty thousand . . . thirty
thousand . . . I must look very pretty against this expanse of nature.
Too bad there's no one else out here now. That man over there at the
edge of the woods seems to like looking at me. Well, my dear sir, I'm
much more beautiful naked, and the price is ridiculously low, only
thirty thousand. Maybe you can bring your friends along, it costs less
then. Hopefully you have lots of good-looking friends, better-look-
ing and younger than Herr von Dorsday? Do you know Herr von
Dorsday? He's a beast—a beast with a repulsive-sounding voice . . .

Come on now, think it over, think it over . . . A human life is
hanging in the balance. Papa's life. No, no, he won't kill himself, he'd
sooner go to prison. Three years at hard labor, or five. He's already
been living in constant fear for five or ten years . . . Trust funds . . .
And Mama has, too. And me, of course.—Who will I be forced to
undress for next time? Or should we stick with Herr Dorsday for the
sake of simplicity? His current mistress is nothing very refined, 'just
between you and me.' He would definitely prefer me. It's not at all
clear that I'm any more refined. Don't put on airs, Fräulein Else, I

could tell some stories about you . . . a certain dream, for example, that you've had three times already—you haven't even told your girl friend Bertha about it. And she can take quite a lot. And what was going on this year in Gmunden, my lofty Fräulein Else, at six in the morning on the balcony? Or maybe you didn't even notice the two young men in the boat who were staring at you? They weren't able to make out my face very clearly from the lake, of course, but they certainly noticed that I was in my underwear. And I was pleased that they saw me. Oh, more than pleased. I felt almost intoxicated. I ran both my hands along my hips, and I even pretended to myself that I didn't know they were looking. And the boat didn't budge from the spot. Yes, that's what I'm like, that's what I'm like. A slut, that's me. Everyone senses it. Even Paul senses it. He would, of course—he's a gynecologist. And the navy ensign sensed it and the painter, too. Fred, the dummy, is the only one who doesn't. That's why he loves me. But of all people I wouldn't want him to see me naked, never, never. It wouldn't give me any pleasure. I'd be ashamed. But that filou with the Roman look—I'd love to undress for him. More than anyone else. Even if I had to die right afterwards. But that wouldn't be necessary. People survive such things. Bertha has survived more than that. I'm sure Cissy lies there naked, too, when Paul comes creeping through the hotel corridors to her room the way I will tonight on my way to Herr von Dorsday's.

No, no, I won't do it! Anyone else—but not him. Paul, even. Or I'll pick someone out at dinner tonight. It doesn't make a bit of difference. But I can't tell everyone that I want thirty thousand gulden for it! I'd be like a tart from Kärntner Straße[7] then. No, I won't sell myself. Not ever. I will never sell myself. I'll *give* myself away. Yes, once I've found the right man, I'll give myself away. But I won't sell myself. I want to be a slut, not a whore. You miscalculated, Herr von Dorsday. And so did Papa. Yes, he miscalculated. He must have seen it coming. He knows people, after all. He knows Herr von Dorsday. It must have occurred to him that Herr von Dorsday would want something in return. Otherwise he could have telegraphed or come here himself. But this way it was easier and more certain, wasn't it, Papa? Anyone who has such a pretty daughter doesn't need to land in prison! And

Mama, stupid as she is, sits right down and writes the letter. Papa didn't dare do it himself. I would have noticed something right away. But you're not going to get away with it. No, you were too sure when you gambled on my familial affection, Papa, you were too sure when you calculated that I would sooner suffer anything, no matter how vile, than let you bear the consequences of your criminal irresponsibility. You're a genius, all right. Herr von Dorsday says so, everyone says so. But how does that help me? Fiala is a nothing, but he doesn't misappropriate trust funds, even Waldheim can't be mentioned in the same breath with you . . . Who was it again that said it? Dr. Froriep. Your papa's a genius.—And I've only heard him plead a case once!—Last year at that jury trial—for the first and last time! Brilliant! The tears were running down my cheeks. And that miserable creature he defended was acquitted. But maybe he wasn't such a miserable creature. All he did was steal, after all, he didn't embezzle trust funds so that he could play baccarat and speculate on the stock market. And now Papa will be standing in front of a jury himself. It'll be in all the newspapers. Second day of hearings, third day of hearings; the defense attorney rose to make his plea. And who will his defense attorney be? No genius. Nothing will help him. A unanimous verdict of guilty. Sentenced to five years. Stein Prison,[8] convict's clothing, shaved head. Visitors once a month. Mama and I will take the train to see him, third class. Because we don't have any money. No one will lend us any. Small apartment on Lerchenfelder Straße, like the one where I went to the seamstress ten years ago. We'll bring him something to eat. Where are we going to get it? We have nothing ourselves. Uncle Viktor will give us an allowance, three hundred gulden a month. Rudi will be in Holland working at Vanderhulst's bank—if they'll still take him.—The convict's children! Novel by Temme in three volumes. Papa receives us in his striped convict's outfit. He doesn't look angry, only sad. He doesn't know how to look angry, actually.— Else, if you had only gotten the money for me—that's what he'll be thinking, but he won't say anything. He won't have the heart to blame me. He's a good soul, it's just that he's irresponsible. His passion for gambling is his downfall. He can't help it, it's a kind of insanity. Maybe they'll acquit him because he's insane. He didn't think twice about the letter, either. Maybe it didn't even occur to him that Dorsday could exploit the situation and demand something awful from me. He's a good friend of the family, on one occasion he lent Papa eight thousand gulden. How could anyone imagine a thing like that of a decent person? Papa definitely tried every other possibility first. What he must have gone through before having Mama write the letter! He ran from one person to the next, from Warnsdorf to Burin, from Burin to Wertheimstein, and God knows who else. He must've gone to see Uncle Karl, too. And they all left him high and dry. All his so-called friends. And now Dorsday is his one hope, his last hope. And if the money doesn't come he'll kill himself. Of course he'll kill himself. He certainly won't allow himself to be locked up. Detention pending investigation, hearing, jury, prison, convict's clothes. No, no! When the warrant for arrest comes he'll shoot himself, or hang himself. He'll be hanging in front of the crossbars of the window. They'll send someone over from the house across the way, the locksmith will have to open the door, and it will be my fault. And right now, in the same room where he'll be hanging the day after tomorrow, he's sitting next to Mama smoking a Havana cigar. How is it that he still has Havana cigars? I hear him talking, reassuring Mama. Don't worry, Dorsday will have the money sent. Remember, I saved him a large sum this winter by intervening on his behalf. And then there's the Erbesheimer case . . . —Truly, I can hear him speaking. Mental telepathy! Amazing. I can see Fred now, too. He's walking past the *Kursalon*[9] in the city park with a girl. She's wearing a pale blue blouse and light shoes and her voice is a little hoarse. I'm absolutely sure about all of this. When I'm back in Vienna I'll ask Fred if he was in the city park with his girl friend on the third of September between seven-thirty and eight.

Where should I go now? What's happening to me? It's almost completely dark. How nice and peaceful. Not a soul far and wide. They're all sitting at the dinner table now. Mental telepathy? No, that wasn't mental telepathy. I heard the dinner gong a little while ago. Where is Else, Paul will wonder. Everyone will notice that I'm not there in time for the hors d'oeuvres. They'll send someone up to my room. What's going on with Else? She's always right on time. And the two men by the window will think, where is that beautiful young girl with the reddish blond hair today? And Herr von Dorsday will get scared. I'm sure he's a coward. Don't worry, Herr von Dorsday, nothing is going to happen to you. I despise you so much. If I wanted, you would be a dead man by tomorrow evening. I'm certain that Paul would challenge him to a duel if I told him what happened. I grant you your life, Herr von Dorsday.

What an enormous expanse of meadows, and how intensely black the mountains are. Almost no stars. Oh yes, three or four—more will be coming out. And the woods are so silent behind me. It's beautiful sitting here on this bench at the edge of the woods. The hotel is so far away, so far away, all aglow like in a fairy tale. And those awful people sitting inside. No, no—just people, poor people, I feel so sorry for all of them. I even feel sorry for the marchesa, I don't know why, and for Frau Winawer and Cissy's governess. She's not having dinner with the others, she ate earlier with Fritzi. What's going on with Else, Cissy's asking. What, she's not in her room either? They're all worried about me, I'm sure. I'm the only one who's not worried. So here I am in Martino di Castrozza, sitting on a bench at the edge of the woods, and the air is like champagne, and it appears to me that I'm actually crying. But why am I crying? There's no reason to be crying. It's my nerves. I've got to control myself. I can't let myself go like this. Crying isn't at all unpleasant, though. Crying always makes me feel better. I cried the time I visited our old French maid in the hospital before she died. And at Grandmama's funeral, too, and when Bertha left for Nuremberg, and when Agathe's little child died, and when I saw Camille[10] at the theater. Who will cry when I'm dead? Oh, how nice it would be to be dead. I'm lying in state in our drawing room, the candles are burning. Tall candles. Twelve tall candles. The hearse is already waiting out on the street. People are standing at the front door. And how old was she? Only nineteen. Really, is that all?—Imagine, her father's in prison. So why did she kill herself? Some filou broke her heart. But how can you say that? She was expecting a child. No, she fell off Mt. Cimone. It was an accident. Good day, Herr Dorsday, you're paying little Else your last respects, too? Little Else, the old woman says.—Why do you ask? Of course I have to pay her my last respects. After all, I paid for her first disgrace. Oh, it was worth it, Frau Winawer, I've never seen such a beautiful body. It only cost me thirty million. A Rubens costs three times that much. She poisoned herself with hashish. She simply wanted to have beautiful visions, but she took too much and never woke up again. Why does Herr von Dorsday have a red monocle? Who is he waving to with his handkerchief? Mama is coming down the stairs, she's kissing his hand. Disgusting, disgusting. Now they're whispering to each other. I can't understand a word, because I'm lying in state. The wreath of violets around my forehead is from Paul. The ribbons reach down to the floor. No one dares to come into the room. I'm going to get up and look out the window. What a big blue lake! A hundred boats with yellow sails.—The waves are glistening. So much sun. It's a regatta. All the men are wearing rowing shirts. The women are in bathing suits. That's indecent. They're imagining me naked. How stupid they are. I'm dressed in mourning, because I'm dead. I'll prove it to you. I'll lie right down on the bier again. But where is it? It's gone. They've carried it away. They've misappropriated it. That's why Papa's in prison. Even though they acquitted him on three years' probation. The jury members were all bribed by Fiala. I'm going to walk to the cemetery now, that'll save Mama the burial costs. We have to watch our expenses. I'm walking so fast that no one can keep up with me. Ah, how fast I can walk. They're all stopping in their tracks on the street looking amazed. How can they look at a dead person like that! What audacity. I'll cut across the field instead, it's all blue with forget-me-nots and violets. The navy officers are lined up on both sides. Good morning, gentlemen. Throw open the gate, Herr Matador. Don't you recognize me? I'm the dead woman . . . you don't need to kiss my hand just because of that . . . Where is my vault? Did they misappropriate that, too? Thank God, this isn't the cemetery at all. It's the park in Mentone. Papa will be glad to hear that I'm not buried. I'm not afraid of the snakes. As long as none of them bites me in the foot. How terrible.

What's happening? Where am I? Was I asleep? That's it—I was asleep. I must even have been dreaming. My feet are so cold. My right one is. But why? There's a little tear in the stocking by my ankle. Why am I still sitting in the woods? They must have sounded the gong for dinner—for the evening repast—long ago.

Oh, Lord, where have I been? I was so far away. What was it I was dreaming? I think I was dead already. And I didn't have any worries and didn't need to rack my brains. Thirty thousand, thirty thousand . . . I still don't have the money. I have to earn it first. And here I am, sitting alone at the edge of the woods. The hotel lights are glowing in the distance. I have to go back. It's terrible that I have to go back. But there's no more time to lose. Herr von Dorsday is waiting for my decision. Decision. Decision! No. No, Herr von Dorsday, to come right to the point, no. You were joking, Herr von Dorsday, of course. Yes, that's what I'll say to him. Oh, that's excellent. Your joke wasn't very genteel, Herr von Dorsday, but I'll forgive you. I'll telegraph Papa tomorrow morning, Herr von Dorsday, that the money will be in Dr. Fiala's hands promptly. Marvelous. That's what I'll say to him. Then he won't have any choice, he'll have to send the money. Have to? Does he have to? Why does he? And even if he did send it he'd get revenge somehow. He would arrange it so that the money would arrive too late. Or he'd send the money and then tell everyone that he'd had his pleasure with me. But he's not going to send the money. No, Fräulein Else, that wasn't our bargain. Telegraph your Papa whatever you like, but I'm not sending the money. Don't imagine, Fräulein Else, that I would let myself be duped by a little girl like you—I, the Vicomte of Prešov.

I have to be careful where I step. The path is so dark. Strange, I feel better than before. Nothing has changed and yet I feel better. What was I was dreaming about? A matador? What matador could that have been? It's farther to the hotel than I thought. No doubt everyone's still at dinner. I'll just sit down at the table calmly and say that I had a migraine and ask the waiter to bring me something to eat. Herr von Dorsday will probably come over to me and say that the whole thing was only a joke. Forgive me, Fräulein Else, forgive me for the bad joke, I've already telegraphed my bank. But he won't say that. He hasn't telegraphed. Everything is exactly the way it was before. He's waiting. Herr von Dorsday is waiting. No, I don't want to see him. I can't stand the thought of seeing him again. I don't want to see anyone again. I don't want to go back to the hotel, I don't want to go back home, I don't want to go to Vienna, I don't want to have to see anyone, not a single person, not Papa and not Mama, not Rudi and not Fred, not Bertha and not Aunt Irene. She's the best of them, she would understand all this. But I'm out of touch with her and with everyone else. If I could do magic, I'd be off in some other part of the world. On a magnificent ship in the Mediterranean, but not by myself. With Paul, for example. Yes, I could imagine that very well. Or I'd live in a villa by the sea, and we'd lie on the marble steps that lead down to the water, and he'd hold me close to him and bite my lips, the way Albert did two years ago at the piano, how shameless he was! No—I'd want to be alone on the marble steps by the sea, lying there, waiting. And sooner or later a man would come along, or several, and I would choose among them, and the ones I rejected would all jump into the sea in despair. Or they'd have to wait till the next day. Oh, what an exquisite life that would be. Why else do I have such magnificent shoulders and such beautiful slender legs? And why am I in this world at all? It would serve them right, every one of them—after all, that's the way they raised me, to sell myself, one way or the other. They wouldn't listen when I talked about becoming an actress. They laughed at me. And they would have been perfectly content last year if I had married Wilomitzer, the director, who's almost fifty. They didn't exactly try to persuade me, that would have embarrassed Papa. But Mama dropped enough hints in that direction.

How gigantic the hotel looks, like an enormous illuminated magic castle. Everything is so gigantic. The mountains, too. It's almost frightening. They've never been so black before. The moon isn't out yet. It won't come out until the grand performance begins, the grand performance on the meadow, when Herr von Dorsday has his slave dance naked. What do I care about Herr von Dorsday? Now really, Mademoiselle Else, what's all the fuss about? A minute ago you were prepared to run off, to become the mistress of men you don't even know, one after the other. And here you are worrying about this insignificant thing that Herr von Dorsday is asking you to do. You're prepared to sell yourself for a string of pearls, for beautiful dresses, for a villa by the sea? And your father's life isn't worth that much to you? It would be the perfect first step. It would be the justification for everything else, too. It was all of you, I could say, who made me this way, you're all to blame that I've become what I am, not only Papa and Mama. Rudi's to blame, too, and Fred, and everyone, everyone, because no one cares about anyone else. A little affection if you look pretty, and a little concern if you have a fever, and they send you to school, and at home you take piano lessons and learn French, and in the summer the family goes to the country, and you get presents on your birthday, and at mealtimes they talk about all sorts of things. But has any of you ever thought for a minute about what's going on inside me, about the things that torment me and make me afraid? Once in a while there was a trace of that in the way Papa looked at me, but it was gone in a flash. And then it was back to his job again, his worries, the stock market—and probably some trashy woman on the sly, 'nothing very refined, just between you and me'—and I was alone again. Tell me now, Papa, what would you do, what would you do today if I weren't here?

Here I am, in front of the hotel again.—How horrible to have to go in, to see all those people, Herr von Dorsday, my aunt, Cissy. It was so beautiful back there on the bench at the edge of the woods when I was already dead. Matador—if I could only recall what . . . that's right, there was a regatta, and I was watching it from my window. But who was the matador?—If only I wasn't so tired, so terribly tired. And I'm supposed to stay up till midnight and sneak over to Herr von Dorsday's room? Maybe I'll meet Cissy in the corridor. Does she have anything on under her nightgown when she goes to his room? It's difficult if you don't have any experience in such things. Shouldn't I ask her for advice? Of course I wouldn't tell her that Dorsday is the man in question—she'd have to assume that I had a midnight rendez-vous with one of the handsome young men here in the hotel. That tall blond one with the sparkling eyes, for example. But he isn't here any more, of course. He just disappeared all of a sudden. I hadn't thought about him again till this very moment. But unfortunately it's not the tall blond man with the sparkling eyes, and it's not Paul, either, it's Herr von Dorsday. So how should I do this? What should I say to him? Yes? Just like that? But I can't go to Herr Dorsday's room.

I'm sure his washstand is covered with elegant little bottles and his room smells like French perfume. No, I won't go to his room, not for anything. Outside is better. He won't matter to me in the least out there. The sky is so vast and the meadow is so huge. I won't have to think about Herr Dorsday at all. I won't even have to look at him. And if he dares to touch me I'll kick him with my naked feet. Oh, if only it were some other man, any man. He could have anything, anything he wanted from me tonight—but not Dorsday. And it has to be him, of all people, him! I can just see his eyes, stabbing and penetrating. He'll stand there with his monocle and grin. No, no, he won't grin. He'll put on a genteel expression. Elegant. He's accustomed to this sort of thing. How many others has he already looked at like this? A hundred, a thousand? But was there ever anyone like me? No, definitely not. I'll tell him that he's not the first to see me this way. I'll tell him that I have a lover. But not until he's sent the thirty thousand gulden off to Fiala. Then I'll tell him what a fool he was, that he could have had everything for the same amount.—That I've already had ten lovers, twenty, a hundred.—But he won't believe any of that. And even if he does believe it, what good will it do me? If only I could spoil his pleasure somehow. How about if another man were there, too? Why not? He didn't say that he had to be alone with me. Oh, Herr von Dorsay, I'm so afraid of you. Won't you kindly permit me to bring someone else along? Oh, no, it doesn't go against our agreement at all, Herr von Dorsday. If I felt like it I could invite the entire hotel and it would still be your obligation to send the thirty thousand gulden. But I'll be content just to bring my cousin Paul along. Or is there someone else you would prefer? The tall blond man unfortunately isn't here any more, and that filou with the Roman look isn't either. But don't worry, I'll find someone else. You're concerned about a lack of discretion? That doesn't matter a bit. I place no value on being discreet. If a person has gone as far as I have, nothing matters any more. Today is just the beginning. Or do you think that after this business I'll go back home and still be the same respectable young lady from a good family? No, no more good family, no more respectable young lady. I'm going to stand on my own two legs from now on. I have beautiful legs, Herr von Dorsday, as you and the other participants in this festive occasion will soon have the opportunity of seeing. Everything is arranged, Herr von Dorsday. At ten o'clock, while everyone is still sitting in the lobby, we'll stroll in the moonlight across the meadow and through the woods to that well-known clearing you discovered yourself. Be sure to have the telegram to your bank with you. I think it's justifiable for me to require this precaution from a sneak like you. And at midnight you can go back home and I'll stay in the meadow in the moonlight with my cousin or whoever it is. You don't have anything against that, do you, Herr von Dorsday? There's no way in the world you could. And if I happen to be dead tomorrow morning, you don't need to be surprised. Paul will send the telegram in that case. That will all be taken care of. But don't go imagining, for heaven's sake, that you, you miserable wretch, drove me to it. I've known for a long time that I would end up this way. Just ask my friend Fred if I haven't mentioned it to him on several occasions. Fred—Herr Friedrich Wenkheim, to be exact, who happens to be the only decent person I've ever known. The only man I would have loved, if only he hadn't been quite so decent. Yes, that's how depraved a creature I am. I wasn't meant to lead a bourgeois existence, and I don't have any particular talent for anything, either. The best thing for our family in any case would be for it to die out. Something awful is bound to happen to Rudi, too. He'll get hopelessly in debt because of some Dutch cabaret singer and embezzle money from Vanderhulst's bank. That's simply the way it is in our family. And my father's youngest brother shot himself when he was fifteen years old. No one knows why. I never met him. Have them show you the photograph, Herr von Dorsday, it's in one of our albums . . . They say I look like him. No one knows why he killed himself. And no one will know in my case, either. Hardly because of you, Herr von Dorsday, I wouldn't do you that honor. Whether it happens now when I'm nineteen or when I'm twenty-one doesn't matter a bit. Or should I get a job as a governess or a telephone operator or marry someone like Herr Wilomitzer or allow myself to be kept by you? It's all equally disgusting, and I'll never go to the meadow with you. No, it's all much too exhausting and stupid and repulsive. Once I'm dead, you will be kind enough to send off the few thousand gulden for Papa, because it would be so sad if he were to be arrested on precisely the same day they bring my body back to Vienna. But I'll leave a letter with my last will and testament: Herr von Dorsday has the right to see my corpse. My beautiful naked girl's corpse. That way, Herr von Dorsday, you won't be able to complain that I cheated you. You got something for your money. It wasn't stipulated in our contract that I still had to be alive. Oh, no. That's not written down anywhere. And so I bequeath a look at my corpse to the art dealer Dorsday, and to Herr Fred Wenkheim I bequeath my diary from the seventeenth year of my life—that's all I ever wrote—and to Cissy's governess I bequeath the five twenty-franc pieces I brought back from Switzerland years ago. They're in my desk next to the letters. And I bequeath my black evening gown to Bertha. And my books to Agathe. And to my cousin Paul I bequeath a kiss on my pale lips. And to Cissy I bequeath my tennis racket, because I'm so noble-minded. And I am to be buried in the nice little cemetery right here in San Martino di Castrozza. I don't want to go back home. Even when I'm dead I don't want to go back. And Papa and Mama shouldn't grieve too much—I'm better off than they are. And I forgive them. I'm no great loss.—Haha, what a funny last will and testament. I'm really touched. When I think that tomorrow at this time, while the others are at dinner, I'll already be dead.—Of course Aunt Emma won't come down for dinner, and Paul won't either. They'll have their meals brought to their rooms. I'm curious how Cissy will behave. But I won't find out, unfortunately. Or maybe we're still conscious of everything until we're buried? I might just be in a state of suspended animation. And when Herr von Dorsday steps up to my body I'll wake up and open my eyes, and he'll be so shocked his monocle will fall out.

But unfortunately none of this is true. I won't be in suspended animation, and I won't be dead, either. I won't kill myself, I'm much too big a coward. Even though I'm a daring mountain-climber I'm still a coward. And I might not even have enough Veronal. How many packets does it take? Six, I think. But ten is safer. I think there are ten left. Yes, that should be enough.

How many times have I walked around the hotel by now, I wonder? And what do I do now? Here I am at the door. No one's in the lobby yet. Of course not—they're all still having dinner. The lobby looks strange without any people in it. There's a hat lying on the chair over there, a Tyrolean hat, very stylish. Pretty chamois-hair tuft. An old gentleman is sitting there in an easy chair. Probably doesn't have much of an appetite any more. Reading the newspaper. He's doing fine. He has no worries. He's calmly reading the newspaper, and I have to rack my brains to find a way to get Papa thirty thousand gulden. That's not true, though. I know how. It's all so terribly easy. But what is it I want to do? What is it I want to do? What will I do there in the lobby? They'll all be coming in from dinner any minute now. What should I do? Herr von Dorsday must be on pins and needles. Where can she have gotten to, he's thinking. Don't tell me she's killed herself! Or is she going to hire someone to kill me? Or is she trying to get her cousin Paul to come after me? Don't worry, Herr von Dorsday, I'm not that dangerous a person. I'm just a little slut, that's all. And you'll have your reward for all the anxiety you've had to go through. Twelve o'clock, room sixty-five. It would definitely be too cool outside. And when I leave your room, Herr von Dorsday, I'll go straight to my cousin Paul. You don't have anything against that, Herr von Dorsday, do you?

"Else! Else!"

What? Who's . . . ? That was Paul's voice. Is dinner over already?— *"Else!"*—"Oh, Paul, hello, how are you?" I'm going to act completely innocent. — *"Else, where in the world have you been?"*—"What do you mean, where have I been? I was out for a walk."— *"Now, during dinner?"*—"Well, when else? It's the nicest part of the day." —What nonsense I'm talking. — *"Mama was worried sick. I stopped by your room and knocked on the door."*—"I didn't hear a thing."— *"Seriously, Else, you caused us an awful lot of anxiety. You could at least have let Mama know you weren't coming to dinner."* —"You're right, of course, Paul, but if you had any idea what a bad headache I had." My voice is simply dripping. What a slut I am. — *"Are you feeling better now, at least?"* —"Can't really say that I am."— *"I'll go and let Mama know right away that—"* —"Just a second, Paul. Would you please tell her I'm sorry and that I'll see her a little later? I want to go up to my room for a few minutes and freshen up. Then I'll come back down and have them bring me a bite to eat."—*"You're so pale, Else. Should I send Mama up to your room?"* —"Oh, Paul, don't make such a fuss over me, and don't look at me that way. Haven't you ever seen a delicate female with a headache before? I'll come down again for sure. In ten minutes at the latest. See you soon, Paul." —*"All right, then, goodbye, Else."* —Thank God he's going. He's a little dense, but he's sweet. Why has the desk clerk come over to me? What, a telegram? "Thank you. When did this arrive?"—*"A quarter of an hour ago, Fräulein."* — Why is he giving me such a—pitying look? Good Lord, what is it going to say? I won't open it till I'm upstairs in case I faint. Don't tell me Papa has— — If Papa is dead, then everything is all right, then I won't have to go out to the meadow with Herr von Dorsday . . . Oh, I'm a miserable creature. Dear God, don't let there be anything bad in the telegram. Dear God, let Papa be alive. Arrested, for all I care, only not dead. If there's nothing bad in it I'll offer a sacrifice. I'll become a governess, I'll take a job in an office. Don't be dead, Papa. I'm ready. I'll do anything you want . . .

I made it to my room, thank God. Turn the light on, turn the light on. It's cool in here. The window was open too long. Be brave, be brave. Maybe it'll say that everything has been settled. Maybe Uncle Bernhard gave them the money and they're telegraphing me not to talk to Dorsday. I'll know in a second. But if I keep staring at the ceiling I obviously can't read what the telegram says. Tra la, tra la, be brave. It can't be avoided. 'Repeat urgent request speak with Dorsday. Amount fifty, not thirty. Otherwise everything futile. Address remains Fiala.' — Fifty, not thirty. Otherwise everything futile. Trala, trala. Fifty. Address remains Fiala. Well, fine, fifty or thirty, what difference does it make. It won't matter to Herr von Dorsday, either. The Veronal is next to my underwear, just in case. Why didn't I say fifty right from the start? I did consider it. Otherwise everything futile. Well, come on, back downstairs, hurry up, don't just keep sitting here on the bed. A slight error, Herr von Dorsday, I'm sorry. Fifty, not thirty, otherwise everything futile. Address remains Fiala. — 'You seem to think I'm a fool, Fräulein Else.' Not at all, Herr Vicomte, why would I? 'For fifty, in any event, my demands would have to be proportionately higher, Fräulein.' Otherwise everything futile, address remains Fiala.

Whatever you want, Herr von Dorsday. Your wish is my command. But beforehand, of course, you'll send the telegram to your bank, otherwise I won't have any security, you see. —

Yes, that's the way I'll do it. I'll go to his room, and only after he's written the telegram before my very eyes will I—undress. And I'll keep the telegram in my hand. Oh, how disgusting. And where will I put my clothes? No, no, I'll undress here and wrap myself in my long black coat that reaches down to my ankles. That will be the most convenient. For both parties. Address remains Fiala. My teeth are chattering. The window is still open. There, it's shut. Outside? I would've caught my death. Beast! Fifty thousand. He can't say no. Room sixty-five. But before I go I'll tell Paul to wait in his room for me. When I leave Dorsday I'll go straight to Paul and tell him everything. And then Paul will slap him in the face. Tonight still. A full program. And then comes the Veronal. No, what for? Why should I die? Not a chance! What fun, what fun, now life is just beginning. You'll be so happy, dear family, you'll be so proud of your little daughter. I'll become a slut such as the world has never seen before. Address remains Fiala. You'll have your fifty thousand gulden, Papa. But next time I'll use the money to buy myself new nightgowns with lace edging, completely transparent, and exquisite silk stockings. We only live once. Otherwise what's the point of looking like I do? Lights on—I'll turn on the lamp above the mirror. How beautiful my reddish blond hair is, and my shoulders; my eyes aren't bad, either. Lord, how big they are. It would be a shame about me. There's plenty of time for the Veronal. —But I've got to go down. Very far down. Herr Dorsday is waiting, and he doesn't even know yet that it's fifty thousand in the meantime. Yes, Herr von Dorsday, my price has risen. I'll have to show him the telegram, otherwise he won't believe me, he'll think I'm trying to make money on the deal. I'll send the telegram to his room with a note. To my great regret the amount is now fifty thousand, Herr von Dorsday, I'm sure that won't matter to you. And I'm convinced that you didn't intend me to take your request seriously. After all, you are a vicomte and a gentleman. I know you will send Fiala the fifty thousand—my father's life depends on it—first thing tomorrow. I'm counting on that. —'Why certainly, mein Fräulein, I'll go ahead and send a hundred thousand, just in case, without expecting anything in return. And beyond that I pledge to take care of your entire family's living expenses from this moment on, to pay your dear Papa's stock market debts, and to replace all the embezzled trust funds.' Address remains Fiala. Hahaha! Yes, that would be just like him, this Vicomte of Prešov. That's all nonsense. So what's left for me to do? It has to be, I have to do it, everything, I have to do everything that Herr von Dorsday demands, so that Papa will have the money tomorrow—so that they don't lock him up, so that he doesn't kill himself. And I'll do it, too. Yes, I'll do it, even though it will be utterly pointless. In six months we'll be in exactly the same position as today! In *one* month!—But by then none of it will be of any concern to me. I'll sacrifice myself this one time—once and only once. Never, never, never again. As soon as I'm back in Vienna I'll tell Papa that. And then I'll leave the house and go—somewhere. I'll ask Fred for advice. He's the only one who truly likes me. But I haven't gotten to that point yet. I'm not in Vienna, I'm still in Martino di Castrozza. Nothing has happened yet. So what should I do? How should I do it? There's the telegram. What should I do with it? I know already. I have to send it to his room. But what else? I have to write him a note. All right, what should I tell him? You can expect me at twelve. No, no, no! I won't give him that victory. I won't, I won't, I won't. Thank God I have the Veronal. That's my only salvation. So where are the packets? Good Lord, don't tell me someone has stolen them! Oh, no, here they are. In their little box. Are they all here? One, two, three, four, five, six. I just want to look at them, the dear little packets. That doesn't obligate me to anything. Even dumping them into the glass doesn't obligate me. One, two—but I'm definitely not going to kill myself. I wouldn't think of it. Three, four, five—that's hardly enough to be lethal. It would be terrible if I didn't have the Veronal along. Then I would have to jump out the window, and I definitely wouldn't have the courage to do that. But with Veronal—you slowly fall asleep and never wake up again, no pain, no agony. You lie down in bed, drink it in one swallow, and everything is over with. The day before yesterday I took a packet, a few days before that I even took two. Shh, don't tell anyone. Today I'll simply take a little more. Only if it has to be, of course. If the thought of going to his room is simply too horrible—But why should it be so horrible? If he touches me I'll spit in his face. That's all there is to it.

But how can I get the letter to him? I can hardly have the chambermaid deliver it. It would be better for me to go downstairs and talk to him and show him the telegram. I have to go downstairs anyway. I can't stay up here in my room. I couldn't stand it for three hours—till it was time. I have to go down and see my aunt, too. Oh, what do I care about my aunt? What do I care about anyone? Please observe, ladies and gentlemen, here's the glass of Veronal. And now I'm picking it up. And now I'm raising it to my mouth. Any time I like I can be on the other side, where there are no aunts, no Dorsday, and no father who embezzles trust fund money . . .

But I'm not going to kill myself. There's no need for me to do that. I'm not going to go to Herr von Dorsday's room, either. Wouldn't dream of it. I'm certainly not going to stand naked in front of an old playboy for fifty thousand gulden just to save a good-for-nothing from the penitentiary. Well, let's decide. Why should Herr von Dorsday have the pleasure? He of all people. If one person is going to see me, then others should, too. Yes! What a marvelous idea! Everyone will see me. The whole world will see me. And then comes the Veronal. No, not the Veronal—why, for heaven's sake? Then comes the villa with the marble steps and the handsome young men and freedom and faraway places! Good evening, Fräulein Else, I like you this way. Haha. The people downstairs will think I've gone crazy. But I've never been this rational before. For the first time in my life I'm being truly rational. Everyone, I want everyone to see me! Then there'll be no going back, no going home to Papa and Mama, to my uncles and aunts. Then I'll cease to be that Fräulein Else they'd like to pander off to some Director Wilomitzer or other. I'll make fools of them all— that beast Dorsday especially—and come into the world a second time . . . otherwise everything futile—address remains Fiala. Haha!

Can't lose any more time, can't lose my courage again. Off with this dress. Who will be the first one? Will it be you, cousin Paul? You're lucky that the man with the Roman look has left. Will you kiss these beautiful breasts tonight? Oh, how beautiful I am. Bertha has a black silk nightgown. Very subtle. I'll be even more subtle. What a marvelous life. Off with these stockings, that would be indecent. Naked, totally naked. Cissy will envy me so much! And other women will, too. But they're afraid. They would all love to, of course. Go ahead, follow my example. I, the virgin, I am not afraid. I'll laugh myself to death over Dorsday. Here I am, Herr von Dorsday. Quick, to the post office! Fifty thousand. It was worth that much, wasn't it?

Beautiful, I'm beautiful! Look at me, night! Mountains, look at me! Sky, look and see how beautiful I am. But you're all blind. I'll get no response from you. The people downstairs have eyes. Should I undo my hair? No. I would look like a crazy woman then. I don't want you all to think I'm crazy. You're only supposed to think I'm shameless, a slattern. Where's the telegram? Good Lord, what did I do with the telegram? Here it is, lying peacefully next to the Veronal. 'Repeat urgently—fifty thousand—otherwise everything futile. Address remains Fiala.' Yes, this is the telegram. A piece of paper with words on it. Dispatched in Vienna four-thirty p.m. No, I'm not dreaming, it's all true. And they're waiting at home for fifty thousand gulden. And Herr von Dorsday is waiting, too. Let him wait. We have time. Ah, it's so nice to parade back and forth naked in the mirror. Am I really as beautiful as I look in the mirror? Come closer, Fräulein Else. I want to kiss your blood-red lips. I want to press your breasts against my breasts. It's too bad that this glass is between us, this cold glass. We would get along with each other so well. Don't you think? We wouldn't need anyone else at all. Maybe other people don't even really exist. There are telegrams and hotels and mountains and railroad stations and forests, but there aren't any people. We just dream them. Only Dr. Fiala exists, and his address. It never changes. Oh, I'm not in the least bit crazy. I'm just somewhat on edge. That's only to be expected before one comes into the world for the second time. Because that former Else has died already. Yes, I'm definitely dead. So there's no need for the Veronal. Shouldn't I pour it out? The chambermaid might drink it by mistake. I'll put a slip of paper next to it with 'poison' on it; no, 'medicine' would be better—so that nothing happens to the chambermaid. I'm so noble-minded. There. 'Medicine,' underlined twice, and three exclamation points. Nothing can happen now. And after I come back upstairs, if I don't feel like killing myself and only want to sleep I just won't drink the whole glass, only a quarter of it or even less. Very simple. It's all up to me. It would be simplest if I were to run along the corridor and down the stairs just as I am. No, someone could stop me before I got there—and I have to be sure that Herr von Dorsday is there, of course. Otherwise he wouldn't send the money, the dirty old man!—But I've got to write him a note. That's essential. Brr, the arm of the chair is cold, but it feels good. When I have my villa on the Mediterranean I'll always walk around naked in my garden . . . I'll bequeath my fountain pen to Fred when it's time for me to die. But for the moment I have something more sensible to do than die. 'My revered Herr Vicomte'—let's not be silly, Else, no salutation, neither 'revered' nor 'reviled.' 'Your condition, Herr von Dorsday, has been fulfilled'— — —'At the very moment you are reading these lines, Herr von Dorsday, your condition has been fulfilled, though not quite in the manner envisioned by you.'—'Ah, the girl writes really well,' Papa would say.—'And so I am counting on you to keep your word and have the fifty thousand gulden transferred by telegraph without delay to the previously-mentioned address. Else.' No, not Else. No signature at all. There. My beautiful yellow stationery! Got it for Christmas. Too bad I have to use it for this. All right—and now the telegram and the letter go into this envelope—Herr von Dorsday, room sixty-five. Why the number? I'll just put the letter in front of his door as I walk by. But I don't have to. I don't have to do anything at all. If I feel like it, I can lie down on my bed now and go to sleep and not worry about anything. Not about Herr von Dorsday and not about Papa. A striped convict's outfit is actually rather elegant. And lots of people have shot themselves. And we all have to die.

But for the time being you don't need to worry about any of that, Papa. You have your splendidly developed daughter, and address remains Fiala. I'll start up a collection. I'll go around with a plate. Why should Herr von Dorsday be the only one to pay? That would be unjust. Each according to his means. How much will Paul put in the plate? And the man with the gold pince-nez? But just don't get the idea that the fun is going to last very long. Immediately afterwards I'll wrap myself back up in my coat, run up the stairs to my room, lock myself in, and, if I feel like it, drink the whole glass in one swallow. But I won't feel like it. It would only be cowardice. They don't deserve that much respect, the beasts. Why should I feel ashamed because of you? Or anyone else? I really don't need that. Let me look into those eyes again, beautiful Else. How huge they are from close up. I wish someone would kiss my eyes, my blood-red mouth. This coat barely covers my ankles. People will see that my feet are bare. What's the difference, they'll see a lot more! But I'm not obligated to do it. I can turn around any time before I get there. I can turn around on the floor above the lobby. I don't have to go down at all. But I want to. I'm looking forward to it. Haven't I been wishing for something like this my whole life?

What am I waiting for, then? I'm ready. The show can begin. Don't forget the letter. Aristocratic handwriting, according to Fred. Goodbye, Else. You look beautiful in that coat. Florentine ladies had themselves painted like this. Their pictures are hanging in galleries, and it's an honor for them.—People might not notice anything when I have my coat wrapped around me. But my feet, my feet! I'll put on my black patent leather shoes, then they'll think I'm wearing flesh-colored stockings. I'll walk through the lobby like this and no one will suspect there's nothing under the coat but me, me myself. And I can always go back upstairs . . . —Who's playing the piano so nicely down there? Chopin?—Herr von Dorsday must be a little nervous. Maybe he's afraid of Paul. Be patient, be patient, everything will turn out all right. I don't know myself what will happen, Herr von Dorsday, I'm terribly curious, too. Light out. Is everything in my room where it belongs? Farewell, Veronal, goodbye. Farewell, my dearly beloved reflection. You're so radiant in the dark. I've already grown completely accustomed to being naked under my coat. It's very pleasant. Who knows, maybe other women sit in the lobby like this and no one knows. I'll bet there are women who go to the theater and sit in their loges like this—for fun or for other reasons.

Should I lock the door? Why? Nothing ever gets stolen here. And even if it did—I don't need these things any more. The end. Now where is number sixty-five . . . ? No one in the corridor. Everyone's still downstairs having dinner. Sixty-one . . . sixty-two . . . those are gigantic hiking boots standing by the door there. And a pair of pants hanging on a hook. How crude. Sixty-four, sixty-five. Here we are. This is where he lives, the vicomte . . . I'll lean the letter against the door so that he'll see it right away. It won't get stolen, will it? There, that's that . . . Doesn't matter, I can still do whatever I want. Just wanted to make a fool of him . . . If only I don't run into him on the stairway now. Oh, no, is that . . . no, it's not him! . . . This man is much nicer-looking than Herr von Dorsday, very elegant with his little black mustache. When did he arrive? I could stage a little re-hearsal—lift up my coat a tiny bit. I'm sorely tempted. Go ahead and look at me, mein Herr. You have no idea who it is you're walking past. Too bad you've just come upstairs. Why don't you stay in the lobby? You're going to miss something. The grand performance. Why don't you say hello to me? My fate is in your hands. If you say hello, I'll turn around and go back. Please say something. I'm giving you such a charming look . . . He didn't say anything. He walked right past me. He's turning around, I can feel it. Call out to me, say hello! Save me! You might be responsible for my death! But you'll never know. Ad-dress remains Fiala . . .

Where am I? In the lobby already? How did I get here? So few people and so many I don't know. Or are my eyes just not focusing? Where is Dorsday? He's not here. Is fate trying to tell me something? I'm going back. I'll write another letter to Dorsday. I'll expect you in my room at midnight. Bring the telegram to your bank with you. No. He might think it's a trap. Could be one, too. I could have Paul hide in my room, and he could point a revolver at him and force him to hand over the telegram. Blackmail. The outlaw couple. Where is Dorsday? Dorsday, where are you? Could he have killed himself out of remorse at my death? I'll bet he's in the game room. Definitely. Sitting at a card table. I'll stand at the door and give him a sign with my eyes. He'll get up immediately. 'Here I am, mein Fräulein.' His voice will have that sound. 'Shall we go for a little stroll, Herr Dorsday?' 'As you wish, Fräulein Else.' We're walking along the Marienweg to the woods. We're alone. I throw open my coat. The fifty thousand comes due. The air is cold, I get pneumonia and die . . . Why are those two women looking at me? Do they notice something? Why am I here? Am I crazy? I'll go back to my room, put something on— my blue dress—and then my coat, just like now, except open. Then no one will imagine that I had nothing on a few minutes before . . . I can't go back. I don't want to go back. Where's Paul? Where's Aunt Emma? Where's Cissy? Where can they all be? No one will notice . . . There's no way anyone could notice. Who is that playing so beautifully? Chopin? No, Schumann.

I'm fluttering around the lobby as aimlessly as a bat. Fifty thousand! Time is passing. I have to find that damned Herr von Dorsday. No, I have to go back to my room . . . I'll take some Veronal. Just a little sip, then I'll sleep well . . . Rest is sweet when the day's work is done. But the day's work isn't done yet . . . If the waiter brings that pot of coffee to the old man there, everything will turn out all right. And if he takes it over to the young married couple in the corner, then all is lost. Why? What's that supposed to mean? He's bringing it to the old man. Hurray! Everything will turn out all right. There go Cissy and Paul! They're strolling up and down outside the hotel, talking happily with each other. He doesn't seem terribly concerned about my headache. Hypocrite! . . . Cissy's breasts aren't as beautiful as mine. She's had a child, of course . . . What are they talking about? If only I could hear them! What do I care what they're talking about? I could go outside too, and say good evening to them, and then flit past them across the meadow, climb up into the forest, higher and higher, all the way up to Mt. Cimone, lie down, fall asleep, freeze to death. Mysterious Suicide of Young Viennese Socialite. Clothed only in a black evening wrap, the beautiful girl was found dead in a remote area below Mt. Cimone della Pala . . . But maybe they won't find me . . . Or not until a year later. Or even longer than that. Decomposed. A skeleton. No, it's better to be here in this heated lobby and not freeze to death. Well, Herr von Dorsday, where can you be? Am I under any obligation to wait? You should be trying to find me, not the other way around. I'll have a look in the game room. If he's not there he's forfeited his rights. And I'll write to him: You were nowhere to be found, Herr von Dorsday, you've voluntarily relinquished your claim; this does not release you from your obligation to send the money immediately. The money. What money? What do I care about that? I don't care one way or the other if he sends the money. I don't have the least bit of sympathy for Papa any more. I don't have sympathy for anyone. Myself included. My heart is dead. I don't think it's beating any more. Maybe I already took the Veronal . . . Why is that Dutch family looking at me so strangely? No one could possibly notice anything. The desk clerk is giving me a suspicious look, too. Maybe a telegram has arrived? Eighty thousand? A hundred thousand? Address remains Fiala. He would tell me if a telegram had come. He's looking at me with the greatest respect. He doesn't know that I have nothing on under my coat. No one knows. I'm going back to my room. I have to get away from here. I have to, I have to! What if I tripped on the stairs—wouldn't that be something? Three years ago a woman swam out into Lake Wörther completely naked. But she left that same afternoon. Mama said it was an opera singer from Berlin. Schumann? Yes, Carnaval. Whoever it is is playing it well. The card room is to the right. Last chance, Herr von Dorsday. If he's there I'll give him a signal with my eyes so that he'll come over and then I'll tell him, I'll be at your room at midnight, you beast. —No, I won't call him a beast. Afterwards I will, though . . . Someone's behind me. I'm not going to turn around. No, no.—

"Else!"— Good Lord, it's my aunt! Keep walking. "Else!"— I've got to turn around, what else can I do? "Oh, good evening, Aunt Emma."—"Else, is something the matter? I was just about to go up to your room. Paul told me— — But just look at you!"—"What's wrong with the way I look, Aunt Emma? I'm feeling fine again. I had a bite to eat, too." She notices something, she notices something.— "Else— you don't have—any stockings on!"—"What did you say, Aunt Emma? My Lord, I don't have any stockings on. You're right —!"—"Aren't you feeling well, Else? Your eyes—you must have a fever."—"A fever? I don't think so. It's just that I had the most awful headache, worse than I've ever had before."— *"You must get to bed immediately, child, you're as pale as death."*—"It's just the lighting, Aunt Emma. Everyone looks pale here in the lobby." She's looking me up and down so strangely. She can't possibly tell—? I have to keep my composure. Papa is done for if I don't keep my composure. I've got to say something. "Do you know what happened to me not long ago, Aunt Emma? I walked out onto the street wearing one yellow and one black shoe." Not a word of that is true. I have to keep talking. But what should I say? "You know, Aunt Emma, sometimes I feel so disoriented after a migraine attack. Mama used to be that way, too." Not even close to the truth.— *"I'm going to send for a doctor just to be on the safe side."*—"Oh, please don't, Aunt Emma, there aren't any in the hotel. They would have to send for one from some other town. Wouldn't he laugh when he found out that they'd had him come because I'm not wearing stockings. Haha." I shouldn't laugh so loud. My aunt's face is twisted with anxiety. She must think I'm crazy. Her eyes are bulging. —*"You haven't seen Paul by any chance, have you, Else?"*— Ah, she's looking for reinforcements. Keep your composure, everything depends on that. "I think he's strolling outside the hotel with Cissy Mohr, if I'm not mistaken."—*"Outside the hotel? I'm going to ask them to come in. It would be nice to have some tea together, wouldn't it?"*—"Very nice." What a ridiculous expression she has on her face. I'll give her a friendly, innocent nod. She's gone. I'm going up to my room now. No, what's the point in that? I can't delay this any longer. Fifty thousand, fifty thousand. Why am I running? Slowly, slowly . . . What am I going to do? What's the man's name? Herr von Dorsday. Strange name . . . Here's the game room. Green curtain in front of the door. I can't see anything. I'll stand on my tiptoes. A group playing whist. They play every evening. Two men playing chess. Herr von Dorsday isn't here. Hurray, I'm saved! No, I'm not. I have to keep looking. I'm condemned to look for Herr von Dorsday for the rest of my life. I'm sure he's trying to find me, too. We keep missing each other. Maybe he's looking for me upstairs. We'll meet on the stairway. Those Dutch people are staring at me again. The daughter is quite pretty. The old gentleman is wearing glasses, glasses, glasses . . . Fifty thousand. It isn't so much, really. Fifty thousand, Herr von Dorsday. Schumann?

Yes, Carnaval . . . Studied it once myself. She plays beautifully. Why 'she'? Maybe it's a he. Maybe it's some famous performer. I'll have a

look in the music room.

Here's the door— —Dorsday! I'm going to faint. Dorsday! He's standing there at the window listening. How can that possibly be? I'm tormenting myself—I'm going crazy—I'm dead—and he's listening to some woman or other play the piano. There are two men sitting on the sofa. The blond one just arrived today. I saw him getting out of the carriage. The woman isn't exactly young any more. She's been here for a few days now. I didn't know that she played the piano so well. She has it good. Everyone has it good . . . I'm the only one who's cursed . . . Dorsday! Dorsday! Is it really him? He doesn't see me. He looks like a decent person now, standing there listening to the

music. Fifty thousand. Now or never. Open the door quietly. Here I am, Herr von Dorsday! He doesn't see me. I'll just give him a sign with my eyes and then lift up my coat a little, that'll be enough. I'm a young lady, after all. A respectable young lady from a good family. I'm not a whore . . . I don't want to be here. I want to take some Veronal and sleep. You were wrong, Herr von Dorsday, I'm not a whore. Goodbye, goodbye! . . . Ah, he's looking up. Here I am, Herr von Dorsday. What eyes he's making. His lips are trembling. His eyes are drilling into my forehead. He has no idea that I'm naked under my coat. Let me go, let me go! His eyes are glowing. His eyes are threatening. What do you want from me? You're a beast. He's the only one who sees me. They're listening to the music. Well, come on, Herr von Dorsday! Don't you notice anything? Good God, there in the easy chair—it's the filou! Thank heaven. He's back again, he's back! He was only gone on a long hike. Now he's back again. My Roman is back again. My bridegroom, my beloved. But he doesn't see me. And I don't want him to see me. Well, Herr von Dorsday? You're looking at me as if I were your slave. I'm not your slave. Fifty thousand! Are we sticking to our agreement, Herr von Dorsday? I'm ready. Here I am. I'm perfectly calm. I'm smiling. Do you understand the look I'm giving you? His eyes say to me: come here! His eyes say: I want to see you naked. Well, you beast, I'm naked now. What more do you want? Send the telegram . . . Immediately . . . Shivers are running over my skin. The woman is still playing. Delightful shivers are running over my skin. How wonderful it is to be naked. The woman is still playing, she doesn't know what's happening here. No

one knows. No one else has noticed yet. Hey you, filou! I'm standing here naked. Dorsday's eyes are as big as saucers. He finally believes it's happening. The filou is getting up. His eyes are gleaming. You understand me, you beautiful boy. "Haha!" The woman has stopped playing. Papa is saved. Fifty thousand! Address remains Fiala! "Ha, ha, ha!" Who is that laughing? Is it me? "Ha, ha, ha!" What faces are these all around me? "Ha, ha, ha!" It's ridiculous for me to be laughing. I don't want to laugh, I don't want to. "Haha!"—*Else!*—Who's calling my name? It's Paul. He must be behind me. I feel a draft of air across my naked back. There's a roaring in my ears. Maybe I'm already dead. What do you want, Herr von Dorsday? Why have you gotten so big? Why are you coming rushing at me? "Ha, ha, ha!"

My God, what have I done? What have I done? What have I done? I'm going to collapse. It's all over. What happened to the music? Someone's put an arm around my neck. It's Paul. Where has the filou gotten to? I'm lying on the floor now. "Ha, ha, ha!" My coat is flying down over me. And I'm lying here. Everyone thinks I'm unconscious. I'm not. I'm fully conscious. I'm completely awake. I'm absolutely awake. I just can't stop laughing. "Ha, ha, ha!" Now you've had your way, Herr von Dorsday, you have to send the money for Papa. Immediately. "Haaaah!" I don't want to scream, but I can't stop screaming. Why do I have to scream?—My eyes are closed. No one can see me. Papa is saved. — *Else!*—That's my aunt. — *Else! Else!*— "*Get a doctor!*"— "*Tell the desk clerk, hurry!*"— "*Good God, what's happened?*"— "*This isn't possible.*"— "*The poor girl.*"— What are they saying? What's all this murmuring? I'm not a poor girl. I'm happy. The filou saw me naked. Oh, I'm so ashamed. What have I done? I'll never open my eyes again. — "*For heaven's sake, close the door.*"— Why do they want to close the door? All this murmuring. I'm surrounded by a thousand people. They all think I'm unconscious. I'm not unconscious. I'm just dreaming. — "*Please be calm, madam.*"— "*Has someone sent for a doctor?*"— "*It was a fainting spell.*"— How far away they all are. They're talking from up on top of Mt. Cimone. — "*We can't just leave her lying there on the floor.*"— "*Here's a lap robe.*"— "*We need a blanket.*"— "*Blanket or lap robe, it doesn't make any difference.*"— "*Please, everyone, quiet down!*"— "*Put her on the sofa.*"— "*Would some-*

one please shut that door!"—"Don't get so excited, it's already shut."—
"Else! Else!"— If Aunt Emma would only be quiet! — — *"Can you
hear me, Else?"—"You can see that she's unconscious, Mama."*— Yes,
thank God, they think I'm unconscious. And I'm going to stay unconscious, too. — *"We have to get her to her room."—"Good Lord, what's
happened?"*— Cissy. What's Cissy doing out here on the meadow?
Oh, no, it's not the meadow. —*"Else!"—"Please quiet down."—"Please
step back a little."*— Hands, hands underneath me. What are they
trying to do? I'm so heavy. Paul's hands. Get away, get away. The filou
is near me, I can feel it. And Dorsday's gone. They'll have to go looking for him. He can't be allowed to kill himself until he's sent off the
fifty thousand. Listen, everyone, he owes me money. Arrest him. —
*"Do you have any idea who the telegram was from, Paul?"—"Good
evening, ladies and gentlemen."—"Else, can you hear me?"—"Don't disturb her, Frau Cissy."—"Oh, Paul."—"The manager says it could be
four hours till the doctor gets here."—"She looks just as if she were asleep."*—
I'm lying on the sofa, Paul's holding my hand, he's taking my pulse.
Of course, he's a doctor, after all. —*"It's not dangerous, Mama. Just
a—fainting spell."—"I'm not staying in this hotel a day longer."—"Mama,
please."—"We're leaving tomorrow morning."—"Right up the servants'
stairway. The stretcher-bearers will be here any minute now."*— To take
me to my bier? Wasn't I laid out on a bier once today already? Wasn't
I dead already? Do I have to die again? —*"Herr Direktor, would you
please see to it that people keep back from the door?"—"Don't get excited,
Mama."—"But it's so inconsiderate of them."*— Why is everyone whispering? Like at someone's death bed. The stretcher will be here any
minute. Throw open the gate, Herr Matador! —*"The corridor is
clear."—"People could at least have a little consideration!"—"Please,
Mama, try to calm down."—"May I be of some assistance?"—"Could
you look after my mother, Frau Cissy?"*— She's his mistress, but she's
not as beautiful as I am. What's going on now? What's happening?
They're bringing the stretcher. I can see it with my eyes closed. It's the
stretcher they use when someone has had an accident. It's the one
that Dr. Zigmondi was lying on after he fell off Mt. Cimone. And
now I'll be lying on it. I fell, too. "Ha!" No, I don't want to scream
any more. They're whispering. Who's bending over me? He smells

good, like cigarettes. His hand is under my head. Hands under my back, hands under my legs. Get away, get away, don't touch me. I'm naked, for heaven's sake. What do you want from me? Leave me alone. I only did it for Papa. —*"Careful now, take it slowly."*—*"Here's the blanket"*—*"Good, thank you, Frau Cissy."*— Why is he thanking her? What has she done? What's happening to me? Ah, this feels good. I'm floating. I'm floating. I'm floating to the other side. They're bearing me, they're bearing me, they're bearing me to the grave. —*"Oh, we're usta it, Herr Doktor. We've had heavier people layin' on this stretcher than her. Two of 'em at the same time once last fall."*—*"Shh, shh."*—*"Would you mind going on ahead of us, Frau Cissy, and making sure that everything's ready in Else's room?"*— I don't want Cissy going in my room! The Veronal! If only they don't pour it out! Then I'd have to jump out the window. —*"Thank you very much, Herr Direktor, don't trouble yourself any further."*—*"I'll stop by later to see how things are, if I may."*—The stairs are creaking, the bearers are wearing heavy mountain boots. Where are my patent leather shoes? Must've gotten left in the music room. Someone will steal them. I wanted to bequeath them to Agathe. Fred is getting my fountain pen. They're bearing me, they're bearing me. Funeral procession. Where is Dorsday, the murderer? He's gone. The filou is gone, too. He's off on a hike again. He only came back to have a look at my white breasts. And now he's gone again. He's walking along a dangerous trail, cliffs on one side and the abyss on the other;—farewell, farewell.—I'm floating, I'm floating. Let them just keep carrying me upwards, farther and farther, to the roof, to heaven. That would be so convenient. —*"I saw it coming, Paul."*— What did my aunt see coming? —*"For the last several days I've been noticing that something like this was coming. She's not at all normal. They'll have to put her in an asylum, absolutely."*—*"But Mama, now is hardly the time to be talking about that."*— Asylum? Asylum?! —*"You certainly don't think that I'm going to travel back to Vienna in the same compartment with this creature, do you, Paul? Who knows what might happen?"*—*"Nothing will happen, Mama, nothing at all. I guarantee you there won't be any problems."*—*"How can you guarantee that, Paul?"*— Don't worry, Aunt Emma, I won't cause you any problems. I won't cause anyone any problems. Not even Herr von Dorsday.

Where are we now? We're not moving. We're on the third floor. I'm going to take a peek. Cissy is standing in the doorway talking to Paul. —*"This way, please. That's right, that's right. There. Thank you. Right next to the bed, now."*— They're lifting the bier. They're bearing me. Good, good, now I'm home again. Ah! —*"Thank you. There, that's just fine. Would you please close the door on your way out?"*—*"Could you give me a hand, Cissy?"*—*"Oh, with pleasure, doctor."*—*"Slowly, now. Here, Cissy, take her by the legs. Careful. And now— —Else— —? Can you hear me, Else?"*— Of course I can hear you, Paul. I can hear everything. But what business is that of yours? It's so nice to be unconscious. Oh, do whatever you want to. —*"Paul!"*—*"Yes, Frau Mohr?"*— *"Do you really think she's out cold, Paul?"*— She's sounding rather familiar. Ah, I've caught you! —*"Yes, she's out completely. That usually happens after fainting spells like this."*—*"Oh, Paul, I could laugh myself silly when you talk like a doctor that way!"*— Now I've got you, you pair of hypocrites, now I've got you! —*"Cissy, be quiet."*—*"Well, why, if she can't hear anything?!"*— How did this happen? I'm lying on the bed naked under the covers. How did they do that? —*"Well, how is she doing? Better?"*— That's my aunt. What does she want here? — *"Still unconscious?"*— She's sneaking around on tiptoe. She can go to the devil. I'm not going let them put me in any asylum. I'm not crazy. —*"Can't she be brought back to consciousness?"*—*"She'll come around soon, Mama. What she needs now is rest. And so do you, by the way, Mama. Why don't you go to bed? She's in absolutely no danger. I'll keep the night watch here with Frau Cissy."*—*"Yes, indeed, madam, I'll be chaperon. Or Else will be, however you want to look at it."*— Miserable tramp. I'm lying here unconscious, and she's making jokes. —*"And I can depend on you, Paul, to have me waked as soon as the doctor arrives?"*—*"But Mama, he won't be here before tomorrow morning."*— *"She looks like she's asleep. She's breathing so peacefully."*—*"Well, it is a type of sleep, Mama."*—*"I'm still so on edge, Paul—what a scandal!—You'll see, it'll be in the newspaper!"*—*"Mama!"*—*"But she can't hear anything if she's unconscious. We're speaking very softly."*—*"In this condition the senses are sometimes unusually acute."*—*"You have such a learned son, madam."*—*"Please, Mama, go to bed."*—*"We're leaving tomorrow, no matter what. And when we get to Bolzano we'll hire an attendant for*

Else."— What? An attendant? Oh, you're wrong there! — "*We'll talk about all that tomorrow, Mama. Good night, Mama.*"— "*I'll have some tea brought up to my room, and in a quarter of an hour I'll look in again.*"— "*That's really not necessary, Mama.*"— No, it's not necessary. Why don't you just go to the devil? Where's the Veronal? I'll have to wait. They're walking her to the door. No one can see me now. The glass must be on the night table. If I drink the whole thing, it's all over. I'm going to drink it right away. My aunt is gone now. Paul and Cissy are still standing by the door. Ha, she's kissing him. She's kissing him. And I'm lying here naked under the covers. Aren't you in the least bit ashamed? She's kissing him again. Aren't you ashamed? — "*Well, Paul, now I know she's unconscious. Otherwise she would have been at my throat for sure.*"— "*Would you please do me a favor and be quiet, Cissy?*"— "*What's the matter, Paul? Either she's really unconscious— in which case she can't hear or see anything. Or she's making fools of us— in which case it serves her right.*"— "*Someone's knocking, Cissy.*"— "*Yes, it sounded like it.*"— "*I'll open the door quietly and see who it is.—Oh, good evening, Herr von Dorsday.*"— "*I beg your pardon, I just wanted to ask how the patient—*" — Dorsday! Dorsday! He actually dares to—! All the beasts of hell have been let loose. Where is he? I can hear them whispering at the door. Paul and Dorsday. Cissy is standing in front of the mirror. What are you doing there? It's my mirror. Isn't my image still imbedded in it? What are they talking about, Paul and Dorsday? I feel Cissy looking at me. She's looking over at me from the mirror. What does she want? Why is she coming closer? Help! Help! I'm screaming, and no one hears me. What are you doing by my bed, Cissy?! Why are you bending over me? Are you going to strangle me? I can't move. "*Else!*"— What does she want? — "*Else! Can you hear me, Else?*"— I hear her, but I won't say anything. I'm unconscious, how can I? —"*Else, that was quite a scare you gave us.*"— She's talking to me. She's talking to me as if I were awake. What does she want? — "*Do you know what you've done, Else? Just imagine, you stepped into the music room with only your coat on, and suddenly you were standing there completely naked in front of everyone, and then you fainted. People are saying it was an attack of hysteria. I don't believe a word of it. I don't believe that you're unconscious, either. I'll bet you can hear every word I'm saying."*—Yes, I can hear you, yes, yes, yes. But she can't hear me saying yes. Why can't she? I can't move my lips. That's why she can't. I can't move. What's wrong with me? Am I dead? Am I in suspended animation? Am I dreaming? Where's the Veronal? I want to take my Veronal. But I can't stretch out my arm. Go away, Cissy. Why are you bending over me? Go away, go away! She'll never know that I really could hear her. No one will ever know. I'll never talk to a human being again. I'll never wake up. She's going over to the door. She's turning around towards me again. Dorsday! He's still standing there. I saw him with my eyes closed. No, I can really see him. My eyes are open. The door is ajar. Cissy is outside, too. Now they're all whispering. I'm alone. If only I could move now.

Ah, I can, I can. I'm moving my hand, my fingers, I'm stretching out my arm, I'm opening my eyes wide. I can see, I can see. There's the glass. Hurry, before they come back into the room. Were there enough packets? I can't let myself ever wake up again. What I had to do in the world, I've done. Papa is saved. I could never be in the company of people again. Paul is peering in through the crack in the doorway. He thinks I'm still unconscious. He can't see that I already have my arm almost completely stretched out. Now all three of them are standing outside the door again, the murderers!—Every one of them is a murderer. Dorsday and Cissy and Paul, Fred is a murderer, too, and Mama is a murderer. They've all murdered me and act as if they don't know. She killed herself, they'll say. *You* killed me, all of you, all of you! Have I got hold of it finally? Quickly, quickly! I have to. Can't spill a drop. There. Quickly. It tastes good. Keep drinking, keep drinking. It's not poison at all. Nothing has ever tasted so good to me. If you only knew how good death tastes! Good night, my glass. Clink, clink! What was that? The glass is lying on the floor. There it is. Good night. —*"Else! Else!"*— What do you want? — *"Else!"*— Are you two back again? Good morning. I'm lying here unconscious with my eyes closed. Never again will you see my eyes. — *"She must have moved, Paul, how else could it have fallen on the floor?"*— *"Could have been an involuntary movement, that's quite possible."*— *"Assuming she's not awake."*—*"What are you talking about, Cissy, just look at her."*— I took the Veronal. I'm going to die. But everything is just the same as it was before. Maybe it wasn't enough . . . Paul is touching my hand. —*"Her pulse is normal. Stop laughing, Cissy. The poor girl."*—*"I wonder if you'd call me a poor girl if I had shown up naked in the music room?"*—*"Why don't you be quiet, Cissy."*—*"Just as you wish, mein Herr. Maybe I should leave so that you can be alone with this naked young lady. No, no, don't mind me. Just pretend I'm not here."* — I took the Veronal. That's good. I'm going to die. Thank God. — *"By the way, do you know what I think? Herr von Dorsday is in love with our naked young lady. He was so upset, just as if it concerned him personally."*— Dorsday, Dorsday! He's the one—the fifty thousand! Will he send it? Good God, what if he doesn't send it? I've got to tell them. They'll have to force him to. Good God, what if it was all for nothing? But they could still save me. Paul! Cissy! Why don't you hear me? Don't you know that I'm dying? But I can't feel anything. I'm just tired. Paul! I'm tired. Can't you hear me? I'm tired, Paul. I can't open my mouth. I can't move my tongue, but I'm not dead yet. The Veronal's taking effect. Where are you? I'm just about to fall asleep. Then it'll be too late! I can't even hear them talking. They're talking, and I don't know what they're saying. Their voices are making such a rushing noise. Help me, Paul! My tongue is so heavy. —*"I think she'll wake up soon, Cissy. It looks like she's trying to open her eyes. Cissy, stop, what are you doing?"*—*"I'm hugging you, obviously. Why shouldn't I? She certainly didn't act shy."*— No, I didn't. I stood there naked in front of all those people. If only I could speak, you'd understand why. Paul! Paul! I want you to hear me. I took Veronal, Paul, ten packets, a hundred. I didn't want to do it. I was crazy. I don't want to die. You have to save me, Paul. You're a doctor, aren't you? Save me! —*"She seems to have gotten very relaxed again. Her pulse—her pulse is fairly regular."*— Save me, Paul. I'm begging you. Don't let me die. There's still time. But soon I'll fall asleep and you won't know. I don't want to die. Save me, please! It was only because of Papa. Dorsday insisted. Paul! Paul! — *"Look at her, Cissy, doesn't it look like she's smiling?"*—*"Why shouldn't she smile, Paul, with you tenderly stroking her hand like that?"*— Cissy, Cissy, what did I ever do to you to make you act so mean to me? Keep your Paul—but don't let me die. I'm still so young. Mama will be so upset. There are so many mountains I still want to climb. I want to go dancing. I want to get married sometime, too. I want to take trips. Tomorrow we'll hike up to Mt. Cimone. Tomorrow is going to be a gorgeous day. I want the filou to come along. I invite him most humbly. Run after him, Paul, he's on such a dangerous trail. He'll meet Papa. Address remains Fiala, don't forget. Only fifty thousand, then everything will be all right. They're all marching past in convicts' outfits and singing. Throw open the gate, Herr Matador! But that's all just a dream. Fred's there, too, next to the girl with the hoarse voice, and the piano is standing out there under the clear blue sky. The piano tuner lives on Bartensteinstraße, Mama! Well, why didn't you write him, child? I tell you, you forget everything. You should practice your scales more often, Else. A girl of thirteen should be more diligent.—Rudi was at the masked ball and didn't come home until eight o'clock in the morning. What did you bring me, Papa? Thirty thousand dolls. I'll need a separate house for all of them. But they can go for walks in the garden, too. Or to the masked ball with Rudi. Hello there, Else. Well, Bertha, so you're back from Naples. Yes, we were in Sicily. Allow me to introduce my husband, Else. Enchantée, monsieur. — *"Else, can you hear me, Else? It's me, Paul."*— Haha, Paul. Why are you sitting on that giraffe on the merry-go-round? — *"Else, Else!"*— Well, don't go riding away from me like that. You can't hear what I'm saying if you ride down the path that fast. You're supposed to save me. I took Veronalica. It feels like ants running along my legs, both of them. Catch him, it's Herr von Dorsday. There he is, running. Don't you see him? He's jumping over the pond. He killed Papa, you know. Hurry, run after him. I will, too. They've strapped the bier to my back, but I'll run anyway. My breasts are trembling so. But I'm running. Where are you, Paul? Fred, where are you? Mama, where are you? Cissy? Why are all of you letting me run through the desert alone? I'm afraid when I'm alone like this. I'm going to fly instead. I knew that I could fly.

"Else!" . . . *"Else!"* . . .

Where are you? I hear you, but I can't see you.

"Else!" . . . *"Else!"* . . . *"Else!"* . . .

What *is* that? A whole choir? And an organ, too? I'm going to sing with them. What song is it? Everyone's singing. The forests and

the mountains and the stars. I've never heard anything so beautiful.
I've never seen such a bright night. Give me your hand, Papa. We'll
fly together. The world is so beautiful when you can fly. Don't kiss my
hand. I'm your child, Papa.

"*Else! Else!*"

They're calling from so far away! What do you want? Don't wake
me, I'm sleeping so soundly. Tomorrow morning. I'm dreaming and
flying. I'm flying . . . flying . . . flying . . . sleeping and dreaming . . .
and flying . . . don't wake me . . . tomorrow morning . . .

"*El . . .*"

I'm flying . . . I'm dreaming . . . I'm sleeping . . . I'm drea . . .
drea—I'm fly . . . . . .

Game at Dawn

I

"Herr Leutnant! . . . Herr Leutnant! . . . Herr Leutnant!" Not until after the third call did the young officer stir. He stretched and turned toward the door, still drunk with sleep, his head buried in the pillows.

"What is it?" he growled. Then, gradually waking up and noticing that it was only his orderly standing in the gloom of the partially opened door, he shouted, "Damn it, what the hell do you want this early in the morning?"

"There's a gentleman down in the courtyard, Herr Leutnant, who'd like to speak to the Herr Leutnant."

"What do you mean, a gentleman? What time is it, anyway? Didn't I tell you not to wake me on Sundays?"

The orderly stepped up to Wilhelm's bed and handed him a calling card.

"Do you think I'm an owl, you idiot? How am I supposed to read this in the dark! Open the curtain!"

Before the command was even finished, Joseph had opened the inside windows and raised the dirty white curtain. The lieutenant, sitting up halfway in bed, was now able to read the name on the card; he put it down on the blanket, looked at it again, ran his fingers through his short blond mussed-up hair and debated with himself for a moment: Tell him I'm not here? Can't possibly do that. There's actually no reason to, either. Just because you invite somebody in doesn't mean that you're friends. And anyway, the only reason he had to quit the service was because of debts. Other people simply have better luck. But what can he want from me?

He turned to his orderly again. "So how does the lieuten. . . how does Herr von Bogner look?"

The orderly replied with a broad, slightly sad smile, "Beg to report, sir, Herr von Bogner looked better in uniform, sir."

Wilhelm was silent for a while, then sat up all the way. "All right, tell—the lieutenant to come in. And ask him to kindly excuse me if I haven't quite finished dressing yet. Oh, and just in case—if one of the other officers happens to ask, Lieutenant Höchster or Lieutenant Wengler or the Captain or anybody else, I'm not in—understood?"

Joseph closed the door behind him; Wilhelm quickly put on a shirt and ran a comb through his hair, then went to the window and looked down on the still empty courtyard. The sight of his former fellow officer pacing back and forth in his open yellow overcoat and dusty brown street shoes, his head lowered and a stiff black hat pulled down over his eyes, made his heart almost ache. He opened the window and came close to waving to him and calling out a cheerful greeting, but at that moment his orderly stepped up to the waiting man, and Wilhelm could tell from his old friend's tense, fearful expression how anxious he was to hear what Joseph would have to tell him. This proving favorable, his expression brightened and he disappeared with the orderly through the gate under Wilhelm's room. The lieutenant closed his window again, as if sensing that the impending conversation might require this precaution, and suddenly the fragrance of forest and springtime that usually filled the courtyard on Sunday mornings but was strangely absent on weekdays was gone. Whatever happens, Wilhelm thought . . . What could happen, though? I'm definitely going out to Baden today and have a nice meal at the "City of Vienna"—unless the Kessners ask me to stay for lunch the way they did last time.

"Come in!" Wilhelm extended his hand to his guest with exaggerated enthusiasm. "How're you doing, Bogner? I'm really glad to see you. Here, take your coat off. Go ahead, have a look around—everything's just the way it always was. The place hasn't gotten any bigger. But there's room enough in the littlest hut for a happy . . ."[1]

Otto smiled politely as if he had noticed Wilhelm's discomfort and wanted to help him out. "I hope there are occasions when the quotation fits your little hut better than it does this time," he said.

Wilhelm's laugh sounded forced. "Not very often, unfortunately. I live a pretty monkish existence. Would you believe it if I told you that this room hasn't been graced by a feminine foot for at least six weeks? Plato couldn't hold a candle to me.—Why don't you have a seat?" He took a few articles of clothing off a chair and put them on his bed. "Care to have a cup of coffee with me?"

"Thanks, Kasda, don't go to any trouble. I've already had breakfast . . . I will have a cigarette, if you don't mind . . ."

Wilhelm wouldn't allow Otto to take one from his own case and pointed instead to a small smoking table with an open pack on it. Wilhelm gave him a light and Otto took a few puffs in silence. His glance fell on the familiar picture of an officer's steeplechase from long ago that hung on the wall above the black leather sofa.

"So how have you been doing?" Wilhelm asked. "Why haven't I ever heard from you? When you left—two or three years ago, it must've been—you promised you'd get in touch every so—"

Otto interrupted him. "It probably was better that I kept to myself, and it definitely would have been better if I hadn't had to come today." He sat down abruptly at one end of the sofa, the other corner of which was taken up by several well-thumbed books. "Because as you can imagine, Willi"—he spoke quickly and his voice had a shrill edge to it—"my coming to see you today at such an unusual hour— I know you like to sleep late on Sunday mornings—there's a reason behind it, obviously, otherwise I certainly wouldn't have allowed myself to—look, to put it briefly, I'm here to ask you a favor as an old friend—seeing I can no longer appeal to you as a fellow officer, unfortunately. You don't need to turn pale, Willi, it's not that serious— it has to do with a few gulden I need to come up with by tomorrow morning . . . if I don't I'll have no other choice but to"—his voice took on a raspy, high-pitched military tone—"well, maybe it would have been best if I had done it two years ago."

Wilhelm felt at a loss. "Come on, what are you talking about," he said in a tone of comradely indignation.

The orderly brought breakfast and left again. Willi filled two cups with coffee. He had a bitter taste in his mouth and felt ill at ease at not having been able to shave and finish dressing. But he had already planned to stop for a steam bath on the way to the railroad station anyway. It would be perfectly fine if he didn't get to Baden much before noon. He hadn't made any specific arrangements, and if he arrived there later than usual, or even if he didn't show up at all, no one in particular would notice, neither the gentlemen at the Café Schopf nor Fräulein Kessner; her mother might be more likely to, actually. She wasn't bad-looking herself, he thought in passing.

"Feel free," he said to Otto, who still hadn't touched his coffee. Otto took a quick swallow before speaking.

"To come right to the point: you may know that I've been working as a clerk for an electric contractor for three months now. Although come to think of it, why should you? You don't even know that I'm married and have a little boy—he's four now. Which means that he was already around when you and I were officers together. No one knew about it. Anyway, I haven't been doing so well since then. I'm sure that doesn't come as a surprise to you. Last winter especially, my son was sick . . . well, I don't need to bore you with all the details. What happened was, I had to borrow money from the cash register every now and then. But I always put it back before it was too late. This time, unfortunately, it was a little more than usual, and"—he paused for a moment while Wilhelm noisily stirred his coffee—"and to make matters worse, I happened to find out that we were going to be audited by the central office on Monday—tomorrow, in other words. We're just a branch, and the amounts of money that go through our office are minimal; and it's really not that much that I—owe: nine hundred and sixty gulden. I might just as well say a thousand, it comes to the same thing. But it's nine hundred and sixty exactly. And I have to replace it by eight-thirty tomorrow morning, or else . . . well, you would really be doing me an enormous favor, Willi, if you could lend me—" He broke off his sentence abruptly, unable to continue. Willi felt a little ashamed for him, not so much because of the minor misappropriation—or defraudation, it would probably have to be called—that his former comrade had perpetrated, but because the man who used to be known as First Lieutenant Otto von Bogner, a few short years ago a charming, well-off, self-confident officer, was now leaning back in a corner of the sofa, pale and insecure, swallowing his tears and unable to go on speaking.

Willi put a hand on his shoulder. "Come on, Otto, don't go falling apart, now." At this not very encouraging opening, Otto looked up at him with a gloomy, almost alarmed expression on his face. "To tell you the truth," Willi went on, "I'm feeling pretty strapped myself. My total assets amount to a little over a hundred gulden. A hundred and twenty, to be as precise as you were. I don't need to tell you that you're welcome to every last kreutzer of that. But if we work at it a little, we're bound to find some other approach."

Otto interrupted him. "Don't you suppose that I've already tried every possible—approach? We don't need to waste time racking our brains—especially since I have a specific suggestion in mind."

Wilhelm looked him in the eye expectantly.

"Suppose that you were in a predicament like this yourself, Willi. What would you do?"

"I don't quite see what you mean," Wilhelm replied in a slightly indignant tone.

"I know, I know, you've never stuck your hand in anyone's cash register, certainly not. Things like that only happen in civilian life. But still, suppose that for some—less criminal reason you absolutely had to have a certain amount of money, who would you turn to?"

"Otto, I'm sorry, that's something I've never thought about, and I hope . . . I mean, I've had debts at times, too, I don't deny that. Just last month Höchster lent me fifty gulden. I paid him back on the first, of course. That's why I don't have anything to spare right now. But a thousand gulden—a thousand—I don't have any idea how I'd get my hands on that kind of money."

"You really don't?" Otto said, looking at him intently.

"I just told you I didn't."

"How about your uncle?"

"Uncle? What uncle?"

"Your Uncle Robert."

"What—made you think of him?"

"It's obvious. He's helped you out a time or two. And you get a regular allowance from him."

"Allowance! That's been over and done with for a long time," Willi replied, annoyed at his former comrade's tone, which, given the circumstances, struck him as extremely presumptuous. "And not only the allowance. Uncle Robert has gotten eccentric. To tell you the truth, I haven't set eyes on him for over a year. And the last time I asked him—and *that* was an exception—for some piddling amount—why, I was lucky he didn't throw me out."

"Hm, I see." Bogner rubbed his forehead. "You really think it's completely out of the question?"

"I hope you're not doubting my word," Wilhelm said somewhat sharply.

Bogner suddenly got up out of the sofa, pushed the table aside, and walked over to the window.

"We have to try it," he declared in a firm voice. "I'm sorry to put it like that, but we *have* to. The worst thing that can happen to you is that he'll say no. And maybe he won't be very nice about it, I'll grant you that. But compared to what's facing me if I don't come up with this paltry little amount by tomorrow morning—it would be nothing but a slight annoyance."

"Maybe so," Wilhelm said, "but it would be a completely pointless annoyance. If there was even the slightest chance—look, I hope you don't have any doubts about my willingness to help you. But damn it all, there must be other possibilities. For example, what about—don't get upset now, I just thought of this—your cousin Guido, the one with the estate near Amstetten?"

"As you might guess, Willi," Bogner replied calmly, "there's nothing doing there either. Otherwise I wouldn't have come to you. To be blunt about it, there's not a single person in the whole world—"

Willi suddenly raised a finger as if he'd thought of something. Bogner looked at him expectantly.

"Rudi Höchster—you should give him a try. He came into an inheritance a few months ago, twenty or twenty-five thousand gulden. There has to be something left from that."

Bogner frowned, then replied hesitatingly, "I wrote to Höchster—it was three weeks ago, when things weren't so urgent—asking for much less than a thousand—he didn't even answer me. Don't you see, there's only one single way out: your uncle." Willi gave a dismissive shrug.

"I know him, Willi—he's such a kind, lovable old gentleman. We even went to the theater a few times together, and the Riedhof[2]—I'm sure he'll remember. For God's sake, man, he can't suddenly have become a different person!"

"It looks like he has, though," Willi broke in impatiently. "I don't know myself what actually happened to him. But people definitely can change in strange ways when they get to be fifty or sixty. All I can tell you is that I haven't set foot in his apartment for over a year, if not longer—and, to be blunt, I never will again, not for anything."

Bogner looked off into space. Then he suddenly turned to Willi as if his mind were somewhere else. "All right, sorry to have bothered you," he said. "So long." He took his hat and turned to go.

"Otto!" Willi exclaimed, "I have another idea."

"Another one? What a joke."

"Just listen for a second, Bogner. I'm taking the train out to Baden today. Sometimes there's a little card game going at the Café Schopf on Sunday afternoons—blackjack or baccarat, one or the other. Obviously I don't get involved very heavily myself, if at all. I've played three or four times, mostly for the fun of it. The main player is Tugut, the regimental doctor—he has incredible luck—First Lieutenant Wimmer is usually there, too, and Greising, from the Seventy-Seventh . . . you wouldn't know him. He gets medical treatment out there, for some problem he's had for a long time. Then there are a few civilians, a lawyer from Baden, the theater secretary, an actor, and an older man—Consul Schnabel. He's involved with a local operetta singer—glorified chorus girl, actually. He's an easy mark. Tugut took him for no less than three thousand gulden at one sitting two weeks ago. We played till six in the morning out on the veranda, with the birds singing all around us. The hundred and twenty that I still have I owe purely to my staying power, otherwise I'd be completely broke.

So here's what I'll do, Otto: I'll put a hundred of that hundred and twenty on the line for you today. I know, the odds aren't exactly overwhelming, but Tugut sat down at the table that time with only fifty, and he got up with three thousand. And there's something else, too: I haven't been the least bit lucky in love for several months now. Maybe that old saying will turn out to be more reliable than people are."

Bogner was silent.

"Well—what do you think?" Willi asked.

Bogner shrugged. "I appreciate your trying to help—I won't say no, of course—although—"

"Obviously I can't guarantee anything," Willi interrupted , sounding exaggeratedly buoyant, "but then it's not much of a risk either. And if I win—depending on how much I win, you get a thousand—*at least* a thousand. And if I happen to hit the jackpot—"

"Better not promise too much," Otto said with a gloomy smile. "But I don't want to keep you any longer now. For my own sake if for no other reason. And tomorrow morning I'll take the liberty of—or maybe . . . I'll wait in front of the Alserstrasse church tomorrow morning at seven-thirty." He laughed bitterly. "We could just 'happen' to meet there, after all."

Bogner brushed aside Willi's attempt at a response and added quickly, "By the way, I'm not just going to sit idly by in the meantime. I still have seventy gulden. I'll put that on a horse at the races this afternoon—I'll buy the cheapest seat I can, of course." He stepped over to the window and looked down at the courtyard. "The coast is clear," he said, his mouth twisted scornfully. Turning his collar up, he shook hands with Willi and left.

Wilhelm gave a soft sigh and pondered for a while, then started to get ready to leave. He wasn't at all satisfied with the condition of his uniform. If he happened to win today, he was determined to buy himself a new dress jacket if nothing else. Considering the lateness of the hour, he decided against the steam bath, but he'd take a carriage to the station at least. Two gulden—that was hardly worth worrying about today.

II

When he got off the train in Baden at noon, his mood wasn't at all bad. Lieutenant Colonel Wositzky, a very unpleasant man when on duty, had conversed with him in a most congenial way at the station in Vienna, and two young girls in his compartment had flirted with him so openly that he was almost glad, for the sake of what he had planned for the rest of the day, that they didn't get off the train when he did. Despite his favorable disposition, however, he was inclined to feel reproachful toward his former comrade Bogner, not so much for having taken money from the cash register, which after all was excusable to some extent given his disastrous situation, but because of the ridiculous gambling incident that had put an abrupt end to his career three years earlier. An officer ultimately had to know, after all, how far he could allow himself to go. He himself, for example, dogged by bad luck three weeks ago, had simply gotten up from the card table, even though Consul Schnabel had offered in the most amiable way to stake him. He had, in fact, always been able to resist temptation and never had had any problem getting by on his meager salary and the small allowances he used to receive, first from his father and then, after his father had died in Temesvar[3] with the rank of lieutenant colonel, from his Uncle Robert. And ever since his uncle had discontinued his allowance, he had simply rearranged his affairs accordingly. He limited his visits to coffee houses, refrained from buying anything new, cut down on cigarettes, and no longer allowed women to cost him anything at all. A minor flirtation that had begun very promisingly three months before had fallen through because one evening Willi had literally not been in a position to pay for dinner for two.

It's actually sad, he thought. Never before had he been as sharply aware of his straitened circumstances as he was today. Wearing a dress jacket that unfortunately had lost some of its original flair, sand-colored pants that were starting to get a little shiny at the knees, and a cap of considerably lower cut than the latest officers' fashion dictated, he walked along on this beautiful spring day through fragrant park grounds toward the country house the Kessner family lived in or pos-

sibly even owned. Today, for the first time ever, he had the sense that
his hope of being invited to lunch—or rather, the fact that this expec-
tation represented a hope—was something shameful.

Nonetheless, he accommodated himself easily enough when this
hope turned out to be fulfilled. Not only did the lunch prove to be
appetizing and the wine excellent; better still, Fräulein Emilie was
seated on his right, and her friendly glances and affectionate touches—
though these certainly could have been accidental—made her a very
pleasant table partner indeed. Willi was not the only guest. The host
had brought along a lawyer from Vienna, a young man who was adept
at leading the conversation in a cheerful, light-hearted, and at times
even ironic tone. The host himself treated Willi politely, though with
a certain coolness. He seemed, in fact, not to be particularly taken by
the lieutenant's Sunday visits; Willi had been introduced to the ladies
present at a Carnival ball the previous season, and it was possible that
he had taken their invitation to stop by sometime for tea all too literally. As for the host's still pretty wife, she seemed to have forgotten
completely that two weeks earlier she had been sitting on a rather
secluded garden bench with the lieutenant and had only pulled back
from his unexpectedly daring advances at the sound of footsteps approaching on the gravel.

During the first part of the meal, the conversation had concerned
a trial the lawyer was conducting for the host in connection with his
factory, and this had involved all kinds of expressions the lieutenant
hadn't quite understood; but afterwards talk shifted to sojourns in the
country and summer trips, and now Willi was also able to say his
share. Two years before he had taken part in imperial maneuvers in
the Dolomites; he told about sleeping out under the stars, about the
two black-haired daughters of an innkeeper in Kastelruth, known as
the two Medusas because of their inapproachability, and about a lieutenant commander who had fallen out of favor before Willi's very
eyes, so to speak, because of a failed cavalry attack. And as often happened to him after three or four glasses of wine, he became less and
less inhibited, more animated, almost humorous, even. He sensed
that he was gradually winning over his host, that the lawyer's tone

was growing less and less ironic, and that his host's wife was starting
to show a glimmer of remembrance; added to this, an energetic nudge
of Emilie's knee against his no longer made any pretense of being
accidental.

As they were having their dessert coffee, a corpulent older woman
appeared with her two daughters, and Willi was introduced to them
as "our dancer from the industrialists' ball." It soon came to light that
the three ladies had also spent some time in South Tyrol two years
before; and hadn't it been the Herr Leutnant they had seen one beautiful summer day, galloping by their hotel in Siusi on a black horse?
Willi didn't quite want to deny this possibility, although he knew
very well that he, an insignificant infantry lieutenant with the Ninety-
Eighth, had never gone galloping by on a proud steed in any Tyrolean
town, or anywhere else for that matter.

The two young ladies were lovely in their white dresses; with
Fräulein Kessner in pale pink between them, the three ran with abandon across the grass.

"Like the three Graces, aren't they," the lawyer said. Once again it
sounded ironic, and the lieutenant was close to replying: exactly how
do you mean that, Herr Doktor? But since Fräulein Emilie had just
looked back from the lawn at him and given him a cheery wave, he
found it all the easier to keep his comment to himself. She was blond
and a little taller than Willi, and her dowry would presumably be not
inconsiderable. But it would be a long time, a very long time, before
things reached that point—assuming he even dared to dream of such
eventualities—and the thousand gulden for his unfortunate comrade
had to be obtained by tomorrow morning at the latest.

And so, for the sake of former First Lieutenant Bogner, he had no
choice but to leave just as the conversation was at full swing. The
others put on a show of wanting him to stay, and he expressed his
regrets; he was expected elsewhere, and first and foremost he had to
visit a fellow soldier in the garrison hospital who was undergoing
treatment for an old rheumatic condition. At this, too, the lawyer
smiled ironically. Would that visit take up the entire afternoon, Frau
Kessner asked with an alluring smile? Willi shrugged his shoulders

uncertainly. Well, at any rate, they would all be happy to see him again in the course of the evening if it turned out that he was able to get away.

As he left the house, two elegant young men drove up in an open carriage. Willi was not pleased; who could say what sort of things might go on there while he was at the coffee house, obliged to earn a thousand gulden for a former fellow officer who had strayed from the straight and narrow? Wouldn't he be smarter not to get involved in that at all and, half an hour or so later, go back to the beautiful garden and the three Graces after having ostensibly visited his sick friend? All the smarter, he thought with a certain smugness, considering that his chances of winning at cards might well have diminished significantly in the meantime.

III

A large yellow racing poster leapt out at Willi from an advertising column, reminding him that at this very moment Bogner would be at the races in Freudenau[4] and might possibly even be on the verge of winning the amount he needed to save his skin on his own. But supposing that did happen, and Bogner kept his stroke of luck to himself so that he could still collect the thousand gulden Willi had won from Consul Schnabel or Dr. Tugut? After all, anyone who had sunk so low as to take money from his employer's cash register . . . And in a few months, even weeks, Bogner would probably be in exactly the same position he was today. And what then?

The sound of music drifted over toward him—some Italian overture or other, of the outmoded type that only orchestras at health resorts ever played. But Willi knew the piece well. Years ago, back in Temesvar, he had heard his mother and some distant relative play it four-handed. He had never gotten good enough himself to be his mother's partner, and the occasional piano lessons he had taken when he was home on vacation from cadet school had come to an end with her death eight years ago. Softly, with a touch of melancholy, the tones carried through the resonating spring air.

He crossed a small bridge over the murky Schwechat Brook and a few steps later came to the broad terrace of the Café Schopf, filled to overflowing with Sunday guests. Lieutenant Greising, the soldier undergoing treatment, sat at a small table near the street looking pale and spiteful; Weiss, the fat theater secretary, was with him, wearing a slightly wrinkled canary yellow flannel suit and his customary flower in the lapel. Willi made his way toward them, squeezing between the tables and chairs with some effort.

"Not many of us here today," he said, extending his hand to them. He felt relieved that there might not be enough for a card game today. But Greising explained that he and the theater secretary were only getting some fresh air to fortify themselves for the "work" ahead. The others were already inside at the card table; Consul Schnabel had driven in from Vienna in his carriage as usual and was there too.

Willi ordered a cold lemonade. Greising asked him where he had gotten so heated up already that he needed a drink to cool off, then commented without any further transition that the girls from Baden in general were good-looking and fiery. Using less than refined language, he went on to tell about a little adventure that he had initiated the previous evening in the gardens by the hotel and that had come to a satisfactory conclusion later that night. Willi drank his lemonade slowly, and Greising, who thought he could tell what was going through his mind, gave a brief laugh and said by way of an answer, "That's the way of the world—other people simply have to accept it."

First Lieutenant Wimmer from the supply unit, who was often taken for a member of the cavalry by people who didn't know any better, was suddenly standing behind them.

"Well, gentlemen—do you really think that we should be the only ones straining our nerves against the consul?" He held out his hand to Willi, who gave the higher-ranking officer his usual brisk salute even though he was off-duty.

"How's it going in there?" Greising asked in a dubious, gruff tone.

"Slow as can be," Wimmer replied. "The consul is hoarding his money like a dragon—and mine too by now, I'm sorry to say. Off into battle, my fellow toreros."

The others got up. "I'm expected somewhere," Willi said, lighting a cigarette and feigning indifference. "I'll just kibitz for a few minutes."

"Ha," Wimmer laughed, "the road to hell is paved with good intentions."

"And the one to heaven with bad ones," Weiss remarked.

"Clever!" Wimmer said, clapping him on the shoulder.

They stepped into the coffee house. Willi cast one last glance back outside, over the roofs of the villas and toward the hills. He swore to himself that he would be sitting in Kessners' garden in half an hour at the latest.

He walked with the others to a dimly-lit corner where not a trace of spring air and sunlight penetrated; he kept his chair pushed far back from the table to make it clear that he had no intention of participating in the game. The consul, a haggard man of indeterminate age with an English-style mustache and sparse reddish hair that already showed a few traces of gray, sat in his elegant light gray suit deliberating with his customary thoroughness over a card that been dealt to him by Dr. Flegmann, the lawyer, who was keeping the bank. His card won, and Flegmann took more bills out of his wallet.

"Never batted an eyelash," Wimmer said with ironic respect.

"Batting eyelashes doesn't change what you have in your hand," Flegmann replied coolly, his eyes half-closed. Tugut, the regimental doctor and division head of the military hospital in Baden, set up a bank of two hundred gulden.

This is really out of my range today, Willi thought, pushing his chair back even farther.

The actor Elrief, a young man from a wealthy family who was better known for his limited intelligence than his talent, let Willi look at his cards. He bet small amounts and shook his head helplessly whenever he lost. Tugut had soon doubled his bank. Weiss, the secretary, borrowed from Elrief, and Dr. Flegmann took some money out of his wallet again. Tugut was about to close his bank when the consul, without counting how much was in it, said "Banco." He lost and reached into his vest pocket to pay the three hundred gulden he owed. "Banco again," he said. Tugut declined, and Dr. Flegmann took over the bank and dealt the cards. Willi still wasn't playing himself, but at Elrief's urgent entreaties "to bring him luck," he bet a gulden on Elrief's hand just for fun—and won. In the next round Flegmann flipped him a card too, and he decided to play. He won again, lost, won, then moved his chair up close to the table between the others, who were glad to make room for him; he won—lost—won—lost, as if fate couldn't quite make up its mind. The secretary left for the theater, forgetting to give Herr Elrief the money he had borrowed from him even though he had long since won back much more than he owed. Willi was winning slightly more often than losing but was still about nine hundred and fifty short of the thousand gulden.

"This isn't going anywhere," Greising commented, dissatisfied. The consul took over the bank again, and everyone sensed at that moment that things were finally going to get serious.

No one knew much more about Consul Schnabel than what his title indicated: he was a consul, to some small republic in South America, and a "wholesale merchant." It was Weiss, the theater secretary, who had introduced him into this circle of officers, and Weiss's involvement with him went back to a time when the consul had convinced him to hire a small-time actress, who had then become intimately involved with Herr Elrief immediately after starting in her insignificant position. Everyone would have liked to take part in the venerable custom of making fun of the deceived lover, but when the consul had dealt a card to Elrief during a recent game and asked him, his cigar between his teeth and without looking up, "Well, and how are things with that little girl friend we've been sharing?" it had become clear that no one would get the better of this man by mocking and jibing him. This impression was reinforced late one evening when Lieutenant Greising tossed off a suggestive remark between two glasses of cognac about consuls to unexplored parts of the world, to which the consul had responded with a penetrating look, "Why are you provoking me, Herr Leutnant? Have you inquired yet to see whether I'm qualified to fight a duel?"

An unsettling silence had resulted from this remark, but, almost as if there were a silent understanding, nothing further came of it, and from then on everyone decided, unanimously and without needing to discuss the matter, to treat him with greater caution.

The consul kept losing. No one opposed his immediately establishing a new bank—not his usual practice—or, when his losses continued, a third. The other players were winning, especially Willi. He put his initial stake of a hundred and twenty gulden aside—that amount was not to be put at risk again under any circumstances. Next he established a bank himself, soon doubled it, and then closed it; with only occasional lapses, his luck stayed with him against the other bankers too, who alternated rapidly. The thousand gulden he had set out to win—for someone else—had been exceeded by a few hundred, and when Herr Elrief got up to leave for the theater where he was performing, making no further comment about this in spite of Greising's mock show of interest, Willi took the opportunity to join him. The others were immediately engrossed in their game again, and when Willi turned around at the door and looked back he saw that the consul, alone among the players, had looked up briefly from the game and was following him with his cold gaze.

IV

It wasn't until now, standing outside again with the gentle evening breeze caressing his forehead, that Willi become conscious of his good fortune—or, to be more precise, of Bogner's good fortune. But there would be some left over for himself, too—enough to buy the new dress jacket, cap, and sword belt he'd been dreaming of. There were even sufficient funds available for a few evening meals in pleasant company, which would be easy to find now. But aside from that, what a gratifying feeling it would be at seven-thirty the next morning when he went to the Alserstrasse church and handed his former comrade the money that would save him. A thousand gulden—the famous thousand-gulden bill he had previously only read about in books, one of which he actually had stashed away in his wallet now along with a few smaller bills. Well, my old friend, here it is. I won exactly a thousand gulden. A thousand one hundred and fifty-five, to be absolutely precise. Then I quit. Talk about self-control! And hopefully, my friend, from now on . . . No, no, he could hardly give his former comrade a lecture. Bogner would take it to heart on his own and hopefully have enough tact not to interpret the day's favorable outcome as permission for continued friendly relations. But in any case it might be more prudent, or even more proper, for Willi to send his orderly over to the church with the money.

On his way to the Kessners, Willi wondered if they might invite him to stay for dinner today as well. Well, dinner or no dinner— fortunately that was no longer a concern. Now he was rich enough himself to invite every last one of them out for a meal. Too bad there wasn't any place to buy flowers. But a pastry shop he walked by was open, and he decided on a bag of candies, and then, turning around in the doorway, bought a second and even bigger one, debating with himself as he did what the proper way to divide them up between mother and daughter would be.

When he walked into the garden in front of the Kessners' house the maid told him that her master and mistress, along with everyone else, had left for the Helenental,[5] probably to go to the Krain chalet. She assumed the Kessners would have their supper at a restaurant somewhere as they usually did Sunday evenings.

A trace of disappointment showed on Willi's face, and the maid smiled, glancing at the two bags the lieutenant was holding in his hand. That's right, what was he supposed to do with them now!

"Give everyone my best and—would you take these, please?"— he handed the bags to the maid—"The bigger one is for Mrs. Kessner and the smaller one for her daughter; tell them I'm sorry I missed them."

"Maybe if the Herr Leutnant took a carriage—I'm sure they'd still be at the Krain chalet now."

Willi looked at his watch pensively, self-importantly. "I'll have to see," he said nonchalantly, giving a humorously exaggerated salute as he left.

Evening was approaching now as he stood alone on the street. A cheerful little group of tourists, men and women with dusty shoes, came trailing past him. In front of a villa, an old gentleman sat on a wicker chair reading a newspaper. A little farther on, an elderly woman sat on a second-floor balcony crocheting and talking to her neighbor, who was leaning cross-armed on the window sill of the house across the way. It seemed to Willi that these few people were the only ones in the whole town who weren't on an outing somewhere. The Kessners certainly could have left a message with the housemaid for him. Well, he didn't want to force himself on them. He had no need to do that, really. But what now? Go straight back to Vienna? That might just be the most sensible thing to do! Or how about if he left that decision up to fate?

Two carriages were standing in front of the spa hotel. "How much to take me to the Helenental?" he asked. One of the carriages was already taken and the other driver quoted a figure that was completely outrageous. Willi decided on an evening stroll through the park.

There were still quite a few people in the park at that hour. Couples, married and unmarried—Willi was sure he could tell them apart every time—young girls and women, alone, in twos or threes, strolled past him, and he met with many a smiling, even encouraging look. But a young man could never be sure that the father, or brother, or fiancé, wasn't walking along behind, and an officer was obliged to be doubly, triply cautious. For a while he followed a dark-eyed slender woman who was holding a little boy by the hand. She climbed the stairs to the terrace of the hotel and appeared to be looking for someone, at first with no success; then she finally noticed people waving to her from a far-off table and, giving Willi a mocking glance, went over and sat down with them. Willi began to look around himself now as if trying to find someone, then walked from the terrace into the relatively empty restaurant and from there to the entrance lobby and the reading room, where the lights had already been turned on. A retired general in uniform was sitting at a long green table. Willi saluted, clicking his heels together, then left quickly when the general gave him an annoyed nod. One of the carriages was still standing in front of the hotel, and the driver announced without being asked that he would take the Herr Leutnant to the Helenental for a reasonable price. "What's the point, it wouldn't pay now," Willi said and set out at a fast pace for the Café Schopf.

V

The players were still sitting in the same grouping as before, as if not a minute had gone by since Willi's departure. The electric light gave off a dull glow from under its green shade. The consul had been the first to notice him coming in; Willi thought he detected a mocking smile playing around his lips. No one expressed the least surprise when Willi pulled his still empty chair up between the others. Dr. Flegmann, who was banker at the moment, dealt him a card as if it were a matter of course. In his hurry, Willi put down a larger bill than he had intended; he won, then started betting more cautious amounts. But his luck changed, and things soon reached a point where his thousand-gulden bill seemed to be seriously in danger. What's the difference, Willi thought, it wouldn't have done *me* any good, anyway. But now he started to win again and didn't need to get change for his large bill; luck stayed with him, and when the game ended at nine o'clock Willi found himself in possession of over two thousand gulden. A thousand for Bogner, a thousand for me, he thought. I'll keep half of my part as a stake for next Sunday. But he didn't feel as happy as it would have been natural for him to feel.

The players went to the "City of Vienna" for supper; they sat outside under the dense green of an oak tree, talking about games of chance in general and famous card games at the Jockey Club played for gigantic stakes. "It is and always has been a vice," Dr. Flegmann maintained with great seriousness. Some of the others laughed, but First Lieutenant Wimmer showed an inclination to take offense at the remark. Just because something might be a vice for a lawyer, he commented, was far from making it one for an officer. Flegmann explained politely that a person could have a vice and still be an honorable man, and pointed out that there were numerous examples of this: Don Juan, for example, or Cardinal Richelieu. The consul was of the opinion that gambling was only a vice if the player wasn't able to pay his debts. And in that case it wasn't really a vice any more, it was a swindle, simply of a more cowardly type. There was silence all around the table. Fortunately Herr Elrief appeared just at that moment, his flower in his lapel and triumph in his eyes.

"Escaped from the ovations already?" Greising asked.

"I'm not on in the fourth act," the actor replied, casually slipping off his gloves, possibly in the manner he had in mind for an upcoming new role as a viscount or marquis. Greising lit a cigarette.

"Would be smarter for you not to smoke," Tugut said.

"But Herr Doktor, my throat is all cleared up again now," Greising replied.

The consul had ordered a few bottles of Hungarian wine, and the players drank to each other's health. Willi looked at his watch.

"Oh, I'm afraid I have to go. The last train leaves at ten-forty."

"Go ahead and finish your glass," the consul said, "my driver will take you to the station."

"Oh, Herr Consul, I really couldn't . . ."

"Of course you can," First Lieutenant Wimmer interrupted him.

"Well, what's the story," Dr. Tugut asked, "are we going to keep playing?"

No one had had any doubts that the game would be continued after supper. It was the same every Sunday.

"But not for long," the consul said.

They've got it good, Willi thought, envious of the prospect of sitting down at the card table again, tempting fortune, possibly winning thousands. The actor Elrief, who was already beginning to feel his wine, gave the consul a somewhat silly, jeering look and extended greetings from Fräulein Rihoscheck, their shared girl friend.

"Why didn't you just bring the young lady along, Herr Thespius?" Greising asked.

"She'll come to the coffee house later and watch us play, if it's all right with the Herr Consul," Elrief said. The consul didn't as much as blink.

Willi finished his glass and got up.

"See you next Sunday," Wimmer said, "we'll lighten your load a little for you then."

That's where you're wrong, Willi thought, it's really impossible to lose if you're careful.

"You'll be kind enough, Herr Leutnant, to send the driver back to the coffee house from the station," the consul said. He turned to the others. "But I don't want it to get as late, or should I say as early, as it did last time, gentlemen."

Willi saluted around the table and turned to go. Then, to his pleasant surprise, he spotted the Kessner family and the visitor from that afternoon with her two daughters sitting at one of the next tables. Neither the ironic lawyer nor the elegant young men who had driven up to the villa in their carriage were there. Everyone greeted him in a very friendly manner; he stood by their table, cheerful and at ease, a smart young officer in pleasant surroundings—feeling, moreover, after three glasses of strong Hungarian wine and with no competitors at the moment, pleasantly "pumped up." They offered him a chair, and he thanked them but declined, gesturing offhandedly toward the exit where the carriage stood waiting. Nonetheless, there were a few questions he still had to answer: Who was that handsome young man over there in civilian clothes?—Ah, an actor?— Elrief?—They had never even heard his name. The theater here was in any event no better than middling, the operettas were the only thing worth seeing in Baden, Mrs. Kessner said. And with an alluring look she proposed that when the Herr Leutnant was here next time they could perhaps all go to the Arena Theater[6] together. "It would be nicest if we could get two loges next to each other," Fräulein Kessner said, sending a smile over to Herr Elrief, who returned it glowingly. Willi kissed each lady's hand, waved over to the officers' table once more, and a moment later was sitting in the consul's carriage.

"Hurry," he said to the driver, "I'll give you a good tip."

The driver reacted to this pronouncement with an indifference behind which Willi sensed an annoying lack of respect. Even so, the horses ran splendidly, and in five minutes they had reached the station. But at that very moment the train, which had just arrived a minute earlier, began to leave. Willi jumped out of the carriage and stood looking at the lighted cars as they rumbled across the viaduct, slowly and heavily; he heard the whistle of the locomotive as it drifted off into the night air, then shook his head, not sure himself whether he was annoyed or happy. The driver sat apathetically on his box and stroked one of the horses with the handle of his whip.

"Nothing anyone can do about it," Willi finally said. "Back to the Café Schopf," he told the driver.

VI

It was pleasant to be riding through the little town in an open carriage; but how much more pleasant it would be, on a mild summer evening some day soon, to be riding out to the country with a delightful female companion. They'd go to Rodaun, or maybe the Red Barn,[7] and have supper outside. Ah, what bliss, not to have to think twice any more about every gulden you spent! Careful, Willi, careful, he said to himself, and he made the firm resolve not to risk all of his winnings, just half at most. As an extra precaution he would use Flegmann's system: start with a small bet; don't go higher until you've won once; never bet everything, just three-quarters of the total amount you have; and so on. Flegmann always started with this system, but he lacked the necessary consistency to carry it through. And because of this, of course, he never got anywhere.

Willi swung himself out of the carriage in front of the coffee house before it had even stopped and gave the driver a lavish tip—it was so much that renting a carriage of his own would hardly have cost more. The driver's expression of gratitude, while reserved, was still friendly enough.

All the players were there, along with the consul's girl friend, Fräulein Mitzi Rihoscheck. Her figure was imposing and her eyebrows overly black, though otherwise she wasn't excessively made up; in a light summer dress, a flat-brimmed straw hat with a red ribbon on her upswept brown hair, she sat with one arm draped over the back of the consul's chair looking at his cards. The consul didn't give Willi so much as a glance when he stepped up to the table, but still the lieutenant sensed that he had noticed his arrival instantly. "Oh, missed your train," Greising said. "By half a minute," Willi replied. "Serves you right," Wimmer said, dealing the cards. Flegmann, who had held a natural eight three times in a row and lost each time to a natural nine, was just leaving. Herr Elrief was still there even though he had no money left. A pile of bank notes lay in front of the consul. "Pretty high stakes," Willi said, immediately betting ten gulden instead of five as he had actually intended. His boldness paid off; he won and kept on winning. A bottle of cognac stood on a small side table; Fräulein Rihoscheck poured a glass for the lieutenant and held it out to him, bleary-eyed. Elrief asked if he would lend him fifty gulden until tomorrow noon at twelve. Willi pushed the bill over to him, and a second later it ended up on the consul's pile. Elrief got up, drops of perspiration on his forehead. Just then Weiss, the theater secretary, arrived in his yellow flannel suit; a whispered conversation resulted in the secretary's paying back the amount he had borrowed from the actor that afternoon. Elrief lost this, too, and, acting quite differently from the way the viscount he hoped to play one day would have, he shoved his chair back in a rage, stood up, swore under his breath, and left the room. When he still hadn't returned some time later, Fräulein Rihoscheck got out of her chair, ran her hand tenderly, distractedly, over the consul's head, and left as well.

With the end of the game near, Wimmer and Greising, and even Tugut, had become cautious; only the theater secretary still displayed some foolhardiness. But the game had gradually turned into a man-to-man combat between Lieutenant Kasda and Consul Schnabel. Willi's luck had changed, and aside from the thousand for his old comrade Bogner he had barely a hundred gulden left. If I lose this hundred I'm going to quit, definitely, he swore to himself. But he didn't really believe it. What do I care about Bogner, he thought. I'm not obligated to him in the least.

Fräulein Rihoscheck appeared again, humming a melody to herself; she arranged her hair in front of the large mirror, lit a cigarette, took a billiard cue and tried a few shots, put the cue back in the corner and rolled first the white, then the red ball across the green cloth. A cold look from the consul called her back to the table; still humming her tune, she took her place at his side again and put her arm over the back of his chair. From outside, where it had been absolutely quiet for some time now, came the sounds of a student song sung in harmony. How are they going to get back to Vienna tonight, Willi wondered. Then it occurred to him that the singers might be

Gymnasium students from Baden. Ever since Fräulein Rihoscheck had been sitting across from him, his luck had slowly begun to take a turn for the better. The singing grew faint and finally faded away; a bell from a church tower tolled the hour.

"Quarter to one," Greising said.

"Let's make this the last bank," Dr. Tugut declared. "One more each," First Lieutenant Wimmer suggested.

The consul nodded in agreement.

Willi played on in silence. He won, lost, drank a glass of cognac, won, lost, lit himself another cigarette, won, lost. Tugut's bank lasted for a long time before finally being cleaned out completely by a large bet placed by the consul. Strangely enough, Herr Elrief appeared again after an almost hour-long absence, and, stranger still, he had money again. With elegant nonchalance, as if nothing had happened, he sat down at the table, like that viscount whose role he certainly would never play, and introduced yet another nuance of elegant nonchalance, one that actually came from Dr. Flegmann: half-closed, tired eyes. He set up a bank of three hundred gulden as if it were something he did all the time, and started out winning. The consul lost against him, against Dr. Tugut, and especially against Willi, who soon found himself in the possession of no less than three thousand gulden. This meant a new dress jacket, a new sword belt, new shirts, patent-leather shoes, cigarettes, dinners for two, for three, drives out to the Vienna Woods, two months of unpaid leave. By two o'clock he had won four thousand two hundred gulden. The money lay there in front of him, there could be no doubt about it: four thousand two hundred gulden plus a little extra.

"That's enough," Consul Schnabel said suddenly. Willi felt pulled in two directions. If they stopped now, he was safe, and that was good. But at the same time he felt an uncontrollable, truly hellish desire to play on, to conjure a few more, *all* of the thousand-gulden notes out of the consul's wallet into his own. *That* would be a bankroll, that kind of money could be the beginning of a fortune! And it wouldn't always have to be baccarat—there were the horse races in Freudenau and the trotting races, there were casinos, Monte Carlo, for example, down on the Mediterranean coast, with exquisite women from Paris . . . While Willi's thoughts raced, Dr. Tugut tried to get the consul to set up one last bank. Elrief, nipping on his eighth glass of cognac, acted the part of host and poured more for the others. Fräulein Mitzi Rihoscheck swayed from side to side, humming a little tune to herself. Tugut picked up the cards that lay strewn about the table and shuffled them. The consul was silent. Then he suddenly called to the waiter and had him bring two new, untouched decks of cards. Eyes lit up all around. The consul looked at the clock.

"We quit at two-thirty on the dot, no matter what," he said. It was five minutes after two.

VII

The consul set up a bank the likes of which had never before been seen in this circle, a bank of three thousand gulden. Aside from the players and one waiter there was no one left in the café. The morning sounds of birds chirping outside came in through the open door. The consul was losing but still able to maintain his bank for the time being. Elrief had recouped his losses completely, and when Fräulein Rihoscheck gave him an admonishing glance he withdrew from the game. The others, all doing reasonably well, continued their modest, cautious betting. Half of the bank was still untouched.

"Banco," Willi said suddenly, startled by what he had said and even by his own voice. Have I gone crazy, he said to himself? The consul turned his two cards over; he had a natural nine, and Willi was fifteen hundred gulden poorer. Then, remembering Flegmann's system, he bet a ridiculously small amount, fifty gulden, and won. Too bad, he thought, I could have gotten back everything on that one play! Why was I such a coward? "Banco again." He lost. "Banco again." The consul seemed to hesitate. "What's gotten into you, Kasda?" Dr. Tugut exclaimed. Willi laughed and felt a kind of dizziness rise to his forehead. Was it maybe the cognac dulling his senses? Apparently. He had made a mistake, of course; he hadn't had the slightest intention of betting one or two thousand all at once.

"I'm sorry, Herr Consul, I was actually thinking—"

The consul didn't let him finish. "If you didn't know how much was left in the bank I'll certainly let you retract," he remarked in a friendly tone of voice.

"How can you, Herr Consul?" Willi said, "banco is banco."

Had he said that himself? Were those his words? Was that his voice? If he lost this hand, he could forget about the new dress jacket, the new sword belt, the pleasant dinners for two; there would be nothing left but the thousand for that swindler Bogner—and he, Willi, would be just as much a pauper as he had been two hours before.

Without a word the consul showed his hand. Nine. No one needed to say it out loud, the number went resounding ghostlike through the room. Willi's forehead felt strangely moist. Good God, it had happened so quickly! But he still had a thousand gulden in front of him on the table, even a little more than that. He didn't want to count it, that might bring bad luck. And in any case, look at how much more he had now than today at noon when he got off the train. Today at noon . . . And nothing was forcing him to risk the entire thousand gulden all at once. He could start with a hundred, or two hundred again if he wanted. Flegmann's system. The only problem was that there was so little time left, barely twenty minutes.

It was silent all around the table. "Herr Leutnant?" the consul said.

"Oh, of course," Willi laughed, folding his thousand gulden note in two. "Half of this, Herr Consul."

"Five hundred?"

Willi nodded. The others made their bets, pro forma. But there was already a feeling in the air that the game was over. First Lieutenant Wimmer stood with his coat draped around his shoulders. Tugut leaned against the billiard table. The consul showed his cards.

"Eight."

And half of Willi's thousand gulden were gone. He shook his head. Was the devil afoot here?

"The rest," he said.

I'm actually completely calm, he said to himself, and slowly looked at his hand. Eight. The consul had to take another card. Nine. And the five hundred was gone, the thousand was gone. Everything was gone.—Everything? No. He still had the hundred and twenty gulden he had come with that noon, plus a little more. Funny, suddenly he really was the same pauper he had been before. And outside the birds were singing . . . just the way they had a few minutes ago . . . when he still could have gone to Monte Carlo. Well, it was too bad, but he had no choice now but to quit, since he clearly couldn't let himself risk the small amount of money he had left . . . quit, even though there was still a quarter of an hour left. What rotten luck. In a quarter of an hour he could win five thousand gulden, the same way he had lost that much.

"Herr Leutnant?" the consul asked.

"Terribly sorry," Willi replied, his voice high and rasping; he pointed at the few miserable bills lying in front of him. His eyes almost looked like they were laughing, and on his next hand he bet ten gulden as if it were a joke. He won. Then twenty, and he won again. Fifty—and he won again. The blood rushed to his head; he could have wept with rage. Now luck was with him again—but it had come too late. Then, suddenly, a daring idea seized him, and he turned to the actor, who was standing behind him next to Fräulein Rihoscheck.

"Herr von Elrief, could you possibly be so kind as to lend me two hundred gulden?"

"I'm infinitely sorry," Elrief replied with an elegant shrug of the shoulders. "You saw yourself, Herr Leutnant, I lost everything, every last kreutzer."

It was a lie, and everyone knew it. But they all seemed to find it perfectly all right that the actor Elrief was lying to the Herr Leutnant. At that point the consul casually pushed several bank notes over to Willi, seemingly without having counted them.

"Please help yourself," he said. Dr. Tugut cleared his throat noisily.

"I'd quit now if I were you, Kasda," Wimmer said admonishingly. Willi hesitated.

"I'm not trying to talk you into anything, Herr Leutnant," Schnabel said, his hand still hovering over the money. With a sudden movement, Willi grabbed the bills and started counting them.

"It's fifteen-hundred gulden," the consul said, "you can trust me, Herr Leutnant. Would you like me to deal you a hand?"

Willi laughed. "Well, what else?"

"How much are you betting, Herr Leutnant?"

"Oh, not the whole amount," Willi exclaimed blithely, "poor people have to hold back. A thousand for now."

He and the consul picked up their cards, the consul with his usual exaggerated slowness. Willi had to take a card and got a three of spades to add to his four of diamonds. The consul turned his hand over and also had seven.

"I'd stop," First Lieutenant Wimmer warned again, and this time it sounded almost like a command.

"Seeing you're more or less even again," Dr. Tugut added.

Even! Willi thought. He calls this even. A quarter of an hour ago I was well-off, and now I have nothing—and they call that "even"! Should I tell them about Bogner? Maybe they'd understand then.

New cards lay in front of him. Seven. He would stand pat. But the consul didn't ask if he wanted a card or not, he simply turned over his own eight. A thousand lost, it droned through Willi's brain. But I'll win it back. And even if I don't, it doesn't really matter. I can no more pay back one thousand than I can two. It all amounts to the same thing now. Still ten minutes left. I could just as well win back the entire four or five thousand I had before.

"Herr Leutnant?" the consul asked. His words echoed hollowly through the room, since everyone else was silent, perceptibly silent. Wasn't anyone going to say 'I'd quit if I were you' this time? No, Willi thought, they can't bring themselves to. They know it would be stupid for me to quit now. But how much should he bet?—All he had left in front of him was a few hundred gulden. Then suddenly there was more. The consul had pushed another two thousand over to him.

"Help yourself, Herr Leutnant."

He took the money, then bet a thousand five hundred and won. Now he could pay back what he owed and still have something left over. He felt a hand on his shoulder.

"Kasda," First Lieutenant Wimmer said behind him, "that's enough."

His voice was firm, almost stern-sounding. I'm not on duty, Willi thought, when I'm off-duty I can do whatever I want with my money and my life. And he put his bet down, a modest one of only a thousand gulden, then turned over his cards: a natural eight. Schnabel continued to study his cards, agonizingly slowly, as if there were all the time in the world. And there was still time, no one was forcing them to stop at two-thirty. Not long ago they had played till five-thirty. Not long ago . . . in the beautiful, distant past. Why was everyone standing around now? It was like a dream. Ha, they were all more nervous than he was; even Fräulein Rihoscheck, who was standing across from him, her red-ribboned straw hat sitting on her upswept hair, had a strange luster in her eyes. He smiled at her. She had a face like a queen in a tragedy even though she was hardly more than a chorus girl. The consul turned his cards over. A queen. Ha, Queen Rihoscheck—and the nine of spades. Those damned spades, they were always bad luck for him. And the thousand gulden crossed the table to the consul. But that didn't matter, he still had some left. Or was he totally wiped out now? He had no idea . . . And once again a few more thousand were lying in front of him. Generous, this consul. Well, why not, he was sure he would get it back. An officer had to pay his gambling debts, after all. A person like this Herr Elrief would always remain Herr Elrief, no matter what—but an officer, unless his name happened to be Bogner . . .

"Two thousand, Herr Consul."

"Two thousand?"

"That's correct, Herr Consul."

He had seven and stood pat, but the consul had to take another card. This time he was in such a rush that he didn't dally, and drew an eight—the eight of spades—to add to his one, and that made nine, there was no doubt about it. Eight would have been enough too, of course. And two thousand-gulden bills crossed the table to the consul—and then came back again immediately. Or was it more? Three or four thousand? It was better not to check, that brought bad luck. No, the consul wouldn't cheat him, and the others were all standing there watching, after all. And since in any case he was no longer sure how much he owed, he bet two thousand again. Four of spades. He had no choice but to take another card. Six, six of spades. Now he was one point over. The consul didn't even have to try, and all he had was a three . . . And the two thousand crossed the table again—and came back again immediately. It was ridiculous. Back and forth, back and forth.—There was the church-tower bell again—half-past. But no one seemed to have heard it. The consul calmly dealt the cards. And there they all stood around the table, the whole company; only Dr. Tugut had disappeared. Ah yes, Willi had noticed him shaking his head angrily before and muttering something or other between his teeth. Apparently he couldn't bear to stand there and watch Lieutenant Kasda gambling for his life. How could a doctor have such weak nerves!

And once again new cards were lying in front of him. He made his bet—exactly how much he didn't know. A handful of bills. That was a new way of taking on fate. Eight. His luck had to change now.

Nothing changed. The consul turned his cards over and had nine. He looked around the table, then pushed the deck away from him. Willi opened his eyes wide.

"But Herr Consul—"

The consul merely raised a finger and pointed outside. "The clock just struck half-past, Herr Leutnant."

"What?" Willi exclaimed, pretending to be surprised. "But maybe we could add on another quarter of an hour, at the very most—?"

His eyes went around the circle as if hoping to find support. Everyone was silent. Herr Elrief turned his head away, looking very elegant, and lit himself a cigarette; Wimmer bit his lip, Greising whistled nervously, almost inaudibly, while the theater secretary commented insensitively, as if it were a small matter, "You really had bad luck today, Herr Leutnant."

The consul had gotten up and called the waiter over as if it were a night like any other. His part of the bill was only for two bottles of cognac, but to make things simpler he announced that he would take care of the entire amount. Greising declined and paid for his coffee and cigarettes himself. The others accepted the offer indifferently. Then the consul turned to Willi, who was still sitting in his chair. He pointed

outside again as he had before when belatedly mentioning the clock's
having struck.

"You can ride back to Vienna with me in my carriage if you like,
Herr Leutnant."

"Very kind of you," Willi replied. And at that moment it seemed
to him as if the last quarter of an hour, in fact the whole night and all
that had happened, had been declared null and void. And this was
apparently the consul's view, too. If not, how could he have invited
him to come along with him in his carriage?

"The amount you owe, Herr Leutnant," the consul added in a
friendly tone, "comes to eleven thousand gulden altogether."

"Yessir, Herr Consul," Willi replied in his military voice.

"We don't need anything in writing, I assume?" the consul said.

"No," First Lieutenant Wimmer said harshly, "we're all witnesses,
aren't we?"

The consul paid no attention either to him or to the tone of his
voice. Willi was still sitting in his chair, his legs as heavy as lead. Eleven
thousand gulden, not bad. Roughly three or four years' pay, including bonuses. Wimmer and Greising were speaking to each other in
quiet, agitated tones. Elrief said something that must have been very
funny to the theater secretary, who laughed out loud. Fräulein
Rihoscheck stood next to the consul and whispered a question to him
that he answered with a shake of his head. The waiter draped the
consul's coat, a broad, sleeveless black garment with a velvet collar,
around his shoulders; it had caught Willi's eye a short time earlier as
very elegant, though somewhat exotic. The actor Elrief quickly poured
himself a last glass of cognac from the almost empty bottle. It seemed
to Willi that everyone was avoiding speaking to him or even looking
at him. With a sudden jerk he got out of his seat. All at once Dr.
Tugut, who surprisingly enough had come back, was standing next to
him. He seemed to be searching for words at first, then finally said,
"You'll be able to come up with it by tomorrow, I hope."

"Of course, Herr Doktor," Willi replied, giving him a broad,
empty smile. He stepped up to Wimmer and Greising and held out
his hand to them.

"See you next Sunday," he said casually. They didn't answer or even nod.

"Are you ready, Herr Leutnant?" the consul asked.

"At your service."

He said goodbye to the others in a friendly, light-hearted manner, and gallantly kissed—it couldn't hurt, after all—Fräulein Rihoscheck's hand.

Everyone left. The tables and chairs on the terrace shone ghostly white; night still lay over the city and the countryside, but not a star was to be seen by now. Over toward the station the horizon was starting to show a trace of brightness. The consul's carriage was waiting outside; the driver, his feet resting on the footboard, was asleep. Schnabel woke him with a touch on the shoulder; he doffed his hat, then saw to the horses and removed their blankets. The officers put their hands to their caps once more and ambled off. The secretary, Elrief, and Fräulein Rihoscheck waited until the driver was ready. Willi thought: Why doesn't the consul stay in Baden with Fräulein Rihoscheck? What does he have her for, if he doesn't stay with her? It occurred to him that he had once heard someone tell about an older gentleman who had had a stroke in his mistress' bed, and he gave the consul a sidelong glance. He, however, appeared to be in vigorous good humor and not in the least in a dying mood; to annoy Elrief, apparently, he said goodbye to Fräulein Rihoscheck with flagrant caresses that seemed out of character for him. He invited the lieutenant to get into the carriage and take the seat on the right side; he spread a light-yellow cover with a brown plush lining over their knees, and they drove off. Herr Elrief doffed his hat once more, with an expansive gesture in the Spanish style and not without humor, much as he had in mind to do when playing the part of a grandee in some small court theater or other in Germany during the coming season. As the carriage turned and crossed the bridge, the consul looked back at the threesome, who were just strolling off arm-in-arm with Fräulein Rihoscheck in the middle. He waved a greeting, but they, engaged in lively conversation as they were, failed to notice it.

VIII

They rode through the sleeping city. Not a sound could be heard but the clip-clop of the horses' hooves.

"A little chilly," the consul remarked.

Willi didn't feel much like carrying on a conversation, but he realized that he had to say something, if only to keep the consul in a good mood.

"Yes, it's always cool towards dawn," he said, "we soldiers know all about that from having to go on maneuvers."

"About the twenty-four hours," the consul began a moment later in a kindly tone, "we don't need to be so precise about that."

Willi breathed a sigh of relief and seized the opportunity. "I was just about to ask you, Herr Consul, seeing that I don't have the whole amount available at the moment, as I'm sure you'll understand—"

"Of course not," the consul interrupted with a dismissive wave of the hand. The sound of the horses' hooves echoed as the carriage passed beneath a viaduct and drove out into the open country. "If I were to insist on the customary twenty-four hours," he went on, "you would be obliged to pay the amount you owe by two-thirty tomorrow morning at the latest. That would be inconvenient for both of us. So let's make it"—he seemed to deliberate for a moment—"twelve o'clock noon on Tuesday, if that's all right with you."

He took a calling card out of his wallet and handed it to Willi, who studied it carefully. It had already become light enough for him to read the address: Helfersdorfer Strasse 5—barely five minutes from his barracks.

"So you mean tomorrow at twelve, Herr Consul?" He felt his heart beating somewhat faster.

"Yes, Herr Leutnant, that's what I mean. Tuesday at twelve sharp. I'll be in my office from nine o'clock on."

"And if it should turn out by then, Herr Consul, that I'm not in a position to—I mean, if it isn't till sometime that afternoon, or possibly Wednesday, that I . . ."

The consul interrupted him. "Oh, that won't be a problem, Herr Leutnant, I'm sure. Since you sat down at the table to gamble, you obviously must have been prepared for the eventuality of losing, just as I was, and if you don't happen to have any private funds at your disposal, I'm sure you have every reason to believe that—your parents won't abandon you."—

"My parents are no longer living," Willi replied quickly.

"Oh," the consul said in a sympathetic tone of voice.

"My mother has been dead for eight years now, and my father died five years ago in Hungary—with the rank of lieutenant colonel."

"So your father was an officer too, was he?" The consul's voice sounded interested, almost cordial.

"Yes, he was, Herr Consul; who's to say if I would have pursued a military career myself if circumstances had been different."

"Remarkable," the consul nodded. "To think that some people's lives lie before them foreordained, so to speak, while other people don't know from one year, sometimes from one day to the next . . ." Shaking his head, he grew silent. Strangely enough, Willi found the consul's unfinished general pronouncement reassuring. And hoping to strengthen his rapport with him still further, he tried himself to find something generally valid and philosophical, as it were, to say; and he commented—a bit rashly, as immediately became apparent to him—that even so, there were instances of officers, too, being forced to change their careers.

"Yes," the consul replied, "that certainly is true, but in those cases it's usually involuntary, and they end up being—or rather, they imagine themselves to be debased, as ridiculous as that may seem, and they can't bring it upon themselves to go back to their previous professions. People like me, on the other hand—by that I mean those who haven't been restricted by any bias of birth, or social standing, or—whatever else. I myself, for example, I've been at the top and then at the bottom again at least half a dozen times. And just how far down I've been—ah, if your colleagues, those gentlemen officers, knew how far, they would hardly have sat down at the same table with me, I wouldn't imagine. I'm sure that's why they preferred, those gentlemen colleagues of yours, not to carry out any terribly thorough investigations."

Willi was silent. He felt utterly embarrassed and was undecided as to how he should react. If Wimmer or Greising had been sitting here instead of him, of course, *they* would have come up with the correct response—they could have permitted themselves to. He, Willi, had to hold his peace. He couldn't very well ask: What do you mean by 'far down,' Herr Consul, and what do you mean by 'investigations'? Oh, he could imagine well enough what the consul meant. Willi was down at the bottom himself now, as far down as a person could be, farther than he would have considered possible just a few hours before. And he was completely dependent on the kindness, the understanding, the mercy of this Herr Consul, no matter how far down he might have been at one time.

But would the consul be merciful? That was the question. Would he be willing to accept regular payments over a year—or over five years—or would he agree to another game next Sunday? He didn't look like he would—no, at the moment he didn't look at all like he would. And—if he refused to show any mercy—well, Willi would have no choice then but to go begging to Uncle Robert. Yes, Uncle Robert—he would have to! It would be extremely embarrassing, it would be absolutely horrendous, but he would have to try it. No question about it . . . And it really was unimaginable that Uncle Robert would refuse to help him, considering that his nephew's career, his existence, his life—yes, the very life of his departed sister's only son was at stake. A man who lived from his annuity income, fairly modestly of course, but nonetheless a man with investments—all he had to do was take the money out of the bank! And eleven thousand gulden certainly wasn't a tenth, not even a twentieth of his net worth. In fact, why not go ahead and ask him for twelve thousand instead of eleven—that wouldn't make a bit of difference. And then Bogner would be saved, too. This thought put Willi in an even more hopeful mood, as if the powers of heaven were under an obligation to reward him immediately for his noble sentiment. But for the time being he would consider this tack only if the consul remained unyielding. And this hadn't been established yet. Willi glanced at his companion out of the corner of his eye. The consul seemed lost in memories; his hat lying on the carriage blanket, his lips half-open as if smiling, he looked older and kinder than before. Wouldn't this be the moment—? But how should he begin? Simply openly admit that he wasn't in a position to—that he had rashly gotten himself into a situation—that he had lost his head, that for a quarter of an hour he had been, to all intents and purposes, of unsound mind? Furthermore, would he ever have dared to go that far, would he have lost control to the extent he had if the Herr Consul hadn't—yes, it was all right for him to point this out—if the Herr Consul hadn't put the money at his disposal, hadn't pushed it across the table to him—completely unsolicited, without the slightest hint on Willi's part—if he hadn't, in a sense, though certainly in the kindliest way, forced it on him?

"Isn't it marvelous," the consul remarked, "to be riding along in a carriage like this so early in the morning?"

"Wonderful," the lieutenant replied dutifully.

"It's a shame, though," the consul added, "that we always think we have to pay the price of staying up all night to do it, whether it's been a night spent gambling or doing something even more foolish."

"Well, as far as I'm concerned," the lieutenant commented quickly, "it's not at all that unusual for me to be up and about this early even without having stayed up all night. The day before yesterday, for example, I was out in the barracks courtyard with my company at three-thirty. We had maneuvers in the Prater.[8] I didn't ride there in a carriage, of course."

The consul laughed heartily, which gave Willi a good feeling, even though it had sounded somewhat artificial.

"Yes, I've been involved in similar things myself a few times," the consul said. "Not as an officer, of course, not even in the volunteer corps—I never got that far. Just imagine, Herr Leutnant, I served my three years back then and never made it past corporal. I'm not an educated man, or wasn't, at least. I've filled in some of the gaps in the course of time—travel offers good opportunities for that."

"You've seen a lot of the world, Herr Consul," Willi said obligingly.

"I can certainly make that claim. I've been almost everywhere—except, of all places, Ecuador—the country I'm assigned to as consul.

But I'm intending to relinquish my title in the near future and take a trip there." He laughed and Willi joined in with some effort.

They drove through a run-down village strung out along the road, between gray one-story houses in poor repair. In a small front garden, an old man in shirt sleeves stood watering his plants; a young woman in a rather tattered dress was coming out of a dairy store, already open at that early hour, carrying a full jug of milk. In a way Willi felt envious of both of them, the old man watering his garden, the woman bringing home milk for her husband and children. He knew that they both felt more at peace inside than he did. The carriage rolled past a tall, featureless building in front of which a soldier in a prison guard's uniform was marching back and forth; he saluted the lieutenant, who returned the greeting more politely than he usually did in the case of lower-ranking soldiers. The consul's glance, a mixture of contempt and recollection, rested on the building, causing Willi to wonder. But what good would it do him now to know that the consul's past had in all likelihood not been exactly spotless? Gambling debts were gambling debts, and even a previously convicted criminal had the right to demand payment on them. Time was running out, the horses were galloping faster and faster; in an hour, in half an hour they would be in Vienna—and then what?

"And characters like this Lieutenant Greising," the consul said, as if completing some inner train of thought, "are allowed to run around free."

So it's true, Willi thought, the man's been in prison. But that wasn't what mattered now—the consul's remark amounted to an unequivocal insult of a fellow officer in that officer's absence. Could he simply let it pass as if he hadn't heard it at all, or as if he were admitting that it was justified?

"I must ask you, Herr Consul, not to make comments about my fellow officer Greising."

The consul gestured disdainfully with his hand. "I find it really remarkable," he said, "that a group of men who adhere so strictly to their code of honor can permit themselves to tolerate in their number the presence of a person who, in full knowledge of what he's doing, endangers the health of another person—an ignorant, inexperienced girl, for example—exposing her to disease, possibly killing her—"

"We're not informed about that," Willi replied somewhat hoarsely, "at least I'm not myself."

"Ah, Herr Leutnant, I don't mean in the least to accuse you of anything. You're not personally responsible for these things, and there's nothing you can do to change them."

Willi tried in vain to come up with a response. He considered whether he wasn't duty-bound to bring the consul's remark to his comrade's attention—or should he first talk privately with Dr. Tugut about what had happened? Or ask First Lieutenant Wimmer for advice? But what did he care about any of this?! *He* was the one who was at issue now, he, Willi, it was his position—his career—his life! Just ahead, in the first rays of the sun, the column of the *Spinnerin am Kreuz*9 was coming into sight. And he still hadn't said a single word that might help him obtain at least an extension, nothing more than a short extension. He felt his companion gently touch his arm.

"I'm sorry, Herr Leutnant, let's drop the subject; when it comes right down to it, it doesn't bother me if Lieutenant Greising or anyone else . . . and all the less so, considering that I will hardly have the pleasure of sitting at the same table as those gentlemen again."

Willi started. "I don't quite understand, Herr Consul."

"Well, I'm taking a trip, you see," the consul replied coolly.

"Soon?"

"Yes—the day after tomorrow. Or I should say, tomorrow, Tuesday."

"Will you be gone for any length of time, Herr Consul?"

"Oh, I suppose something like . . . three to—thirty years."

The main road was already fairly busy with carts and wagons carrying goods and produce into the city. Looking down, Willi saw the glint of the gold buttons on his jacket in the rays of the rising sun.

"Is this trip a recent decision, Herr Consul?" he asked.

"Oh no, not at all, Herr Leutnant, I've been planning it for a long time. I'm going to America—not Ecuador for the time being—I'm going to Baltimore, to be exact; my family lives there and I have a business there, too—which I haven't been able to take in hand personally for eight years, of course."

He has a family, Willi thought. And how about Fräulein Rihoscheck? Does she even know he's leaving? But what do I care about that! There isn't much time left. My neck is at stake. Unconsciously he put his hand to his throat.

"It's really too bad you're leaving so soon, Herr Consul," he said helplessly. "I was actually . . . I was fairly sure"—his voice took on a lighter, almost jocular tone—"that I could count on your granting me a return match next Sunday."

The consul shrugged his shoulders as if indicating that the matter was long since over and done with. What should I do, Willi thought, what should I say? Should I come right out and—beg him? What can a few thousand gulden mean to him? He has a family in America—and Fräulein Rihoscheck—. He has a business over there—what difference can a few thousand gulden make to him?! And for me it's a matter of life and death.

They drove under the viaduct and on into the city. A train was just chuffing out of the South Station. People going to Baden, Willi thought, and beyond that, to Klagenfurt, to Trieste—and from there possibly across the sea to some other part of the world . . . And he envied all of them.

"Where can I drop you off, Herr Leutnant?"

"Oh, don't go to any trouble," Willi replied, "anywhere that's convenient for you. I live in the Alserstrasse barracks."

"I'll take you right up to the gate, Herr Leutnant." He told the driver where to go.

"Thank you so much, Herr Consul, you really wouldn't have had to—"

The houses all still lay in sleep. The streetcar tracks, as yet untouched by the day's traffic, ran smooth and shining alongside the carriage. The consul looked at his watch. "He made good time, an hour and ten minutes. Do you have maneuvers today, Herr Leutnant?"

"No," Willi answered, "today I give training sessions."

"Well, you'll still be able to get a little sleep, then."

"Definitely, Herr Consul, though actually I think I'll give myself the day off—report in sick." The consul nodded and said nothing. "So you're leaving Wednesday, Herr Consul?"

"No, Herr Leutnant, *tomorrow, Tuesday evening*," the consul replied, emphasizing each word.

"Herr Consul—I have to tell you honestly—it's extremely embarrassing for me, but I'm very much afraid that it will be absolutely impossible for me, on such short notice—by tomorrow noon . . ." The consul was silent. He seemed hardly to be listening. "If you could grant me the special kindness, Herr Consul, of allowing me an extension?"—The consul shook his head. Willi spoke on.

"Not for very long, of course, I could give you a written certification, or make out a promissory note, and I would commit myself on my honor that within two weeks—I know there must be a way . . ."

The consul simply kept shaking his head mechanically without showing the least sign of irritation.

"Herr Consul," Willi began again, unable to keep the pleading tone out of his voice, "Herr Consul, my uncle, Robert Wilram, maybe you've heard the name?" The consul continued to shake his head. "Well, I'm not quite sure that my uncle—who I can rely on completely, by the way—I'm not sure that he would have enough on hand at the moment. But there's no question that within a few days . . . he's a well-to-do man, my mother's only brother, he's independently wealthy."—And suddenly, his voice cracking strangely as if he were laughing, he added, "It's really terrible that you're leaving for America so soon, Herr Consul."

"My travel plans, Herr Leutnant," the consul replied calmly, "are absolutely no concern of yours. Debts of honor, as everyone knows, are to be paid back within twenty-four hours."

"I'm aware of that, Herr Consul, I'm aware of that. But still, it can happen at times—there have been other officers in similar situations who . . . It's completely in your hands, Herr Consul, if you could accept a promissory note for the time being, or my word of honor, until—until next Sunday, at least."

"I will not accept that, Herr Leutnant. Tomorrow, Tuesday at noon, is the final deadline . . . Otherwise—your regimental commander will be notified."

The carriage drove along the Ring past the Municipal Gardens, where trees soared in luxuriant green above the gilded bars. It was an exquisite spring morning, with almost no one on the streets as yet. One lone young woman, very elegant in a sand-colored high-necked coat, walked quickly, dutifully, along the fence with her small dog; she cast an indifferent glance at the consul, who turned around to look at her despite his wife in America and Fräulein Rihoscheck in Baden, who in any case was more the actor Elrief's girl friend. What do I care about Herr Elrief, Willi thought, and what do I care about Fräulein Rihoscheck? Though come to think of it, if I had been nicer to her, who knows, maybe she would have put in a good word for me. —And for a moment he seriously considered going straight back to Baden and asking her to speak to the consul on his behalf. Speak to the consul? She would laugh in his face. She knew him, after all, she knew what he was like . . . The only possible salvation remaining was Uncle Robert. That much was certain. Failing this, there was no choice but a bullet in the brain. A man simply had to be clear about these things.

The regular sound of marching feet coming toward them reached his ears. Didn't the Ninety-Eighth have a drill today? Out near the *Bisamberg*?[10] He would have been embarrassed, sitting in an open carriage as he was, to encounter his comrades at the head of their companies now. But it wasn't soldiers approaching, it was a formation of boys, apparently schoolchildren on an outing with their teacher. The teacher, young and pale, gazed with instinctive respect at the two gentlemen riding past him in their carriage at this early hour. It would never have occurred to Willi that he might ever experience a moment in which he would find even a poor schoolteacher enviable. The carriage overtook an early-morning streetcar in which a few men in workers' clothing and an old woman were sitting. A street-cleaning vehicle came toward them; on it was an unkempt man with rolled-up sleeves who swung a hose rhythmically back and forth like a jump rope, wetting down the street with streams of water. Two nuns, their heads lowered, crossed the roadway in the direction of the *Votivkirche*,[11] whose slender pale-gray towers rose toward the heavens. On a bench beneath a tree full of white blossoms sat a young girl wearing dusty shoes; she was holding her straw hat in her lap and smiling as if she had just had some pleasurable experience. A covered carriage with lowered curtains raced by. A fat old woman stood at the tall window of a coffee house rubbing away with a cleaning rag on a pole. All these people and things would normally have escaped Willi's notice, but now they presented themselves to his overwrought senses in almost painfully sharp contours. And all the while the man sitting next to him in the carriage seemed to have slipped out of his mind. Willi cast a cautious glance in his direction. The consul sat leaning back, his hat on the blanket in front of him and his eyes closed. How gentle, how kind he looked! And this man would be—the cause of his death? He really was asleep—or was he putting on an act? Don't worry at all, Herr Consul, I won't trouble you any longer. You'll have your money at twelve o'clock on Tuesday. Or maybe not. But on no account . . . The carriage came to a halt at the barracks gate, and immediately the consul woke up—or at least acted as if he had just woken up. He even rubbed his eyes, a somewhat exaggerated gesture after having slept for two-and-a-half minutes. The guard at the gate saluted. Willi leapt out of the carriage nimbly without touching the running board and smiled at the consul. He even gave the driver a tip, not too much, not too little, in the manner of a gentleman who, when it came right down to it, didn't really care whether he had won or lost at the card table.

"Thank you very much, Herr Consul—and goodbye."

The consul stretched his hand out of the carriage and pulled Willi gently closer, as if he had something to confide in him that not everyone needed to hear.

"I advise you, Herr Leutnant," he said in an almost fatherly tone, "don't take this matter lightly, if you place any value on . . . remaining an officer. Tomorrow, Tuesday, twelve o'clock." Then he added in a normal tone of voice, "Well, goodbye, Herr Leutnant."

Willi smiled obligingly and touched his hand to his cap. The carriage turned around and drove off.

IX

The bell from the Alserstrasse church tolled the hour: quarter to five. The broad gate opened and a company of soldiers from the Ninety-Eighth marched through, turning their heads smartly toward Willi as they passed him. He responded by putting his hand to his cap every so often.

"Where to, Wieseltier?" he said condescendingly to the cadet in charge, who was the last one out the gate.

"Fire department grounds, Herr Leutnant." Willi nodded as if giving his approval and looked after the soldiers for a while without seeing them. The guard stood there still saluting as Willi stepped inside the gate, then closed it behind him.

From the far end of the courtyard came the barking sounds of shouted commands. A troop of recruits was drilling rifle positions under the direction of a corporal. The courtyard stretched out before him, sunlit and austere; here and there a few trees rose up toward the sky. Willi continued his way along the wall, and as he looked up at his room, his orderly appeared in the window, stood at attention for a moment, and then disappeared. Willi hurried up the stairs. Before he was even past the vestibule, where the orderly was in the process of lighting a fire under the coffee pot, he had removed his collar and unbuttoned his jacket.

"Herr Leutnant, beg to report, sir, coffee will be ready right away."

"Fine," Willi said. He stepped into his room and closed the door behind him, then took off his jacket and threw himself onto the bed in his pants and shoes.

I can't possibly go to Uncle Robert's before nine, he thought. Might as well ask him for twelve thousand right away, then Bogner can have his thousand, too, if he hasn't shot himself in the meantime. Although, who's to say, maybe he really did win on a horse race and can help *me* out of the mess I'm in. Ha, eleven, twelve thousand—not so easy to win on a parimutuel bet.

His eyes fell shut. Nine of spades—ace of diamonds—king of hearts—eight of spades—ace of spades—jack of clubs—four of diamonds—the cards went dancing past him. His orderly brought him his coffee, moved the table closer to his bed, and poured him a cup; Willi raised himself on one arm and took a swallow.

"Should I pull off your boots, Herr Leutnant?"

Willi shook his head. "It's not worth the effort now."

"Should I wake you later, Herr Leutnant?" Willi looked at him, uncomprehending. "Beg to report, sir, training class at seven."

Willi shook his head again. "I'm going on sick call, I have to see a doctor. Let the captain know . . . sick call, understand? I'll send the form over later. I've got a doctor's appointment at nine, it's about my eyes. Have them ask Cadet Brill to stand in for me. Dismissed.— Wait!"

"Yessir, Herr Leutnant?"

"Go over to the Alserstrasse church at quarter to eight. The gentleman who was here yesterday morning, that's right, First Lieutenant Bogner, he'll be waiting there. Tell him I'm really sorry, but unfortunately I wasn't able to do anything. Understood?"

"Yessir, Herr Leutnant."

"Repeat."

"The Herr Leutnant says he's sorry, but he wasn't able to do anything."

"*Unfortunately* I wasn't able to do anything.—Wait. Tell him that if tonight or tomorrow morning still isn't too late"—he stopped suddenly. "No, never mind that. Unfortunately I wasn't able to do anything, that's all. Understood?"

"Yessir, Herr Leutnant."

"And when you come back from the church, knock on my door just in case. And shut the window now before you go."

The orderly did as commanded, cutting off a harsh shouted command from the courtyard. When Joseph had shut the door behind him, Willi stretched out on his bed again and shut his eyes. Ace of diamonds—seven of clubs—king of hearts—eight of diamonds—nine of spades—ten of spades—queen of hearts—damn her, Willi thought. The queen of hearts was actually Fräulein Kessner. If I hadn't kept on standing there by their table none of this awful business would have happened. Nine of clubs—six of spades—five of spades—king of spades—king of hearts—king of clubs—Don't take this lightly, Herr Leutnant.—He can go to hell! He'll get his money all right, but then I'll send two friends to see him—but I can't do that, he's not even qualified to fight a duel—king of hearts—jack of spades—queen of diamonds—nine of diamonds—ace of spades—they kept dancing by, ace of diamonds, ace of hearts . . . pointlessly, incessantly, making his eyes hurt under their closed lids. There couldn't possibly be as many decks of cards in the whole world as went rushing past him in the course of this hour.

A knock on the door woke him with a start, and even now the cards continued to rush by his open eyes. It was his orderly.

"Herr Leutnant, sir, beg to report, the First Lieutenant thanks you very much for all your efforts and sends his most cordial greetings."

"Hm. Didn't he—didn't he have anything else to say?"

"No sir, Herr Leutnant, the First Lieutenant just turned around and walked away."

"Hm—just turned around and . . . Did you report me sick?"

"Yessir, Herr Leutnant." Willi noticed that the orderly was grinning. "What's so damn funny?"

"Beg to report, sir, the captain—"

"What about him? What did the captain say?"

Still grinning, the orderly went on, "So the Herr Leutnant has to go to the eye doctor, the captain says, I'll bet he was looking at some girl too hard."

Noticing that Willi wasn't smiling, the orderly suddenly looked worried and added quickly, "That's what the captain said, beg to report, sir."

"Dismissed," Willi said.

As he got ready to leave, he thought through all sorts of different phrases and practiced in his mind the tone of voice he would use in trying to win over his uncle. It had been two years since he had last seen him. At this moment he was barely able to remember what he was like, or even what he looked like; different visual images popped in and out of his mind, with different facial expressions, different mannerisms, different ways of speaking, and he had no way of knowing beforehand which one he would encounter today.

From his boyhood days he remembered his uncle as a slim man, always very carefully dressed and still young—though even at that time he had seemed to him, twenty-five years older as he was, to be very much an adult. Whenever Robert Wilram came for a visit to the Hungarian town where his brother-in-law, then still Major Kasda, was stationed, it was always just for a few days. Willi's father and uncle didn't get along particularly well, and Willi even had a dim recollection of an argument between his parents about his uncle that had ended with his mother leaving the room in tears. They had almost never said anything about what his uncle did for a living, though Willi seemed to recall that Robert Wilram had been a civil servant and had given up his job when his wife had died at an early age. He had inherited a sizable fortune from her and lived independently from then on, spending considerable time traveling to different parts of the world. The news of his sister's death had reached him in Italy, so that he hadn't been able to get back in time for the funeral; Willi had never forgotten the way Uncle Robert had stood with him at the grave, dry-eyed and yet with an expression of dismal solemnity as he looked down at the barely withered wreaths.

Soon after that they had left the town together, Robert Wilram for Vienna and Willi to return to his cadet school in Wiener-Neustadt. From this point on he visited his uncle from time to time on Sundays and holidays, when they would go to the theater or have a meal in a restaurant together. Later, after Willi's assignment to a regiment in Vienna and his father's sudden death, his uncle voluntarily established a monthly allowance for him. The young officer received the payments at a set time each month, with a bank assuming this responsibility whenever his uncle was off traveling. On one of his trips Robert Wilram had become seriously ill and returned home noticeably older, and though Willi continued to receive his monthly allowance regularly, there began to be frequent interruptions of shorter or longer duration in the personal contact between the two, just as the stages of Wilram's life in general seemed to fluctuate in strange ways. At times he was outwardly cheerful and convivial, taking his nephew, as in former days, to restaurants, theater performances, and even to entertainments of a more dubious nature, usually accompanied by some vivacious young lady or other whom Willi generally never saw again. Then weeks would go by in which his uncle seemed to withdraw completely from the world, and if Willi was allowed in the door at all, he would find himself in the presence of a solemn, taciturn man aged beyond his years, who, dressed in a dark-brown, cassock-like robe and wearing the expression of a woebegone actor, paced back and forth in his gloomy, high-vaulted room or sat at his desk reading or working on something by artificial light. On these occasions their conversation was labored and halting, as if they had become strangers to each other. Only once, when they happened to be talking about a comrade of Willi's who had recently taken his life over an unfortunate love affair, did Robert Wilram open a drawer in his desk, take out a number of hand-written pages, and begin to read aloud, to Willi's great surprise, a series of philosophical observations on death and immortality, along with occasional morose and disparaging remarks about women. As he droned on, he seemed completely unaware of the presence of his nephew, who listened to him with some embarrassment and more than a touch of boredom. Just as Willi was trying unsuccessfully to suppress a yawn, his uncle happened to look up from his manuscript; curling his lips into an empty smile, he folded the pages, put them back in the drawer, and abruptly started to talk about other matters that might be of more interest to a young officer. Even after this rather infelicitous encounter, though, they still spent a number of enjoyable evenings together as in former times, or went for an occasional afternoon stroll on holidays if the weather was nice.

Then one day, when Willi was supposed to stop by his uncle's apartment to pick him up, a note came telling him not to come, and shortly after this a letter in which Wilram stated that because of urgent business matters he unfortunately had to ask Willi not to pay him any further visits for the time being. Soon his monthly allowance payments stopped as well. A polite written reminder was not answered, and a second one fared no better; a third note elicited the response that "due to a fundamental change in his circumstances" Robert Wilram regretfully found himself compelled to discontinue any further financial support "even of close family members." Willi tried to speak to his uncle in person. The first two times he wasn't let in, and on the third attempt he caught sight of his uncle, who had just had the servant tell him he wasn't there, flit quickly past the door. This made Willi finally realize that it was pointless for him to make any further efforts, and so he had no choice but to limit his expenditures as much as possible. The small inheritance from his mother that had once been enough to make ends meet was just about gone; still, given his nature, he had never been one to have serious concerns about the future—until now, when all at once, from one day to the next—from one hour to the next, really—the face of care confronted him in its most threatening form.

Feeling dejected but not hopeless, he wound his way down through the perpetual semidarkness of the officers' stairway and at first did not recognize the man who, his arms stretched out in front of him, stood there blocking the way.

"Willi!" It was Bogner. What could he want now?

"What are you doing here? You heard, didn't you? Didn't Joseph tell you?"

"Yes, yes, he told me. But I wanted to let you know—just in case there's still any chance—that the audit has been postponed till tomorrow."

Willi shrugged his shoulders. The news really wasn't of any great interest to him.

"It's been postponed, don't you understand?"

"What's hard to understand about that?" He walked down another step.

Bogner wouldn't let him go any farther. "Don't you see, it's the hand of fate!" he exclaimed. "This could mean my salvation. Don't get angry, Kasda, if I ask you again—I mean, I know you didn't have any luck yesterday—"

"No, I didn't," Willi said with effort, "I definitely did not have any luck." He laughed abruptly. "I lost everything—and then some." His self-control slipping away, as if the man he stood facing was the actual and only cause of his misfortune, he added, "Eleven thousand gulden, man, eleven thousand gulden!"

"Good Lord, of course that's . . . what are you planning on . . ." He broke off, and their glances met. Bogner's eyes brightened. "So you'll be going to see your uncle after all?"

Willi bit his lip. How pushy can you get, he thought, the man has no shame! And he came close to saying it out loud.

"I'm sorry—it's none of my business—I should keep my mouth shut, especially since it's partly my fault in a way—but if you're going to try him anyway, Kasda—whether it's twelve or eleven thousand, that shouldn't matter to your uncle one way or the other."

"Don't be ridiculous, Bogner. I have no more chance of getting eleven thousand than I do twelve."

"But you're going to talk to him, Kasda!"

"I don't know—"

"Willi—"

"I don't know," he repeated impatiently. "Maybe—or maybe not . . . I'll see you later." He pushed him aside and rushed down the stairs.

Twelve or eleven, that was hardly an insignificant difference. *Everything* could depend on that! —He heard a buzzing inside his head: eleven, twelve—eleven, twelve—eleven, twelve! Well, he didn't have to decide until he was face-to-face with his uncle in any case, he would just follow his momentary impulse. But it had been stupid of him to mention the amount to Bogner, or to let him stop him on the stairs at all. What did he care about him? Fellow officers, fine—but they had never really been *friends*! And now his own fate was supposed to become inextricably intertwined with Bogner's? Ridiculous. Eleven, twelve—eleven, twelve. Twelve, maybe that sounded better than eleven, maybe it would bring him luck . . . maybe a miracle would happen— precisely if he asked for twelve. And all the way from the Alserstrasse barracks to the old apartment building in the narrow street behind

St. Stephan's Cathedral, he kept debating with himself whether he should ask his uncle for eleven or twelve thousand gulden—as if the success of his enterprise—of his *life*, in the final analysis—depended on it.

An older woman he hadn't seen before opened the door when he rang the bell. Willi gave his name. His uncle—yes, he was in fact Herr Wilram's nephew—his uncle would, he hoped, forgive the intrusion, but it was a very urgent matter, and he definitely would not disturb him for long. The woman was hesitant at first, then left and came back again surprisingly quickly with a friendlier expression on her face, and Willi, heaving a sigh of relief, was ushered in immediately.

X

Uncle Robert was standing at one of the room's two high windows; instead of the cassock-like robe Willi had expected to find him in, he was wearing a rather shabby, though well-tailored light-colored summer suit and patent leather shoes that had lost their shine. With a sweeping, though fatigued gesture, he waved to his nephew.

"Hello, Willi. Nice of you to stop by and see your old uncle again. I thought you'd completely forgotten about me."

The room was unchanged. Books and papers lay on the desk, the green curtain in front of the bookcase was drawn back on one side, revealing several old leather-bound volumes; the Persian carpet still hung above the sofa, and a few embroidered cushions lay on it. Two yellowed engravings of Italian landscapes hung on the wall, along with family portraits in dull gold frames; the photograph of Uncle Robert's sister, recognizable to Willi from the back by its size and frame, occupied its customary place on his desk.

"Won't you have a seat?" Robert Wilram asked.

Willi stood there erect, his cap in his hand and his saber hanging from its belt, as if he were about to deliver a service report. In a tone not quite in keeping with his posture, he began, "To tell you the truth, Uncle Robert, I probably wouldn't have come today either, if I didn't—well, to be brief, I'm here because of a very, very serious matter."

"You don't say," Robert Wilram remarked in a friendly voice, but without sounding particularly interested.

"For *me* at least it's serious. To come right to the point, no beating around the bush, I did something foolish, something really foolish. I—was gambling, and I gambled away more money than I had to my name."

"Hm, sounds like a little more than just foolish," his uncle said.

"It was thoughtless," Willi agreed, "unforgivably thoughtless. I'm not trying to gloss it over. But the situation unfortunately is this: If I don't pay back what I owe by seven o'clock tonight, then I'm—I'm simply—" Looking like a pouting child, he shrugged his shoulders and stopped speaking.

Robert Wilram shook his head sympathetically but said nothing in reply. The silence in the room was unbearable, and Willi began to speak again immediately. He gave a hurried report of what had happened the day before. He had gone out to Baden to visit a sick fellow officer, had met other officers there—good acquaintances he'd known for a long time—and had let them entice him into playing cards; the game had started out perfectly respectably, but in the course of the evening and through no fault of his own it had degenerated into a wild gambling spree. Willi preferred not to say who the players had been, with the exception of the one he had ended up owing the money to, a wholesale merchant and consul to a country in South America, a certain Herr Schnabel, who unfortunately was leaving for the United States early the next morning and had threatened to report him to his regimental commander if the money wasn't paid that very evening.

"You know what that would mean, Uncle Robert," Willi concluded. Feeling suddenly tired, he sat down on the sofa.

His uncle looked beyond Willi toward the wall. "And how large an amount is involved?" he asked him, his voice still friendly.

Willi was of two minds again. His first impulse was to add on the thousand gulden for Bogner, then suddenly he was convinced that precisely that small additional amount could jeopardize the outcome, and so he ended up saying only how much he himself owed.

"Eleven thousand gulden," Robert Wilram repeated, shaking his head. It almost sounded like there was a trace of admiration in his voice.

"I know," Willi replied quickly, "it's a small fortune. And I'm not trying in any way to justify what I did. It was an act of despicable thoughtlessness—the first one in my life, I believe, and definitely the last one. And all I can do, Uncle Robert, is to swear to you that I will never touch another card for as long as I live, and that I'll try my best to prove my eternal gratitude to you by leading an absolutely respectable life—I'm even prepared—in fact I solemnly declare that I will renounce once and for all any later claims that might arise as a result of our blood relationship, if only you could, Uncle Robert, this one time, just this one time—"

Though he had shown no signs of emotion up to this point, a certain disquiet finally seemed to come over Robert Wilram. Having already raised one disapproving hand, he now enlisted the aid of the other, as if hoping to silence his nephew by this dramatic gesture, and interrupted him in an unusually high-pitched, almost shrill tone of voice.

"I'm very sorry, I'm truly sorry, no matter how much I might want to, I can't help you."

Willi opened his mouth again to respond. "I *absolutely* cannot help you," Uncle Robert added. "Whatever else you might say would be of no avail, so you needn't bother trying." He turned toward the window.

Willi was at first dumbfounded, then, reflecting for a moment and deciding that he couldn't have hoped to vanquish his uncle after only one assault in any case, he began anew.

"I have no delusions about this, Uncle Robert, I know that my request is disgraceful, completely and utterly disgraceful; and I would never, never have dared to approach you about this if there had been even the slightest possibility of coming up with the money some other way. Try to put yourself in my position, Uncle Robert. Everything, *everything* is at stake for me, not just my career as an officer. What other career could I possibly take up? This is all I've ever been trained for, there's nothing else I know anything about. And how could I, as

an officer with a dishonorable discharge—only yesterday I happened
to run into a former fellow officer who's also—no, absolutely not, I'd
sooner put a bullet through my brain. Don't be angry with me, Uncle
Robert. If you could only imagine what this is like for me. My father
was an officer, my grandfather died a lieutenant commander. For the
love of God, I simply can't end up this way! That would be too severe
a punishment for pulling a thoughtless stunt the way I did. I don't
gamble regularly, you know that. I've never owed anyone money. Not
even last year, when I was in a pretty bad way at times. And I've never
allowed myself to be tempted to borrow, even though people have
made direct offers. But an amount like this—good Lord! I don't think
I could ever come up with that kind of money, not even if I were to
pay some exorbitant interest rate. And even then, what would be the
point? In six months I would owe twice as much, in a year, ten times
as much, and—"

"That's enough, Willi," Wilram interrupted finally, his voice even
shriller than before. "It's simply that I *can't* help you—I wish I could,
but I can't. Do you understand? I have nothing myself; as you see me
now before you, I don't have a hundred gulden to my name. Look,
look . . ."

He tore open one drawer after another, the desk drawers, then
the drawers of his chest, as if to prove the truth of what he had said by
showing that they contained nothing but papers, boxes, underwear,
all sorts of odds and ends, but no bills or coins. Then he threw his
wallet onto the desk for good measure.

"You can look for yourself, Willi, and if you find more than a
hundred gulden, you can think—whatever you like about me."

Suddenly he sank into the chair in front of his desk and let his
arms fall onto it heavily, sending several sheets of paper fluttering to
the floor. Willi dutifully picked them up, then let his glance wander
around the room, as if it would be possible to detect something that
was different, something that would reflect the incomprehensible
change in his uncle's circumstances. But everything looked exactly as
it had two or three years before. And he began to wonder if what his
uncle had claimed was really true. Wasn't it possible that this peculiar
old man, who had abandoned him so unexpectedly, so suddenly two

years ago, was trying to protect himself against any further pleading requests from his nephew by telling him a lie and putting on an act to make it seem more plausible? After all, he lived in a well-maintained apartment in the old city with a housekeeper of sorts, his bookcase was filled as always with beautiful leather-bound volumes, all his pictures were still hanging on the walls in their dull-gold frames—and the owner of all these things was supposed to have suddenly become a beggar? What could have happened to all his wealth in the course of these last two or three years? Willi didn't believe him. He didn't have the slightest reason to believe him, and even less reason simply to give up, since there was nothing more he could lose in any case. And so he decided to make one last attempt, though it turned out to be not as bold as he had planned it to be: all at once, in fact, to his own surprise and great shame, he found himself standing before his uncle, pleading with folded hands.

"My life is at stake, Uncle Robert, believe me, my life is at stake. I'm begging you, I'm—"

His voice broke, and on a sudden impulse he picked up the photograph of his mother and held it up imploringly to his uncle, who gently took it out of his hand and, frowning slightly, calmly put it back in its place.

"Your mother has nothing to do with this," he said softly and without a trace of anger. "She can't help you—any more than she can me. If I didn't *want* to help you, Willi, I obviously wouldn't need to make any excuses; I don't accept obligations, and especially not in a situation like this. In any case, in my opinion it's possible to be or to become a completely respectable person in civilian life as well. Honor is something people lose in a different way. But you can't have reached the point yet where you can understand that. Which is why I'm going to tell you once again: If I had the money, believe me, I'd give it to you. But I don't have it. I don't have *anything*. My wealth is gone. All I have now are annuities. That's right, on the first and fifteenth of every month I receive so and so much, and today"—with a gloomy smile he pointed at his wallet—"today is the twenty-seventh." And noticing a sudden glimmer of hope in Willi's eyes, he added quickly, "Ah, you're thinking that I could take out a loan on my annuities. But you see, my dear Willi, whether such a thing is possible depends on the *source* of the annuities and under what conditions they were acquired."

"But still, Uncle Robert, maybe it would be possible, maybe the two of us could—"

Robert Wilram interrupted him vehemently. "Nothing is possible, absolutely nothing." Then he added in a muffled, despairing voice, "I can't help you, believe me, I can't," and turned away.

"Well," Willi replied after a moment's reflection, "in that case all I can do is apologize to you for—goodbye, Uncle Robert." He had already reached the door when his uncle's voice made him stop in his tracks. "Willi, come over here, I don't want you to think that I'm . . . I might as well tell you. To come right to the point, I've signed over all my assets—they didn't amount to that much any more—to my wife."

"You're married?!" Willi exclaimed in astonishment, and new hope glowed in his eyes. "Well then, if your wife has the money, there would have to be a way—I mean, if you tell your wife that it's a matter of—"

Robert Wilram interrupted him with an impatient wave of the hand. "I will tell her *nothing*. Stop pressuring me. It would all be in vain." He grew silent.

But Willi, not of a mind to give up this last bit of hope that had appeared on the horizon, was determined to keep the conversation going. "I suppose that your—your wife doesn't live in Vienna?"

"Oh yes, she lives in Vienna, just not with me, as you can see." He paced back and forth in the room a few times, then said with a bitter laugh, "Oh, I've lost more than a sword belt, and I'm still alive. Yes, Willi—" He broke off suddenly, then started to speak again. "I signed my assets over to her a year and a half ago—voluntarily. And I actually did it more for my sake than hers . . . I'm not very adept financially, whereas she—she's very thrifty, I have to grant her that; she has a good business sense, too, and she's invested the money more sensibly than I would ever have been able to. She put it into some capital enterprises or other—I'm not fully acquainted with all the details, and I wouldn't understand them in any case. The annuity that's paid to me amounts to twelve-and-a-half percent; that's not bad, I can't complain . . . Twelve-and-a-half percent. But not a kreutzer more. The attempts I made at first to get an occasional advance were to no avail. In fact, I had no choice but to stop asking after the second try, because I didn't get to see her then for six weeks afterwards, and she swore that if I ever approached her for money again it would be the last time I'd ever see her. That was the one thing I just couldn't risk. I need her, Willi, I couldn't go on existing without her. Once a week I get to see her, once a week she comes to visit me. She keeps to our agreement to the letter—she's the most orderly person you can imagine. She's never missed once, and the money has always gotten here on time, too, every first and fifteenth of the month. And every summer we take a trip somewhere to the countryside and spend a whole two weeks together. That's in our contract, too. But aside from that, her time is her own."

"And—you don't ever visit her yourself, Uncle Robert?" Willi asked, feeling somewhat embarrassed.

"Oh, of course I do, Willi. On Christmas Day, Easter Sunday, and the Monday after Pentecost. That's the eighth of June this year."

"And if you were to—forgive me for asking, Uncle Robert, but if you happened to get the idea of stopping by some other day—after all, you're her husband, Uncle Robert, and who's to say that she wouldn't feel flattered if you—"

"I can't risk it," Robert Wilram interrupted. "On one occasion— seeing I've already told you everything anyway—one evening it was, I walked up and down her street, by the building where she lives, for two hours—"

"And what happened?"

"She kept out of sight. But the next day a letter from her came, and the only thing it said was that if I took it into my head even one more time to go strolling around in front of her apartment building, I'd never see her again in my life. That's the way it is, Willi. And I know for a fact—even if my own life were on the line, she would sooner see me destitute than give me even a tenth of what you're asking for outside the usual time. I'm telling you, you have a much better chance of getting this consul of yours to show some consideration than I would ever have of softening the heart of my so-called wife."

"Was she—was she always like this?" Willi asked.

"What difference does it make?" Robert Wilram replied impatiently. "Even if I had foreseen all that would happen it wouldn't have helped me. I was her slave from the first moment on, or at least from the first night on—and that was our wedding night."

"Of course," Willi said quietly.

Robert Wilram gave a sudden laugh. "Ah, you're thinking that she was a respectable young lady from a solid middle-class family? Wrong, my dear Willi. She was a whore. And who knows if she still isn't today—for other men."

Willi felt obliged to make a gesture to show that he doubted this; and he really did have his doubts, because after all that his uncle had said he found it impossible to imagine his wife as an appealing young woman. He had pictured her the whole time as a tastelessly dressed older woman, lean and sallow and with a pointed nose, and the thought passed his mind that his uncle might have wanted to give vent to his indignation at her undignified treatment of him by insulting her unjustly. But Robert Wilram cut him off before he could begin to speak again.

"All right, 'whore' is maybe going too far—she was just a flower girl back then. I saw her for the first time at Hornig's[12] four or five years ago; so did you, by the way. Yes, you might just remember her." Willi gave him a questioning look, and he went on. "We were attending a big party there, in honor of Herr Kriebaum, the folk singer; she had thick, curly blond hair and was wearing a bright red dress with a blue bow around the neck." Then, with a kind of grim pleasure, he added, "She had a rather vulgar look about her. Just a year later, at Ronacher's,[13] she looked completely different; by that time she could choose the company she kept. She wasn't at all interested in me, unfortunately. In other words, I didn't have enough spending power in proportion to my age. Well, then things just developed as they sometimes do when an old fool lets himself be swept off his feet by a young woman. And two and a half years ago Fräulein Leopoldine Lebus and I were married."

Lebus—so that was her last name, Willi thought. The moment his uncle had mentioned Hornig's, the red dress, and the curly blond hair, he had realized that the girl he was describing could be none other than Leopoldine, even though Willi had long since forgotten her first name, too. He had been careful, of course, not to let on, because although his uncle seemed to have no illusions about the previous life of Fräulein Leopoldine Lebus, it definitely would have been embarrassing for him to have any idea of how that evening at Hornig's had ended, let alone to find out that Willi, after first seeing his uncle home, had secretly met Leopoldine again at three o'clock and then stayed with her until the next morning. So just to be on the safe side, he acted as if he couldn't really remember much about that whole evening, and, as if trying to console his uncle, commented that it was precisely blondes of that sort who sometimes made very good housewives and spouses, whereas girls from good families and with spotless reputations at times ended up being great disappointments to their subsequent husbands. He even knew of a baroness, a young lady of the finest aristocratic stock, whom a fellow officer had married and who, barely two years later, had been made available to another officer in a "salon" where "respectable women" were obtainable at set prices. This officer, himself unmarried, had felt obliged to inform the husband; the result had been an officers' tribunal, followed by a duel in which the husband was seriously wounded and the wife had committed suicide; Uncle Robert must have read about it in the newspaper, the case had created such a furor.

Willi spoke very excitedly, as if he suddenly was more interested in this incident than his own situation, until his uncle finally glanced up at him with a rather disturbed look on his face. Willi pondered for a moment, and although he knew that Uncle Robert couldn't possibly have the least inkling of the plan that had just surfaced in his mind and begun to take form, he nonetheless considered it best to adopt a calmer tone and drop the subject he had been talking about, which in any case was out of place here. And so he declared, somewhat abruptly, that he obviously would not continue to pressure his uncle after all he had revealed to him. He even went so far as to agree that talking to Consul Schnabel would certainly have greater prospects of success than approaching the former Fräulein Leopoldine Lebus; then too, it wasn't completely out of the question that First Lieutenant Höchster, who had come into a small inheritance, and possibly the regimental doctor who had been one of the players yesterday, might be willing to go in together and help him out of his terrible predicament. Yes, he would have to talk to Höchster especially, he knew that he had barracks duty today.

Willi was on pins and needles. Looking at his watch and suddenly pretending to be in more of a rush than he really was, he shook his uncle's hand, buckled his saber more tightly around his waist, and left.

XI

The first order of business now was to find out Leopoldine's address, and Willi set out immediately for the registry office. At this moment it seemed hardly possible to him that she would refuse his request once he had convinced her that his life was at stake. In all the intervening years he had virtually never thought of her, but now all the events of that evening sprang to life again in his memory. He saw her blond curls against the white of the coarse linen pillow with the red showing through, and her pale, touchingly childlike face, dimly lit the next morning by the first rays of the sun passing between the dilapidated slats of the green wooden blinds; he saw the narrow gold band with the semiprecious stone on the ring finger of her right hand as it rested on the red blanket, the narrow silver bracelet around the wrist of her left hand, and that same hand waving to him from the bed as he left. He had found her so appealing that he'd felt absolutely sure when they said goodbye that he would see her again. But there happened to be another young woman who had longer-standing claims on him in those days; as the kept mistress of a banker, she didn't cost Willi a kreutzer, and, given his financial situation, that was a consideration. And so it turned out that he neither put in any further appearances at Hornig's nor wrote Leopoldine at her married sister's apartment where she lived. As a result he never saw her again after that one night. But whatever might have happened in her life since that time, she couldn't have changed so much that she would simply stand by and let him . . . do what he would have to do if she rejected his request—a request that would, after all, be so easy for her to fulfill.

After waiting a full hour at the registry office, he finally held the slip of paper with Leopoldine's address on it in his hand. He took a covered carriage to the corner of the street where she lived and got out.

The apartment building, four stories tall and relatively new, stood across from a fenced-in lumberyard and did not have a terribly hospitable look about it. Willi went up to the third floor, where a nicely-dressed maid answered the door. He asked if he could speak with Frau Wilram, and when the maid hesitated, he handed her his calling card: Wilhelm Kasda, Lieutenant in the Ninety-Eighth Imperial Infantry Regiment, Alserstrasse barracks. The girl came back a moment later, told him that the lady of the house was very busy, and asked him what it was he wished. Only now did it occur to him that Leopoldine probably didn't know his last name. As he was debating whether he should pass himself off as an old friend or, jokingly, as a cousin of Herr von Hornig's, the door opened and an older, poorly dressed man carrying a black briefcase appeared and headed toward the stairway. Suddenly a woman's voice called out "Herr Krassny!", but the man, on his way down the stairs by now, seemed not to hear her. The woman then stepped out into the hall herself and called Herr Krassny's name again, and this time he stopped and turned around. Leopoldine had already noticed the lieutenant and, as her look and her smile indicated, immediately recognized him. She no longer bore any resemblance to the woman he remembered—her figure was full and imposing, and she seemed to have grown taller; her hairstyle was smooth and simple, almost severe, and, most remarkable of all, she was wearing a pince-nez on her nose, its cord slung around her ear.

"Please step right in, Herr Leutnant," she said. He noticed now that her facial features hadn't actually changed at all.

"I'll be with you in a moment."

She pointed to the door she had come through, then turned to Herr Krassny and seemed to give him some orders or other, in a low voice that was inaudible to Willi but with great insistence. While this was going on, Willi stepped into a bright, spacious room with a long table in the middle; on it were pens and ink, a ruler, pencils, and business ledgers. Two tall filing cabinets stood against the walls on the right and left, and a large map of Europe hung on the rear wall above a small table covered with newspapers and pamphlets; Willi couldn't help being reminded of a travel bureau he had once gone to in some provincial city. But then he suddenly saw the run-down hotel room before his eyes, with the dilapidated blinds and the pillow with the red showing through—and a strange feeling came over him, almost as if he were dreaming.

Leopoldine came in and shut the door behind her; she let her pince-nez dangle between her fingers, then held out her hand to the lieutenant in a friendly way, though with no noticeable emotion. He bent over her hand as if he were going to kiss it, but she immediately pulled it back. "Please have a seat, Herr Leutnant. What gives me the pleasure?" Sie directed him to a comfortable chair and sat down herself in what seemed to be her usual place, a straight chair across from him at the long table piled with ledgers. Willi felt like he was in a lawyer's or doctor's office.

"What can I do for you?" she asked in an almost impatient tone that didn't sound very encouraging.

"Frau Wilram," Willi began after clearing his throat slightly, "I want you to know first of all that it wasn't my uncle who gave me your address, in case you might be thinking that."

She gave him a surprised look. "Your uncle?"

"My uncle Robert Wilram," Willi said pointedly.

"Oh, I see," she replied, smiling and staring straight ahead.

"It goes without saying that he doesn't know about this visit," Willi continued, speaking somewhat faster, "I want to emphasize that."

She gave him a puzzled look.

"I hadn't seen him for a long time, actually," he went on, "though not because of me. It was only when we were talking today that I found out he'd—gotten married in the meantime."

Leopoldine nodded and smiled. "Care for a cigarette, Herr Leutnant?" she asked, pointing at the open box on the table. Willi helped himself, and she gave him a light and then lit her own.

"Well, could you finally tell me what occasion it is that gives me the pleasure—"

"Frau Wilram, I came to see you for the same reason that brought me—to my uncle's. It's a rather—embarrassing one, I'm sorry to have to tell you."

Her expression immediately darkened noticeably.

"I won't take up very much of your time, Frau Wilram. To say it right out: I was hoping you would be able to lend me a certain amount of money for a period of—three months."

Strangely enough, her expression brightened again at this. "Your confidence in me is very flattering, Herr Leutnant," she said, flipping the ash off her cigarette, "although I don't quite know how I've come by this honor. In any case, may I ask how much it would be?" She tapped lightly on the table with her pince-nez.

"Eleven thousand gulden, Frau Wilram." He wished that he had said twelve and was on the point of correcting himself, when it occurred to him that the consul might be content with ten thousand. And so he left it at eleven.

"My," Leopoldine said, "eleven thousand—that definitely is a 'certain amount' all right." She let her tongue play between her teeth. "And what would you offer me as security, Herr Leutnant?"

"I'm an officer, Frau Wilram."

She smiled in an almost kindly way. "I'm sorry, Herr Leutnant, but in business dealings that isn't quite the same as security. Who would vouch for you?"

Willi said nothing and looked at the floor. A brusque refusal would have been no more embarrassing to him than this cool politeness.

"I'm sorry, Frau Wilram," he said, "I'm afraid I haven't thought through all the formal details of this business yet. I'm in an absolutely desperate situation. It concerns a debt of honor that has to be taken care of by eight o'clock tomorrow morning. If it's not, my honor will simply be lost, along with—everything else that's connected with it in my profession."

Noticing a trace of apparent sympathy shimmering in her eyes, he repeated the story of the previous evening that he had told his uncle an hour earlier, choosing his words more carefully this time and expressing himself with greater feeling. She listened to him with ever-increasing signs of concern, even pity. When he had finished she looked at him benignly and asked, "And I'm the only one, Willi—the only human being in the whole world you could turn to in this situation?"

The way she had addressed him, and especially her calling him by his first name, warmed his heart. He sensed that he was already saved.

"Would I be here otherwise?" he asked. "I really have no one else."

She shook her head sympathetically. "That makes me feel all the worse," she replied, slowly stubbing out her cigarette, "but unfortunately I'm not in a position to help you out. My assets are all tied up in various companies. I never have access to any amount of cash worth mentioning. I'm terribly sorry."

She got up from her chair as if an audience had come to an end. Willi remained in his chair in a state of shock. Hesitantly, awkwardly, almost stammering, he asked her to consider, given the presumably very favorable status of her business enterprises, whether one of those companies might not have cash reserves he could borrow from, or whether a claim on some other source of credit couldn't be arranged. Her lips curling ironically, she smiled indulgently at his naïveté in business matters.

"You seem to think these things are simpler than they are," she said, "and apparently you take it for granted that I'd get involved in a business transaction on your behalf that I wouldn't even consider for myself. And over and above that, without any guarantee of being paid back!—How could I possibly do that?"

These last words had a friendly, even coquettish tone to them again, as if deep down inside she was already willing to give in and was merely waiting for one more pleading, imploring phrase to come from Willi's mouth. Convinced that he had found this phrase, he said, "Frau Wilram—Leopoldine—my career, my *life* is at stake."

She gave a slight start, and he sensed that he had gone too far. "I'm sorry I said that," he added softly.

Her expression became impenetrable and she grew silent for a moment.

"I can't possibly come to a decision without first consulting my lawyer," she said finally in a dry tone of voice. As his eyes began to glow with new hope, she made a doubtful gesture with her hand.

"I have a meeting with him today in any case, in his office at five. I'll see what can be done. But I'd advise you not to assume that anything will come of it. I'm certainly not willing to make this into a major issue." She paused again. "I really don't see why I should," she added with sudden harshness. But then she smiled again and held out her hand, allowing Willi to kiss it this time.

"When will I be able to find out what you've decided?"

She seemed to ponder for a moment. "Where do you live?"

"In the Alserstrasse barracks," he replied quickly, "officers' wing, third stairway, room four."

A trace of a smile played around her lips. Then she said slowly, "By seven, seven-thirty I'll know for sure if there's any possibility—" She thought again for a while, then said decisively, "I'll send someone over to you between seven and eight to let you know." She opened the door for him and escorted him into the foyer. "Goodbye, Herr Leutnant."

"Goodbye," he replied, disconcerted. Her expression was cold and distant. As the maid opened the door to the hallway for the Herr Leutnant, Frau Leopoldine Wilram had already disappeared into her room again.

XII

In the short time Willi had spent with Leopoldine he had gone through such varying moods—discouragement, hope, assurance, and renewed disappointment—that he walked down the stairs in a daze. Only when he was outside again did he regain a degree of clarity, and now his situation seemed to him on the whole not unfavorable. There could be no doubt that Leopoldine was in a position to get the money for him if she was of a mind to do so; her whole being was proof enough that it was in her power to influence her lawyer however she wanted. And the sense that she still felt something in her heart for Willi became so intense in him that he suddenly was able to visualize himself at some distant point in the future as the husband of the widowed Frau Leopoldine Wilram, now known as Frau Major Kasda.

But this illusory image faded quickly as he walked along aimlessly in the summer-like midday heat through moderately busy streets toward the Ring. He thought again of the uncongenial office space where they had talked, and his visual image of her, made softer at times by a certain feminine charm, once more took on the hard, almost severe expression that had intimidated him more than once during their conversation. But however things turned out, he was still faced with several hours of uncertainty that he would have to get through some way or another. Why not go ahead and have himself a "high time," as people called it, even though—or precisely *because* he might not have much time left. He decided to have lunch at an elegant hotel restaurant where he had dined on occasion with his uncle in former days. Sitting in a cool, dimly-lit corner, he enjoyed an excellent meal accompanied by a bottle of semi-sweet Hungarian wine, and gradually found himself in a state of cozy well-being that he was unable to resist. Half-awake, half-sleeping, he smoked a good cigar and sat in the corner of his velvet-covered sofa for some time as the only remaining guest, and when the waiter came by offering genuine Egyptian cigarettes for sale, he bought a whole pack on the spot; what did it really matter, after all? And if worst came to worst he would bequeath them to his orderly.

When he stepped out onto the street again, he felt no different than he would have if a somewhat risky but basically interesting adventure were imminent—a duel, for example. And he thought back to an evening—the better part of a night, actually—that he had spent two years earlier with another officer who had to fight a duel with pistols the next morning; first they had been in the company of a couple of girls, and then it had been just the two of them, talking about serious, more or less philosophical matters. Yes, his friend's mood at that time must have been quite similar to his own now, and the fact that the duel had gone well seemed to him a good omen.

He strolled across the Ring, a young, not especially elegant officer, but slim and reasonably handsome, and, as he could tell from the looks he got, not an unpleasant sight for the young ladies of the various social classes. He sat outside a coffee house drinking a cup of strong, black coffee, smoking cigarettes, leafing through magazines, and looking at the people who walked by without actually seeing them; then, slowly at first and unwillingly, but inevitably, he awoke to a clear recognition of reality.

It was five o'clock. Inexorably, though all too slowly, the afternoon continued its advance; the most sensible thing for him to do now would be to go home and rest for a while, to the extent that that was possible. He took a horse-drawn streetcar, got out in front of the barracks, and made it across the courtyard to his quarters without any unwelcome encounters. Joseph was in the vestibule arranging the Herr Leutnant's things in the clothes closet, and begged to report that nothing new had taken place—except that Herr von Bogner had already been there that morning and left his calling card. "What do I need his card for?" Willi said gruffly. The card was lying on the table and Bogner had written his home address on it: Piaristengasse 20. Pretty close, Willi thought. But what do I care whether he lives near here or far away, the fool. Bogner was after him like a creditor—the presumption of the man! Willi was about to tear the card up, then changed his mind and tossed it carelessly onto the chest and turned back to his orderly: Someone would be asking for him, Herr Leutnant Kasda, between seven and eight that evening, a gentleman, maybe a gentleman with a lady, or possibly just a lady by herself. "Understood?"—"Yessir, Herr Leutnant." Willi closed the door behind him, stretched out on the sofa—it was a little too short, so that his feet dangled over the low armrest—and sank into sleep as if falling into an abyss.

XIII

It was already getting dark outside when some noise or other woke him; he opened his eyes and saw a young woman standing there in a blue and white polka-dotted summer dress. Still groggy, he got up and noticed that his orderly was standing behind the young lady, a worried, guilty look on his face, and it was at that point that he heard Leopoldine's voice.

"Pardon me for not allowing your orderly to announce me, Herr Leutnant, but I wanted to wait until you woke up by yourself."

How long has she been standing there, Willi wondered? That tone of voice, that look about her—this isn't the same person I met this morning. She must have brought the money with her. He gestured to his orderly, who left immediately, then turned to Leopoldine.

"You came yourself, Frau Wilram—I'm so happy you did. Please, won't you—" And he invited her to have a seat.

She glanced around the room, her expression bright, almost cheerful, and seemed to find it very pleasant. In her hand she held a blue-and-white striped parasol, a perfect match for her white polka-dotted blue silk dress. Her straw hat wasn't quite in style, broad-brimmed à la Florentine with artificial cherries hanging over the edges.

"This is very attractive, Herr Leutnant," she said, the cherries swinging back and forth next to her ear. "I never would have imagined that barracks rooms could look so nice and cozy."

"They're not all like this," Willi remarked with some satisfaction.

"I'm sure that depends mostly on the occupant," she said with a smile as if she were completing his thought for him.

Feeling awkward and pleasantly excited at the same time, Willi straightened up the books on his table and closed the narrow cabinet door that had been standing ajar, then hastily offered Leopoldine a cigarette from the pack he had bought in the hotel. She declined and eased herself gracefully into one corner of the sofa. She looks delightful, Willi thought. Like a woman of the upper middle classes, actually. Her appearance was no more reminiscent of the businesswoman of that morning than of the curly-haired girl of former days. Where could she be hiding the eleven thousand gulden? She smiled at him almost mischievously as if she had guessed his thoughts.

"What sort of a life do you live, Herr Leutnant?" she asked with seeming innocence.

When Willi hesitated, unsure of how exactly she meant her question, she asked more specifically whether he found military life hard or easy, if he would be promoted soon, how he got along with his superiors, and whether he went on outings to nearby areas very often, such as he had, for example, the previous Sunday. Willi replied that military life was sometimes good, sometimes not so good, that he had no complaints in general about his superiors and that First Lieutenant Wositzky in particular was very nice to him, that he couldn't expect to be promoted in the next three years, and that, as Frau Wilram could imagine, he didn't have time to go on many outings except on Sundays—and as he said this he sighed slightly. Looking up at him with a smile—he was still standing across from her with the table between them—Leopoldine commented that she hoped he had better things to do with his evenings than playing cards. At this point she might well have casually added: Oh, of course, Herr Leutnant, before I forget it, here's that little item you asked me for this morning—but not a word, not a gesture, gave any hint of this. She simply kept looking up at him and smiling agreeably, and he had no choice but to keep the conversation going as best he could. And so he told her about the congenial Kessner family and the beautiful villa they lived in, about that fool of an actor, Elrief, about Fräulein Rihoscheck and all her makeup, and about the late-night carriage ride to Vienna.

"With some nice female companion, hopefully," she said. Oh, not at all, he had driven back with one of the other card players. Next she asked playfully if Fräulein Kessner had blond, brown, or black hair. He couldn't say for sure, he answered. And his tone of voice intentionally revealed that there were no affairs of the heart of any consequence in his life.

"I have the general impression, Frau Wilram, that you think my life is quite different from the way it actually is." She gazed up at him with interest, her lips half-open. "If only I wasn't alone all the time," he added, "I don't think such awful things would happen to me."

She looked at him innocently, questioningly, as if she didn't quite understand, then nodded earnestly, but didn't take advantage of this opportunity either; instead of mentioning the money, which she certainly had with her, or even simpler, just putting the bills on the table without saying much of anything, she remarked, "There's being alone and there's being alone."

"That's true," he said.

To this she merely nodded knowingly. Growing more and more uneasy every time their conversation faltered, Willi decided to ask her how her life had been, whether she had had many nice experiences; he was careful not to mention the older gentleman she was married to and who happened to be his uncle, just as he avoided saying anything about Hornig's, and especially about a certain hotel room with dilapidated blinds and pillows with red showing through. It was a conversation between a not terribly adroit lieutenant and a young and pretty middle-class woman, both of whom no doubt knew all sorts of things about each other—rather embarrassing things—but who were both likely to have their motives for not wanting to go into them, if for no other reason than to avoid jeopardizing the mood of the moment, which was not without its charm and even allure. Leopoldine had taken off her Florentine hat and put it on the table in front of her. Although she was still wearing the same straight hairstyle as that morning, a few strands had come undone and fell in ringlets across her temples, creating a distant reminder of the curly-haired girl of former days.

It was growing darker outside. Just as Willi was contemplating lighting the lamp in the niche of the tile stove, Leopoldine reached for her hat again. This seemed at first to mean nothing in particular, since she was right in the middle of telling about an outing she had gone on the previous year to Mödling, Lilienfeld, Heiligenkreuz—and Baden, of all places. But all of a sudden she put the hat on, fastened it with pins, and, smiling politely, announced that it was time for her to be going. Willi smiled, too, but the smile that played around his lips was unsure, almost frightened. Was she playing a trick on him? Or did she just want to gloat over his discomfort and anxiety for a while and then, at the last minute, give him the good news that she had brought the money? Or had she only come to tell him that she was sorry she hadn't been able to raise the money he needed, and was simply having trouble finding the right words to say it? In any case, it was unmistakably clear that she really did intend to leave, and there was nothing he could do, helpless as he was, other than maintain his bearing and act like a gallant young man who had been paid a pleasant visit by a beautiful young woman and was finding it very difficult to allow her to leave in the middle of the wonderful conversation they were having.

"Why do you want to go already?" he asked, sounding like a disappointed lover. "You don't really want to go so soon, Leopoldine?" he added with greater urgency.

"It's late," she replied. "Besides, Willi," she added in a jocular tone, "I'm sure you have more interesting plans for a beautiful summer evening like this?"

He began to breathe more easily, since she had gone back to calling him by his first name again,[14] and it was difficult for him to hide the new sense of hope he was feeling. No, he didn't have any plans at all, he said, and rarely could he have professed anything with a clearer conscience. Acting a bit coy, she kept her hat on for the time being, stepped over to the open window, and looked down on the courtyard as if it had suddenly become an object of interest. There wasn't, in fact, much to see there: on the opposite side in front of the mess hall soldiers were sitting around a long table; an orderly, carrying a package tied with string under his arm, hurried across the courtyard; another orderly was pushing a little cart with a keg of beer on it in the direction of the mess hall; two officers chatted as they walked toward the gate. Willi stood next to Leopoldine and slightly behind her; her blue and white silk dress with the polka dots rustled softly. Her left arm hung limply at her side, and her hand remained motionless until his touched it; gradually, then, her fingers slipped gently between his. From the wide-open windows of the enlisted men's quarters on the opposite side came the melancholy sounds of a trumpet doing practice runs. Then all was silent.

"It's kind of sad here," Leopoldine said finally.

"Do you think so?"

She nodded. "But it wouldn't have to be sad," he said. She turned her head slowly toward him. He had almost expected her to be smiling, and was surprised to see a tender, almost mournful expression on her face. Suddenly she stretched and said,' "Now I really have to go, Marie will be waiting with supper."

"Hasn't madame ever kept Marie waiting before?" Her smile gave him the courage to ask her whether he might not have the pleasure of her company for supper. He would send his orderly over to the Riedhof to get something, and she could easily be home before ten. Her protests sounded so half-hearted that Willi rushed into the vestibule at once, quickly told his orderly what to get, and was back in the room instantly. Leopoldine, still standing at the window, swung her arm vigorously at that moment and sent her Florentine hat sailing over the table and onto the bed. From this point on she seemed to become a different person. With a laugh, she stroked Willi's smooth hair, and he grabbed her by the waist and pulled her down next to him on the sofa. But when he tried to kiss her she turned away from him vehemently, and he refrained from any further attempts. He asked her how she usually spent her evenings, and she gave him a serious look.

"I have so much to do during the day," she said, "that I'm quite content to have my peace and quiet in the evening and not see anyone."

He admitted that he had no real notion of what sort of business she was involved in; it seemed puzzling to him, in fact, that she had gotten into that sort of thing at all. She refused to talk about it; after all, she told him, he knew nothing of such matters. He didn't give up right away; she could at least tell him something about her life—not everything, of course, he couldn't expect that of her—but he really would like to hear about the kinds of experiences she'd had since the day—the day they'd seen each other for the last time. There were other things, too, that he would have liked to bring up, including his uncle, but something kept him from mentioning his name. He asked her directly, almost overhastily, if she was happy.

She looked straight ahead. "I believe I am," she replied softly. "Most of all, I'm free, and that was always what I wanted most. I'm not dependent on anyone, just like—a man."

"Thank God that's the only thing about you that's manly," Willi said.

He moved closer to her and put his arm around her. She didn't refuse his advances, but her mind seemed to be elsewhere. And when she heard the door open and shut outside, she moved away from him quickly, got up, took the lamp out of the niche in the stove, and lit it. Joseph came in with their food. Leopoldine surveyed what he had brought and nodded in approval.

"The Herr Leutnant must have a bit of experience," she said smiling.

She wouldn't allow Willi to lift a finger as she and Joseph set the table together; he stayed sitting on the sofa "like a pasha," as he said, smoking a cigarette. When everything was ready and the hors d'oeuvres were on the table, Joseph was dismissed for the day. Before he left, Leopoldine slipped him a tip of such substantial size that he first stood there thunderstruck, then saluted as respectfully as if she had been a general.

"Here's to you," Willi said, touching his glass to Leopoldine's. When their glasses were empty, she put hers down on the table with a resounding ring and pressed her lips firmly against Willi's mouth. As he began to get more passionate, she pushed him away.

"Supper comes first," she said, and brought fresh plates.

She ate as healthy people do when they've finished a day's work and can relax and enjoy their food, her teeth strong and white and her manners as fine and well-mannered as those of ladies accustomed to dining in elegant restaurants with distinguished gentlemen. The wine bottle was soon empty, but fortunately the Herr Leutnant remembered that there was still a half-bottle of French cognac in the cupboard, left over from God knows what occasion. After the second glass Leopoldine seemed to be getting a little sleepy. She leaned back in the corner of the sofa, and as Willi bent over her forehead and kissed her eyes, her lips, her neck, she whispered his name—lovingly, as if she were already dreaming.

XIV

It was beginning to get light when Willi woke up, and a cool morning breeze was blowing in through the window. Leopoldine stood fully dressed in the middle of the room, wearing her Florentine hat and holding her parasol in her hand. Willi's first thought was: Good Lord, I must have slept soundly, and his second: Where's the money? There she stood with her hat on and her parasol in her hand, clearly intending to leave the room any second. She nodded a morning greeting to Willi, who stretched his arms out toward her in a gesture of longing. She went over to him and sat down on the bed, a friendly, yet serious expression on her face. He tried to put his arms around her to pull her closer, but she pointed to her hat and then her parasol, which she was holding in her hand almost like a weapon. Shaking her head, she said, "No more nonsense now," and tried to get up. He wouldn't let her. "You're not really going to go?" he said, an emotional edge to his voice.

"Of course I am," she said, brushing his hair back in a sisterly fashion. "I need to get a couple hours' worth of decent rest—I have an important conference at nine."

It flashed through his mind that this conference—what a sound the word had to it!—might have something to do with him—the meeting with her lawyer that she apparently hadn't had time for yesterday.

"Is it with your lawyer?" he asked bluntly, unable to control his impatience.

"No," she replied calmly, "I'm expecting a business associate from Prague."

She bent over and brushed a few wisps of mustache away from his lips, gave him a fleeting kiss, then whispered "Goodbye" and got up. In a moment she would be out in the hall. Willi's heart stood still. She was leaving? She was leaving *like this*?! Then a new hope awakened in him: Maybe she had put the money somewhere, wanting to be discreet, without his having noticed it. Nervously, anxiously, his eyes darted around the room, across the table, to the niche in the stove.—Or could she have hidden it under the pillow while he was asleep? Instinctively he put his hand there. Nothing. Or maybe in his wallet, lying there on the table next to his pocket watch? If only he could dare to look! And all the while he felt, knew, saw the way she had been following his eyes, his movements, mocking him, possibly even feeling a malicious pleasure. For only a fraction of a second did his eyes meet hers. He looked away as if caught in the act. By now she was standing at the door with her hand on the handle. He tried to call her name but couldn't make a sound, just like in a nightmare. He wanted to leap out of bed and rush over to her to keep her from leaving; he would even have run down the stairs after her in his night-shirt, like that prostitute years ago, in a brothel somewhere in the provinces—he could still see the scene before his eyes—who had run after a man who hadn't paid her for her services. And Leopoldine, as if she had heard her name on his lips, though he hadn't said it at all, reached down the front of her dress with one hand while keeping the other on the door handle.

"I just about forgot," she said offhandedly. Stepping back into the room, she let a piece of paper money float down onto the table. "There," she said, and walked over to the door again.

With a sudden jerk, Willi was sitting on the edge of his bed, staring at the money. There was only one single bill, a thousand-gul-den note; that's what it had to be, because there weren't any higher denominations. "Leopoldine," he called out; his voice had an un-natural sound to it. She turned around, still holding onto the door handle, and gave him a rather surprised, ice-cold look that filled him with a sense of shame more profound, more tormenting than he had ever felt before in his life. But it was too late to stop now; he couldn't give up at this point, no matter what might happen, no matter what further disgrace he might bring upon himself. Words tumbled inces-santly from his lips.

"But this isn't enough, Leopoldine, it wasn't a thousand I asked you for yesterday, you must've misunderstood me, it was eleven thou-sand."

Her expression became icier and icier, and Willi unconsciously pulled the blanket up over his naked legs. She looked at him as if she didn't quite understand, then nodded a few times as if she were just now figuring out what he meant.

"Oh, I see," she said, "you thought . . ." She jerked her head briefly, contemptuously, in the direction of the money. "This doesn't have anything to do with that. I'm not lending you a thousand guldens, I'm giving it to you—for last night." And her moist tongue played back and forth along her half-opened lips and sparkling teeth.

The blanket slid off Willi's feet. He stood erect, the blood rushing to his head with a burning sensation. She stared at him unaffected and seemingly puzzled. He was still unable to utter a single word.

"Isn't it enough?" she asked. "What did you expect, anyway? A thousand gulden!—You only gave me ten that other time, remember?"

He took a few steps toward her. She stood at the door motionless. With a sudden lunge he grabbed the money and crushed it in his trembling fingers; it looked as if he were about to throw it at her feet. She let go of the door handle, walked over to him, and stood there looking him in the eye.

"I wasn't trying to make you feel guilty," she said. "I couldn't have expected any more than that back then. Ten gulden—that was enough, really. Too much, even." Her eyes gazed into his with even greater intensity. "Ten gulden too much, to be exact."

He stared at her, beginning to understand, then lowered his eyes.

"How was I supposed to know?" he said dully.

"You could've figured it out," she replied, "it wasn't that difficult."

Slowly he looked up at her again, and now, in the depths of her eyes, he noticed a strange radiance: that same sweet, childlike radiance that had emanated from them that night so long ago. And vivid memories rose up within him—not only of the pleasure she had given him, as many others had before and after her, or of the honeyed words of endearment—those he'd heard from others, too—he remembered the unique experience of utter devotion, the way she had wrapped her slender child's arms around his neck; once again he heard words long unspoken—the words themselves and the tone in which they had been said, in a way he had never heard any other woman utter them: "Don't leave me, I love you." All these forgotten things came back to him again. And just as *she* had done today—this, too, he realized now—unconcerned, without thinking, while she still seemed to be sleeping in sweet exhaustion, he had gotten up from her side and, after briefly debating whether a smaller amount wouldn't be enough, had generously placed a ten-gulden note on the night table; then, feeling her drowsy, anxious gaze on him as she slowly awoke, he had quickly stepped out the door and gone back to the barracks to stretch out on his bed for a few hours. And when morning came—it was not quite time to report for duty yet—the little flower girl from Hornig's had been forgotten.

Yet while the remembrance of that long-past night was growing so amazingly alive in Willi, the sweet, childlike radiance in Leopoldine's eyes had gradually faded. Cold, gray, and distant, they stared into his, and as the images of that night now began to pale, he felt hostility, anger, and bitterness rise up inside him. Who did she think she was? How could she treat him this way? To act as if she really believed that he had offered himself to her for money, like a gigolo who was paid for his favors! And then, to add insult to injury, to play the part of a lecher who had been disappointed by a whore's performance and lowered the price they'd agreed to! As if she doubted for a minute that he would even have thrown all eleven thousand gulden at her feet if she had dared to offer it to him in payment for spending the night with her!

But just as the insult that this miserable woman so well deserved was finding its way to Willi's lips and he was about to bring his raised fist smashing down on her, the insult dissolved unspoken on his tongue and his hand slowly dropped to his side again. Suddenly he realized—and hadn't he suspected it before?—that he would indeed have been prepared to sell himself. Not only to her, to *any* woman, to *any woman at all* who had offered him the money. And so, in all the cruel, deceitful injustice that a malicious woman had inflicted on him he began to sense in the depths of his soul, no matter how much he tried to fight it, a hidden and yet inescapable justice—a justice that went far beyond the miserable little matter he was embroiled in, a justice that was directed at his innermost being.

As Willi looked up and glanced around the room it seemed to him as if he were waking from a confused dream. Leopoldine was gone. He hadn't said a word—and she was gone. How could she have disappeared from the room so suddenly, so unnoticed? Feeling the crumpled bill in his still clenched fist, he rushed to the window and tore it open as if to fling the money after her. He saw her below and was about to call out, but she was too far away. She was walking along the wall, her hips swaying contentedly, her parasol in her hand and her Florentine hat bobbing up and down—she was walking along as if she had just spent a night of love somewhere, as she no doubt had done on a hundred other occasions. Now she was at the gate. The guard saluted as if she were a figure of respect, and she was gone.

Willi closed the window and stepped back into the room; his gaze passed from the rumpled bed to the table and the remains of their meal, the empty glasses and bottles. His hand opened involuntarily and the bill fell out. He caught sight of his reflection in the mirror above the chest and recoiled; it seemed unspeakably repulsive to him that he was still in his nightshirt, with his hair uncombed and rings under his eyes. Grabbing his coat off the hook, he put his arms through the sleeves, buttoned it, and turned the collar up. He paced pointlessly back and forth in his room a few times. Finally he came to a stop in front of the chest, as if ineluctably drawn to it. In the middle drawer, as he well knew, among his handkerchiefs, was his revolver. So it had come to this. For a certain other person, too, who might already have gotten it over with. Or was he still hoping for a miracle? Well, in any case, he, Willi, had done what he could for him—and more. And at this moment it truly seemed to him that he had sat down at the card table only for Bogner's sake, that he had tempted fate only for Bogner's sake, until he himself had become its victim.

The thousand-gulden note lay exactly where he had dropped it before, on a plate next to a partially-eaten slice of cake, and it didn't even look that terribly crumpled any more. It had begun to unfold, and it wouldn't be very much longer till it was smooth again, as smooth as any other unsullied piece of paper—and no one would be able to tell by looking at it that it was no better than what people referred to as ill-gotten gains or the wages of sin. Well, in any case it was his—part of his estate, so to speak. A bitter smile played around his lips. He could bequeath the money to anyone he wanted to; and if any one person could lay claim to it, it was definitely Bogner. Willi laughed compulsively. Excellent! Yes, if anything still had to be taken care of, it was that. Hopefully Bogner hadn't done away with himself prematurely. So a miracle had taken place for him after all! All a person had to do was wait long enough.

What could be keeping Joseph? He knew that the regiment had maneuvers that day. Willi should have been ready by three on the dot, and now it was half-past four; they would have left long ago. He had been so sound asleep that he hadn't heard a thing. He opened the door to the vestibule, and there was his orderly, sitting on a stool next to the little iron stove. He immediately stood at attention.

"Beg to report, Herr Leutnant, I reported the Herr Leutnant sick."

"Sick? Who told you to do that . . . oh, of course."—Leopoldine! She might just as well have gone ahead and told him to report him dead, that would have been simpler.

"Fine. Make me some coffee," he said and closed the door.

What had become of Bogner's calling card? Willi searched for it—in all the drawers, on the floor, in every corner—he searched as if his own life depended on it. But it was no use, the card had disappeared.—Well, so it wasn't meant to be. So Bogner's luck had been bad, too; so their individual fates were inextricably bound together after all.—Then suddenly, in the niche of the stove, something white caught his eye. The card lay there with the address on it: Piaristengasse 20. Not far away at all. And even if it had been farther away!—He'd been lucky after all, this Bogner. What if the card hadn't ever turned up—?!

Willi picked up the thousand-gulden note and looked at it for a long time without really seeing it, then folded it in half and put it inside a sheet of white paper. He wondered for a moment if he should write a few words of explanation, then shrugged his shoulders. Why bother, he thought, and simply wrote the address on an envelope:

Herr Oberleutnant Otto von Bogner. First Lieutenant—yes! He was giving him back his commission, by the power of his own authority. Once an officer, always an officer, somehow—no matter what you might have done; or you *became* an officer again—once you paid off your debts.

He called his orderly and gave him the envelope to deliver. "And make it snappy."

"Any answer, Herr Leutnant?"

"No. Deliver it to him in person and—don't wait for an answer. And whatever you do, don't wake me up when you get back. Let me sleep. Till I wake up myself."

"Yessir, Herr Leutnant!" He clicked his heels together, did an about face, and hurried off. As he started down the stairs, he heard the sound of the key turning in the lock behind him.

XV

The hallway doorbell rang. Joseph, who had long since come back from his errand and dozed off, woke up with a start and opened the door. It was Bogner; Joseph had delivered the envelope from his superior officer to him three hours before as commanded.

"Is the Herr Leutnant at home?"

"I'm sorry, the Herr Leutnant is still asleep."

Bogner looked at his watch. Following the audit, he had felt the immediate need to thank the man who had saved him and had taken off for an hour, but he thought it best not to be gone for any longer than that. He paced back and forth impatiently in the narrow vestibule. "Isn't the Herr Leutnant on duty today?"

"The Herr Leutnant is on sick call."

The door to the hallway was still open, and Tugut, the regimental doctor, stepped in. "Is this where Herr Leutnant Kasda lives?"

"Yessir, Herr Doktor."

"Can I talk to him?"

"Herr Doktor, beg to report, the Herr Leutnant is on sick call. He's sleeping now."

"Tell him Dr. Tugut is here."

"Beg to request, Herr Doktor, the Herr Leutnant ordered me not to wake him."

"It's urgent. Wake the Herr Leutnant, I'll take full responsibility."

After a split second's hesitation, Joseph walked over and knocked on the door. Meanwhile, Tugut cast a suspicious glance at the civilian who was standing in the vestibule. Bogner introduced himself. His name was not unfamiliar to the doctor, as that of an officer who had been dismissed from the regiment under embarrassing circumstances, but he gave no indication of this and said his own name. The two did not shake hands.

Not a sound could be heard from Lieutenant Kasda's room. Joseph knocked harder, put his ear to the door, and shrugged his shoulders.

"The Herr Leutnant always sleeps very soundly," he said as if to reassure them.

Bogner and Tugut looked at each other, and the barrier between them was gone. The doctor stepped up to the door and called Kasda's name. No answer.

"That's odd," Tugut said with a frown and pushed down on the door handle to no avail.

Joseph had grown pale and stood there with his eyes wide open.

"Get the regimental locksmith, on the double," Tugut commanded.

"Yessir, Herr Doktor!"

Bogner and Tugut were alone.

"I can't imagine—" Bogner began.

"You're informed, Herr—von Bogner?" Tugut asked.

"You mean about the gambling losses, Herr Doktor?" Tugut nodded. "Yes, I'm afraid I am."

"I wanted to see how things stood," Tugut began hesitantly.—"If he was able to come up with—do you know, by any chance, Herr von Bogner?"

"No, I haven't heard," Bogner replied.

Tugut went over to the door again, shook the handle, and called Kasda's name. No answer.

Bogner was standing by the hallway window. "Here comes Joseph with the locksmith already."

"You were a friend of his when you were in the service?" Tugut asked.

The corners of Bogner's mouth twitched. "Yes—that certain one, you know."

Tugut ignored his comment. "It often happens when a person has been under a lot of stress . . . presumably he didn't sleep much the night before, either."

"Yesterday morning, at any rate, he still hadn't come up with the money," Bogner said matter-of-factly.

Tugut gave him a questioning look, as if he considered it possible that Bogner might have part of the amount along with him.

"I didn't have any luck myself . . . raising what he needed," Bogner said by way of an answer.

Joseph appeared, followed by the locksmith, a well-fed, red-cheeked young man. He was wearing the uniform of the regiment and carrying the tools he would need. Tugut knocked on the door loudly one last time. They all stood holding their breath for a few seconds, but nothing stirred.

"Go ahead," Tugut said, turning and gesturing to the locksmith, who set about his work immediately. Not much effort was required, and in a matter of seconds the door sprang open.

Lieutenant Kasda lay slumped in the corner of his black leather sofa nearest the window, wearing his coat with the collar turned up; his eyes were half-closed, his head had sunk down onto his chest, and his right arm hung limply over the armrest. The revolver lay on the floor; a narrow streak of dark-red blood had trickled down from his temple, across his cheek, and under his collar. Although all of those present had been prepared for this, they were visibly shaken. Dr. Tugut was the first to approach the body; taking hold of the lieutenant's dangling arm, he lifted it up and let go of it, and it immediately fell back limply over the armrest where it had been before. Next he unbuttoned Kasda's coat, though this was clearly pointless; the wrinkled nightshirt underneath was open down the front. Without thinking, Bogner bent over to pick up the revolver.

"Stop!" Tugut called out, his ear against the dead man's naked chest, "everything has to stay exactly as it is."

Joseph and the locksmith were still standing motionless by the open door; the locksmith shrugged and gave Joseph an embarrassed, uneasy look, as if he felt partly responsible for the scene that had met their eyes when he forced the door open.

Footsteps could be heard coming up the stairway, slowly at first, then faster and faster until suddenly they stopped. Bogner turned his head automatically and looked toward the entrance. An old gentleman dressed in a light-colored, somewhat shabby summer suit walked in through the partially open door, the expression of a woebegone actor on his face; he let his glance wander around the room uncertainly.

"Herr Wilram," Bogner called out. "It's his uncle," he whispered to Dr. Tugut, who was just getting up from the body.

Robert Wilram didn't immediately grasp what had happened. He saw his nephew leaning back in the corner of the sofa with his arm dangling limply and started to walk over to him, already sensing the worst but not yet willing to believe it. The doctor stopped him and put a hand on his arm.

"Something terrible has happened. I'm afraid nothing can be done."

The new arrival stared at him, uncomprehending.

"My name is Tugut, I'm the regimental doctor. Death must have occurred a few hours ago."

Robert Wilram, with a movement that struck everyone present as highly peculiar, suddenly reached into his breast pocket, pulled out an envelope, and swung it around in the air.

"But I brought it with me, Willi!" he shouted. Then, as if he believed he could bring him back to life with it, he added, "Here's the money, Willi. She gave it to me this morning. The entire eleven thousand, Willi. Here it is!" He looked around imploringly at the others. "This is the complete amount, gentlemen, really! Eleven thousand gulden!" He seemed to think that now that the money had been secured they should at least make an attempt to bring the dead man back to life.

"I'm afraid it's too late," Dr. Tugut said. He turned to Bogner. "I have to go and file my report," he told him, then gave a sharp command: "The body is to be left exactly as it was found." Finally he looked at the orderly and said sternly, "You're responsible for seeing that everything stays as it is." Before leaving he turned around once more and shook Bogner's hand.

Bogner said to himself: Where did Willi get the thousand—for me? Then his glance fell on the table, which had been pushed back from the sofa. He saw the plates, the glasses, the empty bottles. Two glasses . . .?! Had he had a woman here for his last night?

Joseph stepped up to the sofa next to his dead master. He stood there at attention like a sentry, but didn't try to stop Robert Wilram when he suddenly walked up to his nephew. Wilram had raised both his hands again, one of them still holding the envelope containing the money, as if he were pleading. "Willi!" he lamented, shaking his head in despair and dropped to his knees in front of him. He was so close to the body now that the aroma of a strangely familiar perfume came wafting toward him from Willi's naked chest and wrinkled nightshirt. He breathed it in, then raised his eyes to look at the dead man's face as if he felt tempted to ask him a question.

From the courtyard below came the regular sound of marching feet as the regiment returned to barracks. Bogner hoped he would be able to leave unnoticed before any former fellow officers entered the room, as was likely to happen. His presence here was superfluous in any case. Sending one last look of farewell in the direction of the dead man lying rigid in the corner of the sofa, he hurried down the stairs followed by the locksmith. He waited at the gate until the regiment had marched by, and then, keeping close to the wall, slipped away.

Robert Wilram, still on his knees before his dead nephew, let his glance wander around the room again. Only now did he notice the table with the remains of the meal, the plates, the bottles, the glasses. In the bottom of one of the glasses a trace of golden-yellow liquid still shimmered.

There were footsteps on the stairway and a confusion of voices; Robert Wilram got up off the floor and turned to the orderly.

"Did the Herr Leutnant have company last night before—"

"Yessir," Joseph replied, still standing at attention like a sentry, "till late at night——one of his fellow officers."

And the nonsensical idea that had passed fleetingly through the old man's mind dissolved into nothing.

The voices and the footsteps came closer.

Joseph stood even more erect than before. The deputation entered the room.

Notes

Casanova's Journey Home

[1]*La Pucelle* (*The Virgin*), a satirical work about Joan of Arc.
[2]Merlin Cocai, pseudonym of Teofilo Folengo (1496?-1544), a writer from Mantua.
[3]Pupilla = ward, protégée (the play appeared in 1757).

Fräulein Else

[1]Italian spelling of a resort town on the French riviera, formerly part of Italy.
[2]Shakespeare's play, a major theme of which is the protagonist's pride.
[3]Ernest van Dyck and Marie Renard were the Vienna Opera's most popular operatic duo during the 1890s. Massenet's *Manon* was first performed in Vienna in 1890, with van Dyck singing the role of the Abbé des Grieux and Renard the title role.
[4]Brand name of a sleep-inducing barbiturate in powder form.
[5]A sly, cunning, not quite trustworthy rogue; the term goes back to English 'fellow.'
[6]A small town in eastern Slovakia, one of the more remote areas of the Austro-Hungarian empire; Else presumably mentions Prešov

here (and later in the story) as a put-down of Dorsday's provincial origins.

7Novel by Guy de Maupassant (1890).

8Vienna's most elegant shopping street, frequented after dark by prostitutes.

9In Stein on the Danube, about fifty miles west of Vienna.

10German lawyer (d. 1881) and author of detective novels.

11The elegant building housing the mineral water dispensing facilities in one of Vienna's major parks (*Stadtpark* = city park).

12Drama by Alexandre Dumas (1852), translated into German in 1886.

Game at Dawn

1From Friedrich Schiller's poem "Der Knabe am Bach" ("The Boy at the Brook"); the full sentence is "There's room enough in the littlest hut for a happy loving couple." Speakers of German quote the two classical poets Schiller and Goethe much as speakers of English quote Shakespeare.

2An elegant restaurant not far from the barracks where Willi is stationed.

3City in present-day Romania; at the time the story is set, it was still part of the Austro-Hungarian Empire and had a large ethnic German population.

4Race track in the Prater, an extensive green area (plus amusement park) near the center of Vienna.

5Wooded area with hiking trails near Baden (Tal = valley).

6Open-air theater in Baden.

7Rodaun: suburb of Vienna, at the time a separate village; Red Barn: a popular restaurant in the vicinity.

8Cf. note 4 above.

9A shrine in the form of an elaborate Gothic column, erected in 1452 alongside one of the main roads leading into Vienna from the south. Concerning the column's name (*Spinnerin am Kreuz* = woman spinning at the cross), the Grimm brothers cite a legend according to which a pious poor woman spun cloth until she had saved enough money to have the monument constructed.

[10]One of the low ranges of mountains on the northern edge of Vienna.

[11]A neo-gothic church built near the inner city in the 1850s, in fulfillment of a vow made by Emperor Franz Joseph following his narrow escape from an assassination attempt.

[12]Middle-class music hall featuring the popular tunes of the day.

[13]Music hall in the elegant Inner City.

[14]At this point Leopoldine switches from the formal "Sie" to the more intimate "du" and maintains this form of address throughout the present conversation.

[15]At this point Leopoldine begins to call Willi "du" again.

Afterword

For the greater part of their lives, the writer Arthur Schnitzler and his fellow Viennese Sigmund Freud corresponded only on rare occasions and never met in person, despite the fact that they lived in the same city, had a medical background in common, and were familiar with each other's published works. Then, in May of 1922, Freud wrote a remarkable letter to his slightly younger contemporary, ostensibly congratulating him on the occasion of his sixtieth birthday but in fact delving into the reasons why he for his part had never sought to establish closer personal contact.

> I think I avoided meeting you out of a certain anxiety about encountering my double. . . . Whenever I became engrossed in your beautiful creations, I felt time and again that the presuppositions, interests, and conclusions I saw behind the poetic images were the same as those I knew to be my own. Your determinism as well as your skepticism—which the people call pessimism—your fascination with the truths contained in the unconscious and with the compulsive nature of man, your shattering of conventional cultural certainties, your intellectual engagement with the polarity of loving and dying—all this struck me as uncannily familiar . . . And so I gained the impression that you understood by intuition—though in actuality it was due to your sensitive observations of your own self—all those things that I had discovered through the painstaking study of other human beings It seems to me that you are in your very essence a psychoanalyst, as honest and unbiased and fearless a one as there has ever been . . .[1]

Freud's admiring words get at the core of Arthur Schnitzler's writing. From the beginning to the end of his literary career, Schnitzler was preoccupied with analyzing members of a society in decline, focussing on their loss of traditional values and changing sexual mores, their maintenance of empty codes of honor and wearing of masks to hide their horror of existence. Arthur Schnitzler, himself aware of his almost symbiotic relationship with Freud, was indeed a psychoanalyst in his own right.

Schnitzler was born in Vienna in 1862, as the first of three children, to Dr. Johann Schnitzler and his wife Louise. In the autobiography of his early years, Schnitzler recounts how, for some unknown reason, he lay on his father's desk for some time shortly after his birth, an incident that later prompted the elder Schnitzler's frequent prophecies that his son would become a writer. These predictions were made in a joking manner, however, since it was a foregone conclusion that Arthur would follow in the footsteps of his successful father, who was not only an internationally respected laryngologist (among his patients were members of the aristocracy and many of Vienna's best-known actors and actresses), but also a co-founder of the Vienna Polyclinic and editor of his own medical journal.

But the young boy's interests and talents clearly lay in other directions. His early enthusiasm for literature and the make-believe world of the stage, the result of frequent visits to the theater with his father, soon inspired him to write his own poems and playlets. He shared his poems, on such lofty classical themes as "The Death of Hector" and "Achilles' Last Words," with his family and received praise for them. But the dozen or so plays that came into being by the time he was fourteen were another matter. The budding dramatist composed them in secret, kept them to himself for the most part, and even resorted on occasion to hiding away a manuscript at his father's approach. In spite of Johann Schnitzler's love of the theater and the writing talent he had displayed at an early age (one of his teachers in Hungary, where he had grown up, predicted that he would become the "Hungarian Shakespeare"), he must have made it clear to his son that there were more fruitful occupations than writing plays. At the age of seventeen, then, having never seriously considered the possibility of pursuing a career as a writer, Arthur Schnitzler enrolled at the University of Vienna to begin the study of medicine.

Not surprisingly, the young man's devotion to his studies was less than exemplary. He went on leading the life of ease he had grown accustomed to, neglecting his classes and instead spending time with friends in coffee houses or at the racetrack, going to plays and concerts, improvising on the piano, and continuing to work on his dramatic pieces. From time to time Johann Schnitzler displayed some sympathy for his son's literary efforts, though often this was merely a reflection of an interest expressed by one or the other of his actor-clients who had heard that the doctor's son had literary promise. On one occasion, however, after the famous *Burgtheater*[2] actor Adolf von Sonnenthal had written a largely negative appraisal of a one-act play by Arthur that his father had given him to read, the young writer suspected collusion; his illustrious parent had criticized his casual atitude toward his medical studies often enough and certainly did not want him to feel encouraged to pursue the insecure, and perhaps somewhat suspect, career of a writer.

After completing his degree in 1885, Arthur Schnitzler became an intern at Vienna's General Hospital. He attended medical lectures at the Polyclinic as well and, beginning in 1888, worked there as an assistant to his father. On the whole, however, his life as a practitioner of medicine offered him no more stimulation than had his years as a student. Given his interest in the workings of the mind, he found his internship in the hospital's psychiatric division highly interesting, but his experience as a surgeon's assistant extremely distasteful. His subsequent successes at the Polyclinic in the treatment of aphonia (loss of voice) through hypnosis and suggestion resulted in a scientific paper on the subject, and at about the same time his extra-medical (and somewhat questionable) applications of these methods—among which were the staging of a "murder attempt" on him by a subject—found literary expression in the one-act play *Die Frage an das Schicksal* (*The Fateful Question*), published in 1890. This and six other loosely related one-acters were united two years later under the title *Anatol*; the title hero's sexual exploits, at this stage of Schnitzler's career still treated with a relative lightness of spirit, set the thematic tone for much of his subsequent writing.

Following his father's death in 1893 Schnitzler left the Polyclinic and established his own practice. From this point on, however, he began devoting more and more of his energies to his literary endeavors, and by the turn of the century he had established a reputation both as a dramatist and a writer of short fiction. Around this time Schnitzler suddenly became the focus of two literary scandals of considerable proportions. The first concerned his novella *Leutnant Gustl*, whose title figure he had portrayed as an arrogant young officer completely lacking in moral fiber and a sense of military honor. Within six months of the appearance of the story in a Viennese newspaper (December 1900), the author had been stripped of his rank as a reserve officer in the Austro-Hungarian Army in which he had served almost two decades before as a one-year medical corps volunteer.

The second scandal revolved around *Reigen* (*Round Dance*), a play consisting of ten dialogues in which the same number of characters do a sexual round dance of sorts, changing partners from one dialogue to the next. When *Reigen* was published in 1903 by a Viennese press, most newspapers refused to review it and those few that did heaped abuse on the play. Later in the same year, a student acting society at the University of Munich was promptly dissolved by the university senate following a performance of three of the dialogues, and in 1904 copies of the book were confiscated and further sales forbidden in Germany. Two days after the Hungarian-language premiere in Budapest in 1912, the play was banned there as well. When the complete *Reigen* was finally staged in German in Berlin and Vienna (1920-21), the public outcry was so great that no further performances were allowed until legal action reversed that decision a year later.

Other plays of Schnitzler's were plagued from time to time by the Austrian and German censors on either moral or religious grounds. By contrast, he experienced his greatest theater triumph in 1911 with the simultaneous premiere of his play *Das weite Land* (*The Vast Domain*) on nine major European stages. Not long after this, Schnitzler began to turn away from the theater and focus more on his prose writings, a shift in emphasis that may have been due in part to the death of his friend Otto Brahm, the director of the Deutsches Theater in Berlin who had pioneered the production of many of his plays. The period between the end of World War I and Schnitzler's death in 1931 saw the publication of his second novel and six of his lengthiest and finest novellas, three of them contained in this volume.

Schnitzler set the great majority of his stories and plays in turn-of-the-century Vienna, returning time and again to the milieu he knew so well to compose yet another subtly penetrating variation on a theme. *Casanova's Journey Home* (1918) is in this sense an exception, but only because its quasi-historical nature required that its action take place in northern Italy. In virtually every other respect—characterization, psychological intensity, thematic content, handling of plot, symbolic use of dream sequences—it is thoroughly Schnitzlerian. It is also one of the author's most intensely personal stories, dealing as it does with the fear of aging and dwindling attractiveness to the opposite sex. Schnitzler himself was a lifelong "Casanova" of sorts, and it is no coincidence that he portrayed his protagonist at precisely the same age (53) as he himself was at the time of composition.

As the author tells us in a brief note at the end of the story, only its general framework and a few details of Casanova's life are based on fact. The historical Casanova had indeed taken first orders in the priesthood, had later been imprisoned by Venetian authorities (as a magician), and escaped from the notorious "Lead Chambers"; he had subsequently wandered around Europe for almost twenty years, meeting many of the most interesting and important personalities of the day and having countless affairs in the process; he had been a diplomat, given himself an aristocratic title, practiced alchemy, and toyed with the cabbala before returning home to Venice as a spy at the age of forty-nine (somewhat younger than suited Schnitzler's purposes). But the main plot line of the novella, the Marcolina-Casanova story with its supporting cast of Olivo, Amalia, and Lorenzi, is Schnitzler's invention. (The Marcolina who appears in several chapters of Volume 9 of Casanova's own *Memoirs* bears no resemblance to the character created by Schnitzler.)

Marcolina becomes Casanova's obsession. The mere mention of a "young niece," even before he has met her or heard her name, is enough to make him want to spend a few days at the country estate of his old friend Olivo, so that he can "have a look at her at close range." And as soon as he hears of a certain Lieutenant Lorenzi, he instinctively knows that the two are lovers. Jealousy and desire begin to overcome him before he has as much as glimpsed either one.

The theme of aging enters in when Amalia, Olivo's wife and Casanova's lover of sixteen years before, declares her undying passion for him—the Casanova of her youth, a Casanova who, for her, will never grow old. But the chevalier, now no longer interested in Amalia, tries to convince her otherwise: Can't she see the wrinkles on his forehead and neck, he asks her, or that he's missing a tooth and has the hands of an old man? His budding infatuation drives him to emphasize to Amalia precisely the things he hopes Marcolina will overlook.

But he has already noticed once, and will soon again, a look of disgust and repulsion in Marcolina's eyes as she begins to become aware of his attraction to her. He has the choice of attributing this either to her chaste nature or to his own deteriorating physical appearance, and for a while he is able to fool himself into believing the former. When he sees Marcolina soon after his talk with Amalia, he feels "a breath of austerity and chastity" emanating from her, and a sense of awed reverence wells up within him, followed by—wonder of wonders!—a momentary loss of desire for her. Given Casanova's nature, of course, this cannot last.

When Casanova first meets Lorenzi, he is puzzled for a moment by the young lieutenant's similarity to someone he knows. Suddenly he realizes that it is himself—Lorenzi is Casanova, as he was thirty years before. But as he carries this thought to its strangely logical conclusion, it becomes apparent to him that if he has returned in the image of Lorenzi, he himself must have died. And the awful truth of this hits him: Casanova, a shadow of his former self, is indeed dead. Later on, once he has discovered that Lorenzi and Marcolina have become lovers, he (unconsciously) takes the next logical step: he attempts, almost literally, to become his younger alter-ego by spending the night with Marcolina. Ultimately forced to accept Marcolina's unspoken but no less devastating judgment—that he is an "old man"—he symbolically kills his rejuvenated self in a duel and escapes to Venice to begin his ignominious "new life."

Of Schnitzler's almost sixty published prose works, *Fräulein Else* (1924) is one of only two written in the form of an interior monologue.[3] Everything that Else experiences is transmitted directly to the reader: whatever passes through her mind, the people and things she sees around her, the conversations she is involved in or overhears, the letter and telegram she receives from her mother, a few snatches of Schumann played on the piano. While the usual narrative perspective is lacking (except to the extent that Else herself can be considered a narrator of sorts), this loss is more than made up for by the intensity with which Else's fate unfolds in and around her and by the direct access we have to all that she experiences.

The setting of *Fräulein Else* is a luxurious resort in the Dolomites of South Tirol, an area that still belonged to Austria at the time of the story's action (approximately 1895) and a favorite vacation spot of wealthy Viennese in particular. Aside from the scenery, then, the setting might as well be decadent Vienna itself with its standard stock of bored, blasé characters interested only in the "good" life of artificial cheeriness and empty affairs.

At age nineteen, Else has learned the games one must play in the high society of her day. Whenever she is in public, she is on stage, as she demonstrates from the very beginning of the novella. "That wasn't a bad exit," she says to herself as she leaves her tennis partners, pleased with a clever retort she has just made. She is acting, too, when she affects a studiedly nonchalant air at the doorman's announcement of the arrival of a letter she has been anxiously awaiting. And she believes that "no one can tell by looking at me" how much worry her family's financial situation habitually causes her..

Having led the privileged life of a daughter of a well-to-do bourgeois family, Else has never outgrown the fantasies of her teenage years. She lives in the dream-world of the theater and French Romantic

novels. Perhaps she has truly been in love only once, she muses—
with the lead singer in an opera. Or was it the character whose role he
sang? Else does not seem quite able to distinguish between the two.
And when she adds that she was also in love with the female lead on
that occasion, it becomes clear that she was in actuality in love with
the *idea* of being in love. One result of Else's dwelling on fantasy
figures is that it is difficult for her to accept the real people she knows,
virtually none of whom, whether deservingly or not, escapes her negative critique.

With the possiblility of scandal and ostracism from high society
facing her family, Else begins to come to grips, at least to a degree,
with the real world. She realizes that she has never learned to do anything of a practical nature and is totally unequipped for a life in which
she might have to fend for herself. Given the predicament her father
and mother (as his intermediary) have put her in, she finds herself
faced with the choice of demeaning herself by accepting Dorsday's
proposal or committing suicide. The variation on this first possibility
that Else carries out has, characteristically, an extravagantly theatrical
element to it and can be seen at the same time as the fulfillment of
one of her recurrent sexual fantasies.

Game at Dawn (1926) is also set at the turn of the century, this
time in Vienna itself, with one central scene in the nearby town of
Baden. Willi Kasda, the main character of the story, is a superficial
and somewhat arrogant young lieutenant with no other source of
income beyond his modest junior officer's pay. Since he subscribes to
the military code of honor and knows the attitudes appropriate to his
caste in various aspects of life, he prides himself on being extremely
cautious when gambling at cards and never allows himself to get seriously in debt. This all changes one Sunday afternoon, evening, and
on into the night, due to a series of fateful events that grow out of a
plea for help from a former fellow officer who has gotten himself into
a financial predicament. What begins innocently enough as Willi's
attempt to help out his comrade—and, given enough luck, to up-
grade his own shabby uniform—ends as a case study of compulsive

gambling. The scene around the card table in a café in Baden is one of the most excruciating that Schnitzler ever created.

From this point on, in fact, *Game at Dawn* consists of one distressing scene after another, each made even more unbearable by Willi's genius for seeing glimmers of hope where none exist. On the long carriage ride back to Vienna, Consul Schnabel, to whom Willi now owes the equivalent of three to four years of military pay and who has "kindly" offered to take Willi along, is cool but cordial. Yet as the Consul's contempt for the military in general and for officers in particular grows ever more apparent, it becomes equally apparent that he will not yield to Willi's request for an extension of the deadline for repaying his "debt of honor." By the time the lieutenant alights from the carriage at his barracks, he realizes that his only option might be "a bullet in the brain."

Willi's visit to his pitiful Uncle Robert, who is utterly subservient to his wife and has signed over complete control of his wealth to her, turns out to be an exercise in futility. But when Willi finds out who Uncle Robert's wife is—Leopoldine, a former flower girl with whom he himself had once spent the night—his hope returns. The ensuing meeting between the two, during which Willi's hope waxes and wanes, results in another night spent together, and this in turn is followed by the novella's second "game at dawn"—a game played this time by Leopoldine, who turns the tables on Willi and treats him as he had treated her years before. Willi is forced to several realizations: that Leopoldine had really loved him, that he had degraded her then just as she has him now, that he was willing to sell himself for the sake of money.

Ironically, it is at this moment of self-disgust that Willi rises to what might be termed a degree of magnanimity: with death staring him in the face, he has his orderly deliver a thousand-gulden note to his former comrade so that at least he will be saved. What remains for Willi to do now is clear, though it is difficult to say whether he is prepared to do it because he has not been able to raise the amount he owes or because he despises himself. Seen in this light, the final irony of Uncle Robert's belated arrival with the money may not be one at all.

Arthur Schnitzler saw the world with extremely skeptical eyes, and his characters inherited this view, as it were, from their maker. Life is unsure, people are on the lookout for their own advantage, no one is to be trusted. Moral values, including even a rudimentary sense of responsibility to others, are difficult to find in a world like this. Some individuals survive (like Casanova), but at great expense to those around them, and even then they are not content. Those who do not (like Else and Willi) are the victims of others, of rigid societal rules, and of their own insecurity and indecision. While his characters may often deceive themselves, Schnitzler never deceives us about them, and this is what makes them so believable—we come to know them intimately, with their few strengths and many weaknesses, in the penetrating light of the author's analytic eye.

Notes

[1] Henry Schnitzler (ed.), "Sigmund Freud—Briefe an Arthur Schnitzler," *Die neue Rundschau*, 66/1 (1955), 97 (my translation).

[2] The state theater of Vienna, originally the theater of the imperial court.

[3] The other was the much shorter *Leutnant Gustl* of 1900.